PARTICL

Jonathan Gathorne-Hardy lives in Norfolk with his wife, the painter, Nicky Loutit. He is the author of a number of novels, children's books, and, among other non-fiction works, a biography of Gerald Brenan, and *The Rise and Fall of the British Nanny*.

BY JONATHAN GATHORNE-HARDY

Fiction

One Foot In The Clouds

Chameleon

The Office

The Centre Of The Universe Is 10 BaedekerStrasse
And Other Stories

The City Beneath The Skin

Particle Theory

Non-Fiction

The Rise And Fall Of The British Nanny

The Public School Phenomenon

Love, Sex, Marriage And Divorce

Doctors

Gerald Brenan: The Interior Castle

Jonathan Gathorne-Hardy

PARTICLE THEORY

A Novel

VINTAGE

Published by Vintage 1996

2 4 6 8 10 9 7 5 3 1

First published in Great Britain by
Hutchinson, 1996

Vintage
Random House, 20 Vauxhall Bridge Road,
London SW1V 2SA

Random House Australia (Pty) Limited
20 Alfred Street, Milsons Point, Sydney
New South Wales 2061, Australia

Random House New Zealand Limited
18 Poland Road, Glenfield,
Auckland 10, New Zealand

Random House South Africa (Pty) Limited
PO Box 2263, Rosebank 2121, South Africa

Random House UK Limited Reg. No. 954009

A CIP catalogue record for this book
is available from the British Library

ISBN 0 09 959771 3

Papers used by Random House UK Ltd are natural, recyclable products made from wood grown in sustainable forests. The manufacturing processes conform to the environmental regulations of the country of origin

Printed and bound in Great Britain by
Cox & Wyman, Reading, Berkshire

To the two Pauls

Part I

1

The plain is in fact in the middle east of the Soviet Union (as it was then), some considerable way above and to the right of Moscow. But from an aeroplane breaking through cloud at 5,000 feet and slowly descending, it looks like the farmland near Chicago. The same vast, dull-coloured squares.

Except here there is no city. Just those great blocks of farmland stretching away, intersected by long canals which drain the autumn rain and the two-foot winter snows when they finally melt, and from which water is pumped during the long, ferocious summers.

When the plane descends still lower, slowly spinning down through the late-autumn drizzle, it is possible to see that the largest of the canals is in fact a river whose most extreme meanderings have been artificially straightened. The two other distant farms disappear into the dullness. The farm below, with its lath and plaster outbuildings and three vast modern barns, arch-roofed in corrugated iron, now seems the only one in the whole desolate plain.

Certainly, it is that to flaxen-haired little Ivan, who is

standing rigidly in the yard. The only one in the world. As he sinks into it, the thick pig muck of the yard flows sluggishly into his boots – but he continues to stand staring, white-faced, underlip curled in anguish.

2

Make a similar sycamore-seed descent above a point eight miles inland about midway round the Suffolk coast.

At first this is a small, dark, green-blue blob in the bare autumn landscape. A miniature landscape: dolls' hills and valleys, mini-brick villages, little churches more numerous than pubs.

The smudged green-blue separates into pine trees. They surround a large Victorian vicarage covered in Virginia creeper, its leaves at this moment birthmark colours – strawberry red, mauve.

It is early evening and the slanting autumn sun is pouring gold into a nursery. A large little boy, surprisingly old for the task engaged in – about seven, even eight – is sitting on a chamber pot. His teeth are gritted, fat fists clenched, eyes closed with effort. Then, with a gasp, he lets out his breath and sits panting. Once again, he draws in another lungful of air, grits his teeth and strains – strains – strains – *strains*.

Suddenly – the resolution! Michael relaxes. Then he stands up and looks eagerly down into the white china chamber pot. What he sees sends him shuffling urgently, trousers round his ankles, to the door.

'Granny!' he yells down the stairs. 'Granny, come quickly, *quickly*!'

'What is it, darling?' The comfortable middle-class voice floats up from the hall. 'I'm coming. Hang on.' Middle-class but with a touch of something, a curl at the edges – Scottish perhaps, or Irish.

Mrs Wordingham arrives panting, her arthritis not yet crippling, but already necessitating a stick. Automatically, she bends and pulls up Michael's shorts and fastens his snake-clasp belt, then accompanies him to the chamber pot.

'Michael!' she cries, delighted. 'Goodness! What did I say about better late than never? I'm proud of you.' And looking down, she smiles at the little boy beside her, flushed with effort, flushed with pride.

She felt her love flow. Long without her ex-naval husband, she could never have admitted it but, terrible as the shock had been, the bomb that had killed her only and extremely difficult son and his young wife in 1941 had proved her salvation. Michael had become everything.

His nanny – a youngish, competent, patient, bespectacled Miss Trudi Goldsmith – had brought the two-year-old little boy down from London to escape the bombs, but leaving behind, unknown to Mrs Wordingham, a large son. Mrs Wordingham gave Michael his bath each night, as she knew his mother had done. Baths equalled love.

Two years or so later Miss Goldsmith abruptly left. It seemed that the entire Allied war effort was being manned – or womanned, rather – by former domestics. Mrs Wordingham had never known anything like it. It had not been like this in 1914. A succession of ludicrous 'servants', each worse than the last, passed through Inkpen Vicarage – wretched single or abandoned women, monstrously underpaid, too crazy or old or ill-adapted to do whatever it was the women who should have been cooks and nannies and parlourmaids were now doing. At first nominally in the care of these unsuitable figures, Michael principally remembered his grandmother appearing suddenly to check that her instructions were being followed – which they seldom were. There were rows. Sackings. Disappearances.

Gradually, in defiance of her entire upbringing, Mrs Wordingham began to look after him more and more herself. She bought, among numerous manuals, *The Truby King Manual of Child Training* and *The Psychological Care of Children* by J. B. Watson. Michael's life became organised down to the minutest detail, from waking to bedtime. The central feature was the chamber pot. Every day, often several times a day, his grandmother would bend heavily forward and peer anxiously in, *Truby King* or one of the other books in one arthritic hand, spectacles held on to her nose with the other. Michael would peer too. Emptiness, apart from the pale puddle of his faintly steaming pee, caused consternation, consultation of *Truby King* and, if empty a second time, Steps: chocolate-tasting aperients or suppositories of a camphor-smelling gel, and once or twice – the enema! But at success – 'Well *done*, darling! That's a really *splendid* one. Clever boy!' Michael wondered at its speedy despatch. Shouldn't they keep it?

Peace brought no alleviation of Mrs Wordingham's other central problem. The domestic servant class appeared to have been wiped out. The last substitute figure, supposedly an ex-teacher, had turned out to be an elderly south London barmaid, sacked for pilfering and alcoholism; before that a bent ninety-two-year-old, posing as eighty, had followed a momentary splutter of energy at the interview by a series of small strokes, until eventually found speechless and paralysed on the pantry floor.

Latest was genteel Mrs Bawdon, a pet-mad former golfing champion shattered by her seventy-year-old husband running off with their life savings and thirty-one-year-old neighbour, whose husband had been killed at the D-day landings. With sagging red cheeks, Mrs Bawdon spent most of her time silently crying, sipping tea in a stifling hot kitchen filled with the smell of damp, geriatric dog.

'Look at that toast!' said Michael's grandmother irritably, pointing to the table laid for tea. 'How often do I have to tell the woman? Now, come to the cloakroom and I'll wash your hands.'

'At least she's better than Mrs Hunt,' she said when they returned to the drawing room. Slowly becoming locked by arthritis, she bent with difficulty to light the fire. She was like some huge, gentle countryside, slope-sweeping downland, cloudy and comfortable. The taut expanse of her skirted bottom filled Michael's vision.

'Shall I get the book ready, Granny?'

After tea, as usual, his grandmother said, 'Pass me another

log, Michael.' The flames leapt, momentarily igniting the fire-back into a constellation of sparks. 'Up you get,' said his grand-mother. Michael climbed on to the arm of her chair and settled himself.

At one time, the first paragraph or two had been devoted to teaching him to read. This rarely happened now. Despite his age, Michael still couldn't really read. In the same way, he could hardly dress himself. He would stand, supine, peaceful, while Mrs Wordingham did up buttons or tweaked his jersey straight. He liked to lean back and let her do his reading for him. In fact, they both preferred it this way.

3

Ivan was five. He stood staring out where the muddy track, very recently tyre-marked, went straight away alongside the flat fields. He stood unconscious of the muck in his shoes, tense, until his fine, almost cream-coloured hair had darkened in the drizzle.

He felt his heart trying to bang its way out of his chest. There was a noise growing in his head, a menacing crescendo.

Suddenly, as though his heart had finally burst through into his throat, he cried out. He was just aware, like a presence at the edge of a nightmare, of the tall, grim-faced, stubble-chinned man watching him from the far corner of the yard.

'Na!' cried Ivan. 'Na! Na! Na!' He clattered through the big, cold, empty rooms. The turret room was small, but it had windows on all four sides. He flung himself across its clammy emptiness on to the bed with the worn black bearskin, its long, hard hairs almost the length of pine needles.

But it was the spongy coverlet underneath he wanted. He pressed his face into it and smelt the onion-sweet smell, pungent and overwhelming – one of the smells of love. All that he had left.

He pressed the coverlet against him, sobbing, took it

desperately into his mouth, sucking, trying to choke his sobs and anaesthetise himself, trying somehow, if only for a moment, to still the terrifying grief which seemed to be breaking him apart.

It might indeed have done that – or allowed him to be broken, since there was now no one to stand between him and iron Boris. But some time after this, Ivan discovered he possessed a secret solace and a secret power.

It was late summer. He had just been beaten. He was standing in the stack yard trembling with stifled fury, pain and the effort not to cry, when he became aware of a superimposed but unconnected agitation. All at once, like a cool wind flowing over him, he was invaded by the most extraordinary sensation of peace. His pain and anger died away. At the same time he became acutely aware of the stacks. They began to glow, the straw was golden, emanating light; gradually, as though condensing out of the gold, he saw a figure appearing in front of him.

It was a boy a little older than him, pale and plump and with a sweet smile. Ivan knew at once his name was Mikhail.

Mikhail became his constant companion. He was calm and slow where Ivan was agitated and overactive, brave where Ivan was frightened. Ivan could see him clearly, but he was invisible and inaudible to everyone else. Although he sometimes came unsummoned, Ivan could make him go at will. Particularly did he make him disappear when Boris was around. Boris was enraged at any suggestion of Mikhail – an extra place at meals, for example, or if he heard Ivan chatting while they both played in the hay.

But how could you hear and see someone if they were 'imaginary'? And Ivan had proof. Mikhail used to help him work, and he was even clumsier than Ivan. There was nothing imaginary about three broken eggs or a gate left open. Ivan had started by pointing these obvious things out. But since arguing invariably meant a beating, he soon gave it up.

4

The reading aloud was as important as the chamber pot. It took place after tea, and then again while Michael lay in bed after his grandmother had given him his bath.

'Now where had we got to?' she would say, peering through her glasses at the pages of *The Golden Thread* or *Tanglewood Tales* or *Coral Island* or *My Dog Crusoe*.

Swiftly, they were both entwined in the sinuous coils of narrative. *The Golden Thread* in particular thrilled him – thrilled them both. Starting with the affecting death of a young mother, it was the story of a little boy lost in a forest. A golden thread, looping through the branches, catching the sun, led him to safety.

There seemed no particular reason why it should have given them such pleasure. It can hardly have been the Victorian symbolism, since Mrs Wordingham did not explain it. (The 'golden thread' was the love of Jesus supported, at crucial points, by the tenets of the Anglican church, similarly symbolised.) Yet certain passages gave Michael a most peculiar sensation, as though touching some distant but imprecise memory of feeling, something both painful and beautiful. It may have been the way she read, the sound. Mrs Wordingham's family came from Scotland. Its accent, now very faint, none the less gave something beguiling, almost hypnotic, to her reading. As a girl and as a young woman she had had an ambition to write. Some of her attempts had been directed at children and even these, transfigured by the magic of her lilt, Michael seemed to enjoy – unpolished as they were.

Mrs Wordingham also played the piano for him, albeit with some difficulty now, her joints knotted and knobbly. 'Now you sit there, by the pedals, darling, in "the boom of the tingling springs".'

'What?' Michael said, nonplussed.

'It's a quotation, darling, from a Very Great Writer.' (Nearly all writers, by that fact alone, were Very Great to Mrs Wordingham.) 'One day you'll read him.'

Michael would sit in the boom and the tingling springs seemed to be speaking to him. She played and sang hymns, songs from the First World War and pieces from her Scottish childhood. 'The Barren Rocks of Aden' did not have words so Mrs Wordingham blew out her cheeks and made the noise of a drum. Some of the songs, for no discernible reason, especially struck Michael. He loved the one that began 'There is a green hill far away/Without a city wall . . .' As he grew older, this intrigued him still more because he realised it did not make sense. Why should a green hill have a city wall? Once, when Mrs Wordingham had sung this to him with particular feeling, with an aching, nostalgic, plangent note that somehow echoed *The Golden Thread*, Michael discovered that he'd peed all over the cushion. At first rather disconcerted, his grandmother quickly saw this as a compliment. It was clear Michael was a child of exceptional sensibility. Possibly even gifted artistically, perhaps in a literary way. She threw herself with extra fervour into the narratives, implanting them. Because, despite the more overt reaction to music, it was these he liked best. And he seemed to want them most when he was in bed.

There was a reason for this. Although Michael loved Inkpen Vicarage, it sometimes also frightened him. At night, out of deep black silence, it suddenly gave loud snaps and cracks or, even more terrifying, long, apparently advancing creaks. At these times, evil spirits blew round it off the sea sound of the wind in the pines.

Once – it must have been a year or so after Michael had come to live there – he was sleeping as usual in the tower room (which wasn't a tower at all; the Victorian architect had just stuck a silly two-sided excrescence out from one corner). Quite suddenly he had been woken in the middle of the night. The room was illuminated and subtly changed. A woman was standing at the end of the bed looking at him. He could not see her eyes because of the gleam on the glass of her spectacles. Gradually the light – which came from no particular source, but was somehow given forth by the room itself, by everything in it –

faded. Had she stretched her hand towards him? Terrified as he was, Michael had slowly crept his own hand out into the cold darkness and turned on the lamp. The room had changed back. The woman had gone.

Two nights later Michael wet his bed. Mrs Wordingham bustled about, cheerful, ostentatiously not blaming. 'It could happen to anyone, darling. To me.' Despite her arthritis, she felt she couldn't ask Mrs Blackstone, the similarly afflicted seventy-year-old laughingly described as a cook, to wash the sheets. Mrs Blackstone was already becoming 'difficult'. Mrs Wordingham washed them herself, inexpertly and exhaustingly in the bath. Her hands like roots, she wrestled the mattress till it hung out of the window.

Michael wet his bed the next night, and the next, and the next, and the next. He wet his bed every night for a month. Mrs Wordingham began to show signs of strain. A lot more sheets had to be bought, two of them rubber. The chamber pot was put on a stool next to the bed, with a torch. Michael went to bed without pyjamas, to facilitate rapid pot access and to lessen somewhat the colossal burden of washing. Then she tried waking Michael and 'potting' him last thing before she went to bed. An extra clothes line had to be strung up outside the kitchen. She found that, after all, she *could* ask muttering Mrs Blackstone to help.

In the second month, she called in Dr Jackson, their new young GP. He examined Michael carefully. 'Nothing wrong with the waterworks,' he reported.

He and Mrs Wordingham talked privately in the drawing room. 'Clearly, there's some anxiety, something bothering him.' Dr Jackson prided himself on his advanced 'psychological' approach to medicine.

'Obviously,' said Mrs Wordingham. 'I've asked him numerous times. His father and mother were killed when he was two. I've talked to him as gently as I can about that. He seems, really, to have forgotten them. But if not, why *now*?'

'Nothing particular happened recently?'

'Nothing at all.'

'I believe,' said Dr Jackson, testing her, 'that there is something, a conducting sheet, connected to a battery – a very mild electric shock is administered . . .'

'No, no, *no*,' said Mrs Wordingham. 'Far, far too sensitive.' Nevertheless, she had to repress a flicker of regret.

'Well,' said Dr Jackson decisively, 'here's the approach I'd advocate. No blame, of course. Praise, in fact. But make him see how you *value* his water, how marvellous it is. A part of him. A part you love. Ask him to keep it for you.'

Oddly enough, dubious as this sounded, it obliquely chimed with Mrs Wordingham's reading. A friend in the village, a slight crank, it is true, had lent her *The Waters of Life – A Treatise on Urine Therapy* by J. W. Armstrong. She had read the book with astonishment and no little disgust.

> Mrs R. Diagnosed (1923) as cancer by the late Dr Rabagliati . . . Fasted on urine and drank five pints a day. Her husband rubbed her from head to foot with his own urine for two hours a day, and packs wrung out in urine were placed over both breasts day and night. *Cure in ten days.*

Perhaps there was something in it. She collected all the pee from Michael's now frequent daily and evening pottings and eventually filled one of her two-pound bottling jars.

'*See* how lovely it is, darling!' she said. 'It's a precious part of you. We mustn't waste it on the sheets, must we?'

Michael stared at her. The whole subject embarrassed him and made him feel ashamed.

'I *love* it!' cried Mrs Wordingham, feeling false but doggedly determined to carry out Dr Jackson's instructions. 'I could *drink* it!'

Michael brightened. 'Are you *really* going to drink it, Granny?' he asked with interest. 'All of it?'

Mrs Wordingham stretched out her club hands and raised the heavy bottling jar towards her lips as if it were some sacred chalice. J. W. Armstrong would have quaffed the lot without a qualm.

'No,' she said, lowering the chalice with seeming regret. 'I'd like to, but it's too precious. We would waste it if we drank it. Especially, darling, we mustn't waste it on the bed. Do you see what I mean?'

Two jars, then three stood catching the sunlight, pale bleached gold upon the windowsill. Then, because they were inadequately sealed, specks, finally rafts of mould appeared on the surface. One day Mrs Wordingham, to Michael's astonishment, even anguish, abruptly threw away all the precious liquid.

Whatever good effects this brief therapy might have had – and it appeared to have had none at all – were considerably undermined by Mrs Blackstone. She was disgusted by what was going on and shortly afterwards gave in her notice.

'If I had my way,' she said to Michael, gripping him tightly with her claw by the upper arm, 'you'd get a good belting. You'd soon learn to control yourself.'

When his grandmother asked him if anything was worrying him, he always said 'No, Granny', because at that moment nothing was. But at bedtime he would remember the woman in spectacles and become frightened. Sometimes his grandmother's stories were sufficient to carry him insulated into sleep. At others he would beg, 'Please, Granny, just one more page – *please*.' Then, still too frightened to talk about it directly, he would skirt dangerously close to the subject. As she lowered the huge downland of her bosom towards him, its sprig of verbena like a little tree, for the goodnight kiss, he'd say, 'Are you *sure* there aren't any ghosts in this house, quite, quite sure?'

'Quite, quite sure, darling.'

'Even in this room?'

'There are no ghosts *anywhere*, darling. I promise you.' The scent of verbena was the scent of love. 'Now tell yourself a nice story and I'll leave the light on in the passage.'

'And leave the door open.'

He heard the heavy creaking as she walked back to the stairs, and then that familiar pattern, rhythm almost, as she descended. One of the sounds of love was always of someone leaving.

He never forgot the woman with the spectacles; however,

gradually the memory lost its power to frighten him and became something permanent but inert. But it seemed to represent or be connected to some far more general body of buried worry, a giant, underground reservoir into whose black depths something penetrated each night like the narrow pipe of an artesian well and up which rushed a thin, warm, unstoppable, sheet-soaking stream.

5

'All flesh is grass,' Boris used to say.

The first time Ivan had looked at him sharply, trying to understand another adult riddle; a male adult riddle, as they usually were.

'The cows eat grass,' said Boris. 'We drink their milk, we eat their flesh. All flesh is grass.'

'What about the pigs?'

'Same thing. Their mash is corn. The swill from the kitchen is potato peel, cabbage stalks. It's all grass.' He looked at Ivan and then, seeing his continuing puzzlement, turned irritably away. 'You'll understand one day.' Adding, in a sentence that was to reappear like a block every time he wanted to find out something important, 'You'll see for yourself.'

Later, when he was in his long night shirt, Ivan discussed this with Mikhail. They agreed it was a lie. Their fingers weren't grass – nor was Boris's iron-hard hand. You might as well say 'All flesh is biscuits' because he'd had a biscuit, shared with Mikhail, before going to bed.

But in the wider context, it was a clue let slip – either accidentally or on purpose.

Quite early in his life, soon after he had conjured Mikhail to be his companion, Ivan had realised that the whole adult male world was a secret society. However, it was a secret society whose secrets he and Mikhail at first thought could be discovered and which, by learning, Ivan would be allowed to enter.

The men of the Taschla Collective quite often paid visits to the farmhouse. Occasionally it was to fight with each other at an evening of the arm wrestling – or arm fighting – which was an old custom in the region and peculiar to it. More often it was to discuss quotas or similar matters with Boris. Ivan noticed that they stood and acted in special ways: with crossed legs or one foot in advance of the other; they pulled their noses or put one hand behind their back; they spat, often, it seemed, in special places. The young boy and his friend copied these and countless other secret actions, to show that he *knew*. He was an initiate too.

'All flesh is grass' was certainly one such secret. Of this they eventually had incontrovertible proof, hearing if not seeing it for themselves. As well as the regular meetings of the Taschla Collective, there were other meetings. These took place late at night, always in the large kitchen. One winter, when Ivan was seven, Boris forgot to have him removed from his bed above the tall, blue-tiled stove. That night Mikhail, whom in fact he rarely saw now, was with him. As the first man entered, his pale, plump, inactive companion shrank down into the little bed. Leaning over, Ivan could hear the password exchanged at the side door. It was 'All flesh is grass'.

At first, Ivan had supposed that it might be to enter this secret male world that he was being 'prepared'. Or if not to enter, then to take the test which would decide whether he could enter or not.

Ever since he could remember – ever since that terrible day which had blotted out all before it and quite soon had itself almost vanished, leaving only the feeling that something terrible had happened – ever since, Boris had been preparing him for something momentous, for some great future test or position. He had said so in as many words: 'Your father left it to me to prepare you.' Had that terrible day been the day his father had died or been killed or whatever it was that had happened to him (a forbidden topic)?

'Prepare' at first meant nothing out of the ordinary. Simply that anything he did – carrying water out to the eleven cows, filling first the little pig trough, later graduating to the long one, cleaning the harness – all had to be done perfectly, 'to prepare you'.

'Yes, but what am I being prepared for?' asked Ivan. He had crossed his left leg over his right while at the same time pulling his nose.

Boris ignored these signs. 'You will learn. You'll see for yourself.'

One thing he was certainly being prepared for was to take his part in the big, hugely popular arm-fighting contests which took place on public holidays. Boris was a champion here, on several occasions the supreme champion, drawing on his pride in his enormous strength, built from years of farm work, his delight in inflicting public humiliation, his aggressive character and consequent hatred of losing. Ivan sometimes thought that to win at arm fighting meant more to Boris than the collective itself. He would quite often see him practising in private, lifting bags of grain up and down or sitting, legs apart, and fighting against some wooden upright to increase his throwing strength.

But, though he perhaps introduced Ivan to it at an unusually early age, this training was no more than many of the local boys went through. Then, when Ivan was ten, something happened that was not ordinary. It was a market day at Pokrowskii, one of the rare occasions when the farms of the Taschla and neighbouring collectives were allowed, despite the war, to sell openly a certain, very limited amount for their own profit. Everyone enjoyed these days. They were outings.

The whole household had gone. Boris's sister Antonina – lean, slightly moustached, smelling of sour cabbage; the four young workers who were billeted with them; little old Na; and a party official who was there for an audit.

It was surprising enough that Boris should decide not to go. There would certainly be arm fighting. As for Ivan, he supposed he was just being punished. There were always punishments. Often it was his overactivity that angered Boris. The way he ran rather than walked back with the eggs, so breaking one; the restless way he got up early; the way he couldn't stay still. Boris and Ivan stood watching the cart trundle into the heat-expectant haze of the early morning. Ivan's arms hung sullenly at his sides.

But instead of punishment, Boris collected a spade and led him silently out of the farm and along the track that led the hundred yards or so to the Wiga, at this early point part river, part canal. On its near bank was a scattered clump of trees: some poplars and several oaks. The ground here was slightly raised. Only a few feet, but it gave a view out over the great plain.

This was the site of the old house – Taschla. When they had been given the farm in the early 1920s, Ivan's father had named it in memory of the village near Samara where he'd been born. At the time of the 1934 collectivisations, furiously resisted, Taschla had been savagely destroyed (as had the great forests – sheared like some enormous beard to make way for grain). The collective of which the farm and nearby villages had been forced to form a part was in reality called the People's Collective of Pokrowskii No. 2. But among the men and all around, it was still obstinately Taschla.

Of the old house, all that remained standing was an earth closet – a rough, windowless brick structure at the end of one of the grass-covered mounds of rubble. It was used by the farm hands, as it had been by the soldiers who had 'installed' it. Inadequately earthed and infrequently emptied, and then only to be tipped down the bank into the slow-moving waters of the Wiga, it could be clearly detected by nose in summer – and was so now by the little boy and the big, grim-faced man.

Boris left Ivan standing apprehensive and slightly puzzled outside the privy door. He ran up on the mound and stood looking slowly all round. Not a soul. Shimmering wheat. A lark.

The smell was even stronger inside the privy. Boris locked them in with an oak branch shoved through two big iron staples. The actual mechanism of the privy was simple: two stained planks, laid, with twenty-five centimetre gap, across a large, sawn-off oil drum with a wire handle. In one corner was the pile of earth the men usually forgot to use.

Boris leant the planks against the wall. Then he took the

twisted wire handle and, bent and grunting with the effort, the odious cauldron swinging between his knees – Ivan could hear the contents slopping about – shuffled a few feet and let it drop with a thud. In winter, the sluggish contents froze solid. Sometimes Ivan had come in and steam was still rising up between the planks.

Now Boris took the spade and began to shovel away the earth floor where the drum had stood. After clearing an area about one metre square and down twenty centimetres or so, he had uncovered a large stone flag. Boris inserted the spade under one end and pressed it down.

'Here, come and hold the candle.'

Ivan did so, and Boris then got his thick fingers under the raised flag. He was a strong man, but Ivan heard him gasp as he lifted the thick flag slowly upright and then wrestle it across so that he could lean it against the wall. Where the flag had been was a gaping black hole. It was like one of Na's stories.

Boris lit the stump of a yellow candle. He handed this to Ivan, and then lowered himself down into the hole. For a moment he hung, grizzled head bent, then dropped.

'Pass me the candle.'

Boris's reaching hand was below him. Ivan lay on his stomach. The hot wax from the candle flowed over his fingers and the flame flared.

'Now, come in feet first. I'll catch you.'

He was nervously lowering himself when he felt Boris's horny grip on his calves and was pulled down, caught roughly at thigh and chest and thumped to the ground. Boris bent and picked up the candle, which he'd put on a ladder lying on the earth floor.

They were in a room about five metres square. It was cool and smelt of damp. Boris walked across to two chests side by side against the far wall.

'This is one of the cellars of the old house. When it was destroyed, your father managed to get hold of some of the things and hid them here.' He lifted the lid of the right-hand chest and held the candle over it. 'They belong to you.'

Ivan looked in, remembering little Na's stories. Jumble, rubbish, heaps. Mostly, looking closer, pieces of painted wood. Not a ruby nor an emerald to be seen.

'What is it?'

'They're icons. Some are old. I believe there's one necklace. They're worth a lot of money.'

'How much?'

'Many thousands of roubles. Even more in the West, in America. Much more. This will help you in your tasks.'

'What tasks, Boris?' Was he about to know, at last?

'You'll learn.'

'Please tell me. What are you preparing me for?'

And then, for the first and only time, Boris set a term to the mystery.

'I will tell you when you're eighteen.'

There was a low opening in the wall nearest the raised flagstone.

'What's in there?' asked Ivan.

'Another cellar,' said Boris. 'It's empty.'

When he'd pushed the ladder back down, replaced the stone, the earth, the drum and the planks, Boris knelt in front of Ivan.

'You are to tell no one.'

'No. I won't.'

Boris took Ivan's shoulders and stood up, lifting him so that they were head to head.

'I shall not beat you if you tell,' he said. 'I shall kill you.' He kept his cold grey eyes fixed on Ivan's till the boy had to look away.

He felt sick with terror. 'I won't tell, I promise,' he said, his mouth dry. Who, after all, was there to tell?

Mikhail hardly came now. And in any case, there was no more point telling Mikhail than in telling Na. Both would know already.

6

'Have we blown your nose this morning, Michael?'

Mrs Wordingham stood poised, a clean handkerchief in her right hand.

'No,' said Michael.

His grandmother reached forward and enfolded his nose between forefinger and thumb as if catching an insect. 'Good blow,' she said.

There was nothing staining the purity of the linen when they both inspected it; but a similar joint inspection of the chamber pot earlier that morning had revealed a splendid something.

'Look at that!' Mrs Wordingham had cried.

It had been a good morning in every way. The bottom sheet had been biscuit dry and apparently fresh (sometimes the night's deposit was dried by his body). Mrs Wordingham bent and sniffed deeply, almost seeming to breathe in and exhale the sheet. Michael, standing watching, felt himself gasp sympathetically.

'Now we mustn't keep Mrs Iken waiting. Stand still while I do up these buttons.' Michael stood obediently, feeling himself tweaked and patted and pulled and squeezed.

Mrs Iken was a woman from the village who came in during emergencies such as the one created by the latest domestic departure.

While she washed his hands in the cloakroom after his cornflakes and bread and marmalade breakfast, Mrs Wordingham chatted around this permanent problem.

'I think we've got a replacement,' she said. 'She's a refugee from Latvia called Elfreda Smitten. I got her through that agency in Ipswich.'

In the drawing room, she showed a totally uninterested Michael the agency papers. 'She's thirty-one. Divorced. She's only been in England a month. I feel so *sorry* for these poor refugees. Even if she's no good at *all*, I feel, we must try and keep her for a while. Now go upstairs and get your hairbrush.'

Michael hated his hair being brushed. 'Tangles!' his grandmother laughed gaily. She was reminded of her girlhood. She sometimes longed to apply her old curling tongs, but Truby King warned that such playfulness could lead to later homosexualism.

Before he returned the hairbrush to the top of his little chest of drawers in the tower room, Michael carefully removed the half-dozen pale, fine hairs caught in the black Mason & Pearson bristles. He carried the hairs over to the window and squatted down. Poking his fat forefinger through a knothole, he pulled up a loose floorboard and leant it against the wall. In the dark space below there were two brown paper bags. Michael picked one out and carefully added his hairs to those already half filling it.

The morning after the woman with spectacles had come to his room, he had found a long hair caught in a screw at the end of his bed. There were two more on the floor. Michael had put them into the empty paper bag which had held his two 'goodnight' sweets. Then he found a fourth hair in the bathroom, but he wasn't sure if it was the ghost's hair or his own. By insensible degrees, he found he was collecting his own hairs. It may have been as compensation for so many other precious parts of himself that were being thrown away all the time. He got pleasure in the secrecy. At first he hid the bag behind his toy cupboard. Later he found the loose floorboard.

The second bag contained bits of china. These were turned up by the plough in Top Field, cultivated for Mrs Wordingham by a neighbouring farmer. Mrs Wordingham had found this collection.

'Oh, Michael, how lovely! But oh, dear, aren't they dirty!' She washed the shattered fragments – some patterned, others white or blue or pink or green – and arranged them in a neat row.

Michael had liked them with earth on them. He felt it fed them. It was part of the mysterious subterranean world they came from. Thereafter he smuggled the earth-stuck pieces of china into the house and, with the same secret satisfaction, hid them under the floorboard. His treasures.

'Come on, Michael darling! It's time for your walk. It's a lovely day again.'

'Coming, Granny,' Michael cried, hurrying plumply and happily down the stairs, consciously replicating, as he did so, the pattern of creaks that followed his grandmother's nightly departures.

7

The children on the Taschla Collective were taught arithmetic, reading, writing, chemistry, physics and history. Then, shortly after the revelations in the privy – and, Ivan felt, obscurely connected with them – a special instructor was sent by the Regional Committee of the Party to instruct them in Marxism-Leninism. Boris was ordered by the Party to house Alexis Kharkov for the purpose. Kharkov was also responsible for Marxism-Leninism instruction in three neighbouring collectives and the Adult Re-Indoctrination Centre at Kologriw nearby.

Alexis Kharkov, aged about fifty-two, was excitable, tall, thin and ungainly. A man of protrusions: forehead, eyeballs, nose, teeth, chin, Adam's apple, everything wobbled, bulged or stuck out. His classes in Marxism-Leninism were extremely boring. Fortunately, they were very brief. It soon became clear that what Comrade Kharkov (as they were told to call him) was really interested in was literature. His luggage had been almost entirely books. What he enjoyed doing, after his perfunctory instructions to his classes of farmers' sons and daughters, was reading aloud fairy stories, folk tales, fables and, often, stories from the enchanting collections Tolstoy had written for children.

One evening Ivan, who loved these sessions and had got into the habit of dropping into the tower room where Alexis lived, discovered a second row of books concealed behind the first on the shelves below the window. They were written in some strange language.

'What are these, Comrade Kharkov?' he asked, still not quite liking to call him Alexis, though the intimacy had been offered.

The teacher at once showed signs of agitation. 'They're perfectly harmless,' he said, his pointed Adam's apple bobbing with nervous, independent life. 'Nothing forbidden there – though I do possess one or two . . . but no need to mention . . . They're English books, some French classics.'

'Would I like them?'

'Oh, yes. These are among, even *are*, the world's greatest literature.'

'Could you teach me to read them?'

Thus it was Ivan began to learn English and French in the evenings both he and Alexis were free. The teacher found his pupil had a gift for languages. Within six months he was reading *Robinson Crusoe*, Rider Haggard and Victor Hugo on his own.

Boris did not approve of this association but, assuming it was in furtherance of Comrade Kharkov's task, did not dare forbid it. It might get back to the Party that he was obstructive. But he regarded political instruction as a waste of time. It interfered with farming. In particular it exacerbated the problem of Ivan. The Ivan he knew was clumsy, obstinate, forgetful and careless. He ran when he should have walked. He was infuriating.

Boris beat him. The more he beat him, the worse Ivan seemed to get. This did not make Boris beat him less. He beat him more. He sensed, rightly, that the clumsiness and forgetfulness were acts of rebellion. But he got pleasure from this. He enjoyed it when Ivan struggled under his hand, just as he did when a puppy being trained yelped and squirmed. It was the frenzied tug of the fish on a line. Once, when Boris was lashing his bare bottom, Ivan, almost mad with fear and fury and pain, had felt his bowels dissolving. He had been unable to hold himself in. The sight had ignited Boris into a sort of frenzy of disgust and rage and delight. He had lashed uncontrollably, flooding with savage joy. The walls and even the ceiling had been spattered with diarrhoea and blood.

Boris's main aim in life, it seemed to Ivan, was to humiliate him. This even applied to the arm-fighting lessons. The sport was more complicated and more subtle than at first appeared. Boris taught him how to lock shoulder and elbow rigid to resist an attack; and it was possible to do this even when bent back at 45 degrees. He taught him to feint and how to feign a feint. He taught him how it was possible to anticipate by vital seconds, vital milliseconds, a surprise attack, sensing with closed eyes minute quivers and tensings. And all this he did, for once, with patience and care. But the real point of each lesson, it was clear, was the final battles between them. Boris always crushed him, with maximum force, as painfully as he could.

Every night, Ivan had fantasies of murdering Boris. He would plan it with Mikhail. Whenever he had a wish – on his name day or served six plum stones or when he saw a magpie – he wished that Boris would die. But not before he'd revealed the secret of what Ivan was being prepared for.

The privy, though secret, had nothing to do with that secret world peopled by adults which he thought he'd detected. It was after all from them, apart from Boris, that the secret had to be kept. But he now sometimes had a glimpse, especially when his hatred of Boris reached a height, of an even more terrifying truth. Nothing existed – at least as he knew it. Everyone, led by Boris, was part of a gigantic conspiracy *to pretend to him that the world was as it seemed.* The farm routines, the farm itself, the Party, the roles everyone played – these were all a show. The events in the privy, Alexis Kharkov, even 'All flesh is grass' and seeing for himself the secret society he thought he'd discovered – these were all blinds to put him off the scent. Behind his back, they whispered, 'He thinks it's true.' Somewhere, there was a real world, inconceivably different, but he was excluded from this for ever. So frightening was this realisation that he could only endure it for short periods of time.

Mikhail – emanation of himself – could, while he still came, comfort him. So could Alexis, and so could Alexis's books, into which he escaped. Soon the very sight of books pleased him and soothed him. He enjoyed touching them, feeling that something of their content communicated itself like this, passing into his fingers and up his arms.

But neither Mikhail, Alexis nor books could save him from Boris. Fortunately, by a further exertion of his power, he had managed to create a fourth member of their household who – though he only learnt this later – did try and save him.

It was not long after Mikhail, and oddly enough in the stack yard again. Ivan had been unusually jumpy and frenetic all day. Boris had shouted at him repeatedly and several times knocked him flying. On the way to the hens late in the afternoon, he suddenly felt as if something, the cool current of a stream, was flowing through him, clearing, cleansing, untangling. The straw particles glowed in the slanting sun and, as before, in the moment of blissful peace a figure materialised in front of him.

It was a little old woman wearing spectacles. Ivan stared at her. She had brown hair and a round, brown, kindly face. The golden light from the straw began to fade, but the woman remained. Ivan was about to go to her when he saw to his horror that Boris was approaching round the end of the nearest stack. At once Ivan focused his power to make the woman invisible before being discovered.

She wouldn't go. Frantically, Ivan strained – go, go, *go*. Too late. Boris had reached her. But instead of anger – which he would certainly have shown, had he come upon Mikhail – he seemed to accept the new figure. They were speaking to each other. Boris was pointing at him. Then he turned and left.

Ivan felt he was waking from a dream. Sounds began to return. He heard the chickens, a clink of metal; he could smell the pigs again, the dry smell of the straw.

This became the pattern for the manifestations of his power: agitation, the sudden onset of calm and strength, intense happiness, the gradual return of reality. But from now on anything he did during the moments of strength passed out of his control. Mikhail had been an exception.

And in fact the kindly little woman was now, under her

own volition, standing in front of him. 'I am Natalia Ivanovna Mikhailova,' she said. 'I am to help look after you.'

'Yes,' said Ivan. He looked at the small nimble face. 'I think I'll call you Na.'

8

When Elfreda Smitten arrived at Inkpen Vicarage, she had no luggage.

'All gone!' she cried in answer to Mrs Wordingham's polite enquiry. 'All iss taken. Elfreda haff only what she iss vearing!'

A big, strong, thin woman, she stood in the kitchen, her legs apart, looking at Mrs Wordingham and Michael, her blue eyes wide and expressive. 'When Russians came, vot they do? They rape all vimin,' she said. 'Elfreda iss raped, many many times.'

'Good heavens!' said Mrs Wordingham. 'Michael, go and put another log on the fire. Carefully now. A small log.'

When he'd gone, Elfreda, who was not slow, smiled at her new mistress. 'You theenk it iss better he not know?' she said. 'People must know these beasts. Rape rape rape they go. He iss big boy.'

'Only nine,' said Mrs Wordingham.

'*Beeg*', repeated Elfreda with emphasis. 'Now, you show me duties. I vill vork.'

Elfreda rapidly became a factor in their quiet life. With a long, thin, lippy mouth slithering about over big broken teeth, with high cheekbones and abundant, coarse and often dirty hair she roughly tied back, she was the first servant Mrs Wordingham had had since 1939 who'd had any energy. Vork she did.

Michael was fascinated by her. She was like something out of a fairy story – a jinni or a sandstorm. She ruffled his hair and pulled his nose and talked to him incessantly about things he could not understand.

'You are not to spend so much time in the kitchen,' said Mrs Wordingham. For the first time in his life he disobeyed his grandmother. Or rather, did not exactly disobey but always found good reasons for another visit.

Dust flew about and landed somewhere else – as did other things.

There would be a loud crash of breaking china outside the drawing-room door as they waited for tea. Then it would burst open and a distraught figure would appear, holding aloft a slice of plate in each hand. 'Now look what haff happened! How can I get trolley over step in hallvay? Always something slide away. But Elfreda pay.'

Mrs Wordingham would get up and bustle to the door. 'Don't worry, Elfreda. It doesn't matter. It's a very old set – most of them are broken.'

When she came back, she'd say, 'That woman! We won't have a cup or plate or jug left soon. But she's had a terrible time.'

None the less, Elfreda was useful. One weekened, about five months after she had arrived, Mrs Wordingham had to make one of her rare visits to London, about the letting of her house in Drayton Gardens. She was also having dinner with her sister. Arthritis, leading to the need for endless pre-ordered taxis and requests for porters, made these visits even more difficult and complicated than Mrs Wordingham's natural desire to make them as importantly difficult and complicated as possible.

She wrote four pages of instructions concerning Michael. An insurmountable problem, owing to misplaced scruples on Mrs Wordingham's part regarding Elfreda, was Michael's bath.

'Let him bath himself – no?' said Elfreda. 'A great big boy he iss.'

'You think so?' said Mrs Wordingham in a worried voice. 'I wonder. It's a big step. I would rather be here.'

'In Latvia children is bathing themselves by ages four or three,' said Elfreda, a trifle scornfully.

'Nevertheless,' said Mrs Wordingham, 'the danger of drowning . . . scalding . . . I don't feel . . .'

'*I* vill him bath give,' said Elfreda.

'Well, that's the point,' said Mrs Wordingham. 'I hardly liked to ask because – well, he is in some respects, in one respect at least, a big boy now, it is true. Are you sure you won't mind, don't feel . . .?'

Elfreda completely ignored these English delicacies, if she was even aware of them. 'Ve vill haff fun!' she cried. 'Vash, vash, vash.'

In fact, however, all she did was run the bath. Mrs Wordingham's attentions and services to Michael she regarded as quite ridiculous.

Michael lay flat in the bath. Nothing happened. No one came. Gradually the water became cold.

'So – still there, a lazy boy! Up ve get. *Vot* a big boy! Elfreda can hardly lift.'

Yet she dried him with peculiar tenderness, bending close so that he could smell her Elfreda smell of onion, cigarettes and hair. She cupped his round white bottom in her sinewy right hand and rubbed the rough softness of the towel to and fro, to and fro, to and fro between his plump open legs.

9

Winter on the plain. A pincer movement. First snow swept in from the east, rank upon rank, tribe after tribe, hordes, swarms – it was the Mongol invasion all over again – until it had covered the land, one metre, two metres deep, three metre drifts, white, everywhere white.

Then the cold came down from the north and northeast, straight from Siberia, from the Arctic. Invader and plain were locked.

The canals became ice. Ivan got out his skates and went skimming through the frozen land. Boris had a pair of the old bone skates that the peasants had used before the Revolution.

The ice was half a metre thick. Even the Wiga froze. Two

phenomena here. The river at this point flowed north for 50 kilometres before curving south to eventually join the Volga (everything joined the Volga in the end). As the water drained and sank, the ice buckled into a curve. Then, three months later, as the thaw began in the south, the water of the Wiga flowed more and more swiftly north. If you were brave or foolish enough to splash out on the dissolving surface, you could see branches and sometimes the bodies of animals rushing underneath. Boris had once seen a dead baby.

The winter suited Boris. He felt at home, relaxed, amid ice and snow. He'd try and race Ivan on his bone skates. To an outsider this hard man might have seemed to be melting.

This especially, and almost physically, at the 'secret' gatherings of the Taschla Collective at night in the big kitchen. These took place every three or four weeks. After the 'All flesh is grass' meeting, Boris allowed Ivan to remain there. 'Time to see for yourself.'

He discovered that, despite the all-important war effort, the collective still sold a good deal on the underground market. It was big business. Produce fetched five, even six times the set prices. There was endless discussion. Quotas had to be juggled, pigs and cows and chickens concealed at the biannual stocktakings, decisions taken about what to grow and breed, when and where to sell. Roubles were handed to Boris for safekeeping and future redistribution.

Ivan watched and listened and, often bored, slept, in his place up beside the tall stove. This gave off a formidable heat, fuelled from the pine logs piled to the rafters in one of the smaller barns.

When the talk was over, Antonina and little Na would come in with plates of cold ham, rye bread, blood sausage and cucumbers pickled the spring before. But Boris himself fetched the big bottle of aquavit illegally distilled in the forests further south.

Sometimes there would be arm fighting. Boris always won. But this was not the real point of the evening. Gradually, the men would get drunk, their faces glistening in the light flung from the open door of the stove. At a certain point, someone would start to play the unique seventeen-string Yaroslav balalaika.

Sad, sweet melodies would flow and ripple, a resonant rippling which made Ivan think of streams flowing swiftly down from the mountains he'd read about but never seen.

Now Boris would come into his own. He had a clear, deep voice. Sweat would trickle down through the stubble on his cheeks, droplets catching the light.

As the fiery aquavit went round, the music too caught fire. Singing stopped. One of the younger men would jump up and dance in the middle while the rest clapped out the rhythm. Faster and faster, whirling, thumping feet and hands in a tattoo – until with a loud cry the dance would end, the young man collapsed in the chair, drenched. Sometimes, if he went out for a moment into the icy night air, he would be actually steaming.

Laughter, talk, swigs from the bottle, another resinous pine log, suggestions called to the player. Even Na would call out from her corner. Then, like a shiver, the first single-handed ripple across the strings . . .

Eventually, Ivan would fall asleep. When at last the men left – and no doubt for their benefit – Boris would reach up and ruffle the boy's fair, almost white, hair.

But Boris was not melting. If he beat Ivan a little less as he grew older, it was not out of increased kindness. Nor was it due to the intercessions of Na, though she did intercede. It was because, through incessant repetition and almost against his will, Ivan at last became quite adept on the land.

His impatient, overactive energy often meant he'd milked and mucked out their eleven cows before anyone else was out. He could plough a moderately straight furrow and be trusted with the reaper and binder (and Taschla was lucky here; on many farms they still scythed the corn).

Indeed, he was tireless at harvest-time. The reaper and binder simultaneously cut the corn and bound it into bundles about the width of a man's waist. These were stacked to dry, seven or eight together, in clumps down the enormous fields.

After a week or so in the sun, they were carted away to the stack yard to await threshing. Just before he left, they had their first visit from the State Tractor Enterprise, with its team of experts. They let Ivan take the wheel. Before that, all the work was done with horses. As one of the big, obedient, hairy-ankled beasts pulled the cart over the stubble, Ivan walked alongside.

'Tpruu!' he would call as they came to one of the blocks of corn. The horse would stop. With a few easy heaves, Ivan would pitchfork the sheaves up into the cart, where Leo or Sergei would arrange them.

'Poshla!' Ivan would shout. The large horse would lean forward and move on, flicking its long black tail to and fro across hot satiny haunches, its slow-moving, hair-draped hooves like swinging tussocks of chestnut-coloured grass.

And as the years passed, Ivan grew strong. In particular, his arms grew strong. As age began to tell on Boris, their practice arm-fighting battles more and more resembled battles. One day I'll beat him, thought Ivan, feeling the hard bulge of his muscle.

The question of his future never left him. It haunted him like a tune you can't remember. It was this that made him eager to get up and eager to get through each day, to get closer to the moment that he'd know. He was impatient to get through the morning to reach the afternoon, through the afternoon to reach the night. But Boris never referred to the subject again.

Certainly, he was not destined to be the manager of a collective. For one thing, thought Ivan, those icons in the cellar were obviously meant for something more exalted than bribing an official, for example, to get an earlier allocation of the tractor team and so gain a march on the rival farms. For another, the other children on the collective stopped schooling at fourteen. But Ivan continued his evenings with Alexis. Fables and fairy tales gave way to Gogol, Pushkin, Zhukovsky; Tolstoy's children's tales to *War and Peace*. He had a large number of Russian translations from the Greek. And Ivan also read further – or they read together, since Ivan still needed help – from Alexis's collection of English and French books: De Quincey,

Shelley, Byron, Racine, Rousseau, Zola, Balzac. They were not exactly classes (Marxism-Leninism was never mentioned) but talk and teaching were irresistibly the same to the tutor. He would move with quick, inspirational jumps from the idea that honour was a drug to Lermontov's generation to De Quincey to 'Kubla Khan' to the nature of reality to Bishop Berkeley to the stupidities of censorship.

Starved of the congenial intellectual company he must have been used to, Alexis fashioned a substitute out of Ivan. Nor was this difficult. With Alexis, as the years passed, Ivan developed a second self, talkative, curious and, as far as literature and ideas and other languages went (they sometimes spoke in English or French), almost sophisticated. He realised years later that his tutor had probably saved his life, but at that time he soon learnt that he had to keep his second self well hidden as soon as he left the tower room.

There were all sorts of rumours about Alexis. The most likely, in Boris's eyes, was that he was a KGB agent planted in the area, unfortunately billeted with them. But in Pokrowskii it was said he was a distinguished university professor who had got mixed up with dissidents and exiled. Other people said he was not really Russian at all (and it is true he had a slight, indefinable accent) but a German who had spied for the Soviet Union and had to flee the West and be given a new 'life' in this remote place. And he was certainly jumpy enough for either spy or dissident. He was always pressing his bulging eyes to the windows. When the inspectors came to do the audit, Alexis locked himself in the tower room until they went.

When he was sixteen, Ivan began to be moved by the great flat plain. Alexis praised the atrocious verses that resulted, while attempting gentle instruction. 'Write what you feel, as simply as you can. What did you feel? Remember what the English poet said? Poetry is emotion recollected in tranquillity.'

What had he felt as the wind swept with a vast sigh through the myriad-stringed green corn? He could remember nothing. He had wondered if they needed more rain. The verses had come later. He decided that poetry was emotion invented in tranquillity.

For some reason this became a key phrase, possibly because, since Alexis disagreed with him, it was a phrase stamped with himself. For the same reason, 'All flesh is grass' was a key, signifying his awareness of the secret world, his silent opposition to Boris. There were key events too which remained intact, marooned in the grey nothingness of his past: standing in the wind and rain watching whoever or whatever it was vanish; some of the moments of his power.

And there occurred a deeper key moment now. Since Alexis invariably forgot to do it himself, little Na used to come into the tower room to light the samovar. There was a book open at an illustration of Napoleon. It was still only five years since the siege of Stalingrad and Alexis was explaining its relevance to Napoleon and so to *War and Peace*. Discussions with Alexis tended to wander.

Suddenly little Na pointed to the picture of Napoleon. It was an idealised portrait of the future emperor as a very young man.

'That's my boy,' said Na. 'That's my Ivan. It's him to a likeness. Well, not the fair hair, but the face. Oh, yes.'

Ivan looked and it gave him a curious sensation, a sense suddenly of not being himself, to find that he could see what she meant.

10

Education, said one of her manuals, is the art of making someone follow without seeming to lead.

'Now suppose you were to be a writer when you grow up,' said Mrs Wordingham guilefully. It was not the first time she had introduced, with infinite subtlety, this notion dear to her heart. 'Sir Walter Scott made a *great* deal of money.'

They were reading *Peveril of the Peak*, but now, when bedtime came, Michael took the book to bed with him.

Realising he was far too sensitive as yet – probably for ever – for the rough and tumble of the local primary and secondary schools, much less the trauma of private boarding education, his grandmother had persuaded four local families to invest in a teacher. Miss Philips, retired but still full of vim, was not cheap – but the rents from Drayton Gardens went up, Mrs Wordingham sold some shares and it proved well worth it. Michael finally learnt to read.

To Mrs Wordingham's astonishment, and not entirely to her relief, Elfreda stayed. After one and a half years the amount of china smashed had become enormous. And more years, apparently, stretched ahead. 'I vill die here – here, in this boring place, far from home, I vill leave my bones,' Elfreda would say gloomily. Mrs Wordingham seriously contemplated cardboard plates and cups.

But the great advantage of Elfreda was that, after the successful bath night, it proved possible to relinquish some of the broad-brush supervision of Michael to her. She cooked him special meals, she washed his sheets, she dressed him and brushed his hair and teeth and then taught him how to do such things for himself; she made him help in the kitchen. She talked to him in her loud voice, smoking continually, requiring a minimum of response, as if he were an equal.

Elfreda stayed because she had nowhere else to go. She was not content. The trouble was, there didn't seem to be another Latvian in Suffolk – not in the whole of East Anglia. Elfreda had not managed to make any friends. Or rather, and this was the real trouble, no men friends.

'Vot is thirty-three that no Suffolk mans vill come?' she said crossly. 'I am still ready!' she would cry. 'I am still young enough – no?'

'No,' said Michael, who still found her sentence construction baffling.

'Vot you mean is yes,' said Elfreda.

'Yes,' said Michael.

'So there you are!' said Elfreda.

No one turned up. Michael occasionally noticed a new, strong smell around Elfreda besides onion, sweat and cigarettes – something raw and clean, almost medical.

One evening when he was thirteen, Mrs Wordingham was asked to a dinner party.

'You'll be all right, darling? Elfreda will give you your supper. I'll look in when I get back. I won't be late. You have your book.'

When she'd gone, Elfreda came and fetched Michael from the drawing room. 'Come,' she said, 've too vill haff party.'

The table was laid in the kitchen in front of the Aga. There was a bottle of rosé wine open. Elfreda helped him to red cabbage and frankfurter sausages and filled his tumbler with wine.

As always, she spoke entirely about the country she had left. 'Such vinters! You vould not belief! Canals frozen, rivers frozen, edges of sea frozen – out ve came and skate skate skate.'

More wine. She was skimming across the surface of his brain, numbing it. Spring came in torrents of words. 'Now crocus came, now melting snow, what joy! Now we haff – what is it you call? You haff chocolate eggs.'

'Easter,' said Michael, feeling the kitchen tilt. The rosé was finished. Elfreda with elastic stride strode to the tall green cupboard beside the Aga and, reaching deep over a jumble of old jams, herbs and spices, produced a bottle of clear liquid. Michael recognised the clean surgical smell.

'Luffers iss time chosen in spring. Don't drink too quick, iss strong,' said Elfreda, her English beginning to slide. 'Soon in the hay, in the fields iss luffers all day long. How never luff iss in Suffolk – oh *no*, not *here*, so likely.' She banged her tumbler irritably up and down.

Michael stood up, watching the kitchen sway. 'I think I ought to have my bath.'

Plump, soft, he was now almost as tall as she was. Her sinewy arm was round his shoulders, each large red hand yanked up into an armpit. '*Vot* a beeg boy,' she murmured.

In the bath, she made him lie fully stretched out. He felt neither shy nor self-conscious. He felt dizzy. He could feel her softly soaping his feet and calves. He was a child again, a baby.

'Now I geeve *real* vash,' whispered Elfreda, kneeling beside the big old bath, sleeves rolled up, arms in the warm water.

The water swirled up between his legs as she soaped with extraordinary gentleness, caressing behind his knees and up the silky insides of his thighs. Swish, swish, swish. Langorous, yet acutely conscious of the sensation she was causing, Michael for an instant opened his eyes.

Elfreda was staring into the bath, rapt, intense, totally concentrated on her task. Suddenly she let slide from the loose side of long lips a glistening rope of silvery saliva which sank swiftly into the water.

It didn't remotely disgust Michael. It simply reminded him, for some reason, of the fairy story about Rapunzel and of the long coiled strand of golden hair she used to let down from the tower for her lover to climb up.

11

The beatings did grow fewer. But when they came, they were more humiliating and therefore more painful. Ivan was beaten three days before he was sixteen. Pride usually kept him silent. This time, he turned at the door.

'One day I'll kill you.'

'What did you say?'

'Nothing.'

'Come here.'

Ivan didn't move, his mouth dry.

'Come here.'

Boris normally used a strap from the harness room or his belt. But he'd just come back from a walk and had cut himself an ash sapling. Na had to remove fragments of bark and wood from Ivan's bleeding backside. When he got painfully to his feet again, he saw that tears had run from under her spectacles.

'Don't cry, little Na.'

'He's too hard on you.'

The only reason he didn't try to kill Boris was that he was waiting to learn what he was being prepared for, his father's last instructions. But he wasn't quite sure what would have happened if his power had come upon him while he was actually being struck. For some reason this had never happened.

After he had created Na (who knew perfectly well: 'I made you, Na.' 'I know, my pet'), it returned regularly every three or four weeks, though it was sometimes set off by some crisis, and had even happened on successive days. Recognising the signs with delight – the agitation, the sudden confusion and mental congestion – he would wait, staring, frozen. The final feeling of exquisite happines would be augmented by a sensation of great clarity and strength, as though all his vital forces had been much increased and then concentrated at the front of his skull.

During the thirty or forty seconds, sometimes as much as a minute, that this state lasted – Ivan still paralysed, speechless – he had magic powers and could do anything. Now he did revenge himself.

Once, he split the roof above Boris's room so that water poured in on his bed. Another time, late at night, when Boris was drinking alone in the parlour, Ivan caused all the pewter plates to leap off the dresser and fly across the room. When one of the cows had her calf taken away, Ivan made her go mad. She broke out of the yard and, nose drooling blood from charging the gate, mouth foaming with frothed saliva, she chased Boris till he was forced to take refuge among the pigs.

As Ivan grew older, the incidents of power gradually became less frequent as, long before this, had the appearances of Mikhail. By the time Ivan was ten, Mikhail had ceased to come. But Ivan knew his companion hadn't really vanished. Somewhere he still existed and this fact was comforting. He sometimes wondered what would happen if he ever did see Mikhail again. Not till nearly forty years later did Ivan read the speculations of Dr Doppell. If two doppelgängers should accidentally meet, they would not recognise each other. This, in the end, was to prove true.

Ivan became fascinated by De Quincey. One spring, he collected seed pods from the tallest poppies, the ones with silky, floppy petals that sprang up with the corn. Alexis had explained that they were opium poppies. He dried the pods, crushed them, smoked them. The resulting head-swim produced no visions.

But three days later, standing out on the flat roof of the tower room, he began to experience the familiar agitation, succeeded in moments by soothing calm.

Transfixed, hands resting on the parapet, Ivan gazed out over the vast flatness of the plain. The blue of young wheat paled in the distance, became dove grey, became sky. All at once he saw a flash of gold. His eyesight rapidly becoming acute, he soon saw that it was the cupola of a church catching the sun.

Ivan knew at once that it was the dream city of the old opium eater starting to become a reality. He managed to add a short row of red roofs, a great tower, a few windows. Then the acuity dimmed; cupola, tower and roofs faded. But Ivan stood for a long time bathed in the delicious aftermath of his power.

In fact, more and more often, this was all he wanted from these experiences: that end glow of vividness, the fusing into an identity with everything around him.

It came once during his weekly bath in the zinc tub. The hot water had run in from the brass tap at the side of the blue-tiled stove; stepping in, standing, Ivan felt the steam billowing him up into the rafters. It came, often, out in the fields. In the autumn, the evening air suddenly sharp, walking back over the stubble, Ivan would startle seven partridges. He could see the glistening red beads of their tiny eyes. Their terror caught at a heartstring and pulled it out, infinitely extended, as they whirred off into the fading light. It came one silent summer afternoon, the air shimmering with heat. Boris was away and Ivan sheetless, sleepless, naked on his bed, watching the flies, when, for a miraculous twenty seconds, he mastered the theorem of their never-still aerial geometry. For that instant he was fly Euclid.

The intensity of these moments added to Ivan's conviction that he was being prepared for something momentous. That he had a destiny.

12

By insensible degrees, it became assumed by Mrs Wordingham and her grandson that he would be a writer.

To encourage Michael, she had shown him a fifteen-page letter his naval grandfather, then nearly eighty (there had been forty-five years between Mrs Wordingham and her husband), had written to *The Times* in 1935. It had proved impossible to publish, owing to length, but had been returned with an appreciative note attached by a pin. Michael read the heading on the yellowing paper: 'Some thoughts on passing the Rock of Gibraltar'.

'We are a literary family,' said Mrs Wordingham.

As her arthritis made it more and more painful to move and, with knotted knuckles, she had to struggle for longer and longer in the garden, she left some general tasks to Elfreda. Nevertheless, she kept a tight grip on the important reins herself: rest times, exercise, state and quantity of daily motions, manners, tidiness, brushing of teeth and hair . . .

Michael escaped into books. Even his grandmother could not pursue him into his head. There was also relief in his collections: bird's eggs, keys, key rings, cigarette cards, matchboxes, stamps. Each time he hinged a new stamp into his album he had a fantasy he was posting a minute part of himself to those distant and exotic places: Tanganyika, Sierra Leone, Canada. He refused to collect English stamps.

But his collections, which littered the tower room, were not immune. The matchboxes, for instance, had to be empty in case he set himself on fire, a castration which removed most of their point.

'Such a pity you gave up that nice collection of old china, darling,' Mrs Wordingham said one day.

'Yes, Granny,' said Michael, conscious that they were standing on the third floorboard he'd levered up that year and that, as well as china, there were now four paper bags filled with his hair beneath them.

Miss Phillips had to leave when Michael was twelve. 'I've taught him all I know,' she said.

Mrs Wordingham again contemplated a boarding school and again rejected it, fearful of bruising nascent talent. This time she succeeded in persuading only one family to come in with her, whose diabetic son was stone deaf, among other impairments. Once again, shares were sold and the rents of Drayton Gardens raised.

Mr Broughton, the first tutor, was not a success. A retired Rugby mathematics master who lived in Inkpen village, set by years of bachelordom, he was rapidly exasperated to find himself landed with one pupil who couldn't and another who wouldn't learn.

Mrs Wordingham, crouching by the keyhole at the end of the first week, her knees in agony, had to restrain herself from hurtling in.

Still trembling, she accosted Mr Broughton after the lesson. 'You seem to be having difficulties.'

'The task is virtually impossible,' said Mr Broughton. 'That boy John should be taught in an institution and your grandson, I'm afraid, has no wish to learn anything at all.'

'No wish to learn!' cried Mrs Wordingham, incensed. 'Miss Phillips found him a model pupil. I thought the task of the teacher was to nurture talent, to draw out.'

'No doubt – where talent exists,' said Mr Broughton. 'There are no signs here that I can discern.'

His successor, Mr Borrow, whose income depended on the job, saw nascent talent everywhere. A gaunt, elderly, droning man who looked like a bat, he quickly found the only course was total *laisser faire*. Michael read or dealt with his collections, John keened to himself in a corner, and Mr Borrow worked at the physics textbook he hoped would make his fortune.

It was Elfreda who stopped Michael wetting his bed. She did this by the simple expedient of asking him to stop.

'You big boy now – beeg, *beeg* boy. You haf no need to vet the bed. You stop for Elfreda – no?'

Michael stopped. He couldn't think why he hadn't done so before. He found he missed the slight resilience of the rubber beneath him, the familiar smell. He'd got too used to sleeping naked to resume pyjamas.

Elfreda was teaching him to cook. 'In Latvia all mans cook,' she said. Weeping, they sliced onions together. 'Vat is thirty-five that no Suffolk mans vill come?' she would ask, and once again Michael would listen to the familiar complaint.

Big as he undoubtedly was, she now gave him his bath every night. The door was always locked first. How different each pathway to exquisite sensation! Sometimes she might still have been chopping in the kitchen, as briskly efficient, as quick and impersonal as a nurse with a full waiting room; sometimes languorous, lengthy, teasing, swishing and swashing, the steamy air heavy with the smell of onions, cigarettes, sweat, the medicinal smell. Once, when it was over, she suddenly froze, staring fixedly into some invisible distance. Michael, still reverberating, lay quite still, not daring to move. He watched, full of an unusual emotion, while tears appeared in her blue eyes and slowly slid down her cheeks.

13

Everything had changed in Ivan's eighteenth year.

He'd noticed for several months that Alexis seemed under some strain. During their evening discussions he was often distant, ash grey.

One morning, when Ivan dropped in to return a book,

Alexis had cut his Adam's apple particularly severely. It wouldn't stop bleeding. He dabbed at it continually with his handkerchief, looking at the specks of blood.

'Ivan,' he said, 'I'm glad you've come. I was going to get you. Listen, you may have noticed I've been . . . well, have you noticed anything?'

'Yes,' said Ivan.

'Exactly,' said Alexis. 'Ivan, I've enjoyed teaching you. I've enjoyed talking to you. I should like you to have my books.'

'Your *books*?' said Ivan astounded. 'Why, what do you mean? Are you leaving?'

'I have to,' said Alexis. He looked at his handkerchief. 'I seem to be bleeding to death.'

'Leaving?' said Ivan. He felt stupid, confused. 'Why? When? I don't understand.'

'This evening. In fact, this afternoon. I can't tell you why.' He paused. 'I wonder if I've got haemophilia on top of my other troubles.'

Seeing Ivan's bewildered face, he came and put his bony hands on the youth's shoulders. 'Of course I could tell you why. But it will be much easier if you don't know. Some men will come when I've gone. Now listen, Ivan. I think it would be best if they didn't find the French and English books. None of those on the shelves is illegal, but there are a number in that cupboard . . . I was going to introduce you to them this year. Some poets, in particular. These are simply typed sheets, and these you should burn. Hide the foreign books. The rest, of course, leave.'

Ivan took refuge in practicality. 'When will they come?'

'Not tomorrow, I hope. Probably the day after.'

'How can I burn and hide in that time? I have to help Boris and the rest get ready for the midsummer market today. Tomorrow *is* the market. I'll put them in sacks and hide them in one of the barns.'

'No, no, these men are far too clever,' said Alexis. 'I've thought of this. I shall tell Boris I am punishing you and have set extra work, and that I wish you to miss the fair.'

'Yes,' said Ivan, 'He'll certainly agree to that.' But the ancient association suddenly reminded him what he could do.

Everyone loved the fair. It was only just light when the household woke. Little Na shook him. 'Never mind, my chicken, I'll bring you something back.'

He stood at the window of the tower room and lifted his hand as the two carts trundled out. Only Sergei, who had taken his place, waved back surreptitiously.

It took him half an hour to conceal the books in the cellars below the shit drum. Everything was as he remembered it. But it was clear that Boris would see the sack at once any time he came there. Ivan therefore hid it in the small adjoining cellar, shovelling over it some of the rubble in a far corner.

He had a strong desire to search the two chests to see if he could find – find what? The message from his father that would tell him his destiny? Or if not that, some other clue – a map, an address in Moscow or Samara, a key, an enigmatic phrase. But fear held him back. Boris would see the chests had been tampered with. More than this, for so long had Ivan looked forward to his eighteenth birthday that he now felt superstitiously he had to wait till then. Thus his father had ordained.

Ivan missed Alexis. His only compensation was the books – but this was considerable. He had never had such a present. For long far too big for the ledge above the blue-tiled stove, he asked if he could move into the tower room. Boris agreed, looking at him with narrowed eyes.

Ivan loved the little room, and loved in particular the two shelves of his books. He was surrounded by friends, by the soul of Alexis if not his bony, clumsy, affectionate body. Two months after his tutor had vanished, Ivan took advantage of Boris's absence in Pokrowskii to get half a dozen foreign books from the privy. He concealed these under a loose floorboard. He did not yet dare bring any of the typed bundles, in case the KGB, if that was who it had been, should unexpectedly come back.

Their visit, the day after the fair, had been extremely unpleasant. Everyone, even Ivan, even little Na, had been closely questioned. And the search, as Alexis had foretold, was thorough. Had there been needles concealed in the stack yard, they would have been found. But it was not this that really upset Boris. He knew the evidence that the Taschla Collective sold on the black market was too well hidden. As for Alexis, the Regional Committee itself had compelled him to take him. It was not Boris's fault if he was – well, whatever it was he was.

Nevertheless, Alexis's disappearance caused the return of a more profound, much older obsession. The obsession was discipline. Once again, everything fell on his shoulders. Without the lessons, the punishments of Alexis – Alexis who hadn't punished him once – Boris saw Ivan going to pieces again. It was this, and one other thing, that precipitated the final crisis.

The first was that Ivan finally won at arm fighting. Boris had long ceased to compete in the local contests, and he had also stopped giving Ivan lessons, saying there was nothing more he could teach him. But Ivan suspected it was also because he was nervous Ivan might beat him. So it proved. One cold, slack afternoon near the end of winter, Ivan asked Boris – it was the first time he'd ever done this – if he would give him a lesson.

'What for?' said Boris suspiciously. 'You know it all now. It's high time you got out there and did some fighting, like I did at your age. Or do you think you can beat me?'

Ivan didn't answer. But the moment they locked arms, he realised he was now stronger than Boris. There was a brief struggle – a lock, an attempted feint, a counterlock – and he found he had pressed the hairy arm of his guardian firmly to the table.

Boris was clearly furious. He got up without speaking and left the kitchen. Ivan was suffused with a deep, calm satisfaction, sharpened by surprise. Now, he thought, if I wish to, I can kill him.

The winter had been exceptionally severe. It seemed it would never end. Each night the temperature fell to minus 29 degrees. Once it went below minus 30, as cold as Siberia.

As though nature had given them a clock which allowed only so many months' stamina against the cold, they all grew restless and irritable. Two of the pigs died for no reason. A purchase of emergency hay was running out. Taschla might have to spend money – black-market money – on more hay or even expensive cow cake.

And then, unfortunately only two days after his victory over Boris, Ivan killed a heifer.

He was crossing the frozen ridges of mud in the yard. He was going to shovel a few precious pitchforks down from the hayloft to the cows and heifers below in the covered yard. The onset this time was quicker than usual. As he reached the gate, he was seized with a moment of premonition. He managed – and this was what was inexplicable, since it wasn't necessary – to get the gate open and then stopped. He stopped and stood staring out over the wastes of frozen snow.

Irradiated with his vision, he stood for twenty minutes in the freezing cold without moving.

He could feel distant warmth. He heard the water beginning to move faster beneath the ice of the Wiginskii. He heard a big log, the size of a man, passing, bumping along the underside of the ice. The snows were beginning to melt 400 kilometres to the south. He could smell the sun.

Half-starved, cows and heifers walked unnoticed past him through the open gate and wandered out, looking for fodder. One heifer, the liveliest, reached the banks of the river. Attempting to get at some frozen rushes poking up through the snow, it slid down the bank. A front leg, the hoof caught in the curve of a root, snapped audibly.

The veterinary officer was fetched by Boris in the sled. The heifer had to be shot. The officer stayed for a meal and then Boris took him back.

He dealt with Ivan on his return, gradually working himself into a cold fury. This indiscipline, this slackness, had been growing ever since Alexis had disappeared. 'Take down your trousers. Get over that chair.'

But Ivan knew that his real rage, the reason he wanted revenge, was that he'd been beaten at arm fighting.

Yet, even though Ivan's eighteenth birthday was in three

months, the harsh voice, the familiar, dread command, moved some lever which seemed to return him irresistibly to defenceless childhood. He struggled, unmanned, with fear. At last he said 'No.'

'What?'

'No.'

Boris advanced, his face suffused. He had to clear his throat. 'Get down those trousers,' he said huskily. 'Get over that chair.'

'No,' said Ivan. He was trembling, but each 'no' made him feel stronger. He half bent his arm, his fist clenched. 'You may beat me. I did wrong. But I won't take down my trousers. If you want that you'll have to do it yourself, and I'll fight.'

They stared at each other. Secretly Boris was relieved, but he knew he could now give full vent to his rage. Ivan, suddenly sensing the relief, realising his power, but trapped by his admission, felt a sort of boiling begin in him.

'Get – over – that – chair,' said Boris.

Silently Ivan laid himself over the big oak chair, gripping one of the thick crosspieces with both hands.

Even through his trousers, the first blow was far more painful than anything he remembered. Boris, in his eagerness, had hit low. It was like having a white-hot bar whipped across the top of his thighs.

But then an astonishing thing happened. The searing pain dissolved into a pleasing warmth. The room was suffused with light. He had a sense of great peace and strength. It had, at last, happened while he was being beaten.

He could hear nothing, he could feel nothing – though no doubt Boris was still striking him. But gradually, as the light faded, he began to see Boris's face on the ground in front of him.

It was a terrified and terrifying face, contorted, chalk white, running with sweat, the eyes staring, the mouth open. He was at a window, pressing frantically against it. He had clawed his way up a high tower and was now desperately trying to get in. One hand scrabbled at the window, both hands. A violent wind was whipping him, whirling his hair, forcing him back. Suddenly, with a shriek, he was blown backwards and disappeared.

The terrible cry echoed round the room. Ivan became aware that it had come from him. He was standing up, holding a bit of the chair in each hand. He had broken the oak crosspiece – a bar of seasoned oak an inch thick – broken it away from the chair and then in half. Boris, white-faced, was standing back, watching him.

Still dazed, Ivan looked from Boris to a piece of chair, and back. It felt as though he had broken a neck, snapped it in half, and he suddenly remembered one of the plays he and Alexis had read together and discussed.

He held up the oak stumps and smiled slyly at Boris. 'It had been so with us had we been there,' he said, and then, laughing loudly, threw the bits to the floor and walked out of the room.

A week later, for the first time in four months, the temperature dropped only five degrees below freezing during the night.

The next morning Boris suddenly appeared in the yard with his skates. Ivan, two leather panniers slung across his shoulders, was trudging to and fro replenishing the pile of pine logs by the stove. He didn't look at Boris, hating him.

'Leave that. Soon the thaw will be here. We'll have a last go on the ice.'

Ivan walked behind, carrying his skates. As usual, neither spoke. Nor had either of them referred to the arm fighting or to the last beating. It would have been extraordinary if they had. But Ivan knew, and knew that Boris knew, that the beating had indeed been the last. This outing was an attempt at reconciliation. I hate you.

In just over two months he would be eighteen. Then he would know. Their breath puffed out, greyly visible, and vanished – smoke from the little engines of lungs and heart and stomach that drove them. Ivan looked out over the unbroken, dirty white, dreary beyond words – corpse white, shroud white, dead white to the grey horizon. When he knew, he would leave.

After three kilometres, Boris stopped at what they called the Wiginskii Lake. This was a place where, cutting away a long corner to make the river-canal accessible to the big grain barges, a clear stretch had been created 180 metres long and 45 metres wide.

Boris was first on with his skates. He hobbled down the bank and then, with the peculiar soundlessness of the bone, was out upon the expanse of ice.

Ivan bent and rapidly pulled the laces tight. He was about to knot them in a double bow when there came a ringing crack and an urgent, hoarse shout.

He looked up just in time to see Boris, only his head and arms visible above the ice, thrashing frantically and then, with no further sound, vanish.

Ivan pulled the bow tight and jumped, fell, down the bank. He sped downstream to avoid the crack and curved up towards where Boris had disappeared.

Nine metres from the hole, he slowed, testing, searching. He could dimly see debris passing swiftly beneath the ice. The current was far more advanced than he'd expected.

Suddenly, in outline, and then all at once horrifyingly clear but ghost–like through the clear thickness, he saw Boris. He was on his back, pressed against the underside of the ice, clawing at it, slowly being forced by the current towards the crouching, staring Ivan. Feet, legs, belt – the beating belt – slid under him, until now his white and contorted face was directly below Ivan, looking up with fixed eyes, the water swirling in his hair. He grasped at the ice. For a moment he was able to hold on to some projection – not seeming to see, yet staring up in terror at Ivan above him. Then, abruptly, he was sucked and swept down out of sight.

Ivan had often wondered what he would do if he found himself in this position. In his fantasies, he had always watched gloating or actively assisted: cheered on the goring bull; severed the unravelling rope.

But now, panting with fear, he hacked furiously with the back of his skates. Splinters of ice spurted. It was useless. Boris wasn't even there.

Skimming to the bank, he thought for the first time, Now

I may never know. Surely, he thought, my father would have left some instructions. It will be in one of the drawers of Boris's table. In one of the chests.

As he ran back he felt stirring in him the beginnings of a wild excitement: I am free! I am free!

Fortunately, by the time he reached Taschla, shock had started. He was shivering, hardly coherent.

'But couldn't you get to him? Hold him up?'

'He wasn't there. He'd gone before I could even get on the ice.'

They brought ropes, a sledgehammer, a pick. They ran about the ice trying to look through, the ice still several inches thick. No one could understand how it had cracked open like that. Old Boris wasn't particularly heavy. If it had been Yuri, now, that one might understand . . .

Ivan knew. It was as clear as that staring face. He was to have nightmares about Boris for thirty years, but he never felt remotely guilty about what he'd done, and nor did he that night as he lay in bed. He just wanted to laugh and laugh and laugh.

14

One night after a particularly turbulent session in the bath, Elfreda playfully whipped the Fairy bubble mixture they sometimes used into rafts of Fairy froth.

'Look vot my beeg boy haff done!' she cried, her blue eyes dancing. 'Haff feel whole bath!'

Michael, when he leant wetly against her as she helped him out, was now the same height. Strands of her coarse hair caught against his cheek.

'How old iss now?' murmured Elfreda.

'Fifteen and seven months.'

'Sixteen iss man,' said Elfreda. 'In Latvia, sixteen iss man. Soon Elfreda vill teach new game.'

'What game?'

'You see by and by. And Elfreda play too this time.'

Mrs Wordingham knew she overprotected Michael – but she was sure that she was right to do so. It was a form of nurturing, of hatching. Michael was her egg. When he was ready, she would hear a tapping from the large shell she was sitting on.

At the same time, and seeing no contradiction, she worried about his solitary, sedentary, indoor life, with his collections and his books. As a grandmother, she did not theoretically approve of mollycoddling. And as her arthritis made it increasingly difficult for her to get out herself, she worried the more.

It was for this reason that a little before his sixteenth birthday she obtained a number of leaflets about holiday camps for boys. One title, Venture Ahoy!, particularly attracted her, owing to its naval associations. Fleetingly, she remembered her husband. The cover photograph showed a three-masted sailing ship with a group of boys waving from the rigging. It was a three-week 'venture course' sailing about the Western Isles of Scotland. The boys learnt the rudiments of sailing and led a vigorous outdoor life under qualified supervisors. This included gymnastics, route marches and swimming.

Mrs Wordingham discussed it with Mr Borrow. He agreed in principle but had a reservation.

'I think Michael would benefit from seeing more boys of his own age, certainly. Poor John hardly qualifies. But I would question the wisdom of him going –' Mr Borrow peered at the leaflet – 'aloft.'

Mrs Wordingham had had similar anxieties. She rang the number on the leaflet and expressed them.

A soothing, male, Glaswegian voice reassured her.

'Never you fear, Mrs Wordingham, the lad'll naer come to *aney* sort of ha-rrum. No one is forced to do *aney*thing they canna do. Sergeant Wiggon is in charge of the lads and he'll no send him up the mast if he canna make it. We expect a lad to try, of course. There's a marvellous sperrit aboard the SS *Atlantic*. But we had a lad wi verteego two courses ago. He had a grand time of it helping in the galley.'

'But could you explain to Sergeant Wiggon, please? My grandson is a delicate boy.'

'Dinney fuss yoursel'. I'll away and tell the sergeant this very afternoon.'

Michael didn't want to go at all. 'I don't like boys my own age. I'm OK here. I hate the sea. Anyway, I can't swim. *Must* I?'

'I think you should, darling. It will be a holiday. It's only three weeks. It will be an experience. Take notes. Think of it as a *holiday*.'

Elfreda, never ill, had suddenly caught flu. A huge drop kept forming at the end of her pointed nose. She encouraged him to go, but also seemed to be explaining something in her flu-thickened croak.

'Elfreda haff through agency found new friend. Conductor. Vill soon visit but soon come back.'

Michael often didn't take in the substance of what Elfreda was saying. Her voice soothed him like the wind in the trees. He was also nervously preoccupied with his forthcoming 'holiday'. What books should he take? Should he take one of his collections?

Jostling for food in a queue soon after he arrived, he found he was in the middle of fifteen Glaswegians sent on the course from a pre-borstal reformatory. Sent, Michael soon assumed, as a punishment. They jostled him to the back of the queue, but the food was so revolting when it was eventually slopped into his mess tin that he couldn't touch it.

The events that followed were so frightening or painful or humiliating that they seemed to blur even as they were happening. Afterwards, he retained only isolated fragments that recurred like flashes of lightning in a storm.

Sergeant Wiggon shouting at him as he clung to the strands of a swaying rope ladder, 'Pull ye'sel up, lad! Up! *Up*! Unclench yer bloody fists. Try, damn you, *try*. Can ye no heer what I'm saying to youse? Up! *Up*!'

'I can't,' Michael said.

Crying at night in his bunk, whispering, 'Elfreda, Granny, Elfreda, Granny.' His urine-wet sheets flapping from the rigging every morning. Panting, lumbering fatly round the stationary deck (they still hadn't sailed) miles behind the others. Sergeant Wiggon shouting, 'Get them fuckin' legs up – up, I said! *Up*, Wordingham!'

The brief respite during the four-day training before they sailed, when he worked in the galley, was destroyed when they did in fact sail. Seasickness. The sight and smell of vomit frying in a pan surrounded by the unhealthy, pale blobs of battery eggs.

Taunts, being punched, threatened, his accent imitated, his pyjamas, unfamiliar and uncomfortable objects his grandmother insisted he take, laughed at, then thrown away. One of the pre-borstal criminals threw his second-best stamp album into the air and it was caught by the wind, stamps fluttering out before it hit the grey-green, heaving waves.

The cold.

Not every spark of humanity had been doused in Sergeant Wiggon's ex-boxer's heart. Besides, Wordingham was interfering with the 'sperrit' of the ship, distracting the lads from seamanship with the easier delights of bullying. When the SS *Atlantic* docked briefly at Kyle of Lochalsh, two weeks into the trip, Michael was put ashore and, after a good deal of telephoning, embarked on a series of trains which eventually arrived at Ipswich. Despite the difficulty she now had in moving, his grandmother was waiting in a taxi.

Already seriously alarmed by Sergeant Wiggon's vague explanations, Michael's appearance shocked her.

'Oh, darling!' she cried, folding him to her bosom. 'What have they done to you? What's been happening?'

A wraith had emerged from the station, a ghost: he'd lost pounds, a stone; his face, always pale, was the colour of white bread.

'Nothing much,' said Michael. In fact, though tired, he had begun to recover the moment he had escaped from the frightful SS *Atlantic* and its fiendish crew. It was what he discovered when they reached the vicarage that precipitated his breakdown.

Elfreda had gone.

'But why? When?' he asked his grandmother. Once again, he felt everything was unreal. It seemed a continuation of the terrible events in Scotland. 'Did you sack her? Has she gone back to Latvia?'

'No. No, I didn't. I don't know. She mentioned a Cambridge conductor.' Mrs Wordingham felt a stab of guilt. She was doing everything wrong. 'I did my best, darling. I looked after her.'

'What was wrong with her?' An extraordinary feeling of desolation was spreading over him, over everything.

'Well, I think she was getting flu when you left. She took to her bed.'

Michael at once grasped a central difficulty. 'Did you feed her?' He didn't think his grandmother could even cook an egg.

'Of course.'

'What on?'

'Raw fish. I looked it up in the old *Encyclopaedia Britannica*. It's the Latvian national dish.'

'What sort of fish?'

'Haddock, cod. I got her a nice raw Dover sole on one occasion.'

'Did she eat it?'

'Towards the end. Then we had a most disagreeable scene.'

Mrs Wordingham hobbled into the house on her two sticks, banging the rubber ferrules angrily down on the red tiles of the hall floor as she remembered the incident.

She had, as usual with a broom, pushed into and across Elfreda's stuffy, curtained room a plate bearing a mound of damp, grey, cold, rubbery cod. A few moments later, on her slow way back across the hall, she heard guttural shouting from behind her. She had returned and poked her head in at the door.

'What is it, Elfreda?'

Elfreda, just discernible sitting up in the evil-smelling semi-darkness, emaciated, wild, furious, shaking, continued shouting.

'Vot haff I to do with more raw fish? All round my bed iss

raw fish. How do I eat raw fish? Vot you think I am? You think I am seal? Is that vot you think – Elfreda is some sort of tame seal?'

There was a sudden crash, just above and to the left of Mrs Wordingham's head. Bits of plate and cod fell at her feet. She might have been killed.

She could still hear Elfreda faintly from the drawing room. Doors slammed. Mrs Wordingham turned on the wireless and decided to wait until she'd calmed down. On an impulse, she got up and locked the door into the hall and also the french windows into the garden.

Michael walked slowly up to the tower room. He realised his feeling of desolation had not been caused by the news. Elfreda's departure had merely brought to the surface a river which ran deep in him all the time.

He wet his bed that night and again the night after. On the third morning after his return he was found to have vanished. The note pinned to his wet sheets was dramatic in its brevity: *Gone. Michael.*

15

Boris's body was found a month later at Manturovo, about ten kilometres below the farm.

Flesh and clothes were mostly rotted or had been eaten away. The belt alone had survived intact and this had caught in a hook hanging down the side of one of the moored and empty grain barges. He could be identified only by the silver crucifix still around the bones of his neck.

Ivan was relieved to find that he could weep at the funeral. His tears were not, of course, for Boris but for himself.

The day after Boris's death, Andrey Voynichov, the second most senior member of the Taschla Collective, had called, apparently to offer his condolences. It quickly became clear that he had come about money. Boris had not only been official treasurer; he had also held all the money from their other activities. This should amount to six or seven thousand roubles. Andrey Voynichov thought it would be sensible if he took charge of it from now on.

Boris had done his paperwork in his austere bedroom. It was soon obvious it contained no money, though some account books were found.

'See,' said the new foreman, stabbing angrily with his forefinger. 'Over eight thousand roubles – 8,545.'

It seemed equally clear that there was no message for Ivan. Nothing obvious, at least, among the sparse, neatly piled or carefully clipped bundles.

Andrey Voynichov left, tight-lipped and suspicious. Ivan immediately returned to Boris's room for a more thorough examination. The only things he found pertaining to himself were his papers: identity card, stamped birth registration and so on.

Voynichov came back that afternoon with three other men of the Taschla Collective. For four days they searched the farm. Ivan helped them, searching on his own behalf. The men tapped walls, prised up loose floorboards, levered flagstones; they pushed long poles under the eaves, up chimneys, down and along drains. They questioned Ivan, Antonina and little Na. They found the ancient skeletons of two new born babies in a roof. That was all.

'We may be back,' said Andrey Voynichov. 'We may have to lift stone from stone, brick from brick.'

The moment they had gone, that very afternoon – it was the measure of his release – Ivan strolled out to the privy by the Wiga. As he had suspected, the roubles were in the second of the unlocked chests: neat bundles of worn notes. Ivan pushed them impatiently aside, digging down. There was nothing else. He now emptied the icon chest. Twenty-six of them, each carefully wrapped in old sacking. No necklace. Some silver, also wrapped; a bag of coins. But no will, no document, not even a scrap of paper with a 'Message to my dearest son from his most loving father . . .'

Ivan stood in the cellar's semi–darkness, the wax from the listlessly held candle running hot over his left index finger. Had the message, then, never been written down? Had it been locked only in Boris's cropped head? He felt an icy chill of fear, under which, rushing and black, a river of despair carried him away. He had been abandoned. He recognised something familiar about the feeling of desolation.

It was this desolation, made tender by self-pity, which swept him again at the funeral. Boris's death, cheating him of his news, of his destiny, had caused it or – it now felt more like this – had revealed it.

And yet – *Boris was dead!* Nothing could take this away. Ivan's delight far outweighed everything else. And soon the habits of impatience and expectancy established over eighteen years reasserted themselves, even though the crucial anniversary itself passed without anything momentous.

After the long winter, the earth took time to revive. The barley they were growing that year was still only just visible, a gold-green fuzz, in April. Then, at the beginning of May, came a long succession of hot, still days, followed by days of damp wind and gentle rain from the south. Suddenly, everything was flowering, mating, swelling; the chickens poured out eggs, the cows' milk was creamier; soon the horses stood head to tail whisking the multiplying flies. Ivan watched the barley bend obediently: twenty billion bright green blades swept left, swept right, flattening in unison. Larks shot upwards like mechanical toys, tiny springs of sound and energy vibrating in the blue sky, symbols of his restlessness.

This restlessness increased still more as the familiar, over-familiar cycle brought each inevitable stage: the barley swelling, the moist grain hardening, the two-coloured corn darkening in waves as the wind swept through it; the midsummer fair; the days of silent, windless heat and fly geometry. The idea that he might now be tied to this wheel all his life horrified Ivan.

Na worried and tried to cheer him.

'They say we might share in a crop sprayer next year,' she said one evening. 'An aeroplane.'

'Why would that make any difference?' asked Ivan.

The solution came one evening a few days after the corn had finally been taken in and threshed and the straw stacked. It was so obvious, Ivan couldn't understand why he hadn't thought of it before.

His visitations came much less often now than when he was young. Sometimes three or four months passed without one. He had been feeling tense and nervy all afternoon. His agitation became so marked when he'd come in from the farm that Na asked him if he felt all right.

Realising all at once what was happening, Ivan left quickly without answering. Out on the roof of the tower room, he could feel autumn. When the first spasm came, the impact was mild. This was not one of the great invasions of power; merely a slow opening to the pervading calm and freshness.

Standing, bathed in benevolence, staring east out over the stubble, staring out over kilometre upon kilometre of darkening, stubble-golden flatness, he saw a distant dull flash. It was the cupola catching the last rays of the sun.

At once he knew what he had to do. He had to go to his city. That was why he had created it. Perhaps that alone was his destiny – to escape from the land. Boris had been bringing him up to be set free.

Ivan was so excited he told Na that very night.

'What city?' The only city Na knew was the capital. 'Moscow, do you mean?'

Ivan realised with embarrassment that his city didn't have a name. 'Ruibinsk,' he said without thinking.

'Ruibinsk?' said Na. 'What an odd name. How far away is it?'

'Oh, about 150 kilometres.'

Na looked at him. She had never disciplined him. She had realised the moment she came that there was too much discipline.

'Wait until Thanksgiving.'

'But that's two weeks. The rains may have come.'

'Rain doesn't matter in a city.'

Ivan became both more apprehensive and more eager as the time to leave grew near. He made Na sew a pouch into the lining of his big sheepskin coat. He had kept the collective's 8,545 roubles. Some plan of this sort must have been forming even then. He would take five hundred roubles.

Na put a clean shirt, a change of trousers and a fur hat into his holdall. Ivan added some books. In the pocket at the side he put two envelopes, and then put these in a larger envelope. These held his papers. He also put in Boris's permit to travel. This entitled him, as leader of the Taschla Collective, to travel 500 kilometres from Pokrowskii. The city of Ruibinsk, or whatever it was really called, could be any distance.

It was still dark when he got up to go, but Na was up before him and had prepared something to eat. She put bread, ham, cheese and two onions in a bag for him.

He picked her up and held her close. She was made of sparrow's bones.

'Write to me. Come home soon.'

'Yes, little Na.'

But he was too excited to look back as she watched him stride out through the farm gates. He could just see a white mist coming off the Wiga to his left, ghostly as his breath.

16

Michael was found two days after he had vanished, wandering round Cambridge in a dazed condition.

Dr Jackson advised care and rest, plenty of food, sleep, freedom from all stress including, for two weeks, freedom from the in fact totally stressless administrations of Mr Borrow. He predicted the renewed bedwetting would soon cease and this it did.

Every night for a fortnight Mrs Wordingham fired into her grandson the yellow torpedoes of Nembutal that Dr Jackson had given her. Michael, always a heavy, long-distance sleeper, slept for fourteen hours at a stretch, and then again at his rest after lunch.

The chamber pot reappeared and once more motions were examined, measured, poked, praised or agonised over. Hobbling on her sticks, she supervised his exercise again. Teeth, hair, clothes, Mrs Iken's food, his collections, his reading – everything was once more subjected to her beams of selfless and now guilt-ridden devotion.

Although her hands were knotted like oak roots, Mrs Wordingham even tried to play the piano to him again, and succeeded despite quantities of smudged notes. Too big to squeeze beneath it, Michael sat on the nearby sofa. Listening to a blurred version of 'There is a Green Hill Far Away', he found that tears had come into his eyes. A little later, exploring the shelves for new books while his grandmother was ordering further Penguins, he came upon *The Golden Thread*. Although the idiotic sentimentality of the tale was now evident, this too retained its curious power over him. In his imagination he attached one end of the thread to Elfreda. Wherever she went, the thread would go too. Eventually he would find her.

And to this end, as soon as Mr Borrow resumed, Michael made it clear he wanted to learn. Mr Borrow was not entirely pleased. The gold-producing physics textbook was only half completed and needed all his attention. Also, apart from physics, all other subjects bored him. By devoting 75 per cent of all their classes to physics, he attempted to solve both problems.

'I want Mr Broughton to teach me again,' Michael said one day.

'Why, darling?' said Mrs Wordingham.

'Because Mr Borrow only teaches me physics.'

'Really?' said Mrs Wordingham, surprised. 'But do you enjoy it?'

'Yes,' said Michael, 'but I need to learn other things.'

Mrs Wordingham had a word with the tutor. Mr Borrow explained that physics was an excellent intellectual discipline for all subjects, including history and English. Physics was none the less slightly reduced. Michael still complained. He'd decided Mr Borrow was no good.

'Now be a good boy,' said Mrs Wordingham. 'Be patient. Give him a chance.'

'But he's had over three years,' said Michael.

'He had such good references,' said Mrs Wordingham.

Once again, she took to crouching painfully at the keyhole. It all seemed fine to her – totally incomprehensible, as lessons should be. But she discovered to her astonishment that Michael possessed a slow, mostly silent, obstinate will of his own. In the end, although she had disliked Mr Broughton with his crass insensitivity to nascent talent, she rang him.

Retirement in Inkpen was weighing on the irascible ex-Rugbean. He agreed, under two conditions: the deaf cripple must go; there would be a trial period of one month.

At the end of the month, he agreed to continue teaching. Michael's attitude had been transformed, to such a degree that Mr Broughton's curiosity was aroused.

'Tell me, Wordingham, what made you decide to work? You have clearly put effort into this essay, way below standard as it still is.'

To Michael, the reason was so obvious it made the question seem almost stupid.

'I want to go to Cambridge,' he said.

'Sir,' said Mr Broughton.

'Sir,' said Michael.

17

Ivan walked all day, with a break to eat. There was little traffic on the broken, deeply pitted road: a few bicycles, some horse-drawn carts, a tractor or two. But once a whole convoy of army trucks ground slowly past. Ivan caught the flash of silver on the officer's epaulettes through the window of the last vehicle.

The man smiled at him. Perhaps I'm to be a general, thought Ivan.

The same endless flatness. Some of the collectives had got their ploughing done. He longed for something new, glaciers, mountains, deserts, jungles, even – astonishing idea! – sea. Whales wallowing and whistling or whatever whales did. Wailing. Wolves. Lions. Locusts. Bears.

But one really astonishing thing did happen. Towards evening, as the rains began, Ivan came to a crossroads. 'Pokrowskii 30 kilometres.' Taschla was about 16 kilometres from Pokrowskii. He had walked 46 kilometres. Ivan crossed directly over the road and stopped, staring in amazement at the sign pointing almost due east: 'Ruibinsk 307 kilometres.'

It existed! Well, not that he'd doubted that. But the name existed. And it was a big place, too, if its gravitational attraction extended 307 kilometres. The rain was coming more strongly now. He thought he saw a barn or perhaps even a house about a kilometre up the straight, narrow Ruibinsk road. Had he seen the name once on a map? National geography had played no part in Alexis's syllabus. Boris had sometimes taken him on his trips to sell produce or when collecting more wood. But these had invariably been to the south, where Boris had relatives. 'Ruibinsk', Ivan realised, was simply another manifestation of his power.

It was a barn. Although in one place the corrugated roof had broken, two sheets slanting down, Ivan could at first see very little. He'd stamped his feet on the earth floor and was hanging his coat across two nails to dry, when he heard a commanding cough from the far end of the barn.

The dark figure of a man was leaning against the large mound of old straw stacked up where the roof was sound.

Ivan wondered if he was the farmer. 'I'm sorry, sir,' he said. 'I didn't see you. Would you mind if I sheltered here for the night?'

'You can sleep up there,' said the man, jerking his thumb over his shoulder. 'I've reserved this place down here for myself.'

'Thank you,' said Ivan. He walked over, holding out his hand. 'I'm Ivan Ivanovitch Khuchevsky.'

The man was elderly, with a lined face. There were several large holes in his dark-blue coat.

'I don't give my name to strangers,' he said. 'What's in that bag?'

'Some ham and bread, a bit of onion.'

'That's all?'

'Trousers, my fur hat in the holdall. My papers. Three books.'

'Papers?' said the man sharply. 'You have papers?'

'Yes,' said Ivan.

'That's good. That's very good. This is a bloody place to get about without your papers.'

'Why, have you none?'

'What do you mean by that?' cried the man, his face suddenly twitching violently. 'No papers? Do you think I'm a criminal or a fugitive or something? No papers? Of course I've got papers.' He slapped his thin, torn coat. 'Identity papers. Work permit. Travel permit. All here. All here.'

There was an embarrassed silence. Ivan had now recognised the man. He was like the men who turned up at Taschla, especially at the harvest, looking for work or even just food. He had the same smell, a choking, thick smell that got up your nose like grease. His hair was thin on top and rather long at the sides. In front, it looked as though it had been planted in sparingly with a pair of tweezers, like the hair on the head of a doll.

'Did you say onion?' the man said abruptly. 'Did I hear the word onion? Ham?'

'Yes,' said Ivan. 'I was going to finish it anyway. Would you like some?'

He noticed that the man, when he thought Ivan wasn't looking, slipped a large piece of bread into his pocket.

'Where are you going?' Ivan asked after they'd eaten in silence. 'I'm going to Ruibinsk.'

'I never tell strangers where I'm going. I wouldn't touch Ruibinsk.'

'Why?'

'Police. Questions. Searches. Arrests. A dirty place.'

It was now almost dark. Ivan didn't trust the man and carried his damp coat up to the top of the stack beside him. The straw was very old, the colour of cheap newsprint, but dry. The rain tattoed on the corrugated roof. Little Na would be sitting by the open door of the blue-tiled stove gossiping with Antonina.

He woke abruptly a few hours later. It was pitch dark. Someone had been close to him. He sat up, his heart beating.

'Who's there?'

The man's harsh voice came out of the darkness. 'Your bag fell down. It might have hit me. You want to watch that. Lucky I was here. You could lose it. Here, I'll throw it back up.'

There was a thump as it landed above him. He reached out, groped, pulled it towards him and at once felt in the side pocket. The big envelope was still there.

'Thank you.'

'You want to watch your possessions,' said the man. 'There's a lot of dishonest people around.'

The barn looked much smaller and more decrepit in the thin grey light of dawn. Ivan lay staring at the broken roof. The rain had stopped. He ached and was cold and itched, and his stomach was rumbling. He wished he hadn't given away the last of his food.

The man had already gone. Leaving where he'd slept a faint, clinging aftermath of his smell.

Ivan collected his holdall and his coat, checking his roubles were there. Outside the barn he looked up and down the long straight road. No one. The man must have started when it was still dark. Ivan knelt and scooped up water from one of the many puddles.

He walked until nearly midday, judging by the position of the diffused glare from the sun blocked behind flat, grey cloud. He'd reached a squalid line of eight or nine houses ending at a crossroads. Above one was a sign that simply said 'Shop' in faded white paint.

Ivan bent his head and walked in. It was rather dark and there was little to be seen on the shelves behind the counter.

Across this leant a large, elderly woman with a kind face, her chins lightly stubbled.

'Do you sell anything I could eat?' asked Ivan.

'Well, what have we now?' She bent below the counter. 'There's some pickled eggs left. I have some bread. The butter's all finished but there's a few onions here.' She reappeared, holding a jar in which some eggs floated in vinegar. 'I'm afraid we're a bit short at the moment. It's that time of year.'

'That's all right,' said Ivan. 'Could you put enough in a bag for tonight in case I can't find anywhere? And do you have anything for blisters?'

'Not blisters. But that'll be your boots. I can sell you some grease for your boots. That'll be 50 kopeks a tin. Where are you going?'

'Ruibinsk.'

'Bless the boy – Ruibinsk! That'll give you blisters enough, no matter how much grease you rub in. You should get Stefan to give you a lift. Hey, Stefan or whatever you said your name was, didn't you say you were going to Jaroslawl? That will take you near Ruibinsk, won't it? Why don't you give this young man a lift and save his poor feet?'

Ivan now noticed that there was a small man sitting on a stool at the far end of the canteen in the semi–darkness. He was wearing a blue cap and biting through a short beard into a blob of green which Ivan supposed was one of the pickled eggs. He finished munching deliberately.

'Could do,' he said at last, in an accent unfamiliar to Ivan. 'Could be done. You wouldn't take up much room. All right. But you'll have to come now. I'm not hanging about.'

'Let the boy get his food,' said the woman, slicing and spreading. 'Why are you going to Ruibinsk?'

'I'm going to –' Ivan hesitated. He had been about to say 'find my destiny' but suddenly realised it would sound pompous and ridiculous; even slightly mad. ' – to try and achieve something there,' he finished.

'Stranger things have happened,' said the woman. 'Here,

I've put two eggs between the bread, and the onion. You can eat while Mr In-a-Hurry drives.'

As they stood by the small, open-backed truck, rusted almost to its skeleton, the bearded man said, 'The engine's a bit noisy. You'd find it quieter in the back.'

Two drops of rain fell from the grey sky on to Ivan's cheeks. 'I'd rather ride with you,' he said.

They roared and shook across the plain all afternoon. The noise inside the cab was deafening. Hot fumes blew back from the engine through rust holes. The bulging, rusty cowling over the gears between them was too hot to touch. Ivan dozed and woke, nodded, slept.

It was growing dark when they stopped abruptly. Ivan was jerked awake. 'I need a piss,' said the man.

They stood side by side, their twin pale-yellow streams arching into the ditch.

'Look,' said the man. 'All this sleeping you're doing – can you drive?'

'A tractor.'

'That's no good,' said the man. 'It makes me want to sleep. It's catching. You've got to shake me. Keep me awake. I've been driving since seven this morning.'

The hot engine fumes swept in like chloroform. Ivan's head lolled forward and swung gently right.

Immediately he was struck a violent blow on the shoulder which knocked his head against the door.

'Don't sleep,' yelled the man. 'Shake me. Keep me awake.'

Ivan, angry, rubbed his shoulder. He watched the bearded man out of the corner of his eye. Before long, no doubt deliberately, he saw him nodding, his eyes closing. Ivan gave him a push.

'That's no good,' yelled the man. 'Shake me! Shake me!' He reached out his hand, gripped Ivan's bicep, and shook him to and fro. 'Like that.'

And so, alternately nodding off and shaking and shoving each other awake, they roared on into the night.

It must have been quite late – ten or eleven – when

flashing lights across the road brought them to a stop. The man turned off the engine.

'What is it?' asked Ivan.

'Ruibinsk. God knows what's going on in that place. I was stopped on the way down.'

Two uniformed figures outlined against the lights came slowly towards the truck. The man turned on the light in the cab and wound down his window.

The face that appeared there had high cheekbones. 'Papers.'

Ivan lifted the holdall from between his feet and pulled the envelope out of the side pocket.

The envelope was empty.

At once aware of the terrible truth, feeling sick with fear, he opened the bag itself and pulled his clothes out one by one. Nothing.

'They're gone,' he said. He looked across to the men at the far window. One of them looked up from scrutinising the form in his hand. 'My papers have gone,' said Ivan. 'I've been robbed.'

The man in uniform came slowly and deliberately round in front of the truck. Ivan wound down his window.

'So you have no papers?'

'No, no, nothing like that. I had papers. All my papers. They've been taken – look, you can see. The envelope is empty. It was a man yesterday. A tramp. He must have climbed up the straw during the night. I knew something like that had happened. He was some sort of criminal, a fugitive. He'd gone by morning.'

The man looked at him. He didn't speak.

'He admitted he had no papers, more or less,' Ivan said. He was beginning to feel unreal.

Still the man didn't speak. He had now been joined by the second man. Neither spoke.

Ivan at last broke the silence. 'But he slept there,' he said.

The two men stared at him expressionless and then walked a little way away and muttered together. One of them looked at his watch. When they came back the second, plainly the senior, spoke.

'Where do you come from?'

'Near Pokrowskii.'

'Do they know you there?'

'Yes, indeed. I've lived there all my life. Eighteen years. On the Taschla Collective. Perhaps you've heard of it? Boris Kozlov was our manager until his tragic and accidental death some months ago.' Ivan couldn't stop himself. For the first time, he felt a strong urge to confess his complicity in the death of Boris.

Once again the two men drew aside and muttered and looked at their watches.

'You should go back to Pokrowskii and get new papers,' said the senior man finally.

'But I have business in Ruibinsk,' said Ivan. 'I have relations here, work to do. At least – '

'If you go into Ruibinsk, report to the police first thing in the morning, is that clear? I'll check in the morning and if you haven't reported by ten o'clock you'll be arrested. Where are you staying?'

Ivan thought wildly. 'Wiga Street,' he said. '19 Wiga Street.'

'Wiga Street? Never heard of it. Where's that?'

'It's a very small street. You know when you're going out of the town towards Jaroslawl – '

'All right, all right,' said the man impatiently. 'We're not going there tonight. You just report. What is your name?'

They took his name. The truck driver, who had pressed himself as far from Ivan as he could during this brief interrogation, started up the engine and they drove off. They stopped again further up the road. The man turned off the engine.

'Ruibinsk starts about a kilometre up that road on the right. You can't miss it.' He paused and looked across at Ivan. 'I shouldn't go to the police if I were you.'

'Why not?'

'They'll arrest you and send you to a camp. How else do you think they get their labour?'

'I don't know.' Such matters were vaguely known, but not talked about at Taschla.

'Get back to your farm. Get new papers there.'

'But I want to stay in Ruibinsk.'

'Not without papers. They'll pick you up in the end. The only people who don't care about papers are the army.'

'The army,' said Ivan slowly. He gathered his coat and his bag. Should he offer money? The man obviously didn't expect anything.

'Good luck,' he said, and for the first time he smiled at Ivan.

Ivan stood and watched the truck drive off. It was like seeing the farm disappear into the darkness.

18

When Michael woke up each morning there would be a note beside his bed explaining what he should wear. The clothes would be laid out over the back of a chair.

He could never understand how his grandmother managed this feat without waking him, though it was true he was a heavy sleeper, already inclined to snore. But her arthritis had now progressed to the point where Dr Jackson had advised the replacement of walking sticks by the newfangled zimmer.

'Ridiculous name,' said Mrs Wordingham, waving the aluminium frame irritably about.

It meant her progress about the house proceeded in a series of thumps. Reluctantly, she was compelled to give up the garden. One compensation was that she could devote more time to concentrating on Michael.

Mr Broughton arrived at nine o'clock. He taught for four hours, leaving enough work to occupy the afternoon and an hour's 'prep' in the evening.

His pupil intrigued him. Mr Broughton found that in physics he had already reached Higher School Certificate standard. Nothing else had really been touched. Yet he learnt with rapidity, seeming to absorb information automatically, almost passively. Mr Broughton chose English and mathematics as the other two Higher Certificate subjects, but also gave a general grounding up to School Certificate standard in all the main subjects.

His pupil had some rather curious personal habits. He would frequently run his hand through his hair, tugging sharply, look at it, and then appeared to put any hairs he had pulled out into his pocket. He also had a tendency, when concentrating or when upset, to drag his fingernails down his left cheek. Mr Broughton decided that these and other mannerisms were no business of his.

By the time he was seventeen and a half, Michael was regularly reaching 60 per cent in his Higher School Certificate papers. In physics he would get 80 per cent. Mr Broughton decided it was time he was tested under proper exam conditions.

They drove together to the large secondary modern in Ipswich which had agreed to let Mr Broughton's pupil join theirs at the end-of-term mock HSC examinations. It was clear that Michael was extremely nervous. He had already drawn blood under his left cheekbone before they arrived.

'Try not to do that, Wordingham,' said Mr Broughton, for once interfering. He was in fact nervous himself. 'You should feel no pressure today at all. These exams are purely for your benefit and mine. I want you to experience the atmosphere. I'm interested in seeing how the staff here assess your work.'

Michael got 25 per cent in physics, 20 per cent in English and 18 per cent in mathematics.

The same thing happened six months later, and again three months after that, by which time Michael was regularly reaching scholarship standard in the papers Mr Broughton set him.

'Panic results in examinations are not uncommon,' the tutor told Mrs Wordingham, 'but I think this is different. It seems to me that your grandson is quite simply frightened by being among other boys of his own age. I can't get him to Cambridge, which would otherwise be perfectly easy, if he gets into such a state at public examinations that he can't function intellectually.'

'Why can't he do the exam here?' said Mrs Wordingham. 'I'll pay for one of those men to come and sit in.'

'That is certainly a possibility. I have considered it. It is usually only allowed in cases of illness. I'll ask. But, in personal terms, I think a little contemporary society would benefit Michael.'

'I'll get John over for tea.'

'I thought he was in an institution.'

'So he is,' said Mrs Wordingham. 'Well, I'll think about it. I'll decide. Don't bother me again about it.'

She had no intention of doing what Mr Broughton suggested. She'd made that mistake once and she wasn't going to make it again. Let a few hooligans loose in Inkpen Vicarage and before she knew where she was, Michael would be strung up at the yardarm again. Besides, Michael had just failed his National Service medical. He was clearly not strong enough yet to mix with his fellows.

Mr Broughton had chosen his moment badly, for another reason. Five months before, Mrs Wordingham, at the instigation of Dr Jackson inspired by the *Lancet*, had undergone one of the first of the new and daring hip operations – joints almost destroyed by arthritis were replaced by ones made of some artificial substance. Mrs Iken had come in daily to see to Michael. The operation had been a total disaster and Mrs Wordingham's thigh had locked rigid. She now swung awkwardly, painfully and very, very slowly round the house like a crippled crab. The zimmer had been replaced by a crutch and a stick. There were days when the long years of erosion suddenly overwhelmed her and she longed, like Long John Silver, to dash people to the ground with the end of her crutch. The desire to dash Mr Broughton to the ground had been almost impossible to resist.

Michael missed Elfreda most of all at bathtime. But soon

after she had left he found by chance, when lying back in the warm water, his eyes closed, imagining that the caresses, the teasing manipulations, the sudden flurry and frenzy and violent frothing were actually her, that in fact she didn't have to be there at all. If indeed she really was not there. The strange thing was that quite often, 'Ven all the swish swish swish and splash splash splash iss over', when the exquisite sensation had finally died away, Michael found that the bathroom was suffused with the delicately mingled odours of onions, sweat and cigarettes and that elusive, medicinal smell.

19

The air was cold and it had begun to rain again. Ivan turned up his collar. There were puddles in the road. But as he walked, discerning the edge by instinct, he realised something very odd. He was walking uphill.

Of course. He'd set Ruibinsk on a hill. How else could he have seen it?

Soon, blacker against the black, there were houses. But there were no people. In the city, in that part of the city, there were no streetlights and no lighted windows. What had little Na meant, rain didn't matter in a city? The road and pavement were slippery with mud. Running his hand along the walls for guidance and support, Ivan had a strong feeling that people were crouching below window level, listening to him pass.

He spent the night halfway up a staircase. A half-open door had banged as he went by. A second door at the top was locked. He ate his eggs and an onion and rye bread in the darkness and then fell asleep.

Woken at dawn by the same door banging in the wind, his clothes still damp, he found the rain had stopped and the skies were clear. There were already quite a number of people, many with bicycles, all hurrying uphill towards the centre of the city.

Ivan had not walked far when he saw a queue outside a restaurant.

The 'restaurant' was, in fact, just a large room filled with long trestle tables. The queue ended at a counter, and by the time Ivan reached it there was no longer any choice. He had a bowl of soup, bread, a mug of coffee.

'Excuse me,' said Ivan, pushing over a rouble, 'do you have a room to let? I can pay.'

'This isn't a hotel. You can try the Committee of Residence in Nevsky Street, but I doubt they'll have anything. Next.' He pushed 70 kopeks back at Ivan without looking at him.

Ivan took his mug and bowl to an empty place at the end of one of the tables by the large, steamed-up plate-glass window. A few moments later he was joined by a young man who'd been behind him.

'Do you mind if I sit with you?'

'No.'

The young man put his bowl and mug down neatly. He had a round face with high spots of pink on each cheekbone. 'I heard what you said about money. How much were you going to pay?'

'I don't know. I've never rented a room. I'd thought five roubles a week. Six?'

'You could share my room for eight.'

'That's very kind. Is it large enough?'

'Not exactly. But I work night shifts in the bicycle factory. After this, I go back to bed. You could sleep there at night. But it's a nice place, considering how some live. It's central. The Tcheksna building on Nevsky Square.'

'Well, thank you. I accept.' He held out his hand. 'Ivan Khuchevsky.'

'Leo Bryullov.' Leo's hand was warm and damp. His short, pale eyelashes flickered slightly as he held Ivan's hand. 'What do you do?' he asked.

'I've come here to get work. What's it like?'

'Not too good for work at all, but I'll ask at the factory.

Otherwise, not bad. Plenty of girls because of the university. Too many police.' Once more his eyelashes flickered. Ivan decided not to tell him about his lost papers.

The Tcheksna building was enormous. Leo, pointing proudly to it across the expanse of Nevsky, said, 'It used to be the seat of the Yaroslav provincial government. Now they've moved that to the prince's old palace so people can live in Tcheksna.'

It was as though some catastrophe had overtaken a nearby town and the entire population had been temporarily rehoused. Ivan and Leo entered by one of three imposing entrances along the street. Clothes hung drying from lines tied across the well of a broad circular staircase, so many that it was impossible to see to the top. Pools of water, stippled with drops, lay on the stone flags.

'I wonder how the bottom clothes ever dry,' said Ivan.

But there was too much noise for Leo to hear him. Children and women clattered up and down. An old man was coughing on the bottom step. There were babies crying, thin, strident radios, the smells of cooking and washing.

At each complete turn of the stair, corridors branched right and left. At the fifth floor, Leo led the way left. Each room seemed to be the dwelling of an entire family. Prams, furniture, piles of clothes were against the walls.

Two rooms from the end, at the side, a straight flight of stairs led to the top two floors of the Tcheksna. By nailing boards, a minute room had been made beneath them. Here Leo lived.

He opened the makeshift door with a key and turned on the naked bulb inside.

'There!'

Ivan looked in. There was just width and breadth enough for a mattress and blankets. Leo's head joined him. 'I'll push my things together at that end so you can get your bag in. And there's an extra nail here you could use.'

'Thank you,' said Ivan.

'We all share the basin at the end and the two latrines.

You provide everything for that yourself. The Pavlovitches live in that room there. I pay her a rouble a day and she lets me share their evening meal. I'll ask her if you can too. Look . . .'

Leo began to look embarrassed. Ivan realised he wanted some money. He gave him 42 roubles for a month and seven roubles for Mrs Pavlovitch.

'Come back about nine tonight,' said Leo, the spots on his cheekbones spreading out. 'I'll give you the key. My shift begins at half past ten. I'll get this place ready before I go.'

Ivan was overjoyed at getting his 'room'. It was proof that his destiny was beginning to take over.

But he only stayed with Leo three days. Each morning, woken at six, he washed as quickly as the queues jostling at the latrines allowed, and set out, expecting something momentous would happen.

The old part of Ruibinsk was built on a steep hillside that overlooked the Volga. It was a warren of narrow streets and alleys, many of them stepped. Although he had created the city, it didn't surprise him that he couldn't recognise any of it. He had only made the seed; thereafter it grew itself. God's task had probably not been so arduous after all.

And the city had grown not only in space but in time, in the same way that little Na had arrived a fully mature woman with a past that was gradually established. It struck Ivan that God must have that power too. Why had this occurred to no one else? Alexis had described some of the difficulties over it in the nineteenth century. Ivan's discovery would have resolved it. The world, the universe, as the Bible indicated, had been created 4,500 years ago, but had grown a great deal older since, just as the animals, once created, were then able to establish their evolutionary descent.

Alert all the time to any hint from destiny, he returned each evening disappointed that nothing really significant had happened. The first night he returned at 10.15. The sheets were still warm. But even cold, they always smelled of Leo.

Smells were the colours in the drab Tcheksna building: damp, paraffin oil, soap, soup, sweat, faecal smells. They seethed about him as he climbed the crowded stairs and threaded the corridor – nappies, fermenting, plaster, piss, cabbage, alcohol, hair – and then in a few minutes, as the nose grew exhausted or accustomed, they vanished.

Mrs Pavlovitch piled her dirty washing in a heap outside her door before dealing with it once a week. Ivan marvelled at her trust. The pile smelt of old, cooked beef fat. On the second evening he ate with them. Vegetable stew. Nothing much was said. The room was partitioned into three by blankets grey with dirt. Mrs Pavlovitch had facial hair. Mr Pavlovitch seemed to be a hundred and four. The reason, no doubt, that their ten-year-old son was a mongol. He smelt of urine and had the face of a blissful tomato.

Ivan was shaken awake on the fourth morning by an agitated Leo.

'The police are here again. They're looking for someone. Get your papers.'

Ivan sat up, blinking under the naked bulb. 'I haven't got any papers.'

Leo opened his eyes very wide, the lashes trembling. Tiny patches of white appeared beside each nostril. 'Is it you?' he said. 'Have you . . . ? Are you . . . ?'

Ivan also felt frightened. It made him impatient. 'Of course not,' he said, pulling his shirt and trousers from the end of the bed. 'They were stolen from me. I was going to do something.'

'You must hide,' said Leo. 'They'll send you to a labour camp. If they find I've been hiding you, they'll send me too. Quick!'

He pulled Ivan out of the room before he'd had time to tie his bootlaces. He only just had time to grab his coat. 'This has happened before. I know where to go. We'll just have time. They were only on the ground floor when I got in.'

He ran down the circular stairs to the third floor and along an identical corridor. At the end, he knocked loudly on what would have been the Petrovitches' door.

'Comrade Minin, are you there? Comrade Minin?'

After a pause, the door opened a crack and a deep voice said, 'What is it? Who is it?'

'It's me, Leo Bryullov. I live on the fifth floor. We haven't met. But I heard you hid people. The police are downstairs searching. My friend has lost his papers. They were stolen. Can you help us?'

The man who came out was small and dark, with a neat black beard.

'My friend here,' began Leo again, indicating Ivan.

'Are you a dissident? What have you done?' said the man sharply to Ivan.

'Nothing. I had my papers stolen. It was a tramp. I – '

'Never mind, never mind,' said the man impatiently. 'Later. You're in trouble. That is enough.'

He disappeared into his room and reappeared with a hammer. Kneeling in the corridor, he extracted three nails from one of the wooden boards and then levered it up. Ivan saw a shallow space. A grave.

'Quick. Get down there. Don't worry if you hear me hammering. It'll only be an hour or so. There's plenty of air. Give your coat to your friend. It's too big.'

Ivan hesitated, then handed the coat to Leo. He wanted to take out his roubles but was ashamed of letting them see how many he had.

The space was about thirty-five centimetres deep and broad enough for him to lie flat on his back. Without saying anything more the man lowered the floorboard and Ivan was in darkness.

There came the sound of hammering. It was far more than three nails. Ivan counted nine. He felt suddenly frightened. He thought, This is my coffin.

He lay there for about half an hour. In fact, it wasn't completely dark, and this for an odd reason. There was about six centimetres of space above him. Ivan could just raise his head. The wall at the end of the corridor should have been about three metres beyond the end of his feet. But the wall must have been built quite recently; or at least more recently than the joists between which he was lying. These continued unobstructed for another fifteen metres or so, and at the far end Ivan could see chinks of light.

He heard muffled footsteps above, the sound of voices. These grew sharp. Someone was shouting, arguing. A door slammed. The footsteps and voices receded. Silence. Darkness.

He must have slept for about an hour. It occurred to him that the little bearded man had been arrested. Leo would return, assume he'd been let out and had then fled. With some difficulty, Ivan managed to get both arms up and pressed his hands against the floorboard.

It wouldn't move. And Ivan was nervous of exerting his full and very considerable strength. Perhaps he'd only slept for ten minutes? The police were still there. They'd come out of the next room – and up he'd burst.

He forced down his heels and raised his bottom, then he pushed with his hands. He could just get himself forwards. With great difficulty, stopping to rest, he began to heave himself feet first towards the chinks of light.

Now the boards above him were much older. There was also far more dust. Suddenly, Ivan sneezed violently. He sneezed twice, each time contracting involuntarily and striking his head on the boards above him.

He was seized by a frenzy of claustrophobia. He was suffocating, drowning, pulling himself along under the ice like Boris. He pushed up with all his force and there was a sudden give and a splintering as he forced the floorboards up – and at the same time a loud, high scream.

Ivan sat up. He was not in a corridor, as he'd supposed he'd be, but in a room. Or rather, in a small part of a room partitioned from the rest by a blanket. In one corner was a bed. A girl was sitting up in it, her knees up, the bedclothes clutched up over her nose but leaving her wide-open eyes. She lowered the blanket a little and gave another scream, but this time it was not so much frightened as curious. An interrogative scream.

20

Mr Broughton disliked what he called the 'adhesiveness' of human beings. He much preferred books and gramophone records. Nevertheless, despite himself, he found himself more and more involved in the affairs of his pupil.

Michael at nearly twenty was tall, oval in shape and already losing his hair in front, either because he had pulled it all out or for hereditary reasons. He somewhat resembled a new-laid egg or much sucked bonbon. His habit of running his nails down his plump left cheek continued, and now he often ate the little rolled-up fragments from under them. He liked the salty taste.

When Michael failed his Higher Certificate twice more – though at Inkpen still regularly reaching scholarship standard – Mr Broughton went to Mrs Wordingham.

'It is not that he will be particularly old. National Service means that many undergraduates now are often twenty or twenty-one. It is simply that unless we do something to overcome his fear in the presence of his contemporaries, I cannot get your grandson into Cambridge. He has now failed three times.'

'Three times!' cried Mrs Wordingham. 'I thought these were trial runs. You never tell me what's going on. In any case, I thought we'd agreed long ago that you would arrange for Michael to take his exams here.'

'We agreed it was a possibility but not a satisfactory one. I suggested other steps. However,' said Mr Broughton quickly, 'I'll see what can be done.'

The examination board replied, asking if there were good reasons, in particular a medical reason, why they should make an exception for Michael Wordingham. Seizing his chance to defeat his imperious and irritating employer, Mr Broughton replied that there was no reason other than the fervent desire of Mrs Wordingham, the grandmother and adoptive parent. In that case, replied the board regretfully – no.

Thus was Mr Broughton hoist. Faced with the board's letter, Mrs Wordingham was clear. 'Then I must ask you to teach him here. You can teach to degree standard, I assume? You would not abandon us now?'

Mr Broughton would gladly have abandoned Mrs Wordingham. Nor could he possibly teach to degree standard. But to resign somehow seemed an admission of defeat at her hands. He had struggled too long to get Michael to Cambridge to relinquish the goal now. Besides, he too now needed the money.

A year later, he secretly capitulated. Mr Broughton had long passed that age when people he'd known when young suddenly begin, astonishingly and inexplicably and maddeningly, to appear in exalted positions. His fag at Rugby had been transmogrified into the Warden of Trinity Hall at Cambridge. Mr Broughton went to see him. Michael was promised a place at the humble little college a year later, let in on an exhibition in the Warden's personal gift.

And yet even in these last months Mrs Wordingham managed to triumph.

'I have of course put Michael down for the physics, chemistry and mathematics tripos,' Mr Broughton informed his employer six months before Michael left.

'Why on earth have you done that? What earthly good are those subjects to a boy who intends to be a writer?'

'I was not aware that Michael did intend to become a writer. He has shown no particular bent in that direction.'

Mrs Wordingham stared at Mr Broughton. The desire to use her crutch on him was again almost overwhelming. At last she took a deep breath. 'Michael will read English,' she said.

To Michael himself, the increasingly imminent prospect of Cambridge, so long postponed, so desperately pursued, was both thrilling and terrifying. The day before he left, his cheek was already streaming and the little mouthfuls tasted of blood. Mrs Wordingham, who had decided she could not manage the journey to Cambridge, slowly limped and thumped about the house. Her own cheek was wet when he bent to her beside the taxi.

'Don't forget a second vest if the temperature falls below

43 degrees,' she whispered. 'I've put extra Ex-lax in your small case. Use the hot-water bottle. Don't forget to use dental thread.'

As the taxi pulled away on its long and expensive journey, Michael flapped his hand back at the waving figure suspended on her crutch. How small his grandmother had become!

But even as he waved, even above the terrifying images of the brutalities that probably lay in store, one feeling dominated above all others, one sentence repeated again and again: I'm coming, Elfreda, I'm coming, Elfreda, I'm coming, I'm coming, I'm coming, I'm coming . . .

21

'Don't be frightened,' said Ivan, scrambling with some difficulty out of the wreckage of her floor. 'Are you frightened?'

The girl had very black hair untidily pinned on the top of her head. He could only see this and her large dark eyes above the sheet. At last she said, 'Yes, I am. I was. What are you doing?'

'Well, that's a bit difficult to explain. At least, both easy and difficult. I was escaping. I've lost my papers. The police came. My friend Leo arranged for me to be concealed in a hiding place beneath some floorboards in a corridor. Then they seemed to forget me. In fact, I have a suspicion that the man who helped me may have been arrested. Perhaps it was the KGB. I saw light coming through these boards ahead of me. As you can see, they are very old. They're full of splits and cracks. In fact,' said Ivan, beginning to walk about, 'I expected to find myself in another corridor. It's really very odd finding myself here like this. Quite unreal. It feels like a dream. In fact, I often feel like that. It may be because I was brought up alone. Perhaps I should explain I was brought up on the Taschla Collective near Pokrowskii. I was the only child. I don't mean the only child in the whole collective, of course – there was Ossip and

Stefan and Anna and Catherine . . . You don't need to know their names. But I was the only child at Taschla. Well, except for Mikhail, but again, he was different. I don't want you to think I'm ignorant – just a country bumpkin. I can see you're probably a student. Is that so?'

Ivan's restless striding about the little partition-room had brought him several times near the girl's bed. On a small table beside it were various books. One had 'Ruibinsk University' stamped on it. The girl nodded. She had let the bedclothes fall back and was sitting in her white nightdress watching Ivan with intense curiosity.

'And are you Sofia Ivanovna Alkhanova?' asked Ivan, reading the name off the front of the exercise book. Again the girl nodded. Ivan looked at his hand and then brushed it down his thigh. 'Ivan Ivanovitch Khuchevsky,' he said, holding it out. He could have held three of her cool little hands in his large, hot, damp one. He felt suddenly ashamed of its roughness.

'Anyway, as I was saying, I've been educated. I can speak and read English. I've read English writers – De Quincey, Dickens, Hazlitt, Coleridge . . . Perhaps I should explain this too. What a lot of explanations! It's really Alexis. My father died when I was very young. I can't remember it, but I think I can remember the occasion, feeling that something terrible had happened. He told Boris, my guardian, what I was to be. It was something special. I think that is probably why he had me educated. Boris was going to tell me when I was eighteen. He wasn't a nice man. In fact, he often beat me.' Ivan stopped. He suddenly felt hot, his face flooding with colour. He stepped hastily away from the bed. 'There's no need to go into that. I always knew I was destined for something special. Perhaps that's why things often seemed unreal, like a dream. I knew they weren't for me. And Boris used to say, "All flesh is grass." Well, of course, I know now what he meant, but to a little boy it sounded odd – as though things weren't what they seemed. I was educated by my friend Alexis. Really, Alexis made me what I am. I could talk to Alexis. In fact, I think it's because I haven't talked to Alexis for so long that I'm talking to you. I mean – so much.

Anyway, then Boris died, as I say, in peculiar circumstances. Did I say that? No? Well, yes, unusual circumstances. He fell through thick ice. It's true, it was nearly spring. But he still hadn't told me what he'd been training me for. Do you see how strange this was? All those years and then at the last moment . . . Anyway, I decided to run away to Ruibinsk to find out . . .'

He stopped. He couldn't understand why he felt so agitated. He must try and calm down. He took several deep breaths.

'Go on,' encouraged the girl, still looking at the young man, boy really, walking about in front of her. He was flushing again. 'That was very brave of you. And very romantic. Did you have adventures getting here?'

The tramp who had stolen his papers, the little bearded lorry driver, quite unremarkable at the time, suddenly, as she nodded and laughed and made him repeat what they'd said, did indeed seem like adventures. But Ivan felt under a compulsion to return to something he knew he should at all costs avoid.

'But do you know why I chose Ruibinsk?' he said. 'Listen, could I call you Sofka? I'll let you into a secret.' He stopped. 'I don't know why I'm telling you all this. I've never spoken to anyone like this before. Perhaps it's because since Alexis left I haven't really spoken to anyone properly. Little Na a bit. But, well – I *invented* Ruibinsk.'

'Invented Ruibinsk?' said Sofka, surprised. 'What do you mean?'

'Well, it's difficult to explain. I expect you thought I was lonely when I was small? Quite the contrary. I found I had this power. I could create people. No, no – I don't just mean an imaginary playmate, though I did that too. No, I could *really* create people. Out of nothing. And this power, which only comes occasionally, grew even stronger. I could make all sorts of things happen – cows go mad, the rivers flood. And one day I created Ruibinsk.'

'But that's nonsense,' said Sofka. 'Ruibinsk's been here for centuries.'

'I know it seems like that. But in fact that past just grew after Ruibinsk was created.'

'Do you mean you created me?' said Sofka. The young man was clearly slightly mad. Or at the least had very strange ideas. At the same time, she was still drawn to him. She was drawn to him the more.

'No doubt it seems odd to you, though my nurse understood that I'd created her. But listen, how else do you explain how I knew the name Ruibinsk?'

'But everyone knows the name Ruibinsk.'

'I didn't.'

'Well, you'd seen it on a map or a signpost and forgotten.'

'No, I hadn't. And how do you explain that I saw it from 300 kilometres away? Do you think I levitated?'

'I don't think you did see it. You saw something else.'

Ivan felt his mind becoming increasingly active and brilliant. 'I suppose you could argue it was just a different way of describing or looking at what happens. You can say "I perceive something" or "I invent something". The thing is there, and whether as a result of your perception or your invention doesn't really make any difference. Bishop Berkeley said something like that.'

'Bishop Berkeley?'

'Yes. He was one of the writers Alexis and I talked about. Actually, I think that Berkeley said you couldn't prove something was still there when you weren't. But let's leave Ruibinsk. I can see it's confusing. I'll tell you something else.' Ivan paused. Now that he was about to tell her his terrible secret, he felt his heart beating faster and faster. He had the taste of blood in his mouth. At the same time, he felt a sense of inevitability. 'I killed my guardian Boris,' he said.

Sofka did now look startled, even alarmed. Once again she pulled the bedclothes up to her chin. 'Do you mean you pushed him through the ice? That you drowned the old man?'

'He wasn't particularly old,' said Ivan. 'No, it wasn't quite like that, but I murdered him just the same. He was beating me. When this power comes, I have a period of agitation, of excitement, rather like –' he was about to say, rather like I feel now, but instead, in case he frightened her, he hurried on – 'and I suddenly felt this while he was beating me. Almost at once, I saw Boris's face in front of me just as it was when he was drowning. I saw his face under the ice, only it was glass, exactly as I saw it a few days later. Do you see what I mean? I *willed* Boris to die, and I *willed* the way it would happen. And a few days later, even though the ice was still thick, it did happen just as I willed it should.'

'But that's not *murder*,' cried Sofka. 'It's strange, certainly. You may have second sight. You foresaw his death, perhaps. But people have done that before. You didn't actually kill him. Those are the powers you're talking about.' And she suddenly did feel he had some power or other, some mesmeric quality which reminded her of someone.

'You don't understand my power,' said Ivan, his voice thick. He could already feel the onset of the great surge of warmth that was about to burst through him. He just managed to say very hoarsely, 'I'll show you', when a wave caused him to raise both hands and reach out as though breasting surf.

His face was flushed, his almost white hair rather wild. He was staring just to one side of Sofka with great intensity, his eyes a piercing blue. Again, he reminded her of someone. There was something beseeching in his outstretched arms and she had a sudden, very strong desire to stand close to him.

But as she got up from her bed to do this, something extraordinary happened. Ivan slowly raised both his arms towards the ceiling. As he did so, Sofka felt herself rising too. She had the sensation of floating along and then of being very delicately lowered down in front of Ivan. His clear blue eyes were still fixed ahead, rapt.

Feeling of, sensation of . . . except that her black hair was now all round her little face, and when she put her hand on the top of her head and then looked round, there was the comb lying in the middle of the floor, obviously knocked out when her head had brushed against the ceiling.

Ivan shook his head as though emerging from a dream. He

looked down at her. From pink, his face had turned rather pale, though extremely relaxed. Although he said nothing, she felt him asking her, 'Now do you understand?'

Also without speaking, she answered, 'Yes, I do.'

Ivan gave a little sigh and, stepping past her, went and sat on her bed. All at once Sofka realised who he reminded her of. This time she did speak.

'I know who you're like.'

Ivan looked up. 'Who?'

'Napoleon.'

'Napoleon?' repeated Ivan, with slow emphasis. 'Are you quite sure?'

'Yes. It was a portrait by David. In one of my history books.'

There was a long silence. At last Sofka said, 'I ought to go to a class. You can stay here. I'll be back at one o'clock. You can have a bath. We're lucky, we have a gas geyser. It costs a rouble a bath, but have one, do.' She'd noticed that Ivan, like most of the people in Tcheksna, smelt of not having had a bath for a long time.

'A rouble!' cried Ivan. 'My money! My coat! Could you get it for me?' He described in detail how to find Leo.

Before she left, Ivan said, 'You don't live here alone?'

'No. My mother and young brother are here too. Our grandfather is dying. They've got a permit to go north and see him. It's already winter there. They'll be gone at least a week.'

The 'apartment' consisted of two rooms. The smaller, back one was divided in two by a blanket and was clearly for her mother and brother. The larger, front one, into which a door opened, was the living area, with cooker, small bath with a wooden lid and a window on to Nevsky Place. The side of this room had been curtained off to make a room for Sofka.

After his bath, Ivan tried to hammer back what was left of Sofka's floorboards. She returned at half past one.

'Your friend has disappeared.'

'Disappeared? He can't have done. You must have looked in the wrong place.'

'No, it was just as you described. But the space under the stairs was empty. Or rather, two young women were moving in when I got there.'

'So – he's run off with my money. I wouldn't have thought he would. No money, no papers. Now I have no choice.'

'I don't think so. I talked to that woman next door – what did you say her name was? It seems the police came for him.'

Ivan wasn't listening. 'I shall join the army,' he said suddenly.

'The *army*?' cried Sofka. 'Are you mad? No one joins the army.'

'They don't ask for papers in the army.'

'Oh, don't worry about your papers. I know someone who can get papers. You can stay here with me in Ruibinsk and be a student.'

'But it was you who said I should become a soldier.'

'Me?'

'You said I looked like Napoleon.'

'I didn't mean as he really was. That was a photograph in a book of an idealised portrait, a painting – really an imaginary likeness. Anyway, what does that matter? If I said you looked like Pushkin, would you have thought I meant you to be a writer? Or like Stalin, a politician?'

'Well, actually, both of those things have occurred to me at different times. But there have been other signs about this recently and before.'

'Wouldn't you like being here with me?'

'Yes, I would. I do. Only . . . well, I know it sounds absurd, but I have to consider my destiny.'

'Destiny, indeed!' said Sofka. 'I've heard that people often die just in the training. Two thirds of the students here are students so that they can get out of conscription. You'll just end up guarding a labour camp in Siberia, hardly better off than the prisoners.'

'Even Napoleon had to begin somewhere.'

'All right, Napoleon, come and help me shop for our supper.'

'But suppose the police see me?'

'Silly, they don't know what you look like. No one's looking for you, are they?'

'They could be. Those men who stopped the lorry . . .'

'If we see the police, we'll move off.'

That night Sofka said he should sleep in her bed while she took her mother's.

He had only been asleep a quarter of an hour or so when something woke him. He was aware of someone standing beside the bed. 'Who's that?'

'Me,' came Sofka's soft whisper from the darkness. He felt the bedclothes lift at the side. 'Move over.'

As he took her in his arms, she felt him trembling. 'Is this the first time you've been with a girl like this?'

'Yes,' whispered Ivan.

'Don't worry,' whispered Sofka, who'd guessed this and been excited by it. 'It's very easy, but we needn't do anything. Let me just lie in your arms.'

In fact, they did not make love until the dawn light was coming in over and through the grey blanket partition. It was indeed so easy that Ivan wondered why he'd ever thought otherwise.

Her arms were round him and he was asleep again. How tender he made her feel. He had an extraordinary white, thin skin and with her fingernail she could trace the delicate harebell-blue veins down the side of his neck and over the top of his chest. She felt for him as if he were a man, yet, although they must have been about the same age, he was also still a boy. How on earth can I get him papers? she thought. She wanted her mother and brother to stay away for a year or two and to keep Ivan to herself.

Everything was easy with her, especially talking about himself. Reflected in her eyes, he was astonished by his life. This only made him more certain his decision was the right one.

On the fourth day, when Sofka returned from her afternoon lecture and hurried to her room, she found a note lying on the bed where he'd said he'd be waiting for her.

I have to join the army. I'm absolutely sure it's what I have to do. I see now that all Boris's disciplines were military. I love you. I love you. I'll come back one day, I promise.
Ivan.

22

Michael loved his grandmother. Yet, to his astonishment, his overwhelming feeling after the strangeness of the first week or two at Cambridge had been one of release.

Dressing in the mornings was for days an extraordinary adventure. He could spend half an hour deciding, choosing, changing. He became something of a dandy and would flip through magazines – *Queen*, *Harper's Bazaar* – for inspiration. Or else, naked, he would tiptoe to his chest of drawers and pluck shirt, pants, a tie, a pullover at random. Of course, detailed instructions, for dressing as well as everything else, arrived in the daily or twice daily letters he received from his grandmother. Michael ignored them. Soon he was barely reading the letters at all.

Always rather laconic, his own letters to her became shorter and shorter. Mrs Wordingham begged for news. In its absence, she was forced to imagine and invent. Two lines suggesting he had watched a rugby match were interpreted as a presage to playing himself. A tin of bruise embrocation arrived, crepe knee bandages, mittens. One thing she insisted on: a detailed record and description of his evacuations. Michael, interested himself, soon developed a shorthand: 'Black. Solid. OK'; 'Omelet'; 'Fragmented, pale'. By the middle of the term his communications, which were usually postcards, consisted of little else, except for rather perfunctory enquiries about her arthritis. Every third or fourth he would include a 'PS Any news of Elfreda? If she writes or rings, let me know.'

Almost as astonishing to Michael as his delight in being

free was the behaviour of the other undergraduates. His reading had given him a vague but menacing impression of university education. Unpopular figures, as his 'Venture' experience had made him realise he was bound to be, were subjected to various assaults: blanket and fountain tossing, compulsory vomiting, 'up' before beaks and proctors, and all described in terms like having his oak sported or being gated, which suggested being broken on the wheel.

Instead, to his delight, the undergraduates ignored him. Urged automatically by his tutor, Professor G, to join something, he became a member of the Train-Spotting Society (the TSS). Their simple obsession with collecting train numbers struck him as a peaceful way of passing spare time and it also fitted admirably with his main reason for coming to Cambridge.

Used for years to his own company, indeed preferring it, Michael was in fact not actually alone. As a daring experiment, and as a gesture towards egalitarian views in the college which he did not share, the Master had allowed in a figure called Poole. Stocky, hairy, with a brilliant if narrow mind and a Yorkshire accent you could cut with a miner's shovel, Poole was the only undergraduate in Trinity Hall from a grammar school. He and Michael shared rooms – a common sitting room with gas fire and institution furniture, off which each had a small bedroom, containing washbasin, bed, chest of drawers and cupboard.

The arrangement worked well. At first deeply suspicious and defensive, Poole soon realised Michael was socially a complete innocent. Reassured on that crucial aspect, he relaxed and they lived their separate lives politely and without fuss. Indeed, Poole came to find something peaceful about his large, considerate and mostly silent roommate, with his air of mysterious activity.

Poole's father had died when he was four, of sclerosis. Conscious that his mother went without luxuries, even without necessities, to augment his minute allowance, he worked eight or nine hours a day, determined to get his First in physics. His only other interest was photography.

Michael genuinely enjoyed discussing the problems of physics, but his polite interest in photography suddenly became real during their second term together. Poole had acquired one of the new colour Polaroid cameras. It was damaged, so that its prints were often just blurred brown washes and smudges, but the speed with which they came sliding wetly out was astonishing. Poole had bought it, second-hand, not to produce photographs but to improve his composition (sheets 6 and 7 in the course offered by *Photographer's Weekly*). Unfortunately, he discovered that the film for this newfangled camera was so expensive that he could never afford to buy any.

Observing the cumbersome apparatus lying unused day after day in a corner of their sitting room, Michael eventually asked diffidently if he might borrow it.

'Go ahead, mate, go ahead,' said Poole in his abrupt Lawrentian way. 'If tha' can afford bloody film, tha's welcome to it.'

It had occurred to Michael that it might please and satisfy his grandmother – whose complaints about the lack of information on his postcards were now bitter – if, instead of his almost coded descriptions, he could send snapshots; it would also substantially diminish the tedium of a tiresome daily chore.

The tiny bathroom-lavatory at the top of staircase B, which Poole and Michael shared with the two rooms below them but which for some reason only Michael ever seemed to use, was extremely dark at the best of times. A single 40-watt bulb glimmered above the basin. Hovering inexpertly above the bowl, his bulk interposed between basin and lavatory, Michael clumsily operated a click mechanism, then waited for the result to unroll automatically, glistening. Unaccompanied by explanatory notes, vague shapes and blodges, indications in various degrees of darkness, began to arrive at Inkpen. Holding them excitedly in her misshapen, trembling fingers, peering through her thick spectacles, a baffled Mrs Wordingham eventually began to discern the outline of various friends, rugger teams, his rooms.

To protect those flimsy records in the post, Michael sliced open the cardboard cylinder from a used toilet roll. Thus was revealed the usefulness of these little drums, usually discarded. Still haunted by memories of his stamp album disintegrating in the gales off Mull, he had left all his collections at home. These intestines of lavatory paper became the first of the Cambridge collections.

But the real contact between Poole and Michael was over Poole's work. Every so often the thickset miner's son would get drunk on quart bottles of Newcastle Brown. He became expansive and generous, and it was during these sessions that he taught Michael to smoke. Poole also became very talkative, though only about one subject. He would sprawl in one of their uncomfortable chairs and talk about the subject that obsessed him, one which he intended to pursue for his PhD. This was the origin of the physical universe. It was the time when Hoyle's theories of continuous creation and the steady state were in the ascendant. Michael, whose interest in physics remained strong, endeavoured to follow the argument. He had persuaded his grandmother to let him have *Science Now*, *Nature* and *Scientific American* and, after being read, the magazines gathered dust under his bed, along with a rapidly growing pile of Mrs Wordingham's letters.

Since the same magazines littered the rooms of Professor W, his English tutor, Michael raised the subject during one of his rambling tutorials. Professor W, a small, sixty-four-year-old, spinsterly, rabbit-mouthed, mouse-moustached, doll-eyeballed, ludicrously overbrained academic, began to look haunted.

'Continuous creation?' he said. 'Yes, of course I've read about it.' He gestured toward the magazines, all unread, many still in wrappers. Michael waited.

'The two cultures reinforce each other here,' said Professor W suddenly, with an air of relief.

'Really?'

'Oh, yes. Oh, yes. In the mid-eighteenth century Swedenborg believed that a divine mind continually created the universe.'

'Oh, really?' said Michael.

'Oh, yes. And the idea wasn't new even then. At least,

related ideas. To be precise, it first appeared about 420 BC in the work of Democritus. He thought there was an infinite number of worlds in which identical men fulfil identical destinies. An infinite number of Democrituses each aware that there were an infinite number of Democrituses. Just as there are now an infinite number of Michael Wordinghams listening to an infinite number of myself.'

'I'm not sure that is exactly Hoyle's position,' said Michael, but he had lost interest in the question. He'd suddenly thought, And are there an infinite number of Elfredas? And if so, are they, in each of those infinite worlds, also lost?

The search for Elfreda was by far the most important of his activities at Cambridge.

23

'I love you,' Ivan had written.

Did he? He'd learnt enough, even in three days, to realise this was what he had to write. But in reality he knew this was just a lesson, a preparation for the Great Love Affair.

But he desired her. Walking quickly to keep warm without his coat, he wished he'd waited for one last half-hour in the little hot bed. There would be no small, soft, eel-slippery Sofka where he was going now.

Ivan stood shivering in the cold wind and stared at the grey stone building. So, this was his destiny? So be it. He clenched his jaw and went up to a young soldier lounging by the big door.

'I wish to enlist.'

The soldier must have been about his age. He had dark rings under his eyes, a sallow skin, a thin, twisted, sarcastic mouth.

'Don't. Run away. Get an exempted job. Cut off your toes. I would if I'd known. I would now if I dared.'

'No. Please. I want to. I've got to.'

The soldier tried to spit, but seemed unable to. 'Don't say I didn't warn you. Go round the side there. The sign says "Stupid bastards this way".'

Ivan went through a door with a board on it: "Recruits".

A hatchway. Behind, a big, grey-uniformed sergeant. Forms.

The sergeant didn't get very far. 'Eighteen and a half? Why the hell didn't you report six months ago?'

'I was working on the farm.'

'You come off a collective? Don't you know that's an exempt occupation? Have you run away? Why are you wasting my time?'

'I haven't run away. I was allowed to leave. I want to be a soldier.'

'Don't make me laugh. Let's begin at the beginning. Give me your papers.'

'I haven't got any. They were stolen.'

'Ah, I *see*.' The sergeant's face, which had become quite animated with curiosity, now fell back into grey rhinoceros folds.

'No, you *don't* see. They were stolen. I had them. You can check,' said Ivan, standing up in his agitation. He felt his entire future career was at stake. It was essential not to be branded from the start as some sort of wrongdoer.

'Don't worry. Don't worry,' said the sergeant. 'We're not too particular here, as I've no doubt you know. But certainly we'll check. Where was this collective of yours?'

At the end of this interrogation, since he was not a conscript but a volunteer, Ivan had to choose a term of years which he would serve. How long would it take to become a general? He thought five years, but he signed the form for ten, since this seemed to offer advantages in terms of money and leave.

Once again the plates of flesh on the sergeant's face cracked and moved. 'So you really mean it,' he said. 'Well, it's a tough life but I've enjoyed it. We've only had one other volunteer this month, and none the month before. I'll see you're together. Section F.'

They took away his clothes and shaved off his hair. He had to shower with four other naked, shivering youths.

They were shouted into line to get their uniform. The boy next to Ivan said, 'Christ, I can hardly lift this coat.'

'Sign here. You'll need it where you're going.'

'Where's that?'

'Somewhere fuckin' cold.'

No sooner had they dumped their kit on their beds than they were yelled into line again and marched to the dining hall. Ivan's heavy-duty working trousers and top were too big and seemed to be made of canvas. The long vest scratched and itched.

He couldn't eat the grey, greasy lump of rubber on his plate. He mopped round it with the bread and swallowed the mug of hot black bile.

'You're lucky. This is a meat day.'

It was the young guard with the thin, elastic mouth who'd told him not to join. He'd sat down opposite Ivan and was watching him not eat.

'I'm not hungry.'

'So I see. You will be. What section are you in?'

'F.'

'Oh, yes. I heard you were to go either to Tsilma or Tunguska.'

'Where are they?'

'They never tell you exactly where anywhere is. I've heard Tunguska is hell. They're both in the north, northeast.'

Ivan suddenly thought, Perhaps I'll meet Sofka's mother and brother. Things like that happen.

'When will we go?'

'Soon. Nothing goes on here. You just sit about. The army is either hell or sitting about. Training is hell.'

There were thirty-five of them in Section F. Forty centimetres separated the two-tier bunks, boards not springs. Ivan had had no idea people could make so much noise sleeping. It was like a jungle: honking, gurgling, sudden cries, creaking. He lay for a long time listening, his mind crowded and confused, running his hand again and again over his bristling scalp. At last he found himself thinking a single strong thought: This is my destiny. Just before he fell asleep, he imagined Sofka wriggling down into his bunk.

Four days later they were on a train.

On each side of the aisle seven wooden seats faced the front, seven seats the back; three men to each wooden seat. Sections F and G were in the same carriage, the last in the train. At its back there was a small platform with an iron balcony open to the air. You could stand and watch the rails unreeling into the distance.

The carriage was noisy and hot. Many of the faces in his lot already had characters, or at least roles. Nikolai Andreivitch, the boastful, burly, dark-skinned, sharp-eyed son of a shoemaker, was the wit and bully. Lanky, thin, nervous Andrey Boinov was teacher's pet, sergeant's arse-licker, victim. Vasili, six foot five, six years older than the rest of them, built like a blacksmith, gentle, slow, was their respected strong man, father, unofficial noncommissioned officer. He was the only other volunteer.

And Ivan, what or who was he? Prince Myshkin? Perhaps – to them at any rate, if not to himself. Not that they would have heard of Myshkin, but they regarded him as an innocent idiot, partly because of his inability to master the complicated webs, straps, belts, pouches, packs, buckles, bolts, knots and loops, or indeed to deal with any single item of their continually augmented equipment. The whole section had to help get him on parade.

It was also because of a brush with the shoemaker's son Nikolai. Ivan couldn't believe his ears, the second night after he'd joined up. Nikolai's gang had apparently got this girl, tied her legs behind her head, gang-fucked her. Three times each. She'd loved it. Begged for more. Daniel, Nikolai's mate, used to have girls on the line. When the whistle went for the ten-minute break – two of them at once in the toilet. Great stuff. Randy Daniel had once . . .

They'd all done such things, at seventeen. Were they

inventing? Only lanky Andrey Boinov stammered out he hadn't yet had . . . he was . . .

And Ivan? 'You've listened to us. Are you asleep or something?'

Ivan felt himself blush in the darkness. After a pause, he said, 'Whatever I've done is my business, not yours, Nikolai Andreivitch.'

'Oh, yes? The others have told. Are you another virgin and ashamed of it?'

'Whether I am or not is also no business of yours, though I didn't know there was anything to be ashamed of in that.'

'Oh, dear, so we do have another frightened virgin, do we? Another little mother's boy. "There was a frightened little mouse . . ." ' began Nikolai Andreivitch, one of whose weapons was satiric doggerel.

Suddenly Vasili grunted from the bottom bunk along from Ivan, 'Leave him be. And shut up! You're keeping me awake with your rubbish. That goes especially for you, Nikolai Andreivitch.'

Their coach was shunted on to the back of a different train going north and east. When joined, it was too hot. As soon as it was uncoupled it grew too cold. Hours passed in sidings.

Every five or six hours, they stopped and were marched into some little station waiting room or just lined up on a platform and dished out what Ivan was learning passed for food in the army. They used the rapidly overflowing and stinking latrines, or pissed over a bank.

In the middle of the third night of what now seemed an endless journey, they reached the snow. Suddenly the rumbling trundle of the wheels became softened, almost soundless. Only Ivan appeared to notice. The other soldiers remained motionless, contorted in sleep under the dim light of four tiny bulbs. He rubbed away the moisture on his window. Winter.

He extricated himself from his seat, got his fur hat out of his kit bag, and picked his way over the legs and arms sprawling across the narrow aisle. He wrenched the rear door quickly shut to prevent the gush of cold air waking them.

Wide white fields, dark blocks of woods, single strokes of black trees against the white, all of a sudden a house crouched black. Once, the fleeting orange dot of a light. The air was biting and Ivan pulled the fur flaps over his ears and fastened the strap under his chin. The train made a soft rushing sound and a great plume of snow spurted up behind it, an endless fountain like the wave behind a speeding ship.

Gradually, Ivan realised the great expanse – blocked out starkly in black and white – was changing. Mighty waves formed frozen in the cold, tilting up higher and higher, then swooping down. For the first time in his life, he was seeing hills, valleys and mountains.

He stood for a long time, oblivious of the intense cold, on the platform at the back of the silently rushing train, Napoleon racing through the night to join his armies in the north.

24

Dear Elfreda,

I'm in Cambridge! I've got here at last! I'm at Trinity Hall, Staircase B, Room 4d. My bedroom is off the sitting room. The door is directly opposite the door you come in by. The bathroom is at the top of the staircase. Only I seem to use it, so it is very private. There's a bolt on the door and I am going to fit a second, stronger one.

I am larger than when you left, but I know that will please you. I am now six foot one inch tall and I weigh twelve stone. My hair is inclined to fall out but I keep it. You will recognise me. If you see me in the street, come up to me, of course. I shall do the same.

You can communicate by letter to the college, or leave a note in the 'W' pigeonhole at the porter's lodge, or slip one under the door of my room. And of course you can write to me at Inkpen Vicarage. My grandmother's arthritis seems to get worse each year. You remember how active she was? She is now contemplating a wheelchair (motorised). We often talk about you, of course.

Elfreda, there is one thing I must ask. I often wonder if you left so abruptly because my grandmother sacked you? Or was it anything to do with her behaviour? If so, I would find it hard to forgive her. If you get this, that is one of the first things I would like to know, apart from where you are, of course.

I remember the time you were with us very well. I have often thought about you since you left. I think about you every night and often during the day and as a result I am never lonely. I very much hope I see you again. When you get this, or more likely a copy of it, please communicate at once. We will have so much to talk about and do. Don't forget.

I look forward to your reply.

Love,

Michael

25

Mid-morning on the sixth day, three trucks took eighty filthy soldiers from Tunguska railway station – a wooden shed with a siding behind it beside a single-line track – to the notorious Tunguska training camp.

Notorious? For what?

Isolation, for one thing. A large space cleared and wire-fenced in the valley-wide pine forest which then continued for hundreds of kilometers. A hundred wooden huts in five rows of twenty. Parade ground. Bare mountainside to the north, with rifle range and assault courses. Station an hour by truck. Nearest human habitation 400 kilometres away in Vilvny.

Brutality for another. Brute conditions, brute food, brute

NCOs. Up at five. On parade 5.30, the parade ground still dark, harsh under arc lights; stamp stamp, shoulder arms, order arms, at the double, about turn, *about* turn, half asleep, jets of breath, order, shoulder, order, shoulder, stamp stamp, stamp stamp, stamp, stamp, stamp, stamp, yelling, running, sweating – for an hour.

Programme Monday 29 November (temperature at night minus 32 degrees celsius). Reveille 5.0. Parade 5.30–6.30. Eat 6.30–6.45. Drill 6.45–7.45. Weapon training 7.45–8.30. Kit inspection 8.30–9.0. Drill 9.0–10.0. Lecture 10.0–11.0. 11.0–12.0 punishment parade, eat, prepare for range. Range 12.0–4.0. Eat 5.0. Recreation (i.e. cleaning equipment) 6.0–7.0. Night march 7.0–10.0 Bed 10.30.

On the range, the rifle metal was so cold before firing it would stick to flesh. Any relapse at any time anywhere – dirty belt, dirty neck, dirty rifle, lateness, slowness, nodding off at a lecture – incurred three days, five days, ten days of heavy fatigue duty: up at 4.30 to clear frozen latrines, dustbins, carry coal, clear laundry; more fatigues midday; extra guard duty at night, alone outside the main gate, the air crackling with cold, imaginary wolves, in a haze of exhaustion.

Permanent state at Tunguska: the haze of exhaustion.

Emblem: close-up corporal's mouth, full of broken teeth, stinking, screaming abuse.

Sounds: trains at night, boots on snow, the camp generator, sea sound of wind in pines.

Rumours: Sgt Gribov got one of his recruits twenty-eight days in the cooler because he refused to be buggered. A recruit in Hut 35 was found dead at reveille of pneumonia (previously diagnosed as malingering). It was said no one had ever escaped from Tunguska, but a week ago two men made a run for it. Dogs were set after them and did indeed catch up with them. But too late. They had already been killed and half-eaten by wolves. All three-year conscripts were to serve four years. Corporal Khaskar had been found murdered. The whole of Section B was suspected and sentenced to the Zur Labour Camp. Suicides since September – four.

Hut 67 was the centre of their lives; the big iron Donetz

stove was the centre of Hut 67. Every morning, the turned-down flaps of the coarse grey blankets were hard as boards from their frozen breath. The seven-day coal issue lasted three days. Thereafter, there was a roster for stealing fuel. Most people got wood. Ivan had discovered a place in the coal compound where it was possible to pull aside the corrugated sheeting. The perimeter fence was also full of holes. Where would escapers go except into the maw of wolves?

Life was so hard there was no time for animosity. At any moment any one of them might need help – need to be supported, even carried on a route march, pushed awake on the range, lent a belt or can of polish, a cigarette or a clean rifle.

Each had his mate. Big Vasili, the other volunteer, was Ivan's. Volunteers were not admired in an army of conscripts, but Vasili had got drunk when his wife left him. He'd knocked out the two police who had tried to arrest him. It was during one of the crackdowns on alcoholism. He was given a choice: a year in a labour camp or five years in the army.

Ivan told Vasili that he'd run away from his collective because of the brutality of the overseer. He also said he'd lived with a girl in Ruibinsk for three months. He felt ashamed of both lies; at the same time, they didn't feel like lies.

Big Vasili was his friend, but Ivan had got the others on his side by a piece of luck. One Sunday Nikolai Andreivitch, seeking to bully, had challenged Boinov to arm wrestle with him.

'Why don't you pick on someone your own size?' Ivan said. 'I'll fight you.'

He won with ease. One by one, eight of the other men – the eight with Andreivitch made up a group – had a go at him. Ivan beat them all. Thereafter, though he didn't join them, they looked at him with respect.

One night, something woke Ivan. The bottom of the Donetz was open and, cast by its fiery glow, a giant, demonic shadow was leaping on the wooden walls and ceiling of the hut.

It was Vasili. There was rust in his rifle. Thinking to clear it, he had tried to pull a large piece of sock through the barrel. It had stuck. The more he pulled, the tighter it had become. A rifle was sacrosanct. Normally so calm, the big, slow man had suddenly become frenzied. He'd heated a metal rod red hot and was trying to force and burn his way down the blocked barrel.

Ivan sat up and watched. He could hear Vasili panting. He got out of his bunk and walked over to him. His friend was pouring with sweat. Ivan saw at once what was wrong. Vasili was driving the block down the barrel from wide to narrow, wedging it firmer.

'Let me,' he said in a low voice. He took the rifle and slid the cooling rod in at the barrel mouth alongside the pull-through cord. A few sharp blows with a boot and the blackened piece of sock fell out.

Those nights in the hut. Sometimes, too tired to sleep, Ivan would be awake thinking of Sofka. The fire would remind him of the blacksmith when the Taschla horses were shod. The clouds of smoke streaming from the burning hoof. The blue-tiled stove. Little Na.

The clanking of couplings as the long trains slowly made their way west across the silent, frozen valley.

The deepening darkness as the Donetz stove went out.

The cold.

The seven months Ivan spent at Tunguska were far worse than anything he would have believed possible; at the same time they were no more than he'd expected. Napoleon would have to pass through fire – and ice.

The other recruits received letters. The distribution of mail every three weeks created occasions of sadness and humiliation for Ivan. Suddenly it occurred to him – why not write to little Na? Thereafter, the distributions of mail were even more painful, disappointment being added to his other emotions.

Then, at the end of January, came a reply. Ivan actually wept when he saw she had used a page from one of Alexis's exercise books. He hadn't even been sure she could write (astonishing ignorance of God about his creations!).

She didn't seem to have taken in that he'd begun his life's work. There was some local news: the big sow had farrowed, the new overseer had been confirmed – Andrey Voynichov – and they were to get the use of a crop-spraying plane. But the burden was: when would he come home?

Astonishingly, that too seemed just possible. Then likely. Finally certain. All recruits would get a week's leave in June, volunteers would get two weeks. They would then receive their postings. Marshal Chuikov – one of the heroes of Stalingrad and now a full marshal of the Soviet Union – was to inspect the camp and take the salute.

Training stopped at the end of April. May and early June were devoted to drill and cleaning the camp. Even pebbles were whitewashed. The entire perimeter was soused in chemicals to keep at bay the notorious Siberian mosquito. Selected sections rehearsed various training routines again and again. The last week was devoted entirely to their equipment.

Ivan's power had not manifested itself again since the time with Sofka. This seemed quite natural to him. The frequency of the visitations had grown less as he'd grown older. But the real reason was that when he was young they had been necessary to remind and convince him of his destiny. Once he'd embarked on it, they had become unnecessary.

Caught up in the Tunguska fever, he'd supposed his excitement just part of the general excitement and the prospect of two weeks' leave. But as they marched out on the parade ground, which had been literally polished like an enormous dance floor, Ivan recognised the familiar symptoms.

He managed to hold them at bay until just before the end. By then his agitation was so extreme that his teeth were chattering and his rifle butt slippery with sweat. From a great distance, he heard the final word of command.

Ivan was rising swiftly into the air. Carrying himself effortlessly upwards, registering in passing that this must have been how he'd managed to see Ruibinsk, he realised for the first time how beautiful the district of Tunguska was. The austere, sharp-angled mountains, still glistening at some points with snow, slid down and tucked into the dark-green pines as into an enormous bed. There to the right was the railway like a thread; that point where it crossed a second thread, a forest track, was where Vasili had caught him as he fell sideways almost unconscious on their return from a night exercise. Vasili had virtually carried him home on one mighty blacksmith's arm. But then Ivan, blessing the continuing strength of his own arms, had carried all Boinov's equipment plus his anti-tank gun the eight kilometers of a route march. What memories! What times!

How peaceful it was floating in the clear sky. Ivan glanced down. The parade ground was empty, except for a single figure on whom three NCOs were now converging. Reluctantly, he allowed himself to be reeled in.

The wide open, meat-coloured mouth of the sergeant. Gold fillings. Inaudible.

Ivan, his eyes still extremely acute, observed that the juts and ledges of the marshal's face, till then rigid, were for the first time alive and working. Was that a smile? Watching Ivan being marched off alone, he bent and said something to the camp commandant, Colonel Eremenko.

But the oddest thing about the episode to Ivan was not the levitating – which, after all, he had done a number of times before – but that on his return to the ground he found he'd snapped his rifle in half at the butt. The strength of his arms always surprised and slightly embarrassed him.

The breaking of the rifle was, it seemed, the real crime. It angered them – but it also astonished them. The rifle was examined and found to be sound. Perhaps astonishment, even secret admiration, mitigated the seriousness with which they took the offence. Or perhaps Marshal Chuikov interceded on Ivan's behalf. In any event, his punishment was mild. His leave was cancelled. He would spend the two weeks in the cooler doing fatigue duties during the day. Then go to his posting.

Cleaning, shovelling coal, peeling potatoes, scrubbing floors, emptying bins – it was a good deal less onerous than training. He missed Vasili and the rest of Section F, but they'd meet up soon. The wooden bunk in his cell was the same as in Hut 67, except there was a light on all night.

Then, on the fourth day of his detention, Ivan had his revelation. He was scraping grease from one of the big pans in the officers' mess kitchens. All at once he thought, I shouldn't be doing this. He stopped and stared round at the big coke-burning range, the rows of pots, the bloodstained chopping block. In a space of perhaps three seconds he realised he'd made a ridiculous mistake joining the army. He realised why. He realised what he should be doing.

It had nothing to do with not seeing Na or Sofka or his punishment. He'd simply misread the evidence. Or rather, invented it. The real evidence had been so obvious, so close, he'd missed it.

What was the most extraordinary thing Boris had done for him? Have him taught English. Why had he done this? So that Ivan could go to the West. Subsidiary proof: Boris saying that the icons would fetch a lot more money in the West. Indeed, now he thought about it, he couldn't remember Boris – who after all *knew* Ivan's destiny – ever even mentioning the city or the army.

Ivan set the pan down and picked up another. He would have to escape. And easier here than in Minsk or Moscow or Berlin or the borders of China or wherever they were to be posted. Since escape was thought pointless, he was hardly supervised. He was simply sent off to report to the latrines or guardroom or cookhouse or wherever else there was work for him.

The following afternoon he was again told to go to the officers' mess and, if he finished there before six o'clock, to report to the fuel depot.

His task at the mess was to sweep out the junior officers' rooms, empty ashtrays and wastepaper baskets, make beds.

Ivan looked in at the kitchens after collecting a brush and refuse sack. By chance, they were empty. He was able to grab a loaf of bread, a lump of pork and some cheese. He shoved these into the sack.

He next went down the row of small bedrooms – cubicles really, none larger than his own cell – putting the waste tins into the corridor. In the third, he found a stout, fur-lined jacket behind the door, with fourteen roubles in the inner pocket. Junior officers were poorly paid. He only found a total of forty-six roubles in the other thirty cubicles.

Ivan put the roubles in his pockets and resisted the temptation to take the jacket, thus risking early discovery. He shouldered the sack and, carrying a bucket and brush, set off through the lines.

It was well known you could go anywhere unquestioned through the camp if you were carrying a bucket and brush. This was especially true of Ivan, who'd become something of a figure since his escapade in front of Marshal Chuikov. Jokes on the lines of one-man parade and rifle-smasher accompanied him from chore to chore.

At the last line of huts he turned towards the bottom left-hand corner of the camp, where a deep refuse pit had been dug. He threw in the brush and bucket, slid down the far side and with beating heart ducked through the clouds of mosquitoes and a hole in the perimeter fence at the bottom.

It was cooler under the pines. There was a good deal of young growth here, dense and thick. Panting, slapping his neck and face, Ivan pushed through it; then, as the trees grew taller, it withered into emptiness – pine trunks with dead lower branches, gloom, the mosquitoes giving up.

Ivan hurried on at an angle and soon came out on the track down which they'd often set out on exercises or route marches. He stopped to listen, then set off at a steady trot.

He reached the railway line in two hours. Twenty-five minutes' rapid walk up this and he came to the long, twisting incline which eventually led up to Tunguska station. He hoped that one of the trains, one with a full load, would be sufficiently slowed by this to let him jump aboard. He chose a spot just before a corner with a longish view to the left. The train would be further slowed by the corner.

It wasn't until he was sitting in the sun against a pine trunk, roughly concealed by unfurling bracken, slapping at mosquitoes, that Ivan realised how frightened he'd been. The running had been nothing – he'd run twice the distance in full equipment – but his heart was pounding. Would they pursue him? When would they pursue him? The officers' mess might contact the detention cells. On the other hand, nothing might happen till he was due back at 7.30. When would the roubles be missed? There was not much the officers could spend it on.

Fear often made Ivan sleepy. Besides, he'd got up at 4.30. The slight wind sounded softly through the tops of the pines but didn't reach down to him like the sun. Ivan nodded, dozed, slept.

When he woke it was dark and much cooler. He sat forward and listened. There was only the wind. He stood up, wishing that after all he'd stolen the jacket, and stepped across to the track. The railway line was cold and hard and dead against his ear.

He stepped back to his tree and pulled the bread, pork and cheese from the sack. He should have taken a knife. To defend himself with, apart from anything. His chewing was deafening. He stopped to listen. Chewed. Listened.

The wolves would creep up silently. The dogs from the camp would bark, then, as his scent became stronger, yelp. He'd see lights coming up the track, men shouting. He'd scramble up into the tree. The dog would be on hind legs, barking furiously up at him. A torch beam would be directed upwards, two beams, dazzling . . .

There was nothing but silence and the soft wind. Slowly, a quarter moon floated up over the black pinetops. For two hours, three, Ivan sat, straining his ears and eyes. Astonishingly, once again he slept.

This time he was woken by a confused dream of a train that was suddenly a real train. Ivan started up, clutching his sack with the remainder of his food. No doubt about it. Punching its way through the forest – rattle clank, rattle clank, rattle clank. Now he could see the beam of light thrusting ahead, now the engine; the whole train was pounding towards him.

It was going too fast. It couldn't be boarded. The engine roared alongside, the roar altering pitch on the instant, the ground trembled. Ivan glimpsed the fire, a man shovelling, then truck after truck rattling past rapidly, emptily. As the last came level and passed him, he leapt out and ran desperately in pursuit of a swinging chain. Its red light receded, vanished round the corner. Ivan stopped and stood, his fists clenched.

But hardly was it out of sight than there came a loud clattering and banging and clanking of trucks hitting together and pulling apart and an outburst of steam. Once again, Ivan ran forwards.

The red light glowed ahead of him. But even as he rounded the corner there was a series of rapid, explosive steam and engine bursts and it began to move again. Ivan forced himself to run faster. The red light. Faster. He was close. They were going at the same speed. The red light was pulling away. Ivan flung himself forwards and just managed to catch the swinging chain. It nearly wrenched itself out of his hand. He dropped the sack and flung up his other hand, pulling up so that he swung forwards and then back, his feet beside the racing wheels.

26

Michael had his letter to Elfreda Roneoed two thousand times in a small workshop off King's Parade. He placed each letter in a stamped envelope and then addressed it: 'Elfreda (nee Smitten)'. At the bottom he wrote in minute, neat handwriting, 'If moved, please forward.'

He had bought a street map of Cambridge and divided it into eighteen numbered squares. Nearly every afternoon and most evenings he set out with two large paper bags full of envelopes. During his first term he systematically posted letters into every building in squares 1 and 2, though towards the end of term it meant he often stayed out until the college gates closed at 11.30.

He distributed the first two thousand letters in five days. Roneoing was not particularly cheap. Luckily he found that the college possessed a duplicating machine, which he could use at a fraction of the cost. He also discovered he could buy stamps at the porter's lodge and put them on the bill. For a month he simply copied addresses from the telephone book and posted huge bundles of letters – until he grew nervous at the size of the bill and took to the streets again. Almost his entire allowance went on activities connected with his search.

Michael found it enormously exciting, despite moments of despair. Every morning he hurried to collect his letters, shoving the one from his grandmother with increasing irritation unopened into his pocket. His disappointment was soon swamped by hope – *tomorrow*! Every walk, the next face could be hers. A pleasing tension was added to his long postman's tramps. And just as queueing can seem a form of progress, each day seemed to bring him closer to finding her. Even an endless queue would be bearable provided one did not know it was endless, and Michael was at first certain Elfreda was somewhere in Cambridge.

Or almost certain. He thought it likely her enormous vitality, her love of gaiety and her wit might also mean she'd be much sought after in London. His train-spotting helped here. His enquiry about a season platform ticket had amused the station master into giving him one. The porters became accustomed to the large, pale, balding young man who sat on Platform 1 beside the ticket collector's shelter, apparently as interested in the people as the trains.

He had another clue – Elfreda's mention of a conductor. But conductor of what? Endless bus rides and endless concerts occupied him, with embarrassing questions after performances or journeys and letters to various musical societies and the City Bus Company.

He devoted about 75 per cent of his time to Elfreda. This was possible because Mr Broughton had taught him so well that at first he found the work comparatively easy. He also quickly discovered that really all that was necessary for his essays was a skilful amalgam of his critical reading.

' "The Excremental Vision" – good title, Wordingham,' said Professor W. 'And written with feeling, too.' Since Michael had cribbed the title from an obscure book on Swift, he merely nodded. But from then on his essays finished even quicker, being not just an amalgam of other people's ideas, but, if they were sufficiently obscure, of their words as well.

Yet, when even these speedy transactions seemed a waste of time, the vacations were far worse. Hurrying back after his first term, eager to see his grandmother, his collections, the garden, he rapidly wished himself back at Trinity Hall. Her endless little attentions irked, then infuriated him. 'Don't tweak me,' he'd say angrily. Nor, as always when he asked, had she any news of Elfreda. Soon the project itself was threatened.

'One hundred pounds!' she cried one teatime, waving the afternoon's post clumsily in her clubbed fist. 'Michael, darling, how did you manage to spend one hundred pounds on stamps? How was it *possible*, darling?'

'Not difficult,' said Michael. 'Letters. Postcards. The odd parcel.'

'But one hundred pounds, darling. And letters to who?' said Mrs Wordingham. Drayton Gardens rents were in for another hoick.

'Oh, fellow train spotters,' said Michael vaguely. 'I've still got friends from the Venture course. Mr Broughton. John. Stamp dealers.' And then, as Mrs Wordingham continued to stare at him incredulously, he had a brainwave. 'And I'm taking a postal course in creative writing. Didn't I tell you?'

'No! Oh, *Michael*,' cried Mrs Wordingham, 'that explains it. No, you didn't. How sensible! How exciting! I'm thrilled. How's it going?'

'Very well. They're very pleased. Of course, it's only exercises as yet. I shall leave serious writing till I come down.'

'So late?' said his grandmother, with a note of disappointment. 'But perhaps you're right. Your grandfather didn't write his "Thoughts on passing the rock of Gibraltar" until he was seventy-five.' She laughed. 'We both agreed that *was* a bit late.'

Nevertheless, Michael decided to spend the whole of the long vac working in Cambridge. His grandmother's disappointment was intense. 'You're too conscientious,' she said when he informed her on the telephone. 'I was so looking forward. I'd thought we could . . .'

'Professor W thinks it vital I should,' said Michael. 'He thinks I might get a First. And I find it much easier to concentrate on the writing course if I'm here. I'm about to start short stories.'

Even this didn't comfort Mrs Wordingham. 'It means I

won't have seen you for six months. No – nine. I'll write, of course, but it's not the same.'

In the end, Michael promised to go to Inkpen for the last week of the long vac.

At Cambridge, with nothing else to do, he found he was able to deliver over five thousand letters a week as well as cover the station and fit in a few concerts and bus rides. Like branches in winter swept clean of leaves, the inhabitants of the city stood out far more clearly when the myriads of undergraduates had been blown away.

There was one embarrassing incident. The Warden's sister-in-law, an elderly widow, bored, lonely, opened one of Michael's letters when it fluttered through her letter box. Intrigued, she showed it to the Warden.

Sir Charles, about to set off for Spiros, was intrigued too. Trinity Hall was a small college and he thought he knew who had rooms on Staircase B. He felt in a small way responsible for Wordingham's presence in Cambridge, and certainly the Christian names were the same.

Padding out to check up on Staircase B, he was astonished to find the undergraduate still in residence.

'I'm staying up to do a few weeks' work, sir,' said Michael, uncomfortably aware of the envelopes covering his table. 'Professor W felt I should.'

'Very good. Very commendable, Wordingham,' said the Warden. 'But not too long. A holiday is important. Now –' he looked at the letter in his hand – 'this is no business of mine. None at all. It just so happened, my sister-in-law, quite by chance . . .' He held out Michael's letter, feeling embarrassed. It *was* no business of his. Nevertheless, in a way perhaps it was.

Michael felt himself blush, and drew the fingers of his left hand sharply down his cheek. He could think of nothing to say.

'You're doing nothing wrong,' said Sir Charles. 'But I only wondered – is everything all right? Perhaps I could help. Or the Reverend Phipps . . .?'

'The thing is, sir,' said Michael. What was the thing? How could he explain? 'I'll explain. The reason was – well, Elfreda and I met in the vacation. She came to work for my grandmother. We fell in love. In fact, we had an affair. Then, she had to go. I know she's in Cambridge.'

he heart. Yes.' Sir Charles knew
d himself on being able to change
nething to do with it. In his day,
lept with each other if they were
ng. Now – well, only last term a
n someone's rooms at one in the
tly. He would do so now.
you find her, not in college after
.m. I would only question your
"
d the post office. You see, sir, I
n area.'
- well, Wordingham, don't forget
e Greek islands myself.'
one of the chairs and lit a ciga-
mbling. He felt as if he had had a
arden had said, he had done, was
nhaled deeply, ran his nails down
he also began to feel released, as if

a had done constitute an affair?
Vordingham had shrunk from all
of such matters. She considered it
t ever fell to her, she would post-
marriage. The sexual passion was
artistic creation and it would be
few books under his belt first.
nal experience that men reached
their peak of sexual performance and need at the age of sixty-six. There was no hurry.

In fact, Michael had been seduced the term before. At least, partially seduced. He had been disturbed at the first lecture on the Romantics by a newcomer: a girl too small, it was true, and with spectacles, but with the same long, pointed nose, wide, lippy mouth, high cheekbones and untidy, coarse hair pulled back from blue eyes.

Henrietta Mirren was American. She reacted to the large, pale, shy young Englishman whose eyes she felt on her during the four subsequent lectures by going up to him in the foyer and saying, 'Would you care to take a coffee with me?'

They got on. Michael found it enough to look at her, to exaggerate her Elfredian features. She shared another of these – the medicinal smell, in her case from the half-bottles of Smirnoff she bought and consumed most of herself. Henrietta felt soothed by his silent attention, and intrigued, even excited by the gnomic, ambiguous, English quality of his response. She said, 'What I like about you, Michael, is that you don't see me as a sex object. I bet I could get into bed with you and you wouldn't lay a finger on me.'

'No,' said Michael; 'I mean yes.' She even, Elfreda-like, muddled him syntactically.

The reply was elucidated a month later, during a bout of flu. Michael's temperature was 102. Henrietta dropped in to help. 'Would you like me to get your pyjamas washed?'

'I don't wear pyjamas in bed,' said Michael.

'Is that so?' said Henrietta speculatively. She paused. 'You like me to cook you a boiled egg tonight? Soft English style?'

'Well . . .' said Michael.

'Don't give it another thought,' said Henrietta. She came back at eight with some eggs, bread, a salad and a whole bottle of Smirnoff. Michael had no appetite. He dozed, half aware of Henrietta's chatter. When the Smirnoff was three quarters finished she undressed and got into bed with him. There was some fumbling on her part and they both fell asleep.

Michael woke first, feeling slightly better. Henrietta was snoring lightly. So that was what going to bed with a girl and sleeping with someone meant. Jammed against the wall, he wished his bed was bigger.

'You'd better wait till 10.30 before you leave.'

'I can't wait,' said Henrietta, brushing her hair violently. 'I feel too ill. I need coffee. I need a drink. I'll walk about a bit and pretend I'm a tourist. You can get away with anything in this town if you've an American accent.'

Before she left, she stood looking down at him from the door. 'I guess you're a bit low-sexed,' she said. 'Or even impotent. Don't get me wrong, Michael. I *like* that. I don't want relations between men and women to have to be sexual. I feel you and I meet as equals, as *people*. That's why you can listen to me. Most men can't listen.'

When she'd gone, Michael lay feeling the flu still in him. Low-sexed? Impotent? He who could fill whole baths with his semen? So likely, as Henrietta would say.

He wondered whether to invite her into his bathroom but decided against it. When at last he found Elfreda, he wanted to be able to say, 'I have made love to no one else but you.'

27

Sofka was aware of the tapping on the door but remained asleep, hoping that her mother would do something about it.

Suddenly she thought, Police! I must get to them before mother hears. She was halfway to the door before she realised the police would never tap softly like that. In any case, why should the police call on them? It was someone at the wrong door. It was her friend Anna from the floor below.

Not until the door actually opened did it suddenly occur to Ivan that he might not be welcome, even turned away. Or it might be her brother or mother.

The little face was smaller and much further below him than in his dreams.

'It's me, Ivan. You remember?'

There was a pause. At last she whispered, 'Ivan?'

'Yes.'

There was a long pause. Then she stepped back and held the door open. Ivan opened his mouth. The sight of her at once excited in him a desire to tell her everything that had happened to him, all his plans, his new destiny. 'I –' he began.

But Sofka put her finger to her lips. She was looking intently at him as though searching. Finally she whispered, 'So you really have come back?'

Ivan looked at her face, still childish and thick with sleep, her tousled black hair. 'Yes,' he said.

Sofka, irradiated with happiness and sadness, looked back at him. He was no longer a boy. His face was gaunt and with his burning blue eyes and cropped head he looked like a criminal on the run. She guessed he would not stay long.

'Do you have anything I could eat?' said Ivan in a low voice, looking suddenly from side to side. 'Bread? Anything? I haven't really eaten for days.'

'Sssh,' whispered Sofka. 'You'll wake my mother. There may be some supper left over. I'll look. Go and sit on my bed.'

He was so hungry, he couldn't talk while he ate. Twice she got him more bread. The third time she went back, taking his plate, he heard voices. He sat nervously, unable to distinguish words.

Sofka came round the blanket and up to him, smiling. She put her mouth so close to his ear her breath tickled. 'I have a lecture at 8.30. I've told my mother I don't feel well. She'll be gone in half an hour.'

'What about your brother?'

'He doesn't live here any more. Why don't you get into the bed?'

A faint smell of hot milk came through the blanket. Subdued voices. At last the door clicked.

As Sofka eel-wriggled down the narrow bed beside him, against him, Ivan thought, How real real life is compared to dreams.

28

It took Ivan three days and a night to get within striking distance of Taschla. He got two lifts, both of about 80 kilometres, before the lorries turned off. For the rest it was walking. Sofka had 'lent' him some old clothes of her brother's, but he'd kept his tough army boots and his legs were like iron.

He reached the barn where he'd spent his first night on the morning of the fourth day. The closer he got to home, the more excited he became and the faster he walked. But he decided to walk the last 50 kilometres by night. He could easily be recognised and there was no knowing what the authorities had been up to.

The barn was more or less exactly the same. The broken sheets of corrugated iron hung a little lower. The straw was untouched. He half expected to find the tramp there. It was really pretty shocking, thought Ivan, walking towards the straw. You wouldn't get a barn abandoned like this on Taschla.

He climbed up into the straw and then heaped up a barrier so that he'd be out of sight from the barn door. He didn't want to deal with any tramps – or anyone else, if it came to that. As he did so, something white caught his eye. He moved some straw and saw an envelope. *His envelope.* He opened it and pulled out the contents: permit to travel, birth certificate, identity card . . . everything, all his papers. Not even damp.

Ivan stared in amazement and growing excitement. They must have fallen from the second envelope when the tramp threw his holdall up to him that night. Or perhaps the tramp had realised he couldn't risk passing as Ivan and had tossed the envelope up before he left. That was the most likely. He'd been a fool not to check the big envelope. But this, if anything, was proof. If he'd had his papers, he'd have stayed in Ruibinsk. He wouldn't have met Sofka. Above all, he wouldn't have realised he had to go to the West. Here, in his hands, was the clearest sign that his destiny was at work.

Ivan set off as dark was falling. He could still make out the signpost: 'Pokrowskii 30 kilometres.'

He reached the long track which led down to Taschla soon after dawn. Heart beating, he took in the trees by the privy, the familiar profile of the buildings, the stack yard, while still half a kilometre away. A cock was crowing. Nothing had changed.

As he drew near, he could almost see the sleep rising like the shimmer over wheat in summer. They wouldn't be up for half an hour yet. He'd risk the back door, the one near the rear of the piggery.

But pressing his ear to the door, he could hear faint sounds in the kitchen. Antonina, up early? Or little Na? Ivan turned away. He'd hide till nightfall. Then he turned back, unable to resist. The door, at which the men had once in turn murmured 'All flesh is grass', had always opened easily.

After all, it was little Na, not Antonina. How warm the kitchen was, warm like a loving heart.

'Psssst.'

She took no notice. Ivan stepped inside. 'Na,' he said softly. 'Na'.

The little woman jumped, nearly dropping her pan, then turned. When she saw Ivan, her eyes opened in terror. Then, putting down the pan, she came towards him, her tired face slowly becoming radiant with relief.

Ivan felt tears pouring down his cheeks. He picked her up. Sparrow Na! They were both crying. 'Oh, you naughty boy,' she was saying. 'Oh, my naughty, naughty, naughty, *naughty* boy.'

He put her down at last. 'Why naughty?'

'We've had the police here. We've had the military police. How they searched! Do you remember that time Andrey came looking for the money Boris kept? Why we haven't all been shut away over you, I'll never know. What have you been up to? I knew you'd come back. You'll always come back to Na. You're thin. We must feed you up.'

'Who's here?'

'Andrey Voynichov is still the manager. He lives here now. Stefan's gone. We've got a couple of new boys. Antonina's not well. That's why I'm up. It takes me longer. You'd better go to my room. They'll be down soon. No one will go there.'

Two hours later she brought him a tray laden with food he hadn't seen since he'd left. And when he'd finished it, she brought him more.

'Now,' said Na, removing the tray from her little table, 'what have you been up to? The army, indeed!'

When he'd finished a short, edited account, Na was once more filled with anxiety.

'The *West*? What do you want with the West? What is all this rubbish?'

'Oh – you would object,' said Ivan, wanting her approval, angry at being made guilty. 'Boris would have approved.'

'Boris?' said Na, looking extremely surprised.

'Of course. Obviously he wanted me to go. Why else do you think he had me taught to read and write English?'

'Oh, that,' said Na. 'If you ask me, that was all a misunderstanding. Anyway, how would you get there? And besides, you've chosen quite the wrong time.'

Ivan heard only the sentence that suggested he could change her mind.

'I'll find a way.' He stood up and began to walk about her familiar little room. 'My papers are still valid. Once I'm away from here where I can be recognised, I'm safe. I'll get a job on a fishing boat.'

'Safe?' said Na sharply. 'On all their lists? But you don't listen to a word I say. Always so impetuous. Why go now, when we're doing so well? Why, this afternoon the sprayer plane comes at last. Think of that!'

'You think that plane can solve everything.'

He was able, later, to see from her window the single-engined, double-winged plane drone in low across the flat fields and bump to a stop along the stretch that had been rolled flat for it just beyond the farm buildings. The plane was much larger than he had expected. Soon after it had landed, a tanker came down the track and drove out to the field. This would be the fertilising agent and insect sprays. There had been much talk of these amazing new chemicals before Ivan had run away. Yields could be doubled, trebled, it was said. Huge new quotas were in mind. Special new bonus payments rumoured. But none of this interested Ivan, nor would it concern him.

For an hour the plane flew all over Taschla, returning from time to time to have the long cylindrical containers fastened below its wings refilled from the tanker. Refilled – or was it re-fuelled? It suddenly struck Ivan that Na might after all be right.

She was, at that moment, watching with him. 'There you are,' she said. 'Now we'll see something.'

'Look, Na,' said Ivan, 'when he's finished, I want you to bring him up to me here.'

He had to threaten to walk out and get the man himself before she agreed.

Ivan knew he was about to take a terrible risk but he was not frightened. He knew – as he was to know many times in the future – that he was in the grip of his destiny.

He felt it strongly again when the pilot came in through the door. He was a thickset man of about thirty-five with one of those crafty, greedy peasant's faces that could be outwitted by something he would be quite unable to comprehend – complete honesty.

'Leave us, Na,' said Ivan. He shook the man's hand. 'Ivan Khuchevsky.'

'Andrey Gzibov.'

'Listen,' said Ivan, 'I'm in bad trouble. I also happen to have a lot of money. I want to bribe you to help me.'

Gzibov didn't say anything. He just nodded, as though he'd known it would be something like this.

'Is your plane reliable?' said Ivan.

'The AN-S5? There's nothing better. You could go to the North Pole in an Antonov if you were minded.'

'So?' said Ivan. 'So it can go far. How far?'

'On a full tank – that's 1,273 litres – she'd take you about 1,200 kilometres. With a tail wind you might do 1,300.'

'I see,' said Ivan. 'A kilometre to a litre. And how much crop spray do you carry?'

'About 1,000 litres.'

'Could you fill the spray tanks with fuel and join them up to the fuel tank?'

Gzibov thought. How slowly he thought! At last he said, 'Might be done. You'd need a pump. It would cost you.'

Ivan looked straight into Gzibov's little blue eyes. 'I'm a deserter from the army. I intend to fly to the West – to Finland. If you agree to fly me, I'll give you . . .' He paused. He could see into Gzibov's mind. It was thinking, I can do myself a bit of good turning this chap in. 'I'll pay you 8,000 roubles, and all in used notes.'

It was an enormous sum. Far more than Gzibov could have saved in a lifetime. In two lifetimes. Gzibov's mind was immediately wiped blank. It was like some coarse, white material on to whose middle had been emptied a mug of purple dye. Ivan watched the stain spreading.

'How do I know you've got such money?'

'I'll show it to you.'

'But what will happen to me? If I get caught I'll be sent to a labour camp. And I don't want to stay in the West.'

'You won't get caught and you won't be sent to the camps. I haven't worked out a route in detail yet, but the round trip is about 2,300 kilometres.'

'But what if we come down before we get there?'

'I thought you said your plane was reliable.'

'It is. But a margin of 300 or 400 kilometres isn't much. Suppose there's a head wind? I might have to land in a hurry on the way back. What then?'

But Ivan could sense the feebleness. The stain had almost reached the outer edges. Gzibov wanted to be convinced. 'Look,' Ivan said. 'You'd be sent back to your district. But what would that matter? I don't know about your lot, but Kozlov at Pokrowskii would let you get away with murder for 500 roubles.'

He saw Gzibov relax. 'Oh, of course – bribes.' He paused, thinking. 'I'd need a lot in advance.'

'I'll pay for any work on the tanks,' said Ivan. 'And I'll give you 2,000 roubles in advance.'

'Make that 4,000.'

'We can discuss that. Will you do it?'

'I'll have to talk to my younger brother. He's the mechanic. When can you show me you've got the money?'

'Come back in two days. And don't forget, even those downstairs don't know I'm here. Only the old woman who showed you up.'

Twenty minutes later, the plane took off again. Now he was in danger.

He spent that night and the next in the privy cellar, with candles and a couple of blankets. If the police came, they'd come at night. He also moved the roubles and the icons up into Na's room.

Poor Na. When he'd told her what he wanted her to do, she was too frightened to remonstrate. All she said was, 'What's happened to you? You weren't like this as a boy.'

'I was. I had to hide it.'

'Yes, that Boris was too hard on you. I told him so, many times.'

'I know you did.'

Twice he was nearly discovered; once on the stairs, once in the kitchen, moving before the household had finally settled.

But the police didn't come. Instead, on the third day Gzibov returned. From the window, Ivan saw him walking about over the fields with one of the new men.

Eventually, a nervous Na showed him in. Gzibov said, 'I told that chap out there the fertiliser valve was faulty. I've inspected it and said it will all have to be done again.'

'Very clever of you.' He waited.

'Let's see the money,' said Gzibov.

Ivan went to one of Na's deeply recessed wall cupboards and pulled out the small hessian bag. He emptied it on to the bed. 'Each bundle contains 100 roubles. If you want to count, tie them up again.'

Gzibov stared at the heap. Then he lowered himself very carefully as though about to hatch something. He counted all the notes in one of the bundles, then, measuring for thickness each time against this one, counted all the bundles. Every now and again he undid a bundle and peered at a note or two, to show he knew what he was about.

At last, with a sigh, reluctant to stop fingering them, he stood up.

'All right,' he said, 'we'll do it. The fuel tank's a big job. Cost you 500 roubles.'

Ivan knew this was a huge exaggeration, but he nodded. 'How long?'

'About a week. And we'll want 4,000 in advance,' said Gzibov. 'I'll take that now.'

Ivan knew by this, which he knew anyway, that they would cheat him if they possibly could. He smiled. '2,000 in advance,' he said, 'and not until I'm sure the tanks are done.'

'In that case the deal's off.'

'Very well,' said Ivan. He began to drop the bundles of roubles one by one into the big bag. 'I'm sorry about that,' he said. 'I'll have to give all this to someone else.'

Gzibov watched in silence. At last he said, '3,000 in advance.'

'2,000,' said Ivan.

There was another long silence. Ivan tied up the mouth of the bag. Suddenly Gzibov laughed. He came and put his hand on Ivan's shoulder. 'I was only testing you,' he said. 'You can certainly do business, for a chap your age. No hard feelings?'

'No hard feelings,' said Ivan, smiling faintly. 'Do you have a compass in your plane?'

'Yes,' said Gzibov.

'Good,' said Ivan. 'Come back in a week or so. Bring your brother. Come in the evening. We'll leave before the sun's up. About five. And don't forget – I'll check those tanks.'

Each night, Ivan walked the farm in the darkness. He knew it so well it was like walking about in his head.

His only map was an old world atlas left behind by Alexis. They would fly NNE. By ruler, the border with Finland was 1050 kilometres away. Suppose there was nowhere to land? His destiny would see them through.

The plane returned five days later at seven in the evening. The tanker arrived half an hour later. After an interval, the two men came into Na's room. Gzibov's brother was several years younger, pink, not so certain.

There was a last confrontation.

'Right,' said Gzibov, when they'd gone over the map. He seemed perfectly confident in Ivan's rudimentary – barely existent – navigational instructions. 'So – let's have the advance.'

'Not yet,' said Ivan.

'You mean you want to check the pump and the fuel? Very well – but after that, the advance. We agreed 2,000 in advance.'

'Yes, but in advance of what?' said Ivan. 'In advance of our arrival in the West? Nothing would be easier for you than to take the 2,000 roubles after I've looked at the fuel and bugger off. You could even take it after we've taken off and then just circle round and dump me.'

'You mean we don't get 2,000 roubles in advance?' said Gzibov.

'You do,' said Ivan, 'but not quite so easily. You know perfectly well I can't really check your work, but if you haven't fixed it we'll run out before the border. I've arranged to ring Pokrowskii and get a message to Na. Wherever we land, I should be able to do that before the end of the day – unless we have in fact reached the West. If there is no message by eight o'clock, Na will hand over 2,000 roubles to your brother.' Almost none of this was true, but the dark stain of 8,000 roubles had by now penetrated Gzibov to the very centre. 'You'll get the balance – 6,000 roubles – on your return, but only when you hand Na a signed note from me.'

There was rather a long silence. Then Gzibov gave a slightly overloud laugh. 'Nothing wrong with your head,' he said, 'except over that map. Let me have another look at it.' He held it close to his face. 'We can't fly on this. Give me three days.'

In fact, it took them a week. Ivan guessed that they still hadn't even bothered to fix the fertiliser tanks. Once again, they arrived late in the evening.

Ivan and Na were up at 4.30 the following morning. He was too excited to eat, but swallowed some hot tea. Na, for once, for the only time, was almost unable to speak. As he held her, she whispered, 'You'll come back?'

'Yes – one day.'

'You promise?'

'I promise.'

Ivan joined the men on the field, carrying under his arm the two big parcels of icons, each one carefully wrapped in fresh newspaper.

They had to stand for some time beside the plane before Gzibov would take off. Slowly the farm buildings, from the middle one of which Na would be watching, appeared out of the mist, until all at once it cleared rapidly. It was going to be a fine day.

At first the giant fields of Taschla seemed all there was. Then, as they rose higher and higher, the land of the other farms and the long intersecting canals came into view. As the plane vanished into cloud at 1,000 metres it was above a patchwork of vast, dull-coloured squares, very like the farmland near Chicago.

29

Michael obtained a Third, to no one's surprise but his grandmother's.

'But I thought your tutor said a First, darling,' she said, as they scanned *The Times* together. 'Do you suppose there has been a mistake? Should you appeal?'

'No,' said Michael. 'The trouble is, I really gave more time to my writing course during the last year than I did to work.'

Mrs Wordingham allowed herself to be soothed. 'Look,' she said. 'Poole. Wasn't that one of your friends? I think I have a rather smudged photograph of him. *He*'s got a First – that's something.'

Michael's social life – Henrietta and Poole – had dwindled, really, to nothing. This was due almost entirely to the fact that sections 13 to 18 on the Cambridge map grid comprised the increasingly far-flung suburbs. Unable to ride a bicycle, Michael had to undertake lengthy and boring journeys by bus and on foot before he could begin to distribute his letters.

And his heart was no longer in it. Elfreda would never have consented to live in these dreary purlieus, somehow the urban equivalent of the dismal and miasmic marshlands upon whose ancient sites they'd gloomily grown. The queue, it seemed, was endless after all. Or perhaps the end was elsewhere. He could feel the golden thread that joined them being tugged from London.

Anxiety about this and other things – principally the neglect of the Cambridge collections, which were in danger of becoming chaotic – meant that by the end of the third year Michael was smoking thirty to forty cigarettes a day. He had returned to Inkpen with relief and, as always, anticipatory feelings of love and interest.

His grandmother had greeted him in her new wheelchair. Softly, they had brushed cheeks.

'Perhaps you could push me sometimes, darling,' she said, anxious to make real a long dwelt-on fantasy. 'There are places in the garden I can't reach.'

'I doubt it,' said Michael, 'at least not for several weeks. I have terrible blisters.'

'Oh, dear, too much rugger, I suppose,' said Mrs Wordingham.

'Rugger is a winter game.' Michael, again as always, was slightly appalled to note how swiftly irritation dissolved all other feelings.

'Anyway, don't bother, darling,' said Mrs Wordingham. Pathetically she gripped the knurled inner rim and with hands like roots slowly began to turn herself towards the house.

Michael limped guiltily after her. 'I'll do it, I'll do it,' he said.

'It's so lovely to have you here again,' said Mrs Wordingham, closing her eyes.

Certain it was already under way, Michael had sworn to himself not to refer to his major plan for a month, but it burst out of him on his third evening, provoked partly by anger at his grandmother's inefficiency and partly by overlong interrogation about his clothes.

'I don't *need* Aertex pants,' he said irritably. 'Have the top tenants moved out of Drayton Gardens yet?'

'Good heavens, darling, I don't suppose so. It's not urgent, is it?'

It had always been agreed that at some point Michael would settle in London, with an allowance until he 'found his feet', and pursue a literary career.

'Urgent? Of course it's urgent. I must be in by the end of next month at the latest. I wrote and told you in the very first letter last term.'

'It was a postcard,' said Mrs Wordingham. 'You only ever send postcards. They're so short. It wasn't clear.' She'd vaguely seen him staying at Inkpen a year.

'I'll ring Smiley and Pinkerton first thing in the morning,' said Michael. 'I thought all this had been arranged months ago. I must start my writing.'

'Why can't you do it here?'

'Because I can't.'

The tenants hadn't even been given their statutory six months' notice. He wouldn't be in till the end of January. Michael stumped angrily and heavily upstairs. He'd have to make a start on unpacking the seven tea chests containing the Cambridge collection.

Part II

30

Refugees from the East bloc still made news in the 1950s – and the manner of Ivan's escape had been spectacular.

He was interrogated at length and eventually granted political asylum – a process much facilitated because the Provost of King's, a man of influence, had been struck by newspaper photographs of the young man. If he wished to continue his education, said the Provost, there was a place for him at Cambridge.

Ivan accepted at once. Had not Boris had him educated? Hadn't Sofka suggested he go to university? The term had already begun, but by chance a small room had suddenly been vacated on Staircase K. When they apologised for its size, Ivan laughed. 'In Ruibinsk I lived for six months in a cupboard under some stairs. Not alone. I shared. We had the same sheets. Things are very different in Russia.'

This was just the sort of reply a refugee from the Soviet Union was expected to make. For a while, Ivan was something of a celebrity. Yet he was often lonely and homesick. He was saved by Rawbones.

Rawbones was, in fact, Sam Raeburn. Ivan called him Rawbones partly because he at first misheard and mispronounced his name (not until his third year was his English more or less perfect); but also because it suited him. He was almost fleshless. What there was was bone-coloured – blanched white from expenditure of energy. Even his hair and wispy nicotine-stained moustache were white, as white as Ivan's. Perhaps that drew them together, too.

Rawbones was a painter in his late thirties, and lived with his third wife in a large, rented house that was so full of leaks and cracks, it seemed to be collapsing. It was full of children born of past husbands and wives, past houses, past collapses. Rawbones's huge paintings kept out the wind.

Ivan hadn't realised that someone like Rawbones was possible. He seemed to radiate light. His spare, tall, sinewy body, his white hair, often seemed actually luminous with energy. Either his eyes, or the constant stream of his ideas, or his long, alcohol-shaken, nicotine-stained fingers seemed to charge anyone near him with a sort of intellectual electricity. He only had to come into a room and people instantly wanted another drink and a cigarette. His recklessness made Ivan, made all his friends, feel guilty and cowardly if they weren't equally reckless. It was the time when people were beginning to try and give up smoking. Rawbones stepped up his consumption. He also took a vicious, very cheap black tobacco from Albania, which he rolled tight in liquorice paper. A looked, and smelt, as if he were smoking bootlaces. When Ivan was away from Rawbones he found he remembered him as an event – a thunderstorm, say, or an elpileptic fit.

Ivan saw a great deal of the whole ramshackle family. Rawbones took him up, inviting him to meals, to stay the night, to let the night turn into a weekend or a week – and all this when it was most needed, in the vacations. Ivan found that Rawbones not only mainlined talk, injecting himself straight into Ivan's arteries, making his heart thud and his brain crackle, but he also listened. He listened with the same intensity that he talked. His magnetism, the gravitational force of his interest, were irresistible. Ivan opened his mouth and his entire past life came rushing out, sucked out like a stream of iron filings. Rawbones called him a holy innocent, something which Ivan knew to be untrue but which, because he was ravenous for echoes from that past, made him love the battered, unsuccessful painter. Despite the difference in their ages, for the first time in his life since Mikhail and Alexis, Ivan felt he had a best friend.

But he had many acquaintances who called themselves friends. He had become a fashion and taking Russian in the Tripos allowed him plenty of time for acquaintances. Young men – boys, really – like Mikie Manton, with a sallow face like a spoon, and three cars; Dermot, Caspar, 'Heigh-ho' Harry the Earl of Strathbane, another oval-faced Scots boy apparently called Ilk, 'Pootsie' Pomeroy, Peregrine ('Perry') Percy – all very young, very rich, very noisy, very easy, very generous, very kind and very silly. Perry Percy's family had, among numerous dwellings, an enormous castle on the north Norfolk coast. On a few warm autumn nights phosphorescence briefly lived its brilliant liquid life along the long, long waves as they rolled and broke upon that shore.

But that was the only time in three years that Ivan was asked to one of their houses. It baffled him. At the vacation they vanished. He heard nothing.

Himself about to decamp, Rawbones said almost nonchalantly, 'Forget it. You simply haven't the foggiest idea about the English upper classes. They're hermetically sealed. You haven't a hope of really being accepted. It's not just having to go to their ridiculous schools from the age of eight; you practically have to have had the same nanny – and that's just a start. Girls are your only hope.'

Ivan felt a door slam, a momentary and familiar pain. Only later did he realise that Rawbones, with his last sentence, had suggested a way in – or out.

31

The top-floor flat at 92 Drayton Gardens consisted of a small kitchen and bathroom, a spacious sitting room looking out over the plane trees and an almost equally large bedroom with a view of roofs and down along a series of perfunctory little gardens three storeys below. There was also a windowless cupboard/room, and a flat roof which could be reached by a metal ladder whose rickety limbs unfolded precipitately with a finger-crushing clatter.

Michael used the cupboard/room to store his piles of science magazines, his grandmother's letters, his Cambridge notes and essays, and the work he'd done for Mr Broughton. There remained space for more. A tea chest, converted into a table for the sitting room by a chintzy remnant of Mrs Wordingham's, held his china collection; his two thousand books filled the long, floor-to-ceiling shelves he had had put up on the longest wall, while his stamp albums and postcard albums, the unfurled lavatory cardboard store, the collection of cuttings and numerous other embryonic collections were ranged neatly round the walls. In the bedroom he kept the small sacks of hair and other items of a personal nature, rolled toothpaste tubes, *objets trouvés* in skips, boxes of used paperclips, re-usable envelopes and the like.

Was this obsessive, as Mrs Wordingham had irritably observed while the collections were being loaded into the removal van? Michael doubted it. He realised her remark was prompted by hurt feelings. Nor did he feel obsessive; he had no sense of frenzy, of being driven. On the contrary, he felt calmed. When, after a month or so, the flat was in some sort of order, Michael thought he'd never experienced such peace. Or would have done, but for one thing – the telephone.

Mrs Wordingham's life was, perforce, very restricted. She would suddenly wake in the night shot through with horror – when had Michael last been to the dentist? For some extraordinary reason she had supposed Cambridge would deal with this.

She must have been mad. Rigid, sweating, she imagined hovering in the darkness before her a mouthful of rotting teeth.

She rang Michael at nine o'clock. As she had feared, he hadn't seen a dentist for three years. He promised to go. Fears, warnings, advice, sudden ideas for his wellbeing, or the simple desire, so long frustrated, for a chat – these could strike at any odd moment throughout the day. Mrs Wordingham would ring. Michael would reply.

One morning Michael said, 'Granny, please don't telephone so much. I'm all right. I'm nearly twenty-five. You must let me control my own life.'

Was this the tapping on the egg? Mrs Wordingham thought not. Besides, she couldn't help herself. Love must exercise – or die.

After three months, Michael asked if his telephone might be made incapable of receiving incoming calls. To this unusual request, the engineers suggested he go ex-directory. Michael felt this would be too wounding. Would he like a telephone that could be plugged in and unplugged? No. He saw at once this would involve a lot of stooping and straightening, and he now weighed fifteen stone. He had a feeling an unplugged telephone would make him feel marooned.

Eventually, at some cost, the engineers complied. Michael rang his grandmother to explain.

'But why, Michael? What's the point?'

'I find I shall save money.'

'How? How can you save money?' Mrs Wordingham was certain this couldn't be true. She was being purposely confused.

'When people call me, they involve me in expense. Only this morning the agency from whom I got Mrs Inch rang to say I owed them £25 booking fee. In this way, I can control things.'

'You're obsessed with control,' said Mrs Wordingham crossly.

Denied the contact of incessant telephone calls, she once more took painfully to letters, her pen gripped in a clublike hand. Instructions, suggestions, questions, orders flowed from Inkpen as from a command centre: don't eat fat, don't fill your hot- water bottle upright, have you registered with a doctor? As months and years passed, she was ordering his life down to the smallest particular: time to have a haircut; time to send the laundry, time to collect it; the week's news arrived on Monday, a postcard on Thursday with a pair of nail scissors, an exercise chart and article on smoking cut from a newspaper on Friday (Michael now smoked two packets of twenty a day). She told him, or suggested to him, what he should read, what films to see, programmes she'd noticed on the wireless, what clothes to wear. Was he cool enough? Warm enough? She enclosed a thermal vest (fond, inaccurate memory! He could hardly get it over his hand).

Michael replied rarely, or not at all; when he did, only a few laconic sentences in writing now so minute she had the greatest difficulty reading it. She didn't even have the solace of smudged photographs. For want of facts, she gradually created a life for him in London which was almost entirely imaginary.

Every five or six months, the longing to see him became intolerable and Mrs Wordingham would send her grandson frantic telegrams begging him to come and see her. Guiltily, Michael would eventually comply.

32

'There are eels in the river. One winter I saw a farmer with a whole pail of them he'd caught. They were swimming round and round.'

'Eels?' Ivan trailed his hand in the brown water. Specks showed up against his pale palm. It was his third year at Cambridge.

'Yes.'

'I had a girl once who reminded me of an eel.'

'Is that the one you lived with in a cupboard for two years?'

'Yes.'

There was a long pause, while the boat drifted.

'I do rather wish you *wouldn't* tell me about girls you've had.'

'I'm sorry, Clarissa. You're quite right. It was long ago. I cannot help remembering sometimes.'

On his bed, in his tiny bedroom, her head was on his stomach and she lay curled naked, coiled and Clarissa'd warmly down his thigh and leg, asleep. Her golden hair lay where it had swirled, as if blown, in a soft wave down across his other thigh. The knee-high corn, like the pelt of some enormous beast. As the wind grew stronger, it would seethe, the corn seething under the sun; a wind coming sweeping in from the distance in long, rolling waves, wave succeeding wave across the corn, successive armies, troops flowing across the plain. And as it grew golden, and then almost dark ripe, thigh-high, and the wind blew, it had its own sound, not like the sea, or the wind in pines, but higher, more sibilant – the wind hissing through ripe corn. And much earlier, it had been a house, a forest, a world of stalks. Someone was calling him in for supper. Was it little Na? Ivan! Ivan!

He was being shaken. 'Ivan! What's the matter? What's wrong?'

He couldn't see her face. Distorted, as though the present was under water. Only the past was clear.

'You're crying, Ivan. What is it?'

'Nothing,' said Ivan. 'Your hair reminded me of corn. That's all.'

33

Darling Elfreda,

I often have the feeling that you are trying to find me too. At night lying in bed or in the bath – especially the bath – I think you are about to come in through the door (which I leave unlocked for that reason). I listen, I brace myself, the floor creaks, the door is about to open . . .

Sweet Elfreda, if you have been there, and have then tiptoed away, too shy to make your presence felt – *never do that again, Elfreda. Come in. I love you. I want you.* And I, if I find you, and find myself, as I surely shall, outside your bathroom or your bedroom, I will do the same.

All my love, *all of it,*
Michael

These letters, short, long, many of them, he had copied and sent to likely addresses: police stations, hospitals, the Latvian Society (an invention), Salvation Army headquarters. One weekend, on a rare visit to his grandmother, he put one in a bottle and threw it into the sea.

He could not search the whole of London, as he had searched Cambridge, but the habit of searching died very slowly – indeed, it never completely died. As he padded to and from the small Trattoria Calvino where he ate many of his meals, or returned from the laundry, he studied every face, the back of every head. Sometimes he saw her in the nape of a neck and broke into a run or stood transfixed, palms spread, while she advanced, slowly transforming, towards him.

34

Ivan had first met Rose-Anne, who had arrived from London, halfway through his first term at Cambridge. She was, initially, really just two very large, young, buoyant breasts simply flying upwards longing to escape from a blue silk shirt bulging taut and thin as a French letter. She stood, as a result, yanked up on tiptoe so that each slender calf curved elegantly with the tension.

Ivan, who had not had effective contact with a girl since Sofka seven months before, stared and stared. He was introduced, spoke in his still charmingly Russian English, stared – and was suddenly swept away by the chattering current.

Nevertheless, at the start of his last term three years later, she sent him an invitation to her wedding.

He heard about the wedding four years later still, but heard about it in reverse, as it were, in the news of her divorce. He had never received the invitation. She'd sent it c/o Rawbones, who, just after the trauma of his fortieth birthday, had vanished hurriedly to Spain, leaving seven massive paintings as grotesque overpayment of a year's rent and no forwarding address.

Ivan was devastated to find him gone. Rawbones had been his only close friend, the only one he felt he could rely on, a second Alexis. Daily, then weekly, he expected a letter, even a summons, at least a word of explanation. There was nothing – not after a month, not by the end of the term. He also discovered at least five other people who regarded Rawbones as their best friend. They, however, were not alone as Ivan was.

What was the nature of Rawbones's friendship? Did its very intensity preclude anything in the nature of a backward look – rather as an intense, narrow beam of light, moving on, leaves darkness in its wake, whereas some milder, more extensive source allows a longer aftermath of diffusion?

But why then were so many included? Was it automatic, turned on by whoever caught the tripwire, a chemical discharge responding to the presence of the human spirit? In which case he, Ivan, was equally automatic himself. Had Rawbones come in through the door, slightly drunk, glowing, a foul-smelling bootlace between two quivering nicotine-brown fingers, a bottle in the other hand, or a glass requiring a bottle, he would have forgiven and responded instantly. The very idea made him jump up restlessly.

Or was it perhaps this class thing that seemed to obsess them all so much?

He'd noticed they often did that. They'd say something really quite abusive, penetrating and accurate about it all – as though they themselves were a totally different species.

In the end, with the sadness becoming familiar to the exile – a sadness which also seemed to strike down deep into the dark river of his past – Ivan decided that in warning of the hermetic sealing which would cut him off for ever from Dermot and Caspar and Perry, Rawbones had really, or also, been giving a warning against himself.

35

Michael and his grandmother did not talk a great deal on his infrequent weekend visits. Mostly he sat reading in the chair opposite her, occasionally throwing a log on to the fire at her request.

Mrs Wordingham did not mind. The moment he arrived, her anxieties vanished. At last she could see the results of her handiwork, the fruit of her letters. The sight was both reassuring and rewarding – on the whole.

'You seem to be putting on weight, Michael.'

'Probably.'

'Do you do those exercises?'

'What exercises?'

'I sent you an exercise chart: something like Chair and Desk Exercises for the Sedentary Man. Don't you remember? It was designed for office workers in the Canadian air force.'

'I must have missed it.'

Long silence, the fire's comfortable crackle, the flapping cotton of its flames punctuated by her questions, questions that seemed as if she were musing aloud.

'I wonder when you'll begin your book?'

Michael turned the page. Mrs Wordingham said, 'Darling, do you know when you'll begin your book?'

'Soon. I have to get my notes sorted. The end of the year.'

'Oh, Michael! I'll be so thrilled. You'll write and tell me?'

'Of course.'

'Darling,' she'd say fondly, looking at him without her spectacles on as he turned another page.

When he left, usually as a concession on Monday morning, her once plump form, now frail, diminutive and twisted by arthritis, vanished into his corpulent embrace.

'Come again soon,' she whispered through tears and into his cardigan. 'Write to me.'

'Yes, Granny. By the way, do you ever hear from Elfreda?'

'No, darling.'

36

It was hurt over what he regarded as Rawbones's betrayal as much as his advice on the impenetrable nature of British society that made Ivan decide he wanted to work abroad.

None the less, the job was obtained English fashion, through someone he'd met at Cambridge. Francis Wyatt was a charming, diminutive and clever homosexual, feminine in everything except his arms, which were those of a navvy. He had an uncle in Reuters and a vague attraction to Ivan. Francis obtained a post in Paris and persuaded his uncle to recommend Ivan, on the strength of his Russian, some articles in *Varsity* and his promise he'd learn French in a month.

In fact, it took two months. But Ivan knew this was not his destiny. It was a holding job, a pause, a vantage point. Except for one element – Ivan always knew there was a possibility that he was destined to be a writer. This was because of one of his 'key sentences'. This was the phrase he used to describe a number of experiences or memories, often deep in his past, which were in fact often wordless. Wordless, but radioactive. He could, for instance, still just see himself as a very small boy standing in the rain, in the yard, his shoes filling with muck, Boris at the corner of his eye. And where there were words they were either meaningless, trite or enigmatic. "All flesh is grass." It was the force or meaning that they concealed which was important. The key phrase to do with writing was 'emotion created in tranquillity'.

Despite its springboard position, Reuters followed the pattern of all his subsequent jobs. Excitement and certainty, followed by a slow disillusionment (masked, often from himself as well, by increasingly energetic activity) over one, two, three, even four years, and ending in a thunderclap realisation that he'd made a ridiculous mistake. To be followed almost at once by a sudden revelation: Of course, *that* is what I should be doing.

These convolutions were quite independent of anything his employers might be thinking. Indeed, they often seemed to take place just as he was becoming most successful. Ivan was very surprised to be told, when he handed in his resignation at Reuters after three and a half years, that they had been grooming him to become their Moscow correspondent.

A few mornings before, as he came to work in a light spring sunshine along the bank of the Seine, he'd noticed as always, almost without allowing the observation to become conscious, the curious flow of feelings this stretch of his walk always produced. It was the stretch that passed the bookstalls and book carts. Quite often he stopped to look. Sometimes he bought something.

Books always soothed Ivan. He never felt alone in a room full of books. Partly this was because they talked to you if you opened them. And in this respect, the books he loved (he'd even managed to bring some from Russia) had faces. But his feelings of warmth and peace also came because they reminded him of Alexis's jerky sweetness. Handling books, sitting among them, he felt safe, as if he'd escaped with Alexis into the tower room, safe from Boris.

That morning, Francis lit the fuse with the idle remark that his younger brother Stephen was starting a second-hand bookshop in London's old docks, and needed a partner. Walking back in the evening, as he entered the reverberating stretch, Ivan felt the charge go off – bookseller! Of *course*!

Frances made a telephone call. Ivan sold the last icon and caught the 8.0 p.m. train from the Gare du Nord. Already he felt relief at leaving the febrile, insular French. The dining-car wine was delicious. Soon, when he looked out at the sliding suburbs, he saw only himself looking in.

37

It was in fact not until the end of his second year in London that Michael was finally able to force himself to try and begin his book.

He bought a dozen loose-leaf files, several quires of lined paper, a hole-punch, ink, a small notebook for ideas. The space round his desk had become cluttered with objects rescued from skips and demolitions on his walks to and from Calvino's and other occasional outings – a towel horse, some perfectly good strips of carpet, a useful plastic plate rack and the like – and these he cleared into his bedroom.

For an hour he sat in front of a sheet of paper. After two hours he wrote in his tiny handwriting at the top: 'Tuesday 21 January, 12.30 p.m. Unable to make a start. No hurry. Raining.'

The second day much the same thing happened, except that he finally drew a small face above 'Wednesday 22 January, 12.15 p.m. Little or no progress. No concrete ideas as yet. Some snow. Constipated.'

On the third day, after waiting an hour, he copied from an article on scorpions he'd torn out of *Science Now*, an item that had interested him. 'They can manage without a meal for long periods: the record for fasting belongs to a scorpion that lived for 17 months on one housefly.' After this, Michael wrote 'Admirable.' Then, smiling faintly to himself, he added, 'Last time I weighed myself I weighed 18 stone 5 lbs. Still constipated.'

On the fourth day he waited only half an hour before copying out a passage from Gombrowicz. Without attribution, naturally. The homage of a composer's 'quotation' of another composer's phrase is increased by the assumption it will be recognised. He noted he was still constipated. 'Will dose tonight.'

The constipation cleared with a vengeance on the fifth day and – Pepys had set a precedent here – Michael described this too.

These descriptions echoed the ones some years before at Cambridge but, suddenly seeing the point of all this, Michael also treated them as exercises in observation and prose. Here the variety fascinated him: one day floating deep, shaped into a series of intertwining snakes like an Indian temple sculpture; at others the very reverse of Indian sculpture, lighter, surface-clinging, more homogeneous and compact, a cumulus, say, or large rust-coloured brain; at still others floating foamy raftlets of astonishingly different hues, orange, black, cream yellow, flecked red, once – but this, it is true, was when he'd accidentally used to clean his teeth and then swallowed a fiery cream bought to treat fibrositis – blue.

As at Cambridge several years before, he extracted these descriptions from his journal and put them on a postcard every week for his grandmother. The condensation required not only meant strict editing, but shrank his already microscopic hand to something that resembled – what? Specks, dots, electrons. Mrs Wordingham's eyesight had deteriorated as if anxious to keep pace with her arthritis. There was talk of eventual blindness. Peering through an enormous magnifying glass, bought specially to supplement her powerful reading spectacles with their thick lenses, struggling to define these overdisciplined spermatozoa as they wriggled minutely across the tiny half of a postcard or even a sentence, she deduced that Michael had visited an art gallery, Poole had called, was that the word 'arthritis'? Probably.

While this interest lasted – and, though brief entries never ceased, after a while other things took centre stage, as it were – but when he was writing as much as half a page or more a day on the subject, Michael found he was oddly reluctant to abandon the field work and, each time he eventually turned away, finally causing the whole field precipitately to vanish, he had a sense of loss, a feeling of regret, which he somehow felt, without quite being able to trace why or when, went deep into his past.

38

Ivan's three-year stint with Stephen Wyatt nearly foundered on the first day when he saw the bookshop – or 'Bookwharf' as Stephen preferred to call it.

This was a cavernous warehouse by the Thames, 120 feet long, 100 feet broad and 50 feet high. Shelves filled it like the spars of a ship. There were hoists and cranes and cradles and clamps and piles of pallets and forks with bulb-tipped two-foot tines curved like bull's horns for shifting the monstrous mountains of books.

Stephen had discovered you could buy barges of books. Some people buy almost worthless shares in companies which own the mineral rights to vast stretches of empty desert because, 'something must be there'. Stephen bought barges of books, and partly for the same reason. Intimacy quailed in the face of such numbers. Stephen pointed to one of the alpine ranges. Each book had cost approximately .0001 of a penny. Sell them for one penny each and there was a profit of 1,000 per cent. Ten pence would be 10,000 per cent. And, like the desert shares, every now and then the something that must be there *was* there. In a five-ton consignment of books bought from three bankrupt girls' schools, two demolished hospitals, a liquidated printer and a dozen 'contents' sales, Ivan found a first edition of *Wuthering Heights*.

For three years this new aspect of things seemed to satisfy him. He hardly took in the fact that throughout the period his share of the profits hardly altered. A third went on his crummy flat. He couldn't afford a car. He couldn't afford new trousers. One afternoon, toiling at the bookface of a newly moored delivery (30,000 old textbooks and a ton of assorted encyclopedias) he suddenly thought, Why am I doing this? I must be mad.

He'd got to know a Scotsman called Davie McBride. One evening, after numerous drinks, Davie intimated he was on to 'a guid wee thing' and could cut Ivan in on it if he was so minded.

The guid wee thing was old people's homes. A licence to print money? It *was* money, 'puir and simple. I canna open them fast enough. I need a guid-looking chap like you to supervise that – Hastings, Bournemouth, Brighton . . .'

Next day he took Ivan round one of his 'homes'. It was followed by lunch in his 'surgery', the whisky in medicine glasses.

'Listen to me, Ivan. Now you're in the West, you might as well enjoy the fruits of the capitalist system. What are you earning?'

Ivan told him. 'God in heavens, man, is that all?' cried Davie. 'I'll pay you three times that and a cut of the profits. Here, give me your glass.'

Money. Of course. Why on earth should it need Davie to point out something so blindingly obvious? What did the West mean to someone like Boris, to the whole of Russia, if it wasn't money? Why would Boris have drawn his attention to how much the icons would fetch in the West if he didn't mean Ivan's destiny was to become rich?

And there had been another sign, one of those oblique signs by which his destiny revealed or confirmed itself. One of the old ladies nodding round the television set had for a fleeting moment reminded him of little Na.

Ivan's job setting up old people's homes lasted two years. It merged seamlessly, over lunch at Wheeler's in Brighton, into advertising. Pursuing 'discreet' advertising (a typical Davie contradiction in terms), he'd become friendly with the managing director of the agency he'd used. It seemed they needed someone to organise premises in Paris – rent the space, get basic office staff. 'Same sort of thing you've been doing for Dr McBride. Advertising is booming – but the Continent is going to be the key. What are you paid?' Chris Wilkinson looked like Wellington. 'Heavens *above*, Ivan, we'll double that.'

Paris took a year. Francis Wyatt was delighted to see him (and it was from him he learnt of Rose-Anne's marriage via her divorce). Paris was followed by Frankfurt, Frankfurt by an aborted foray into Athens, and then Chris sent him to Madrid. He joined Ivan on one of their many crisscrossing flights. 'This is our Peninsular War,' he said. 'I've decided to buy the Plaza Agency. Ivan, you've been with us nearly four years. I'd like you to join the board. Can you speak Italian? I think we should open in Rome.'

Yet, it was something to do with the travelling that excited him, not the work at either end. It satisfied the side of him that had always hurried through the morning, his meals, the day. Travel was all hurry, even at its most peaceful.

When he had an affair with an air hostess, Ivan felt he was making love to his medium. Leila's father owned a large international travel agency in Bonn. Ivan was now fluent in German, Spanish, French, English and (least of all) Russian. In a few years he'd be within sight of forty. As usual, Boris's distant hand could be detected.

'Six months at the counter, Ivan, to learn what our clients are like – then we work together. You and Leila make a fine pair.' Helmut Krebs beamed and squeezed Ivan's upper arm.

With each launched traveller, Ivan felt he despatched a small part of himself. Suddenly one afternoon (the two-year affair with Leila was going badly wrong), he realised that this was indeed what he wanted to do. Extrication was embarrassing but swift. It simply involved joining the tour operator who'd bought his tickets through them. They did Hellenic tours and – rare then – tours in South America.

Over four years, the tours began to decline. Ivan started to double as a courier. Three years into this, Everest-high above the Atlantic (his highly paid courier job took him everywhere – this time it was Buenos Aires), he thought, Yes, at last, this is what I like. The little bottles of free champagne. The hot magenta sun through hotel curtains. Wine on his own in toothmugs in wagons-lits. The feeling of being out of touch with reality.

He did not just like it; it was his destiny. It exemplified his entire life. Boris had never had an explicit message, it had always been implicit – implicit in Boris himself. The message had been: Escape me. Run for your life. There was no goal but that – continual, carefree, goal-less flight. And it misted the sadness of the expatriate – the desolation that used to sweep him. For someone who had no country, it was appropriate to belong to them all, if only through their airports.

Typically, Ivan's certainty reached its peak just as he was about to change direction.

40

As time passed, Michael found it was less a matter of collecting than of being unable to throw away. As things mounted, the appropriately named Mrs Inch (4 ft 11 in in her high heels) grumbled a good deal, though it meant in effect that her work steadily became less. And she could pass between the tottering piles like a wraith, like a cloud of the smoke with which his smoking filled the flat. Michael's bulk was always dislodging a rack of wire coat hangers or a box of '10p off' coupons.

Poole wrote once a year. He was a senior research fellow in theoretical cosmology at Sheffield University. He was getting married soon – had Michael any news on the girl front? Happy Christmas.

Michael wrote back. Hadn't he read Hoyle was under threat – theoretically? Poole should remember Elfreda – but no, he remembered now, they'd never met. Yes, marriage very much on the cards. Happy New Year.

It was a white lie. Poole's question had been one expecting the answer no. Michael wasn't going to be humiliated. If, indeed, it was a lie. Surely the point was the heart should be full, engaged. And he could still feel the tug of the golden thread joining them. One day they would come together, of that he was completely certain.

From time to time he did a spell of train spotting at Liverpool Street; partly nostalgia, partly to add to his collection of train numbers, partly on the off chance she'd be visiting friends in Cambridge. But, of course, the main collecting was out on the streets, down the escalators, on the tops of buses, in the building sites and demolition dumps. Here you could find almost anything – from a wisp of cotton and the occasional hairpin all the way up to an abandoned mangle or the Baby Belling with two hotplates unaccountably abandoned on a park bench. And as he walked, collecting, he always had half an eye out for Elfreda.

He read a paperback every two days, and naturally they piled up too. At this point he read Djuna Barnes, the Pauls

Bowles and Binding, Borges, Beckett. Elliptical, enigmatic, gnomic, ambiguous, cryptic – they chimed with his life-mode, his feelings about himself. Odd how they all began with B.

41

Ivan's decision to run safaris in the Serengeti was taken in the teeth of all the signs, which pointed across to quite a different shore of the Atlantic.

One of his clients was, among much else, the chairman of Uni-Vac Holdings Inc., Chicago. Ivan C. Strassburg had to do a lot of travelling himself. Quite often Ivan would find himself in the adjoining first-class seat to his namesake. Never revealing that he was often carrying a Uni-Vac package the tycoon could have saved thousands by transporting himself, Ivan chatted. They got on well for reasons that had nothing to do with Strassburg's views, which were usually outrageous.

On the fourth such occasion, Ivan C said, 'I could use you, Khuchevsky. Tell me, whadder ya earn?'

In one second, Ivan realised, he would be offered a job with Uni-Vac Holdings Inc. 'What about those safaris you were telling me about last month?' he said.

'You wanna job with Venture Interior?' said Ivan C, sounding surprised. 'I was going to say – but dun matter. Let it go. Have you had any sorta experience with animals?'

'I was a tour operator for several years,' said Ivan, 'often not unlike working with animals. And I was brought up on a farm.'

'Ho ho ho,' honked Ivan C. Strassburg. 'Elephant farm? Lion farm? But I don't see why not. Makawawa can teach you. There's nothing difficult.'

Ivan's staff on Venture Interior were all from the Tschambula people, who were a breakaway branch of the Masai, or so they said. They didn't look like Masai. The name meant 'Men with strong arms', which made Ivan feel vaguely that he might perhaps get on with them.

Venture Interior catered for the very, very rich. The very, very rich loved to think they liked discomfort and danger. Four or five extended, air-conditioned Safari Range Rovers would drive them 30 miles into the Serengeti. Previously gathered thorn bushes would be rolled in a protective ring and champagne would be taken from the ice boxes while tents were erected and fires lit of thorn and bush scrub. Two chefs prepared dinner. Ivan opened claret. His job, as in his tour-operator days, was to keep everyone happy.

And safe. No food could be left unboxed. A lion, an elephant, he learnt, could smell a fragment of chewing gum at 300 yards. Ivan shared guard with his assistant Makawawa and two of Makawawa's cousins. Makawawa and the cousins would sleep. They seemed able to wake at the passing of a moth, but not for months was Ivan able to master such tricks. During his two hours, he would sit tense, a rifle across his knees, his face hot from the fire, listening, peering. Once, as he sat under the velvet sky, a huge bull elephant was all at once *there*. Ten yards away, motionless. Looking. It was as though the darkness had suddenly condensed. Then the five and a half tons glided away and evaporated back into night. Extraordinary creatures, impervious to thorns, it seemed, or able soundlessly to remove them.

Another time, eight months after he had got there, Ivan was roused by wealthy screams. He emerged from his tent to find Makawawa (who for once had slept through the moth-soft sounds of approach) trying to soothe an hysterical Lady Cranthorpe, who had caused considerable trouble already. She had woken to the crackle of wrapping paper and, reaching out, seized in both hands some rough-skinned extremity of the invader. Mistaking the nature of the organ in the half-light of dawn, and with an imagination no doubt inflamed by racial prejudice, the elderly countess insisted that she was being raped. In fact the trunk of one of those immense and usually gentle creatures was delicately plucking, as they can, her

Charbonel & Walker chocolates one by one from their elegant container foolishly left open beside the bed.

Ivan used to wonder if the stupidity of the very, very rich was what it seemed – pure genetic stupidity – or simply another form of arrogance. He was astonished that during his two years with Venture Interior they only had one death.

It was in June, theoretically some weeks before the onset of the dry season, but already water holes had dried up and the whirling dust ghosts were appearing and vanishing in the Serengeti heat. At this time the animals became restless, setting off on long treks to find water and more than normally plagued by insects. The lions, the rhinos, some of the elephants were more likely to be dangerous. Ivan gave his usual speech, the burden of which was, 'Don't leave your Range Rover.'

Soon after the party had stopped to observe a solitary bull elephant standing flapping its ears under an acacia tree, he was horrified to see a diminutive figure tottering towards it from the last Range Rover. It was Frau Hedwidge Meyers, widowed mother of a German industrialist. In one hand she carried an orange parasol. Ivan watched as the batty, sun-hatted multimillionairess swayed to a halt in front of the rogue and then, waving her ridiculous umbrella at it, appeared to deliver a lecture. After four or five gesticulating and waving minutes, she took a step forward. The big elephant began to whisk its trunk irritably from side to side.

Ivan raised his rifle. He had no doubt which of the two he would rather shoot, but doubted he could hit either. He hadn't fired a rifle since Tunguska. Fortunately, he could see the barrel of Makawawa's rifle protruding from the Range Rover behind him.

And then, to their astonishment, the elephant flapped its ears, lowered its trunk, turned away and ambled slowly off into the heat.

A great gust of relief-impelled fury swept Ivan as he came towards the idiotic old woman.

'Do you realise you might have got us all killed?' he shouted in German. 'An elephant of *that* sort can turn these vehicles over like *that.*' He snapped his fingers at her. 'If you do anything so stupid again I shall take you back to base and see that you're flown home at once.'

Frau Meyers laughed her light, idiotic laugh and waved the orange umbrella at him. '*Mach dich nicht selbst verrücht, du dummer Verl!*' she quavered, '*Hör auf dich verrücht zu machen!*' The animals and us are one. Brothers and sisters. I too am a lion, a gazelle, an elephant. They know that. I speak to them.'

Three hours later, while his smaller party was having lunch, Ivan saw one of the other Range Rovers racing towards them across the savannah. The group had split in two, Makawawa taking two cars to observe a pride of lions, while Ivan had pursued some giraffe. The Range Rover whirled up to them, dust pluming behind it as in a Western.

'Oh, Missa Van! Oh, Missa Van! Quick! Quick!' The cousins' English, far more rudimentary than Makawawa's, was rendered incomprehensible by panic. Interpreting their graphic gestures and mostly using their dialect, which he'd begun to pick up, Ivan pieced together what was happening as they raced back.

Makawawa's party had watched the lions for an hour or so, filming and photographing, then withdrawn some way for lunch. All at once, one of the party, Lord Rootham, had cried out and pointed. In the distance they had seen old Frau Meyers just vanishing behind the outcrop of scrub and rock which hid the lions from view. In one outstretched, shaking hand she was holding a ham sandwich.

Makawawa had seized his rifle and leapt into a Range Rover, at the same time shouting to his cousin to go get Missa Van.

When Ivan arrived, it was all over. As far as life and death went, it had all been over as Makawawa rounded the bend. He had simply seen a mass of rending, tearing, gnawing, crunching, swallowing, snarling lions. He could hardly shoot the whole lot and they refused to be driven off.

Indeed, they only reluctantly slunk away when Ivan and Makawawa returned together. The two men searched the crushed and torn-up grass. There were a few flecks of blood but of Frau Meyers there was no sign. They couldn't even find the orange umbrella. The only thing they found, untouched, was the ham sandwich.

Ivan only saw Ivan C. Strassburg twice in his entire time with Venture Interior. The first was now, when the tycoon flew in to deal with the kerfuffle over Frau Meyers's death. So conclusive was the evidence and so distinguished the witnesses (Lord Rootham was a retired Lord Chief Justice of India, 1935) that this was fairly straightforward.

Ivan said the woman had been an arrogant, ignorant fool.

'Now remember this, Ivan,' said Ivan C, wagging his ringed forefinger, 'at Venture Interior we have only the cream of society, the *cree-um*.'

'Exactly,' said Ivan, 'rich and thick.'

Ivan C stared at him. 'Ho ho ho!' he honked. 'Very neat. Very neat. Ho ho ho!'

Ivan, deciding not to reveal the plagiarism, smiled faintly. Strassburg had glaring faults. He was dictatorial. He was a Texan racist. He had a coarse streak. 'I cayan't stand those great lips they have on them,' he said. 'Slobber slabber, slobber slabber – d'ya ever see the sexual orifice of a female baboon on heat, Ivan?'

'I *beg* your pardon?' said Ivan, shocked back into a phrase he'd heard and memorised at Cambridge in 1952.

'Baboon's cunts, that's what they put me in mind of,' said Ivan C, watching one of Makawawa's many cousins pass them on his leisurely, elegant way.

Despite this and much else, Ivan still liked him – perhaps because their meetings were so infrequent. In fact, he saw very little of the stupid rich either. Hardly anyone came in the dry or wet seasons, that is, August, September, April or May. And there were long gaps besides these. Strassburg wouldn't have minded if no one came at all. The point of VI was to facilitate business deals elsewhere. In the long, empty weeks, Ivan drove about the Serengeti with Makawawa and perhaps a cousin or two, exploring and planning future Venture sorties.

Gradually, he found the immensity of Africa wrapping itself around him until he sometimes felt he was disappearing.

During the long, long nights, he had moments of intense loneliness and would sit under the twinkling blaze of stars and wonder if once again he'd made a terrible mistake. At other times, those same stars seemed more comforting and close than the empty darkness and he would suddenly feel certain something momentous was going to happen, that once again his destiny was about to become clear.

In fact, of course, the night was anything but empty and quite the reverse of silent. Once, quite early on, he'd been sitting in the darkness some way from their fire. They were near a large marsh off the Mbalangeti River and the quacking of the frogs was added to the usual African cacophony: the distant roaring of lions and shrilling of cicadas, the cries of hyena, the smashings, crackings and gruntings as some huge animal – hippo or rhino – crashed about. Suddenly Makawawa, sitting as usual silent beside him, put his large, soft lips close to Ivan's ear. 'You hear lioness? Two lioness?'

Without waiting for a reply, he slipped off into the night. Ivan followed. After fifty yards, they stopped. Some way ahead, Ivan heard a quiet grunt-cough. Makawawa shone his torch, there was a glow of green eyes and then a crashing as the two animals made off through the reeds and bushes.

'How do you do that, Makawawa?' Ivan asked when they got back to the fire. 'Would you teach me?'

'Yes, Missa Van. Not today. Tomorrow.'

Another time, two months later, they were walking together in the highlands of Nyamuma along the edge of some rainforest. All at once Makawawa pointed casually to a big *majaba* tree 500 yards ahead, as far as Ivan could see untenanted. 'Maybe we see big killer bird,' Makawawa said.

Sure enough, as they drew near, out of the apparently empty branches soared on five-foot wings one of the giant kites quite common in September – or was it a buzzard? – and then made swift beating progress back the way they'd come.

'Makawawa teach Missa Van day after tomorrow,' was the comment this time.

There was some block. Was it perhaps tribal law not to pass on lore of this kind?

Breakthrough came in an odd way, not long after this incident. It was very hot. Ivan was lying against the back wheel in the shade of the Rover, trying to keep awake and learn about the Serengeti. From the book it had clearly been a honey buzzard. He heard the boys laughing and shouting near the river. To dispel sleep, he stood up and walked towards the sound.

There was a short stretch of grey, sandy beach revealed by the river's shrinking. Here the trunk of a large tree lay stranded. They had rolled two boulders opposite each other along one side and, using the trunk as a table, were arm fighting.

Ivan stood and watched. Makawawa always won. The two boys were eighteen or so. Makawawa must have been about forty, very strong but not in the arms particularly; in the legs. They should have been called the Oschambula – 'Men with strong legs'. He won because he was stronger. There was no skill.

Ivan wandered forward. 'I'll give you a go, Makawawa.' When had he last done this? Surely it had been in Málaga that time, the time he saw Rawbones. Three drunk Spaniards, one of them a picador. He wasn't as strong as he'd once been, but his skill he'd never lose.

He sat on his boulder, shifted his elbow about in a minute depression and put his arm up. He took Makawawa's smooth, dry, black hand in his own slightly moist, pink one. There was a gleam in Makawawa's eye. It was always fun defeating the boss.

They tensed. The older of the two cousins raised his hand and then brought it down smartly, at the same time giving one of their sharp, guttural exclamations.

Ivan, guessing Makawawa would attack at once, locked. Makawawa did attack. Ivan closed his eyes and held him. Two minutes. Three minutes. He felt, sensed, a minute tremor run down the black man's arm. He was tiring. Ivan would seem to relax. Makawawa would seize an instant's rest and then attack again, expecting victory.

So it happened, but Ivan's attack came a fraction before Makawawa's, while he was still holding Ivan and trying to recover. Ivan had forced him flat before he'd had time to react.

The second bout was easier. Ivan was now fairly sure he was the strongest. He also guessed Makawawa would try a change of tactic and start off holding firm. He therefore attacked as soon as the shout had been given. As he suspected, exerting full strength he could gradually force Makawawa back.

The contest was effectively over. Makawawa was in any case probably tired from fighting his cousins. Ivan played with him for a while and then flattered him again.

'It's not just strength, Makawawa,' he said. 'I learnt this as a boy. It's an art.'

'Art? Art?' said Makawawa in a disgruntled voice and rubbing his arms. 'What that there?'

'A skill,' said Ivan. 'Something you learn.'

'You teach Makawawa?'

'Yes – if you teach me how you hear in the night and how you see so far.'

'Yes,' said Makawawa. 'Tomorrow.'

'Not tomorrow. Today. Now.'

42

'How often,' Michael wrote in his journal for Wednesday 15 August, 'are the decisive moves in our lives dictated by chance?' It seemed a bit sententious. After some thought he added, 'Either frequently or never.'

The entry was prompted by an event, a train of events, that had begun at the end of June. He had been wandering vaguely round Drayton Gardens while his sitting room, where he had been cataloguing all afternoon, cleared of tobacco smoke. Suddenly, abandoned on the pavement, he'd found a three-pound Kilner jar complete with rubber seal.

That night, before going to bed, he couldn't find his

chamber pot (it was becoming increasingly easy to lose things in the flat). He squeezed the Kilner jar beneath his bed instead. He used it. The next morning he rested it on the windowsill, where it caught the morning sun. How beautiful it looked, how crystal clear and fresh, how golden. Why, you could almost drink it.

Drink it! Some deep memory stirred in him, inchoate and – though he struggled – uncapturable. Proust was wrong about involuntary memory. It was seldom definite; it was as though the past had been gently brushed and had given off that curious and nostalgic sensation as pinched thyme gives off its scent. And the woman with glasses . . . ? Was *glasses* the key, disguising themselves as spectacles? Was he meant to drink this nectar that glowed so golden in the sun? Once again, he had that strange sensation, not a feeling but an echo of feeling.

That night he used the Kilner jar again; and again the following night. But by the time it was full, it was already becoming cloudy. Michael poured it away, and this time he recognised the feeling from the past that washed briefly through him, and did remember it. Regret.

It so happened that about ten days before all this, he'd found on the seat of the bus going to Liverpool Street a detective novel. It was a form of literature that, for no particular reason, he'd hardly ever read, but starting it he was soon gripped. The novel was set in Kenya and during it the finally unmasked murderer used water-purifying tablets.

Having emptied and washed the Kilner jar, Michael rang a number of chemists and eventually located water-purifying tablets in John Bell and Croydon. As he had suspected, liberal use of these seemed to kill whatever agent had caused the clouding and the unpleasant smell. But effective preservation raised a new problem – Mrs Inch.

Michael had noticed that Mrs Inch had a decidedly puritan streak. If you were a collector you couldn't draw the line just because something might offend the squeamish. Mrs Inch didn't seem able to appreciate this. Michael decided to hide the jars till full and then store them on the flat area of the roof. At a stroke he nearly doubled his storage space, at least for a certain class of object. And, as the jars accumulated, he found that after his slow, creaking ascent with a fresh one, then standing among them and marvelling at the way they caught and refracted the slanting rays of the sun, he often had an extraordinary sensation of peace, a feeling of coming home.

Thus did his tasks multiply. The room/cupboard was becoming so full of Mrs Wordingham's letters that he decided to make space by storing the science magazines in his collection of tea chests and stacking them along one wall of his bedroom. This meant finding a new place for the miscellaneous objects already piled there awaiting cataloguing and eventual storage. Cataloguing was often difficult. How, for example, would he have catalogued the Kilner jars before providence dictated their use – with jam jars, or with larger receptacles like the big tea tins and smaller cardboard boxes, or possibly as a new category of their own?

And all this activity, the steady accumulation, the often necessary cleaning, the sorting and storing, the necessity at times to conceal from Mrs Inch, the shoring-up of some unsteady heap or pile, the need now, in much of the flat, to move with circumspection so as not to bring the piles and stacks crashing down, all this was echoed, almost repeated, by the necessity of noting down what he had done in his journal.

And, in a single instance, of course, one of the most important of his tasks, and its repetition in his descriptions was echoed yet again, when it was condensed on to his weekly postcard to his grandmother.

43

Ivan discovered that most of Makawawa's skills were really a question of what you considered important. They had nothing to do with sharper ears or keener eyes or a more sensitive nose.

When Ivan had first come to England all those years ago, and first gone to a cocktail party, he'd heard nothing at all. Or rather, he'd heard everything. The English cacophony. Quite rapidly, he'd learnt to single out 'Pootsie' Pomeroy's fluting notes, or concentrate only on Dermot's ridiculous drawl; the rest became a sort of silence. Makawawa needed to hear a lion or a lioness at night or he might die, so he heard one. Knowledge could be involved. He hadn't seen the honey buzzard in the distant foliage, but he had seen a coppery brown flash out of the corner of his eye, six minutes before. The copper brown honey buzzard always chose to land in the highest tree.

It was often a question of not doing as much as doing, just as a faint star is easier to locate when not looked at directly. Or it was a question of trusting instinct. The fact that you were being looked at could be transmitted to the back of your neck as easily by an animal as by a human being.

It sometimes reminded Ivan of the coming of snow at Taschla. There was a whiff of coldness in the air so faint it was like a smell, like the memory of a smell. In fact, it couldn't really be detected consciously. Ivan used to find that suddenly he just knew that winter was coming. In the same way, Makawawa seemed suddenly, by instinct, to *know* that water was ahead of them, often several miles ahead. Though it was also true that there was sometimes a minute increase in haziness, in *thickness*, of the air above the water – only detectable if not looked at full on.

And while Makawawa taught him, Ivan taught Makawawa. He showed him how to lock elbow and shoulder to hold an opponent with the least expenditure of energy. He showed him how to delay the final flattening so that his adversary would fight back uselessly and tire himself. He gradually taught him how to detect milliseconds in advance that an opponent was about to attack. Some tricks, for some reason, he didn't teach – an omission he later regretted.

Ivan had not thought about Russia for years but sometimes now, as he and Makawawa fought, it would suddenly bring back his childhood sessions with Boris. He would be seized by sudden fury and to Makawawa's surprise would grind painfully into the tree trunk or rock on which they were tussling the black arm of his friend.

Because he did, finally, regard Makawawa as his friend. The Tschambula were not physically, as far as he could see, remotely like the Masai. They were black and negroid while the Masai, who'd come south from Egypt two or three thousand years ago, were thin-lipped, tall and lighter in colouring. Ivan's *Guide to the Serengeti*, written by an anthropologist, suggested that the Tschambula might once have been made subject to the arrogant invaders but had eventually managed to fight free. Makawawa would now spit on his palms before greeting Ivan – a Masai compliment and sign of closeness. His young cousins had their plaits stuck together with red clay while Makawawa's head was shaved – a sign, as with the Masai, that he was married.

One slack afternoon in March, Ivan asked him where his wife was. Makawawa answered what he supposed was the question behind the question. Not for several years did Ivan realise how natural an assumption this was.

'Missa Van want woman? Yes. Yes. You like Jambuna?'

He arrived back with Jambuna three days later. She must have been eighteen or nineteen, very black, her plump, lozenge-shaped breasts still firm, her huge lips permanently slightly open in a wide, pink-centred smile, lithe as a python and without a word of English. Her language, thought Ivan, is not words.

She loved making love and Ivan was sometimes slightly relieved she only seemed able to be with him every five or six days. Even on safari, she would silently slip into his tent and wriggle under his mosquito net in the middle of the night and he would at once be grappling with her sinuous, oily body smelling at first faintly of ripe melons. Once, arching above him (so that he remembered Venice), she had involuntarily let out a series of high, thrilling cries. Mrs Edgar P. Sanders, on safari with her husband, the Senator from Bloomington, Indiana, complained that she had been woken by a hyena shrieking outside her tent and might have been eaten alive.

The rains came – too late and too little, it seemed, but none the less intermittently impressive. Once, while the giant indigestion of a thunderstorm rolled and rumbled round them, the water did not fall but seemed to be fired down from the black and writhing heavens.

For a few weeks empty water courses raced into turbulent, frothing flood water. Pools and huge, shallow lakes appeared across the flat plains of the Serengeti. Clouds of pink flamingo the colour of lipstick lighted daintily along their shores. Ivan preferred the storks with their even longer legs and their slow-flapping, heavy but elegant dream flight.

In the welcome gaps between safari groups, Makawawa practised arm fighting with increasing intensity. He also asked Ivan what else he could do. Ivan, whose arms had slowly developed their extraordinary strength through years of heaving corn and humping sacks and carrying calves and all the other work on the farm, had never really bothered with anything additional, but he showed Makawawa certain tension exercises he remembered Boris used to do; lifting rocks and logs, press-ups and pull-ups. Ivan joined Makawawa in the exercises because he didn't like to be beaten, which occasionally happened. Makawawa was not a tactful winner.

It was becoming clear that there was some purpose in all this. Makawawa agreed. 'Missa Van know soon. Tomorrow.'

The rainy season brought the great hordes back to the Serengeti central plains on their vast wheel of migration – south from Togoro, east from Ndebaka and Sabora. It was now the only place left in Africa where you could see a plain roamed to the horizon by zebra, wildebeest, antelope or the mild-mannered buffalo with their centre-parted horns. And puffing in the wake of these wild hordes came the very, very rich, vaccinated, inoculated, sprayed, insured, mosquito-netted, pilling and injecting and creaming and complaining.

Then, as the ponds, then the lakes, then the rivers evaporated in the fierce equatorial heat, so the very, very rich dried up and vanished too. The Serengeti shimmered, its rocks melting under the laser sun. The long grasses withered and turned as white as Ivan's hair until, under that colour-destroying sun, they looked like flames and when the hot, dry wind moved from the west, the great plains seemed to run with pale fire.

One afternoon at the end of August, Makawawa asked Ivan to come with him in the VI Range Rover. They left the Serengeti, skirting Olduvai Ravine, and went east across Olbalhal. The ground rose, it became minutely cooler, trees became more numerous. They were heading for Tschambula country.

Short of it, and short of any real ascent, Makawawa left the track and bumped for five or six miles north under acacia trees graceful as dancers. They passed a small flock of sheep guarded by a small boy. Soon after this, Ivan saw ahead a small boma.

A boma was something too humble to call a village: a huddle of half a dozen huts in a ring surrounded by a temporary thorn hedge. A few skeletal cows and some bare-necked chickens. Naked children. Flies.

There was talking, bowing, spitting on hands, hands laid on heads. More talk. Ivan spat and bowed.

At last they were led to one of the huts. These were always the same: branches bent into a bell shape, plastered with cow dung on which hides had been laid. Inside they were dark, very low and smelt of cheese.

This particular hut was full of smoke which, despite the heat, came from a small fire smouldering in its middle. Ivan entered behind Makawawa, stooping and coughing. Gradually he made out what he recognised as the paraphernalia of magic hanging and lying about – mummified skins and heads of animals, bones, herbs. A very old man, himself almost mummified with age, was propped against the side of the hut. Bald, he had a few long hairs on the chin. One tooth. Both eyes were opalescent with thick cataracts.

Makawawa knelt and banged his head on the ground in front of this creature. He muttered, banged his head, gestured at Ivan to bang his head. Then they sat in silence. At last, from the heap of wraps and rags, there came a reedy voice.

'Detu say give her your hand,' said Makawawa. 'She tell you what happens.'

Ivan humped himself nearer and held out his hand. It was like *She*, he suddenly thought. Detu groped about, found his hand and tugged him to come closer. She felt his face. She spoke.

'Detu say you came from far, far away across many lands and worlds,' said Makawawa.

'It's true,' said Ivan.

Once more the ancient figure ran her fingers over his face and down to his hand again. It was like being touched by bones covered with a faint film of warmth. All at once, she began to speak in her high singsong.

Ivan felt very peaceful. He felt he was becoming transparent, his life was transparent, like a pool. Unable to see anything in the present, Detu stared endlessly into the future, as it stirred before her in her cloudy globes.

And then Makawawa was pulling him outside and they were in the Range Rover again.

'I must have fallen asleep,' said Ivan. 'She hypnotised me, knocked me out with that smoke. What did she say, Makawawa?'

'She say you very strong. She say one day you save my life. She see you passing near little hill, green hill, long time no come. She say you be big general in army one day. She say many things Makawawa no understand.'

'General?' said Ivan, with a curious feeling of *déjà vu*. Was this Napoleon come again to haunt him? 'In what army? When?'

'You learn by an' by, tomorrow, I think,' said Makawawa, with his deep pleasure in postponement.

But in fact proof of the old witch's percipience in one prophesy came surprisingly soon.

A small safari group was due, despite the dry-season heat. They were all out preparing: choosing a site with shade, storing water, cutting thorns – not so much to make a proper surround as to protect the Range Rover tyres, which lion and hyena liked to chew.

When preparations were more or less complete, Ivan wandered off with his rifle. Shooting was forbidden in the Serengeti, though an exception was sometimes made for food. But Ivan felt an exception could also be made for someone who always missed.

When he returned, a small drama was in progress. Makawawa and the boys had been joined by a stranger. This man, clearly a Masai but with a peculiarly light skin, was none the less of massive build, with the huge shoulders and swollen biceps and forearms of a body builder. Makawawa and he had set up two of the camp's folding chairs alongside a tablelike outcrop of rock.

The contest looked certain to be unequal, but Makawawa had learnt a lot. Twice he won: once by an extended lock followed by a sudden attack, the second time by feinting (one of Ivan's favourite moves). The boys went wild, hooting and leaping. Makawawa quite literally crowed, in his irritating way.

The big Masai was expressionless. He put up his arm for a third throw. Ivan, drawn in, stepped closer.

This time there was no escape for Makawawa. His big opponent simply gripped his hand and exerted his enormous strength. Makawawa tried to lock but just failed and was forced out; tried again, for a moment stood firm, then once again couldn't hold. Gradually, his arm was forced down, down, until at the end, he gave up and let himself be flattened.

But the victor, instead of stopping and releasing him, simply hunched his great shoulders and half rose in his chair. Without thinking, hardly aware he was doing it, Ivan raised his rifle and fired.

The bullet struck the rock three feet behind Makawawa and ricocheted in a shower of splinters. But the crack, the shock, made both men leap up.

Ivan ran forward. 'Don't you try and harm my friend,' he said angrily in his rough Swahili. 'I saw what you were doing. Get out. Go!'

The man looked at him, coldly furious. Ivan was suddenly reminded of Boris when he'd defeated him all those years ago.

The fury of a challenged bully. Then the Masai opened his thin lips, spat at Ivan's feet, pulled his long spear off the rock and strode off into the bush.

It was the only injurious trick in the repertoire. Once defeated, the loser should immediately be let free. If the winner refused to disengage and continued to press and twist, serious damage could result – at best, a sprained wrist; at worst, a torn ligament or even a snapped radius or ulna.

Ivan explained. 'Anyway,' he said, 'who was that Masai?'

'Not Masai. Tschambula. Man call him Sapi.'

'Sapi. He reminded me of someone I knew long ago. I don't suppose we'll see him again.'

'I think may happen,' said Makawawa. 'Yes. Will happen soon.'

'When?' said Ivan. And then, as Makawawa was about to speak, he said, 'No, don't tell me. Tomorrow.'

'Haw haw haw!' crowed Makawawa. 'That right, Missa Van – haw haw haw!'

44

Nothing happened on his birthday, except a card and a present from his grandmother – some useful item selected from a catalogue. This would be preceded a month or so before by a letter begging him to spend the happy day at Inkpen, followed, since he never opened the letter, by a telegram, or usually two or three telegrams (and later telemessages) and finally, forced out of him by the increasing frenzy of the messages, by his telephone call.

'I can't this year, Granny, I'm sorry.'

'*This* year? You don't come any year. We haven't had a birthday together since you were nineteen. Why not?'

'I'm terribly busy.'

'We could have a cake,' pleaded Mrs Wordingham. 'Crackers.'

'Next year perhaps,' said Michael.

He didn't mind birthdays – at least, he didn't mind the first forty-five or so. He felt he aged but he didn't change. Does anyone? 'The person who looks out on the dew and the snow is always the same.' Hadn't Elfreda said that, his poetic Elfreda? One of her flights? Or was it a Latvian proverb? Or had he made it up himself?

The moments when he suddenly wondered if he'd invented Elfreda were the worst. Poole-like theories of quantum transience and parallel dimensions reeled in his head. Then sanity returned. The fires of love flared up again.

But one year Mrs Wordingham sent a greetings telemessage which was five pages long. It cost her £25. It outlined in some detail her intention of coming up to Drayton Gardens to celebrate his birthday with him. 'If the mountain won't come to Mohammed,' it ended somewhat tactlessly, 'Mohammed must come to the mountain.'

Appalled, the mountain hurried to the telephone.

45

Tomorrow always comes.

Late in April, as his second rainy season swept the Serengeti, Ivan was approached by Makawawa with a serious request: would Missa Van please accompany him on a trip into Kenya?

'How long will it take?' said Ivan. 'You know Mr Strassburg is coming out in about ten days. We have to be back at least two days before that.'

'No, no, Missa Van,' said Makawawa. 'No ten days. Oh, no. Three days. Maybe *two* days. We be back.'

Several times during the past four months his assistant had taken a few days off 'on Tschambula business' and vanished across the savanna. Makawawa intimated that this was the last of such absences and the most important – in some way their climax. Curious, Ivan finally agreed. Three days only.

But the journey hadn't begun before he'd stopped it. Makawawa expected them to walk! Ivan knew the Tschambula 'walk' – a sloping half-run which they seemed able to keep up effortlessly for 50 or 60 miles.

A quarter of an hour later, they set off again in a Venture Interior Range Rover. Once more Makawawa, who was driving, took them in the direction of the fortune teller Detu, past Olduvai Ravine and across the Olbalbal. But this time he continued west and then north, the road winding up between Ngorongoro crater and Oldeani. The trees grew taller and denser, the grass and scent of the bush vanished. Soon, the road was winding through rainforest. They were entering the region dominated by the Tschambula.

About 15 miles into this, Makawawa suddenly turned off the road and forced them into the undergrowth. He slashed branches and thick, spongy-leafed fern fronds with his machete and concealed the Range Rover, finally cutting a long blaze in a big *majaba* tree close by.

'Now we walk short way,' he said. 'Very short.'

In fact, it must have been a good ten miles. Close to where he'd hidden the Rover, a track vanished into the forest, zigzagging up through trees dripping with recent rainfall. Now they were wreathed and twined about with jasmine and giant convolvulus and roped together with lianas. It was also clear from the deep churning that a lot of people had recently passed up the same way, people and animals – Ivan recognised goat and sheep droppings.

At last, as Ivan squelched and slipped irritably upwards in his wake, Makawawa explained where they were going. It seemed that every five years the Tschambula chose a new or confirmed the old leader. For this purpose they gathered at a sacred and secret spot deep in their territory. It was to this they were heading.

'But why take me?' said Ivan. 'They won't want me there.'

'Oh, no mind stranger,' said Makawawa. 'Not Ikoma or Hebe people, not Masai or Wambula. But no mind white man interested Tschambula. You see.'

'I shall go straight back if you're not telling me the truth,' said Ivan. 'I'm not going to force myself on your people.'

It was late afternoon, having climbed to some considerable height, when they finally broke clear of the forest. The trees came up to the very lip of a small, shallow crater, except where, at its far side, about half a mile away, a stream or some past convulsion of what was clearly a long-extinct volcano had cut an exit. The crater formed a small amphitheatre surrounding a central, smaller, steeper amphitheatre, which held a small lake from which the stream ran. The black, still waters of the lake gleamed in the sinking sun like polished steel. The green grass of the larger and shallower natural bowl was covered with people, tents and sheep and goats and the usual scrawny chickens, all milling noisily about, their cries and bleating and shouts rising up with the spiralling, twisting blue woodsmoke and smell of roasting flesh into the evening air. Ivan guessed at least a thousand Tschambula were gathered before him.

To his surprise, they did indeed take little notice of him as he followed the hurrying figure of Makawawa between the rough hide tents. Covered in mud and flecks from the rainforest, perhaps he hardly stood out. But he thought it had more to do with the unusual mixture of features among the Tschambula; it was clear seeing them en masse that at some point they must have interbred with the Masai.

Makawawa stopped at a small circle of hide tents. Women came forward – his wives, four of them. From a tent to one side stepped Jambuna, her lips like smiling cushions. Makawawa beamed, presenting Ivan. When the bowing and spitting and patting had finished, Makawawa disappeared into one of the tents and came out a few minutes later swathed in the long, brown, cloak-like sari of his people. The two men sat side by side, a wooden bowl of brownish milk between them. Makawawa passed the bowl to Ivan. It had a curious smoky taste, not entirely pleasant.

'Makawawa,' said Ivan, 'I want to know what's going to happen. How do you choose your new leader?'

Makawawa gave a broad grin and raised his right arm bent as for arm fighting.

'I hope you don't expect me to take any part,' said Ivan, suddenly suspicious. 'Because I won't.'

'Oh, no, no. Missa Van. That is not allowed. Oh, no. Missa Van help Makawawa fight and win tomorrow.'

Gradually, by determined questioning, Ivan forced Makawawa into explicitness. Only the elders of the Tschambula could take part – that is, those over forty. Eliminating contests had been going on for the past five months, and it was to these that Makawawa had gone on 'Tschambula business'. Thanks, he said, to Ivan's coaching he had now reached the last twenty-eight. These were due to fight the next day.

It had begun, according to Tschambula history, a hundred years before; or perhaps two hundred years before. Once, the Tschambula had been like the Masai. Personal standing depended on the number of men and women killed. One day a great master – a *bwana makuba* – had come among them. A white man. He had pointed out the trouble they were getting into with neighbouring tribes and among themselves, too, since it didn't matter where a warrior gained his victims. The *bwana makuba* had taught them arm fighting. That, Makawawa said, was why the Tschambula were so much more civilised than the arrogant Masai.

'Detu say Missa Van save Makawawa. Missa Van bring luck. You teach Makawawa final tricks.'

There were no final tricks. Ivan had, after that single near disaster, taught him everything. All he could say now was, 'Don't fight, don't practise, rest, relax.' But he also asked if that murderous Tschambula whose name he'd forgotten was to compete.

'Sapi, oh yes. Oh yes, Sapi fight. He think he win. Makawawa beat him this time. Oh yes.'

Ivan doubted this, but he nodded in agreement. Once more they ran over the escape and counter to the arm-breaker. But Ivan gathered this wouldn't be needed. Each contest had three umpires, not to speak of the two thousand other watchful eyes.

Walking about muddy and rank with sweat, Ivan longed for a bath or a shower. Jambuna didn't mind; on the contrary. Gripped in her hot, slippery, melon-smelling, sex-smelling, salt-tasting limbs, panting on the heap of hard, undressed hides inside the little tent, stinking of dung and skins, Tschambula love was a stew. Halfway through the night it suddenly rained.

The old crater was dense with early-morning mist. Gradually, as it thinned and cleared, it became possible to see more and more of the little fires dotted among the tents. It was as if those slender orange pencils were themselves dispensing the mist. There were increasing sounds and surges of activity, men running to and fro, and excited humming – they were bees about to swarm.

Only the Tschambula could make a group of fourteen couples, competing in a series of contests each lasting, at most, fifteen minutes, take all day.

The first fourteen fights took place simultaneously at various sites about the camp. Everything else took place beside the little lake, about 100 yards wide. Here the ground sloped more steeply in what had obviously been the central vent of the old volcano. A single ancient acacia tree spread the outstretched hands of its foliage beside the lake. Some way from them, in full view of the encircling crater, the Tschambula had rolled a large, flat-topped rock, along one side of which were two rock seats. Here was the focus, the stage, the ring.

Makawawa won his first bout quite easily. His opponent was another of what Ivan could only call the more negroid-featured Tschambula. He was strong, but he had little skill. Makawawa beat him in three straight throws. To Ivan's relief, instead of his usual crowing and haw-hawing, he behaved with dignity in victory, bending his head politely to be patted and spitting respectfully on his palms before patting in return.

But what most surprised and impressed Ivan was Makawawa's evident standing among the Tschambula. He was clearly a man of importance. He seemed to have an active following of some fifty warriors, who accompanied him and supported him vociferously. Wealth among the Tschambula consisted in sheep, goats and cattle and was expressed in wives. But, Ivan guessed, with Strassburg's generous wage, Makawawa had the enormous additional advantage of cash.

Now the action moved, with maximum excitement and chaos, to the central arena. The Tschambula poured in until the flat fighting rock was surrounded by a sloping black wall of buzzing, chattering faces. Black faces reflected in black water. The seven remaining couples, two by two in turn, came in through the single gap made by the stream in the side of the crater. Their supporters, leaping and chanting and waving their spears, came with them. It was not arm fighting any more. This was battle to the death.

It all took time. The bands of supporters had to be forced back and sat down some distance from the rock. The three aged umpires had to totter about, making sure each fighting warrior was sitting fair and square. Finally, two hollow hardwood sticks were struck sharply together to signal the start of each bout.

These were fought in complete silence. So perfect were the acoustics that it was possible to hear the panting of the two opponents at the topmost and most distant rank of spectators. At the final throw, as the victor was known, a deep roar swept like a wave over the two fighters. The supporters of the winner leapt up and yelled and stamped. Only the two central figures stood quite still. Then, outwardly composed, they bowed and patted and spat and bowed and withdrew, each accompanied by his private band, to cram down some fifty feet from the fighting stone.

Makawawa's first bout in the central arena was won only after a considerable struggle. Like the first one and the one that would follow, it was the best of five throws – the first to reach three. The last two bouts were the best of seven, first to reach four. Makawawa's opponent was much taller than he and his longer arms gave him a leverage advantage. But they had heard he lacked stamina – and so it turned out. Makawawa lost the first throw, despite using, as Ivan had advised, blocking tactics. But in the second, he established a powerful lock which he held for four minutes and then won with a sudden attack. By the third and fourth throws, his opponent was exhausted.

The end of this round left seven contenders. Lots were now drawn – pebbles in a gourd, one of which was black – and the winner went through without contest. Makawawa picked the black stone.

His supporters shouted and stamped. Not only was this respite a considerable physical advantage, it was a sign.

'Now you see, Makawawa win easy easy,' he crowed, clasping Ivan to him.

'I hope so. Yes, I'm sure you will. But Sapi's still there.'

'Sapi – him,' said Makawawa, spitting into the mud.

Ivan had been watching Sapi closely. The whole of the Tschambula watched him closely. A particularly dense silence fell when he fought. Although his supporters were less numerous than, for instance, Makawawa's, they made more noise. It was clear he was expected to win the contest. And he was impressive. He appeared totally calm, almost indifferent. Between each throw, he sat for a minute, sometimes longer, completely still, his eyes closed.

'See Sapi tired. He fall asleep,' said Makawawa scornfully.

'I don't think he's sleeping,' said Ivan.

There was nothing tired about Sapi's fighting. In this round – the first of the bout of seven – he won with four straight throws. He made it appear effortless. But Ivan noticed something unusual about his style. When he embarked on a crucial throw, he flung his left arm out and back. This had the effect of twisting his body more viciously into the attack. It might also serve to distract his opponent. But it seemed to Ivan that this sideways fling of the left arm came a fraction of a second, a fraction of a millisecond, before the attack. It might, therefore, also serve to alert an opponent. He pointed all this out to Makawawa.

They were now well on into the afternoon. Hours seemed to pass between fights, even between throws, when each fighter was allowed up to walk, massage arms, recover. Then supporters and officials (and anyone seemed able to adopt or relinquish this role) jostled and laughed and argued. Objections would be made. The umpires discussed and argued and finally reached a decision. A bout or even a single throw might have to be refought. More hours passed.

By the time the last but one fight came, large torches – long poles with bundles of some resinous fibre flaring at their ends – had been stuck in the ground all round the table stone. Two couples were left to fight. The winners would meet in the final bout. Sapi went first, his opponent an enormous man with arms like logs. As usual, in dead silence, Sapi forced him down in four straight throws.

Now it was the turn of Makawawa. His opponent was, it seemed, the current chief, Ole Senda. He was a grizzled figure, perhaps Ivan's age, with deep, ancient scars down his left arm, probably from a lion. Ivan wondered if the necessity to concentrate on his right arm had led to his fighting success. The difference between the two was striking.

They were well matched. Makawawa won the first throw with a lightning and ferocious opening. Ole Senda came back with a long lock broken by a quick feint and a forward throw. The next two throws were also shared. In the final one Ole Senda disclosed a new wiliness. He feinted and then, an extremely risky move, feinted again and then attacked. Makawawa, caught out, was forced back to 45 degrees. He locked, fought, and locked again for three minutes, but was at last forced to concede. Ole Senda had won.

Makawawa returned to Ivan's side in the middle of his supporters, extremely dejected.

'Never mind, you did very well,' said Ivan. 'I've never seen a move like that before. You'll win next year.' In fact, unable to see how Makawawa could have continued as his assistant had he won, he was quite relieved.

'Now Sapi win,' was all Makawawa could say.

Indeed, the last two bouts were an anticlimax. For the first time there was even chatter and talk during the fighting. Sapi defeated his first antagonist in four straight throws. More torches were planted and flared in the darkness. In the last fight, Ole Senda held him twice but was then swept away. The noise was considerably less deafening than at some of the other results. Ivan guessed that Sapi's was an expected but not a popular victory.

Its effect on Makawawa was, however, extreme. Throughout Sapi's two fights he'd been muttering to himself, banging his forehead, bending his arms and shaking both clenched fists and then muttering again. As the scattered applause died away he suddenly jumped up, ran out to the big table rock and scrambled up on it. There he let out a great cry and into the astonished silence launched an impassioned and lengthy harangue.

Except it was soon not so much harangue as song. He was using the monotonous singsong the Tschambula employed when recounting their legends and stories at night. But whatever he was saying certainly gripped. Ivan could feel a murmur of excitement running through them, breaking into cries as Makawawa changed his note a third time and began to chant, gradually building to a climax. All at once there was dead silence. Ivan shivered.

They were all looking at him. Makawawa was pointing at him. The men close to him drew away.

Makawawa jumped off the rock and ran over to him. 'Quick, Missa Van, you come here. You tell them.'

'Tell them what?' said Ivan, not moving. 'What have you been up to out there, Makawawa?'

Makawawa didn't answer, but simply pulled Ivan up and dragged him out into the centre. Then he let go of his hand and stepped back, pointing. A murmur went round the Tschambula. It was suddenly very bright under the flaring torches with their swirling smoke and resinous smell. Ivan felt unreal and disembodied. Perhaps he would float away.

Makawawa and the three elders were talking. Then there was silence and they all looked at him.

'What have you been telling them?' said Ivan.

'I tell them you great fighter. You fight Sapi. I tell them you the new *bwana makuba*. You come back as promise. You lead us as promise.'

'I'm not going to fight anyone,' said Ivan. 'I'm not the *bwana makuba*, as you know perfectly well.'

'How you know? Detu see it.'

'Nonsense! Detu said nothing about this.'

'I no tell you.'

'Oh, rubbish, Makawawa,' said Ivan, but even as he spoke an extraordinary suspicion began to form in his mind, making his heart beat and his mouth dry.

The three elders were clearly growing impatient. One of them said something to Makawawa. 'He say again, will you fight Sapi? Fight tells truth.'

'No,' said Ivan, as the suspicion became a certainty.

Before Makawawa could reply, Sapi, who had been standing listening and who clearly had some English, spat at Makawawa's feet and said something.

'Now he say you coward,' said Makawawa.

'He's quite right,' said Ivan. 'Nevertheless, I've changed my mind. I think I will fight him. Yes, I will. Oh, God!'

46

The gathering emergency necessitated a visit, though one was not due, in Michael's view, for several months.

'But you can't come up,' he said more or less as he came through the door, as usual unable to wait the tactful three or four hours he'd enjoined on himself.

'Why not?' said Mrs Wordingham.

'I mean physically, of course, Granny,' said Michael. 'How would you manage the train? The taxis? You presumably don't plan to try the underground. And I'm afraid I can't come and get you. I have far too much to do at the moment. Libraries. Meetings.'

'Meetings?' cried Mrs Wordingham, momentarily sidetracked. 'You never told me you had meetings. How exciting, darling! Who with?'

'Various people. Scholars in the field.'

'Perhaps I could meet some of them? We could ask them to the birthday party. I've already asked Mrs Deekin in the village if she'd make a cake.'

'No,' said Michael. 'Anyway, there isn't going to be a birthday party. You can hardly get up and down stairs; you can't possibly manage a trip to London.'

'Yes, I can,' said Mrs Wordingham.

'How?'

'I shall come by ambulance!' said his grandmother triumphantly.

'Ambulance?'

'Yes – ambulance. I've discovered that it is possible to hire a private ambulance. The cost is considerable, it is true. But it will be worth it.'

'You seem to have forgotten that there are four and a half, really five flights of stairs up to my flat,' said Michael. 'They are steep and have sharp turns. I find them taxing myself. How do you plan to negotiate all that?'

'I shall be carried on a stretcher,' said his grandmother. For the first time in years she felt she had the upper hand with her grandson. 'I have found out that is possible. Indeed, they often have to do it. I can have oxygen if I like – that's £35 extra. I can even have a doctor in attendance, but that's £250 per day.' Her plans had been three months maturing. They were foolproof. 'The ambulance comes complete with revolving light and siren and full emergency facilities, including blood.'

Michael got up and began to walk heavily and agitatedly around the drawing room. He stopped by the piano. 'Listen, Granny, I can't let you go through all that. I'll find some time and come down here for my birthday. We can have the cake here. We could even have a party. We could ask Mr Broughton, if he's still alive.'

'That's sweet of you, darling, but I want to see you in your flat. I want to see your work, your book. Besides, I need an outing. I feel I haven't been out of here for twenty years.'

'I'll stay a week if you like,' said Michael.

'That would be lovely,' said his grandmother. 'Why don't we do both? You could travel back with me in the ambulance. But I'm quite determined to come and see you. I want to be able to envisage you at your work.'

'I see,' said Michael, envisaging this himself.

47

Sapi had refused to fight there and then. He was tired. They would meet tomorrow.

His childish taunt had nothing to do with Ivan's decision. The reason for this was more profound.

The only thing that Boris had taught him had been to arm fight. Naturally, he had taught him to work on the farm – that was necessity. But the only thing he had personally instructed him in outside the routine of their life was arm fighting. And even then he had done it with a purpose. 'One day you will learn why.' Of course, he couldn't have foreseen the Tschambula. No doubt he had simply had an instinctive feeling that Ivan would one day need this skill. It was an example of the future shaping the past, so common with men of destiny.

It was this realisation, which came to him – as often before – in the space of a few seconds, that stopped Ivan remonstrating with Makawawa. His friend was, after all, right in his way.

Events, which up till then had moved with exasperating slowness, now suddenly and terrifyingly raced. Ivan had hardly fallen asleep than he was woken by the lingua franca of dawns around the world – the cockerel's melancholy, strident trumpet call. He knew from the dull tattoo on the hides that it was raining. Ivan had a light breakfast, prepared by Jambuna, consisting of a gourd of the smoky-tasting brown milk. He had another at midday, which seemed to arrive in about half an hour. Not till mid-afternoon did it stop raining. 'Time we go,' said Makawawa.

His assistant's supporters had transferred their allegiance *en bloc* to Ivan. He walked among them in a state of complete unreality. Perhaps I'll float above them, he thought again. He was stripped to the waist and Jambuna and Makawawa had washed him all over. 'He see you how white,' cried Makawawa, 'he see you *bwana makuba*. He get frightened.'

If Sapi was frightened, there were no signs of it. He stood menacingly still beside the fighting rock, muscular, expressionless. The elders fussed about them. The rock and two seats and the ground about them had been dried. Ivan was conscious of the pressure of eyes, the dense blackness of the massed faces. He was sitting down. He put up his arm and felt the warm satin of Sapi's arm as they came together. He had a sudden feeling that they were about to become not opponents but lovers.

Sapi would either block and test, the conventional opening, or, confident of his strength, attack at once. Ivan guessed he would suppose the first of Ivan and do the second himself. He half closed his eyes and laid himself open to Sapi's nerves, muscles, blood.

The short, hollow clack of the wooden starter, the glimpse of Sapi's outflung left arm and his attack all came almost simultaneously – but not quite. In the fraction between outflung left arm and attacking right, Ivan sprang in. He felt the inner click as Sapi, forced to his surprise back at 45 degrees, locked. Ivan locked in return and seconds later Sapi counterattacked. He was strong, stronger than Ivan, but he could be held. Ivan held him. Let him tire himself. After five minutes, Ivan felt Sapi's arm quivering. He took a deep breath and slowly forced his opponent down.

The roar that greeted this first throw was an expression of surprise as much as anything else. It was clear that the Tschambula had expected Sapi to sweep Makawawa's white man away like dust. Now they had a fight to watch. There was a hum of expectation as the two men circled and then sat down again.

The art of the feint was simple and depended on surprise and speed. If an opponent felt his arm suddenly pulled instead of pushed, his instinctive reaction was to pull back. The feinter had to strike immediately, utilising this. Ivan's rare use of the feint had always been characterised by speed and daring – always, that is, thirty-three or thirty-five years ago.

His daring had consisted in the distance he pulled his opponent's arms, thus, if lucky, provoking an equally violent instinctive reaction. So it was now. He yanked Sapi to his right and instantly reversed. Before Sapi could recover or even lock, Ivan had slammed his arm down on the rock.

This second victory was greeted in complete silence. Even Makawawa's supporters were silent. It suddenly seemed the stranger might win. And now an awed muttering ran round the watching Tschambula: '*Bwana makuba*, *bwana makuba*, *bwana makuba*.'

Ivan was aware of none of it. He hardly even noticed the lighting of the resinous fibre torches on their poles round the fighting rock, or the swirling smoke and flames that poured from them. He was gathering himself for renewed effort, half in trance, trying to sense what Sapi would do.

Sapi was in fact about to take a considerable gamble. He started the third bout as he had the first, by flinging out his left arm and attacking with his right. Not expecting the same thing twice, Ivan was fooled. He failed to lock and Sapi forced him down with considerable violence.

In the same instant, without thought, sensing the sudden ripple of continuing force along his opponent's arm, Ivan flung himself forward on to the rock and turned a complete somersault, trying to twist Sapi's right hand as he wrenched his arm free.

At once there was uproar. Sapi's supporters ran forward, showing by sweeping gestures that Ivan should be disqualified. Makawawa, guessing what had happened, rushed in shouting that Sapi had hoped to break Ivan's arm. Ivan demonstrated the same to the three elders by twisting his right hand with his left. These distinguished figures gestured and discussed and listened. Finally it was decided in Ivan's favour. It had all happened too fast for certainty, but the senior elder – looking at least a hundred, but sharp-eyed – had seen Sapi's shoulder hunch up as he came down on Ivan. The white man was given the throw.

Three to nothing. Perhaps the desire for a new *bwana makuba* had something to do with the decision. But the next two went against Ivan. In the first, wet with sweat, his elbow slipped on the rock. In the second, Sapi fooled him by a clever double bluff. He flung out his left arm but instead of attacking, he feinted. Ivan pulled back and Sapi forced him down.

Three–two. Ivan decided to gamble himself. Sapi had hoped by cheating that, though he might lose a throw, he'd cripple his opponent. A bully's way out, a Boris way out. But Ivan had a feeling, judging by a certain tremor before the start, and the way Sapi held his hand, that the reverse had happened. His own somersaulting, wrenching twist free had damaged Sapi.

He decided to risk a direct, unsubtle trial of strength. At the first lock he knew he was right. Sapi couldn't maintain it. Ivan felt the shift, the weakness. At last, as so nearly with Boris thirty-three years before, it would be a complete victory, without skill, without subterfuge. He was the strongest. Sapi was not Boris, but looking up, looking at the cold eyes, the bristling hair, the thin mouth, the sweat catching the light as it trickled through his stubble – for a moment Ivan saw Boris. With a surge of fury, staring him in the face, now not needing to concentrate with half-closed eyes, Ivan forced him relentlessly back. Back – back – down – down – till, with a gasp of pain, Sapi gave up and Ivan pinned him to the rock.

Confusion followed, hours of confusion. Or perhaps he was too exhausted to discern the pattern. Fires were lit round the rock. He heard now, for the first time consciously, a chant in which the word Masai was repeated endlessly – Masai and *bwana makuba*. They had begun to drum. The smell of roasting lamb mixed with the black smoke and sharp smell of the torches. Makawawa stayed close beside Ivan, speaking for him, shouting, giving orders, pulling people forward. Had Makawawa perhaps planned all this long before? Everyone seemed to want to touch him and be touched and patted by him. He ate the meat but refused the smoky milk, now foaming. It was more revolting when fermented. Milk and blood fermented. Water, please, Makawawa. Makawawa shouted. Days seemed to pass. Ivan longed to sleep.

'Makawawa, why do they keep on calling on the Masai?'

'One day, *bwana makuba* lead us victory over Masai. That he promise. Now you *bwana makuba* here. Tschambula kill Masai.'

'That's absurd. The Masai are a fighting people, tens of thousands strong. The Tschambula are tiny.'

'Detu say so too.'

'Detu rubbish! I certainly shan't help you do anything like that.'

But Makawawa wasn't listening to him. The drumming had become insistent and seemed to be beating a sort of coherence into the crowds, the gently shuffling walls of staring black faces and smoke and noise and darkness in front of him. Lines were forming of men stamping to the drums. They were carrying spears. Was this the start of a war dance?

To his left, Ivan caught sight of Jambuna crouching down among a crowd of other women, her eyes on him. He beckoned to her. They could now, in a crude mixture of Swahili and Ivan's few words of Tschambula, just converse.

'We go to tent,' he said.

No one stopped them. Jambuna led him, stepping lightly.

It had suddenly become quite clear to Ivan that he'd made a terrible mistake from which he had to extricate himself as quickly as possible. Typical that the realisation should come at the apparent moment of triumph. Or perhaps not – it was the very completeness of the triumph, the nakedness of the position he was now in, that made the mistake obvious.

They built up the fire and sat in its light before the tent.

'I have to go now. Go at once,' said Ivan. 'Jambuna, you know car? Range Rover?' He made the noise of an engine and turned an imaginary wheel. Jambuna nodded. 'I need key,' he said, turning an imaginary key. 'Key, like this, you know? You remember? Makawawa has it. In his white man's clothes. Get it for me.'

She was gone only a few minutes. Ivan pulled on his shirt and jacket. His arm ached and he felt very tired.

'I have to go. Don't tell Makawawa till morning. Take me to the path through the forest.'

She didn't say anything. Even though they could speak now, after a fashion, her real language remained, as he'd guessed, wordless. At the edge of the forest, Ivan said, 'Goodbye, Jambuna. You go back. Remember, don't tell Makawawa till morning.'

'Jambuna come too.'

'No, Jambuna.'

'Jambuna come too.'

'No.'

'Jambuna come too.'

He couldn't have done it without her. She seemed able to see in the dark or what, despite the fitful moon, was dark as far as Ivan was concerned; as he slithered and stumbled and squelched behind her, swearing and panting, she stepped nimbly ahead. Several times she caught him. She guided him round corners and waited for him to get his breath.

Dawn broke an hour before they reached the main track. Ivan knew the Tschambula would celebrate most of the night and then pass out but, even though totally exhausted, almost dropping, he felt he had to be off. He was fleeing. The Range Rover started at once.

'Goodbye, Jambuna. I'll come back. I'll send for you in a few days.'

But it was clear she knew she'd never see him again. She looked at him with her large, black-olive eyes, her soft lips bulging and slightly parted. She reached out and lightly touched his forehead with the tips of her fingers, turned, walked ten or fifteen yards and then her slim, black, mud-spattered form vanished into the forest.

Ivan watched her go, suddenly swept by sadness. For the first time he was conscious of the mud that, like a manifestation of past sorrow, had filled his shoes.

48

'I think I told you my grandmother will be coming to tea in two days' time,' said Michael.

'Yes,' said Mrs Inch.

'The problem lies in some of the larger things, the actual objects, of the collection,' said Michael. 'My grandmother is incredibly old-fashioned.'

'Yes,' said Mrs Inch. She hoped Mr Wordingham's grandmother would insist that the lot was thrown out. The *lot*. But she knew better than to say so. If Mr Wordingham wanted to do it, that was his business. Michael decided the only thing to be done was to sacrifice his bedroom, which he would keep locked. He wasn't going to be subjected to his grandmother's sarcasm about being obsessive for a second time in his life.

All notes, newspapers, cuttings and journals not already there, as well as old copies of *Science*, *Nature*, *Scientific American* and, latterly, the *New Scientist*, would have to be moved into the sitting room, from which Baby Belling, tins, wire coat hangers – the huge collection of assorted hardware accumulated from his life or painstakingly garnered from skips, building sites and indeed the entire outside world covered by his perambulations – all had to be relocated in the cupboard room and in his bedroom. Space created in the sitting room, for their tea and general manoeuvring, was thus taken up elsewhere. Mrs Inch tramped sullenly to and fro, obeying directions. She had recently taken to secretly throwing away small items in order to relieve her feelings.

Michael was continually amazed and delighted at some of the things they turned up. 'Look at this,' he'd say to Mrs Inch. 'Amazing find! The things people throw away.' Mrs Inch would look and make an ambiguous noise in her throat.

'Could you come again tomorrow? There's still quite a bit to do.'

'I can only make the afternoon, Mr Wordingham. I do Mr and Mrs Ainsworth in the morning.'

The shifting around wasn't finally completed until the

lunchtime of the day Mrs Wordingham was due to arrive. Michael had a quick snack at Calvino's and hurried back. Despite himself, he found he was looking forward to his grandmother's visit.

The ambulance had rolled up, prompt to the second, at three o'clock. Michael had found Mrs Wordingham sitting chirpily in the back. Beside her, on the padded seat, were her handbag and a large iced cake. She beamed at him, her eyes enormous behind her powerful 'seeing' spectacles.

'It's been such *fun*, Michael darling! Come in and kiss me. See – that's the oxygen cylinder. There's a new bypass round Chelmsford. Completely blocked, of course. I made Bob use the siren. We sailed through! Bob, this is my grandson Michael, and Michael, this is David, his assistant.'

'Hi,' said Bob familiarly. 'I'd better have a quick look at the premises, if you don't mind.' Both men had uniforms of a vaguely medical tinge, somehow rather bogus. They followed Michael through to the door and together peered up the stairs.

'She don't weigh much,' said Dave.

'Yer, but we'll never manage a lift up that lot,' said Bob. 'It'll 'ave to be the stretcher, Mr Wordingham. But she's a game one, she is. What's 'er age then?'

'Seventy-eight . . . Eighty . . . Something like that,' said Michael. 'I'm not sure. It might be eighty-four or eighty-five. I forget.'

'Is she now? Well, there you are,' said Bob.

'I've left the flat door open,' said Michael. 'It's at the top.'

Mrs Wordingham, nervous but highly stimulated, did everything asked of her.

'Now them straps will hold yer,' said Bob. 'Yer keep a hold of them. But if yer feel yer slipping, on a corner, say, just push on my stomick with yer feet, OK?'

'OK,' said Mrs Wordingham, doing her best to grip the straps. 'Michael, pass me my handbag.'

'I wouldn't do that, Mrs Wordingham,' said Bob. 'You just keep a hold of them straps. Yer grandson can take the bag.'

'No, Michael has to carry the cake. We can lock the bag in the ambulance. Michael, get my reading spectacles out of it and give them to me, there's a darling.'

The two men lifted the stretcher out of the ambulance. Michael collected the cake. Mrs Wordingham was gently lowered and Bob locked the ambulance, then they picked up the stretcher again. Mrs Wordingham gripped her straps and they set off for the house, followed by Michael with the cake. A man had stopped to watch the curious scene.

The first two flights passed without incident, though Mrs Wordingham was clearly rather alarmed at the angle with which they negotiated the two 180-degree bends.

'Up a bit, Dave,' shouted Bob. 'Swing the head round. That's it. Tilt. Tilt to the left.'

Michael was reminded of furniture removers.

But at the third 180-degree turn, Dave struck one handle of the stretcher sharply against the ornamental banister knob. Mrs Wordingham's head was jerked round, causing her 'seeing' spectacles to shoot off her nose and, grabbing, she flung her reading spectacles after them.

'Help!' cried Mrs Wordingham, 'my spectacles! Quick, Michael!'

Michael tried to jump forward but, stumbling, dropped the cake and stepped heavily with his right foot on the reading spectacles, and with his left foot on the 'seeing' spectacles. There were two successive, audible crunches.

'Oh, Christ,' said Michael.

'What's happened?' cried Mrs Wordingham, who could see nothing now but whiteness, vague shadows. 'My spectacles! Michael!'

It was all sorted out in his sitting room, in so far as it could be sorted out.

'But how did they break?' said Mrs Wordingham, groping in her fog and eventually making contact with the spectacles Michael was holding out to her. 'They can't break. They're unbreakable. They often slip off the bed and don't break.'

'I trod on them,' said Michael. 'I'm sorry.' Guiltily he felt a gust of his usual irritation.

'Trod on them? On both of them? How?' said his grandmother, aware that she too was feeling emotions habitual when they were together – exasperation mixed with agitation and a loss of control.

'I just trod on them. I was trying to get at them and I dropped the cake and trod on them. I'd better go and see to the cake.'

'You better leave that to us, Mr Wordingham,' said Bob, who was becoming uneasy being present at this intimate scene. 'Where's the kitchen? Cloth, dustpan and brush, you know?'

'It's along the corridor to the right,' said Michael. 'Thanks.'

'And Bob, get my bag from the ambulance,' said Mrs Wordingham with sudden inspiration. 'I may have put another pair of spectacles in it.'

But they weren't there.

'We'll just have to make the best of it,' said Mrs Wordingham. 'At least I'm here. In fact, where am I, Michael?' It looked to her as if someone had immersed her in a tank of milk also occupied by indistinct shapes.

'My sitting room.'

'That will be the big room at the top of the house. It used to be my bedroom. A lovely room, I remember.'

'Yes.'

Mrs Wordingham reached out behind her as if exploring her surroundings and made contact with a pile of something which at once came slithering to the floor.

'Watch out, Granny!' cried Michael. The slithering had provoked more toppling and sliding. Mrs Wordingham heard her grandson struggling, shuffling paper, breathing heavily near her.

'What is it, Michael?'

'Magazines, research material. They're piled high. Don't flail your arms about like that. This room is full of research material.'

'Oh, Michael,' Mrs Wordingham breathed. After a short pause, she said, 'Is that the rather curious smell I smell?'

'What smell?'

'A musty smell,' said Mrs Wordingham, sniffing.

'Possibly. I can't smell anything.'

There was another, longer pause. 'Michael?'

'What?'

'I know I can't really see your book properly like this. But might I just hold it?'

'I suppose so.' Michael fetched one of his journals from a pile beside his desk and gave it to her. Mrs Wordingham turned a few pages, running her fingers over them.

'Michael,' she said hesitantly, 'I know you've told me several times but I can never quite remember – what is it *precisely* that you're writing?'

'Well, I've hardly begun yet. I'm still at the collecting stage, collecting facts, research.'

'Yes, but what will it be *eventually*?'

'It's partly autobiography,' said Michael, taking the journal from her and putting it back beside his desk.

'All first novels are autobiographical, I believe.' She spoke with satisfaction, as if he'd passed some small test.

'A bit of science,' said Michael. He hated his grandmother tweaking at his life like this.

'Ah, I *see*,' said Mrs Wordingham. 'Of *course*, now I remember. Science fiction. A novel of science fiction. So *that*'s it. I knew I knew.'

'If that's what you want to call it,' said Michael.

Bob and Dave, well-meaning but clumsy, had swept up a good deal of the stairs with the cake. They had the birthday party round the sofa off a virtually intact tea trolley Michael had salvaged only a month before. He gave his grandmother one of the least contaminated whole chunks of cake. Then Bob and Dave, who, with a sense of almost Blitz-like classlessness, Mrs Wordingham had insisted join them, suddenly sang 'Happy Birthday'. Mrs Wordingham joined in, her voice unexpectedly deep. Michael remembered how she used to play the piano to him.

'Well, Mrs Wordingham,' said Bob, 'if we've to be back by eight as requested, we'll 'ave to be goin' soon.'

'Oh, dear, I suppose so,' said Mrs Wordingham. 'Where are you, Michael? It's been so lovely. We must do it again.'

Michael did not answer. He held out the two crushed pairs of spectacles. 'Do you want your glasses?'

'What good are they to me?' said Mrs Wordingham impatiently. 'They're ruined. Useless. Thank goodness I have spares at home.'

Michael held the spectacles for a moment, looking at them absently. 'I think the frames might still be of use,' he said, 'if only for the little screws.' He put them on his desk. He'd fit them in somewhere when he'd got the flat back in order again.

'I suppose there's no chance of you coming back with me like we discussed?' said Mrs Wordingham.

'No,' said Michael. 'I've an appalling amount to do here. I'm months behind as it is.'

The journey downstairs was even more hair-raising than the ascent. Mrs Wordingham gripped the straps and rammed her feet into Bob's buttocks, thankful she could see almost nothing. Just vague darker areas moving like ghostly dolphins in her sea of milk.

In the ambulance again, she elected to stay lying on the stretcher under the blanket. She said she felt exhausted suddenly. She reached up her arms and Michael placed himself between them for the kiss.

'It was lovely seeing you, darling. We had fun, didn't we?'

'Yes, Granny,' said Michael.

49

Ivan C. Strassburg wasn't in the least surprised when Ivan said he wished to leave Venture Interior. Indeed, he said it was just as well.

'I'm winding this thing up, Ivan,' he said. 'Damn thing

didn't make a damn bit of difference to anything. I never really felt you were suited here. What I'd had in mind before you asked for this was the Uni-Vac Think Tank in Chicago. In fact, we're looking for new blood right now.'

As his namesake spoke, Ivan suddenly realised he had a strong desire to settle down. He was sick of rushing about. He wanted to amass money for his old age. And he also realised – in a flash, a revelation, he realised – well, why on earth hadn't he gone to America before? To come to the capitalist West and not go to America! There was something Russian about America.

The abandonment of the Think Tank sessions astounded and exhilarated him. After one particularly rippling session, he compared himself to a Yaroslav seventeen-stringed balalaika. And then the money! To be paid thousands of dollars a week for lounging about and talking off the top of his head. Even more astoundingly, it worked. Lying on a leather sofa and free-associating one afternoon, Ivan described, with his eyes shut, the horses on the Taschla collective (he had just returned from seeing Rawbones in New York). He remembered sitting on the cart behind the glossy satin haunches, the long, black, coarse-haired tails whisking left, whisking right, whisking left, then one tail suddenly lifting, the grey out-bulging of the massive encircling sphincter slowly revealing the tender, fig-red inner rim, followed by the inexorable, steady outthrust of the protuberant brown blunt head, glistening and shiny like a just peeled conker . . . From this description was eventually developed the famous Uni-Vac extruder top which, under pressure from the industrial glue, opened outwards, deposited its rapidly solidifying load, and rolled back, to leave the grey outer surface, unlike its rivals, bone dry.

The average useful life of a Think Tank member was 2.9 years. Ivan became increasingly bored and, as a result, increasingly abandoned.

'Ivan, two more years of this and you'll *really* unhinge,' said Professor Edward S. Sarnoff after a particularly wild session in the Think Tank.

The professor had a yen for free association, as he put it, and liked the extra $25,000 a year his two mornings brought in. But as well as teaching at the University of Chicago, he had the power of patronage there. Ivan's restlessness at Uni-Vac was reaching fever pitch. How could he ever have believed that 'settling down' was what he needed?

Six months later he accepted a four-year lectureship in cultural affinities.

'Your remit is broad, very broad,' Sarnoff said with a smile. 'Really, Ivan, provided you deliver and then publish your lecture at the end of each fall semester, you can do what you like. The theme is different cultures and the US. And, as you see, the stipend is not ungenerous.'

Ivan had never earned so much money in all his life. At the same time his first two lectures, although a success with the students, began to worry the faculty. They seemed rather slight at $85,000 each, plus free on-campus apartment, travel allowance, free medical insurance and numerous other academic perks.

'Perhaps you should try and *home in* a bit more next time, Ivan,' said Sarnoff tactfully. 'For instance, I think perhaps what the faculty might like could be something about the US contra Russia.'

'Russia?' said Ivan. 'But I don't know anything about Russia.'

'Oh, ha ha ha ha ha.' Sarnoff was delighted. The European sense of humour. 'Why, you *are* Russian, Ivan. Oh, dear.'

'Am I?' said Ivan.

For six months he toured the vastness of his adopted land (but one he had never, in so many words, actually joined), meanwhile reading, with astonishment, about Russia. It was true he knew nothing about it – yet at every point he found things that tugged at him, that reverberated.

Returning from one of his expeditions late in the autumn, his little plane had to circle the vast, flat, dull-coloured squares of farmland which surround Chicago. As it slowly descended like a sycamore seed through the drizzle, as the few farm buildings disappeared into the dullness, Ivan found he was crying. His tears allowed him suddenly to see clearly, as tears often do. Russia and America were mirror images of each other – the one corrupted by money, the other corrupted by the lack of it, the longing for it, the need for it. His sudden hunger to be down, embedded in the squares of corn land below, meant he wanted to go back to Russia.

This sudden desire was, of course, pointless since it was impossible. But it was followed, naturally enough, by an equally strong longing for London, England, Cambridge, the Thames, Rawbones. Particularly, perhaps, Rawbones.

Six months later Francis Wyatt, now head of Reuters' London bureau, had found him a place as consultant to the Eastern European section. Although neither of them knew it, this was about to become a volcano. It seemed almost ridiculously appropriate to come full circle like this. And appropriate, too, to long-displaced Russian Ivan, to be always slightly outside, observing but not of events or places, never to have a goal, always to have goals – the next riot or earthquake or step of repression. His destiny was on course again.

Not in fact that it had ever really strayed off course. As always, the past was his bible. As the past grew longer, his bible grew larger too, the range of references, the clues, more complete. The step to the latest position, since it came from the one before, which in turn had come from the one before that, meant that each past job, past love affair, the events of each succeeding day, receding backwards now for many years had been necessary to reach this final goal. Ivan had no sense that he had wanted this life. He saw it as the unfolding of a plan, each step of which had been foretold and laid down long ago. The pattern itself was his destiny.

At the same time this sense of purpose and movement had another, almost opposite effect. Even as he sat down that first day in his chair in the Eastern Section of Reuters, London, he was aware – as usual – of a slight unreality hovering at the edges.

50

Since Michael's last visit, and since her own fraught expedition to London, Mrs Wordingham had had a stair lift installed at Inkpen, a broad wooden seat that was carried up and down by means of an electric motor and a ratcheted trackway screwed below the banisters.

Michael read the instruction plate and then managed to balance himself on one buttock on the ridiculously inadequate seat. He gripped the banister with his left hand and pressed the start button gingerly with his right forefinger. There was a loud fizzing, Michael was aware of sparking out of the corner of his eye, finally a smell of burning and silence. The stair lift hadn't moved.

He got off and stared at it. The metal arm which fastened the seat to its track had buckled and the seat hung at an angle. When he pressed the start button again, nothing happened.

Michael plodded guiltily up the stairs. After he had knelt and kissed his grandmother, who now spent all afternoon resting on her bed, he said, 'I'm afraid I may have broken that lift thing on the stairs, Granny.'

'Good heavens!' cried Mrs Wordingham, 'How ever did you do that? It's only been in four months.'

'I don't know. I may be too heavy for it.'

'Oh, it can't be that,' said his grandmother. 'The leaflet said categorically it would carry up to twenty-five stone.'

'Yes, well. Perhaps . . .' Michael let his voice tail away. He was uneasily aware that the useful foot scales he'd rescued some years before from a demolition whirled their needle round to the twenty-stone limit. 'I suppose it could be a fuse,' he said.

'Well, don't worry, darling,' said his grandmother. 'But you must ring Mr Payne to come and see to it. I can hardly get up and down stairs without it now. Now come and sit on my bed and tell me about London. I still miss it, you know. *Such* fun!'

Her bed tilted under him. So had his bed tilted when he was a boy as she had sat to read to him. A wave of love flowed through her and surged out to him.

'Did you do what I suggested over the plugs?' she asked gently.

'Yes,' said Michael.

It was the knowledge that she was in a controlling or at least powerful advisory position, via her letters, that reconciled her to his long months in London. She recommended detailed courses of action – visits to the dentist, repainting the top landing, rewiring, expeditions to Kew, the possibility of yoga classes – and then imagined him following her advice, imagined she detected confirmation in the weekly postcards, and would suddenly think of what could go wrong and write detailed instructions about how to extricate himself from whatever it was she had imagined.

'Granny,' said Michael, 'I need more room. I think I'm going to have to take over the flat below.'

'More *room*?' said Mrs Wordingham. 'How? Why? Are you getting married?'

'No,' said Michael.

'I don't understand.'

'It's research,' said Michael. 'My collections and my research.'

'Are you near the end of the book, of the first draft? Already? I thought you'd hardly begun.'

'No,' said Michael. 'Yes. There's still some way to go. But the research is immense. You saw for yourself. I need hundreds of books, files, cuttings. I'm making very full notes, very, very full. It will all come in.'

'But couldn't you use the drawing room more, or put some things in your bedroom? It can't be *that* full.'

Only two mornings before, Michael had realised it was now effectively impossible for him to get to his bed. Each time he forced his way through the precarious wall of newspapers, old newspaper cuttings, magazines and magazine cuttings, unreturned library books, detective paperbacks, the piles of receipted bills, flattened lavatory rolls, rolls of saved string and boxes of saved corks and screw bottle tops – piles which, with many others, now completely shut off the windows and his cupboard, so that he kept most of his clothes on the end of his bed – he often brought so much of it crashing down that in the morning it took him a good quarter of an hour to re-pile himself out, as it were, and into another line of tottering barriers along the passage to the kitchen similarly constricted, past a sitting room or drawing room, as his grandmother still insisted on calling it, which was itself now nothing but a narrow lane leading to a desk piled high, nearly ceiling-high, with unpaid bills, journals, current cuttings and magazines and assorted correspondence.

'It *is* that full,' said Michael tersely. 'Even the roof is full.'

This was true, but not strictly true. The Kilner jars had seemed increasingly small for the magnitude of their task as time passed and a few months or a year before he had managed to secure 107 twelve-gallon glass demijohns from a bankrupt lead-acid factory. The roof space was overfull, but all but one of the demijohns were empty. The price had been considerable.

'And Granny, is there any possibility of you increasing my allowance? The research, the filing systems, libraries – it's all very expensive.'

'But darling, if I ask Mr Pinkerton to give notice to the second-floor tenants, that will reduce my income from Drayton Gardens by a third. And I've sold a lot of shares over the years. I don't know what I'll do.'

However, Mrs Wordingham did know what she'd do. Inkpen village, from being a 'dormitory' village, had recently been designated an 'Ipswich overspill dormitory town'. Mr Crisp, who owned the farm next to the vicarage, had apparently sold a small patch of one of his fields for an absolutely astonishing sum. Mrs Wordingham's big twenty-acre field was directly in the path of a proposed development.

'I'll talk to Mr Pinkerton about it,' she said. 'Now, darling, how long are you staying?'

Michael took a deep breath. 'I thought I'd go back on Tuesday afternoon.'

'Oh, darling, how lovely! What a lot we'll do! We could go to the sea.'

'I'd stay longer if only I had less work.'

'It will be easier when you've more room,' said his grandmother, smiling fondly at him. 'Now, I must get up. Pass me that shawl.'

'I'd better go and ring Payne. I can help you up and down the stairs.'

As he rose ponderously to his feet, there was a brief flash from the bed and something small fell with a thud on the carpet. Michael stooped, knelt, rose, panting slightly. He held a jeweller's glass in his plump fingers. 'What on earth do you use this for?' he asked.

'Oh, my glass,' said his grandmother. 'I use it, Michael, to try and read your infuriating letters. You must try and write larger. It's absurd. Don't you read my letters about it?'

'Yes,' said Michael.

Before he left the room he turned and said casually, 'Do you ever hear from Elfreda, Granny?'

'No,' said Mrs Wordingham.

51

Although in the end it was love that would help precipitate the final twist of his destiny, for many years, however passionate, however empty, Ivan's love affairs seemed quite threadless. There was no general picture. That doesn't mean there weren't quite often individual lessons, of course.

He had thought Karen, for instance, thirty-five, behind thick spectacles, really much preferred her four dachshunds. (Once, while they were making love, one of the dachshunds jumped up on the bed and, probing deep, licked into his bare bottom.) It was always understood that one day one or the other of them would wish the affair to end. For this reason, although they 'lived' together, Ivan sometimes spent a night or two in his own flat. He was in any case quite often away (it was the start of his stint in the old people's homes). Karen would suddenly take the dogs to her mother in Hove for three days. Their eventual parting – when it would take place, what would initiate it, what they would most remember – was the most interesting and exciting thing about the affair. It almost seemed they were together in order to part. To Karen, especially, it seemed of no consequence at all. She could pack a few knickers and be off tomorrow. 'I can't exist without tension,' she said once. 'No, Ivan, don't laugh, just because I'm so domestic. It's true.'

When, after two years, Ivan had to take a series of extended trips to Paris and then to Frankfurt, it suddenly seemed the right moment. Karen agreed at once. She asked him round to say goodbye, casual as that. The ground-floor tenant had jammed the lock of the front door. They'd rung to get it broken open. But he could get up by the drainpipe again, as he'd done so romantically at first before it had got unsafe. She'd had it mended, secured, last week.

Ivan was nineteen feet up when the pipe broke loose. In fact, it wasn't even attached. It simply floated away backwards, Ivan clinging.

By chance he landed in a large privet bush, smashing it to bits. Lying winded, bruised, dazed, blinded – that is to say, essentially unhurt – he realised with astonishment that Karen had tried to murder him.

When he was thirty-eight he met and for a year lived with on and off (in Buenos Aires) a woman who embodied all his sexual fantasies. He realised that, with one exception, he had really only been dabbling. Now he was engulfed. Drunk. When she left, he was heartbroken and relieved.

For a while, the convulsions remained addictive. But it took years of searching before he met in a casualty ward a forty-year-old American nursing sister, whose appearance and manner (those cuffs!) gave no indication of seismic qualities. She too delighted him with the earthquake of her orgasm.

Ivan, wishing to part amicably, repeated with gratitude the compliments he'd often extended in bed. Sister Mary was not feeling amicable. 'It's not sex men like,' she said in her brisk, clinical little Manhattan voice, her eyes diamond-tipped behind their lenses. 'You men don't like sex as much as women, even when you think you do. What men want to do is think they've given a girl pleasure. It's pure conceit. I know if I *really* wanta please a man, I've only to yell and heave about a bit.'

Feeling vaguely insulted, Ivan brooded about this for several months. In the end he decided Sister Mary was wrong. Women's cries, their flowing spasms, fulfilled men's fantasies – Marie-Carmen had taught him this. Fantasy was the male sexual fuel. That was why there were magazines of sexual fantasy for men and not for women, and why women didn't write on walls.

Still later, when Rawbones had come back into his life after one of his many absences, Ivan discussed it with the quivering, ageing roué.

Rawbones didn't agree. Women had fantasies too, he said, just as much as men. How many times had Rawbones entered the lists? wondered Ivan. Ten thousand times? Ten million? His face was orange now, rather than red, orange-green and criss-crossed with hairline fractures.

'Men like sex,' said Rawbones. 'Some men like it a lot. Some have a lot but don't particularly like it. Some men don't like it or need it at all. It isn't so much that women like pleasure more than men. They like pretending pleasure in order to enslave men. It's about *power*,' said Rawbones, speaking from his huge experience.

'I see,' said Ivan. 'So each wants what it hasn't got and can't have.'

Destiny was a habit, a game – yet he couldn't stop playing it. If it ruled how he lived, should it not rule how he loved? What was the pattern? Was he in fact able to love at all? Ivan had noticed that he never loved at the time. The 'love' got lost in the love affair – in its fears and confidences, its guilts and jealousies and discoveries, excitements and boredom and angers, in its sex. It was only afterwards, when it was over, that the love became visible, as it were, and he realised he had loved. Love was always in the past.

In fact, Sister Mary gave him the first clue. It was late at night when she left his apartment in Chicago. The Sister Mary love pattern consisted of Marie-Carmen, Jambuna, Rose-Anne, his now seldom thought-of wife (*that* hadn't been dabbling) and so on back to Sofka. All patterns ended at Sofka, since that was where they all began.

Sofka. As he returned to that distant figure, a small shutter opened in his mind and allowed him to see back across the past. Calmly, lying in bed, just as years before he had suddenly and without effort seen the rhomboidal geometry of the flies above his head, so now he recognised the pattern of his love. The whole pattern, not just the Marie-Carmen pattern or the Karen pattern or the Rose-Anne pattern, was obvious. It had been obvious for years. How had he missed it? The pattern was leaving – to leave or be left. It was more precise than a pattern. It was a goal.

As he realised this, Ivan was flooded with a deep, familiar and ancient desolation. I shan't sleep, he thought – but in fact he was asleep a few minutes later.

When he woke in the morning, the sadness was still with him. But another realisation had attached itself to the sadness. The terror of leaving, the terrible pain of loss – these had become the goal because only through them could he really feel intensely any emotion at all.

52

Michael sometimes felt he was neglecting Elfreda, yet not a day passed when he didn't think about her. In a long relationship there must be ups and downs, variations in intensity. You can't be at white heat all the time. Sometimes he was practically tepid. At others . . .

Well, sometimes, with no outside intervention, he'd find he was smelling of her. He would be sitting writing his journal at his desk, or about to take a bath – naturally enough, that was when it happened most often, as he undressed – when he would spontaneously give off that subtle skin-sorcery of hers, that mingled aroma of rich, pungent, stewy kitchen smells: shallots, rabbit, pheasant, Parmesan, fungus; into which came, coiling and wafting, mingling but distinguishable, her heady, vapoury bathroom smells, oily, moist, powdery, soft; and finally, cutting through, distinct, sudden, clear, bladelike smells from a still or surgery, like a wind off a Latvian glacier or over the tundra of a Latvian steppe.

Elfreda – and who else? It was true he saw very few people. Practically no one, indeed. Mrs Inch. No one. But one Sunday, fortunately just after he'd moved into the flat below, Poole turned up. A postcard preceded him. Michael laid in Newcastle Brown.

'So how's things, lad? You've put on weight, I see. Lost a bit o' hair. Likely I've changed a bit, too.'

Michael ran his hand nervously over his smoothness, a pulling-out-hair gesture with no hair to pull. He drew his nail down his cheek.

'Not bad,' he said. 'Cigarette?'

'A've given up, lad. So what do you do, Mike?'

Michael swallowed the fragment of skin that had lodged beneath his nail. 'I'm writing a book,' he said.

'A *book*?' said Poole. 'What are you writing on?'

'Mixed,' said Michael. 'Autobiography. Perhaps some fiction. And you?'

'We're at the cutting edge, lad,' said Poole. 'We're starting to make waves in Sheffield.'

It was as though they were still at Cambridge together. Poole had now been a professor for over twenty years, but his conversation had always resembled a lecture. As he drank the Newcastle Brown, Michael had a sensation familiar to him from reading *New Scientist*, that he was understanding something he didn't understand.

'Of course it all depends on what you mean by being in "the same place",' said Poole. 'Quantum mechanics would allow for a particle, a ganger particle, say, or a photon, to be in two places at the same time. Two worlds.'

'I seem to remember years ago you talked about an infinity of worlds.'

'Parallel worlds, an infinity of worlds. That's right.'

'Can they contact each other?'

'Look,' said Poole, gesturing heavily. 'Quantum mechanics has shown' (he pronounced it 'shone') 'that a pair of particles can be separated by enormous distances and still not be independent. In fact, lad, theory is so fluid at this point in time that I'd say *anything* is theoretically possible. Chap in our department was arguing the other day that interdependence of particles under certain circumstances could be a theoretical basis for Jung's collective unconscious.'

'Goodness,' said Michael. 'I was wondering – '

'Collective unconscious could well 'ave sound theoretical basis. I think it's a nonsense, frankly, but I see what he means.'

'I was wondering. Do you suppose, if one of these other worlds, the parallel worlds, passed close together, they might want to join each other? Like two libraries want to join if they're on opposite sides of the street?'

'Two *libraries*?' said Poole, uncomprehending. 'What's two libraries got to do w'it?'

With a slight inner sigh, Michael remembered what a profound lack of poetry, or even ordinary romanticism, there was in Poole's powerful mind.

'Only a metaphor,' he said. 'An idea I once had. No, but if two parallel worlds brushed against each other, could someone be sucked from one to the other?'

'Well, there's questions of dimensions here. But it's arguable, yes, definitely arguable.'

'Then, suppose you invented, that is, discovered one of these other worlds, parallel worlds,' said Michael, becoming increasingly stimulated. 'Suppose you got in touch. Do you suppose what you thought could influence it?'

'Well, if there can be, theoretically, reciprocal contact, there can be reciprocal influence. Theory would allow that. As I say, Michael, theoretically almost anything is possible at this point. There's another chap in the field, Everett-Wheeler, has a theory that the universe spawns a multitude of new universes every quantum decision. There'll be papers about that too some time. But I'm getting tired, Michael. You should read some of the latest work on ganger particles. I forget the man's name. Where's your loo, lad?'

Poole spent the night on the sofa. He'd gone when Michael got up, leaving a note of laconic thanks and promise 'to send chap's name'.

Michael remained extremely stimulated by Poole's visit. For several days he wrote about it in his journal and, at intervals, for years. Apart from his copying from his reading, it was almost the only time he'd had something to write about other than the repetitious cycle of his days. At first he felt he was in the thick of a series of explosive revelations.

'Parallel worlds,' he wrote, that first morning after Poole had left. As they whirled past, veered near each other for an instant at close to the speed of light, would the spiralling skirt of one galaxy pluck an innocent figure from across the dimensions? Or could ideas, memories stream out and bombard the passing other? That could explain ghosts.

His imagination worked seldom. It could lie dormant for years. Then suddenly – these flights. He lay awake for hours, his mind erupting.

'Infinite,' he wrote next morning, 'that is the clue.' It meant that every single possible manifestation of character, every permutation of events could somewhere, in one of this infinite number of parallel worlds, be taking place. And therefore, since *infinite*, everything that man could *imagine* could be taking place. And this could explain a certain curious quality about invention – that it seemed to be given. It arrived or was uncovered. This might mean that the whole of creative literature was really an account of events that were actually taking place at the time – or had taken place several million light years before, since messages even in the brain could only move at that unexceedable maximum. Writers were not creators but reporters. And, of course, these worlds had histories, which extended back, as far as you were concerned, the moment you 'created' them – that is, tuned in to them; and futures which extended forward long after you ceased to write or even exist.

If that was indeed what happened, Michael thought as revelations continued to explode in his head. His writing had become so small and concentrated, he couldn't even read it himself. Perhaps in some way the distant ganger particle or photon depended on its other/same self. The writer was indeed a creator. In which case his world would die with him. Or was God a writer, *the* writer? That would seem to be the suggestion in Genesis. In which case God lived – 'I am, therefore God is'. On the *other* hand, scribbled Michael, with a sense of losing control of the threads, perhaps the world (worlds) *could* continue after the death of the creator, in this case God. Once created, as I think I've already said, they immediately grow a past and a future. So you could argue that the world *was* created 4,500 years ago, and immediately grew 15 billion years older.

Poole's postcard arrived five days later. 'Great evening. Like old times. Doppell is the name of the chap you want. *Particle Theory and Parallel Worlds*, Harvard, $70.'

53

Ivan was never certain why he had married Rose-Anne. He thought in the end it was probably pity, though, as in most liaisons, sex at first concealed all real feelings.

Or perhaps there was no emotion involved. He met her again at another of Rawbones's gatherings, a few weeks before the end of his advertising career. It was in Rawbones's gloomy, chaotic basement flat off Earl's Court. Her straining blue silk shirt tightly tucked in, attracted him by its broad, white, nurse-like cuffs. Perhaps it was that – the clinical detachment. (Certainly those same cuffs on Sister Mary nearly twenty years later signalled something similar.) Or was it the way she was standing incongruously speechless, somehow quintessentially English to

Ivan's eyes? If he could never be accepted by them, as Rawbones continued to assert, at least he could make love to them.

At supper two nights later he studied her face, not listening while she talked about her job. She had a face like a vole or a ferret, with tiny, glistening eyes and a little mouth pulled in by strings. If you could release those strings, thought Ivan, what would happen? He felt if he could make her eyes wider, her soul might hop out and fly into the sky.

Unusually for him, he drank a great deal of wine. As Rose-Anne helped him into her car, she thought she heard him mutter, 'I suppose I ought to fuck you.' In fact Ivan, whose English still tended to go slightly with drink, had tried to say, 'Oh, Rose, a bit of luck I met you.'

Transformed into a humiliating imperative, the remark greatly excited Rose-Anne. To be treated as part of the meal, roughly, coarsely, a task, a duty . . . She drove rapidly back to her flat. When they arrived, she was breathless, dry-mouthed, and wasted no time at all in setting her breasts free, so that they came tumbling out and up before Ivan's intoxicated eyes, bursting to the surface like large buoys loosed from the seabed.

Two months later Ivan and Rose-Anne were married. He soon found that in many respects his wife had been more or less totally destroyed. He learnt that the English middle class had evolved a series of special, very powerful engines for this purpose. Chief among these was the mother. This terrible creature, now seventy-four years old, mauve-faced, distracted by food and alcohol, riddled with petty snobberies and absurd regrets, incapable of warmth or affection, had despised her only, late-born child from birth. She had despatched her, already two thirds crushed by a series of incompetent, frequently sacked nannies, to a strict little girls' preparatory school in the frozen north. This had been followed by a strict little boarding public school. The process had been completed by a series of (apt name) finishing schools.

Only one thing had escaped, because the engines were too frightened or too embarrassed to admit that it existed – her sexuality. As a result it had learnt to stand in for everything else. Making love to Rose-Anne was therefore a great deal more than that. It was not precisely a conversation, since nothing specific could be expressed. But it was an act of communication. She somehow managed, through the act of love, to press upon him the essence – the sweetness and gaiety and sensuality and tenderness – of what, everywhere else, had been destroyed; and also to express everything that she had been thinking and feeling that evening, that day, that week, sometimes perhaps for years. When it was over, her relaxation was not due just to the release of physical tension but to the resolution of frustration and the expression of pent-up thoughts.

Ivan tried to explain this to her early one morning. Rose-Anne smiled but, naturally, said nothing.

54

It was four years before Michael was compelled to move down again, into the first-floor flat at Drayton Gardens.

This brought advantages and disadvantages. One difficulty was that the daily journey to the roof now became extremely arduous, even dangerous, since the metal clatter-ladder was beginning to buckle. He also found it depressing, since it meant he was confronted each day by the increasingly disordered collections. Apart from reminding him how far behind he was with the cataloguing and sorting, there was the simple matter of sweeping and dusting. Mrs Inch had categorically refused to enter the top two floors any more.

Michael solved the arduous climb by moving the remaining empty demijohns down into the first-floor flat. The basement and the flats on the ground and first floors had a spacious extra room built out from the back. Here he had shelves installed along the walls from floor to ceiling and a rack of them down the middle. The demijohns fitted nicely here, with space for new ones which he collected if he found them, or, much more usually now, bought.

He got into the habit of spending some time there towards the end of each day. A moment of meditation. He found that his worries and anxieties were miraculously soothed away. The silent jars of golden, faintly opalescent liquid seemed, especially those catching a gleam of evening sun, almost to glow. The knowledge that it was all part of him, like shelves of books all of which he had written, and the underwater quality of the silence, filled him with peace.

It was a peace that was horribly shattered that same evening. Michael had squeezed himself into his chair to write up the journal, when suddenly the doorbell went off like a bomb. Michael jumped, then braced himself to endure until the caller gave up.

The caller did not give up. The bell shrilled and screamed. Michael put his hands over his ears, as much to shut in an extraordinary idea that was growing in his head.

Who was it? Apart from Poole, the other day, that is year, or rather several years before, the last visitor had been . . . the last caller of this sort . . . damn that bell, he couldn't think . . . had been . . . was . . . well, he couldn't remember the last time. No one had called within living memory – except for Poole.

Michael couldn't any longer control the idea. The idea was Elfreda. He had to see if it was Elfreda. Trembling now with terror and excitement, he thumped down the stairs.

It was a woman, but it was not, surely it couldn't be Elfreda. Unless . . . Michael peered fearfully at the haggard figure collapsed against the bell. There was a strong smell of drink.

'Ain't ya gin' t'ask me in?' Slurred as it was, to his huge relief the accent was American.

'Say, doan say you doan *recognise* me, Michael?'

'Well, I'm sorry, I'm afraid –'

'Mr No Pyjamas doan recognise Henrietta?'

In the kitchen, which was becoming fairly cluttered with

his collections, she put her thin, wrecked face in her bony, dirty hands and leered at him. She was clearly very drunk. She had also aged appallingly. She looked sixty, even seventy. And along with grey hair, lines like sword cuts and bags under her eyes like scrotums, she seemed to have acquired a peculiar malevolence. 'D'ya have any drink in this goddamn house, Michael? Anything? Bottle ends?'

'No,' said Michael. 'I'm afraid I don't drink very often. Have a cigarette.'

Her hand trembled so much that he had in the end to give her the matches. It took ten matches.

'What the fuck is all this rubbish?' she asked, blowing out a great billow of smoke and alcohol fumes.

'It isn't rubbish.'

'Well, what the hell's that, then?'

'It's a Baby Belling. Oddly enough, I've another like it. I could give you that one.'

'What's the point of it? Why d'ya do it?'

'It's very useful.'

'No, why the fuck d'ya collect all this – *this*?' She waved her cigarette.

Michael thought. Oddly enough, the question had never occurred to him – or rather, hadn't seemed worth asking. It was obvious, like all imperatives. But he heard himself saying, mesmerised by her, 'I suppose I feel safer like this.'

But Henrietta had lost interest. She drew noisily on her cigarette, looking about her. Suddenly she said, 'Can I use the bathroom?'

'What – with me?'

'With *you*?' Henrietta stared at him and then began to cackle. 'Oh yeah yeah yeah yeah yeah.'

Once again she seemed to lose interest. There was a long silence. Then all at once she snapped, 'Don't do that! Don't eat yourself like that. It's disgusting.'

'Eat myself?' said Michael. 'What are you talking about?'

'Eating your cheeks like that. It's revolting. You pulled off a great slice of cheek and stuffed it in your mouth. No wonder you're so fucking fat. Do ya eat your turds as well?'

Michael stood up. He found he was shaking. 'I think . . .' he said.

'Auto-cannibalism,' said Henrietta, giggling.

'I think I must ask you to leave now,' said Michael.

'OK, turd eater, OK. There's no drink here anyway. Lend me five quid and I'll go to the pub.'

Michael gave her ten.

55

Rose-Anne joined Ivan in Milan while he was setting up the office there. They used to drive down and spend long weekends in Tuscany.

Rose-Anne ticked off the things they saw in her guide-book. 'I'm one of nature's swots,' she used to say.

One Saturday at the end of August they were in Castellina. It was the fiesta. A stage had been erected for the band at the side of the little square. Thick cables trailed across the cobbles to loudspeakers. There were trestle tables.

Night fell. Slowly people began to amble towards the outside of Castellina. A man had lifted his little girl on to his shoulders and her baby fists were clenched in his black curly hair. Rose-Anne was making conversation, taut as a guitar string.

The fireworks rippled into the black sky and fell in crackling cascades of diamond, green and gold. The last rocket climbed so high it reached the stars and brought them tumbling down in a silver shower. The final explosion had been deafening. Their ears were ringing.

They were part of a crowd. Ivan and Rose-Anne drifted back with them, drinking from a bottle. A distant crump crump crump crump came from the band.

The little square looked like an opera set under the floodlights. There were thirty or forty couples waltzing. The cheap, very loud loudspeakers gave the music an echoing, tinny quality, introducing sudden twangs, elongations and crackles. One old man spun in slow, drunk bliss on his own. Adolescent girls danced together, as heifers mount each other.

'Come on,' said Rose-Anne.

'But I can't waltz,' said Ivan. 'It's the one dance I can't do.'

'Nonsense,' said Rose-Anne.

He found she could make him waltz. It was like a miracle. She didn't lead him; she was quivering light on his arm. The turns seemed inevitable.

They drank and danced and sat and danced until there was hardly anyone left. Even the band had stopped. Taped waltzes came crackling and compelling through the speakers.

'I can't,' said Ivan. 'I'm exhausted. You'll have to dance alone.'

Heady with wine, Rose-Anne walked on tiptoe into the floodlights. She brought her heels down and spun with military precision. The almost empty cobbled square was a parade ground. Her shoulders were as flat and steady as those of the subalterns at Tunguska afraid their crowns might roll off.

Ivan watched her dance in floodlights. He was thinking of the open door of the blue-tiled stove. Of Boris singing, the bright drops of sweat finding their way slowly down through the stubble of his beard.

56

Henrietta's visit went on reverberating for years. The move to the ground floor, when it came, did not even bring temporary relief to Michael as the other moves had.

He was a year behind with his cataloguing. The first floor, a holding area, as he saw it, was really just a dump, a tip, little better than a skip. It smelt.

In a gigantic reorganisation seven years before, he had concentrated rust-proof solid objects on the roof, burying the old Kilner jars and about six demijohns, and devoted the top two floors to papers. But now the accumulation of these, of magazines, clippings, cuttings, unopened letters, journal manuscripts and so on, grew more and more chaotic and difficult to control. For some years Michael had been fairly sure he could put his finger on anything he needed. Now he was not sure at all.

Valuable pieces of information, notes he had made or clipped, would suddenly turn up in unexpected places, in the wrong piles. Only two weeks ago he'd found one such simply blowing about. 'On average,' it read, 'two and a half tons of toad are squashed on Britain's roads each year.'

The words of Henrietta rang in his ears – why? He seemed to have, to have had for years, since very small, a collecting frenzy – but again, why? Was it a disease? Was it guilt? Perhaps he was hiding, under his collections, an awareness that he did nothing. Or that he was nothing. That he'd done nothing and been nothing for twenty-eight years – or was it thirty-eight years, or forty-eight?

Now often smoking sixty cigarettes a day, he took up reading detective novels again, something he'd stopped. He could read two a day and the piles of these grew alarmingly. But he questioned this too. Why detective novels? Did they symbolise the fact that he was searching? If so, for what? Was he concealing some crime? If so, again, what? Against whom? Perhaps himself.

Not that he read only detective novels. He sought a solution in physics again, and for a while this held out hope. Dr Steinway G. Ganger allowed parallel worlds. A doppel particle could exist in both or several or even in two places in the same world – and all this at the same time. A person could be seen as a collection of such particles. And suppose the same person met themselves – something theoretically possible? There was, of course, no reason why two doppels should know or even recognise each other – on the contrary. (This, as aforesaid, was eventually to be proved.)

Kurt Gödel went further. In fact, his solution to Einstein's field equation also allowed time travel and this let him argue that time was unreal and therefore that our space-time- oriented world was also not real. Michael often felt totally unreal. So to feel unreal was a legitimate reaction, indeed the only legitimate reaction, to reality. I feel I am not, therefore I am.

But despite such momentary reassurances, his feelings of inner chaos continued to increase. He had the feeling sometimes, as he wrestled with his collections, that he had only created an outer representation of his state of mind. More and more he only went out late at night to avoid seeing people or being seen by them. But he similarly loathed the furtive way of life that this entailed – the creeping, the fear. Months passed – once nine months – before he could face his grandmother, despite her continued threats to visit him again. He was often very lonely. Sometimes for a whole month together he copied into his journal the same single phrase. 'I have locked myself into a dungeon and I cannot find the key.'

The only good thing in his life, the only *sane* thing, was Elfreda.

Darling Elfreda,

One of the things I loved most about you was your playfulness – your jokes, your *games*. I wonder whether we haven't been apart long enough now. Surely our love has been tested and not found wanting? My life is often dark at the moment. Very dark. I need your games and your lightness to brighten it. To lighten my dark, sad life.

About four years ago, perhaps more, I thought you'd come. The bell went – but alas, it wasn't you. It was a friend from the old days. Sadly deteriorated, I'm afraid to say. As far as I could see she'd sought me out in my eyrie to abuse me and seduce me in equal measure.

I sometimes have a fantasy that we meet in some garden, late at night, in our mackintoshes. It is raining.

We are naked under our mackintoshes. And then, Elfreda, you open your mackintosh. I open mine . . .

Goodnight, Elfreda. If you get this, come as soon as you can. Why not collect a mackintosh on the way? I'll pay. Just a game, my sweetheart.

All my love. Oh, all all *all* my love, my sweet, my precious, my *playful* sweet Elfreda.

57

Ivan met Rawbones again about six years before he went to Chicago. It was in the south of Spain, in a restaurant near the bullring in Malaga. Ivan was alone, having got rid of the party he was conducting for the evening. (Two nights later, in that same restaurant, he was to be challenged at arm fighting again.)

Rawbones looked much older. His lined face, unshaven and as coarse as a goat skin, was now a curious green-mauve-red, contrasting oddly with the red tablecloth. He looked like a very ancient, overactive lizard, a thousand-year-old chameleon beginning to have difficulty changing colour. He behaved as if they had been apart about a day and, just as he'd guessed he would even during their first long parting, so did Ivan.

RAWBONES: 'What are you doing here? Quick, come and join me. How marvellous! I was about to leave. Have a drink. *Señor – una autros botella de vino tinto. Para me, tambien, una cognac grande.*'

IVAN: 'How are you? You look –'

RAWBONES: (interrupting) 'Drunk. I've been drunk for a week, or a month. I can't remember. Perhaps it's a year.'

Immediately, Ivan remembered. He'd never seen anyone who could get and remain as drunk as Rawbones and still continue to – well, continue. Everything about him, every cell in his body, became drunk: his eyelids, his teeth, his clothes. Although he could still function, he became completely unpredictable, like a huge overloaded computer that had started to blow fuses or a dangerous bull two thirds of the way through the corrida. He would talk very carefully, listening and nodding, or else talk wildly and often nonsensically; he would become aggressive or sentimental or amorous or incoherent or stupid or obstinate or despairing or furious – or brilliant. There would be sudden incandescent magnesium flares of talk, cascades, Catherine wheels. He would pass out. Ten minutes later he'd start up, apparently completely sober, although stinking of alcohol, and have another bottle. He would gobble enormous meals, eating anything to hand – whole cheeses, loaves. He could go on for days on end. Companions would suddenly start to vomit uncontrollably or be taken to hospital. Rawbones would move on to find fresh partners. No one had ever lasted the course.

'I'm here with Jean, my wife,' said Rawbones, rolling one of his black bootaces to the tightness of fuse wire. 'My fourth wife. Or is it my fifth? Yes, fifth. Some one finds oneself not counting as wives. We've got two magnificent rooms right on the sea. Two steps and you're in. I'm painting an enormous picture of the room. We can't leave. We haven't any money to pay the rent. I'll leave them a painting or two. You'd love it, Ivan. In the morning there are French letters all along the shore like the ghosts of cocks.'

At the end of one of these nights Ivan would remember nothing except the sensation of forgotten revelations, lost but momentous insights and intimacy. He would leave (or be helped to leave) for bed and unconsciousness, vaguely aware that Rawbones was on the telephone to the next person or ordering a taxi.

That night, in Malaga, quite late on, the arena scattered with snipped bootlaces signalling for another bottle, Rawbones suddenly said, 'I've made the most extraordinary discovery.'

'What?' said Ivan.

'Fucking is the only thing that matters. I don't mean one of the things, or an important thing, but the *only* thing. Randiness is next to godliness. Randiness *is* godliness. Do you know what Wilkes said? I'm reading a book about marriage, not that *that's* anything to do with sex, but it quotes Wilkes. Wilkes said, "Life can little else supply/But a few good fucks and then we die." '

He looked very serious for a moment, squinting slightly as a wave of alcohol must have washed across the cortex. Then he repeated it. 'Life can little else supply/But a few good fucks and then we die.'

'Is that all you do?' said Ivan.

'What d'ya mean?' said Rawbones, rather belligerently.

'I mean, is that all you do – fuck?'

'All I do?' said Rawbones, with a bitter laugh. 'You must be joking. Jean hasn't let me *near* her for three months. *Nada*. I love her – can't you understand that?'

'Of course I can,' said Ivan, 'But you said that all that mattered was fucking, that's all.'

'Fucking doesn't matter a *fuck*,' said Rawbones. 'You can love someone without fucking them. You love them more if you don't fuck them.'

'Well, I know that too,' said Ivan, becoming impatient. 'It's simply that you're contradicting yourself. I don't understand you.'

Rawbones stared at him, his face congested, swaying a little even though he was sitting down. When he spoke, his voice had altered, become offhand, distant.

'Don't you?' he said. 'I just want to be liked. I thought that was the clue to everybody.'

58

The moment that saved Michael came about in rather an extraordinary way.

Partly because his twenty-nine stone now meant movement was quickly exhausting, partly because that very bulk itself meant the bending and close peering needed for accurate analysis and description were difficult, indeed, in the close confines of the ridiculously small lavatory in the Drayton Gardens flats, next to impossible, Michael had taken to using a chamber pot. That is to say, a bucket.

The regret at despatching, he imagined to be universal. With him it was a sadness, a sense of loss and waste, that had roots so deep he couldn't begin to discern their origins – only register their tug. It was one morning when he was consigning a particularly splendid specimen to oblivion that he suddenly thought – it came with the thunderclap force of a revelation – I don't have to.

He didn't have to. It could be preserved. And in that instant – in the next few minutes – the whole kaleidoscope of his life was shaken into an entirely new pattern. Or rather, in a series of unconnected flashes, rapid mental leaps, revelation after revelation, he now suddenly saw the pattern that had always been there. He was a collector who collected himself. It had begun with his hair. And what else motivated other collectors if it was not self? Self-love disguised, it was true, but self-love none the less, spreading out and transforming objects, invading them, making them glow, for a Getty, say, with a peculiarly Getty glow. And, really, was it not a considerable part of all art, this celebration of self, albeit at a remove again, as reconstructed memory, reused experience, as reaction of sensibility? To that extent, the collecting of himself neat, straight, was closer to the bedrock of art.

And closer in another way, since unconscious. The fact that *he* had collected everything, the mountains of paper, the multitudinous objects, the fact that the unacknowledged quotations were *his* choice, meant that Duchamp-like he'd inevitably stamped it with the pattern of himself. And this explained that impression he'd increasingly had that his collections somehow mirrored his state of mind. It meant also that he had already, as it were, 'written' a great deal – was almost, as Drayton Gardens filled up, at the end of his work – and in this he resembled Proust, the architecture of whose great book, whose book itself, was not apparent until the revelatory moment at its end. Of course, he was not Proust, yet Michael saw he had not been entirely wrong in thinking in terms of a book. *I* am my book, he thought. He had achieved what he'd set out to do without realising he was doing it.

And the marvellous thing about his revelation was that it necessitated no alteration in his way of life. It was simply a different way of looking at it.

Except that his life did change. He took over the basement flat, and this time the sense of peace and space was considerable. Here he had installed the shelves and racks for an even larger, even, in the dark stillness, a calmer and more restful series of meditation rooms. The frenzy left his collecting. He even found he could throw things out, though usually only scraps. He threw out the second Baby Belling. He gave up reading detective novels.

And he decided to devote the time that emerged from his new relaxed state to Elfreda. He realised he'd neglected her for years.

59

Ivan remembered that time in Venice. She had been on top of him. Ivan had reached out and – against habit – turned off the light. She was arched back in a muscular arc, ebony, a black woman, a savage, then bearing down, sliding down, grinding her teeth once. When it was over, they lay in each other's arms, slippery with sweat, panting in the darkness.

Ivan was almost asleep, Rose-Anne still across him, when she whispered in his ear, 'Why did you turn the light out?'

Ivan said, 'I can see you better in the dark.'

60

She influenced him, thank God, even though they were so far apart. Sometimes Michael had a curious feeling, a gooseflesh of the neurons, an echo – just as two ganger photons can influence each other from parallel universes or across the ether when billions of light years apart.

But there were also terrible times.

He thought that there must be something about him that kept Elfreda away. Perhaps it was physical. She had commented then on his thinness. Surely he had rectified that? Unless – was he now too fat?

But of course it would be something she disliked *then*, all those years ago. Perhaps he had failed to express his love. Women minded, apparently. Yet had he not rectified that too, with his letters? 'Darling Elfreda, Darling Elfreda, darling, darling, darling . . .'

At other times he tortured and yet excited himself with terrible fantasies; Elfreda unfaithful, him a witness, face against the glass, clinging to a ledge. Elfreda ogling, drinking, hotting herself up. He could just see the excited creature, pelvic bones flying through her dress. Elfreda *in flagrante*, at it, on the job. Grinding his teeth, Michael imagined what he'd do to her, to her man – or was it her dog? Or the edge of her sink?

What did she look like now? She'd been, what? Ten years older than he? She'd be in her late sixties, skin like a sloughed-off snake. He didn't want this raddled, sixth-hand Elfreda, screwed to a ravelling. He wanted them to come together like two youthful top gymnasts.

Like a medieval monk fighting with the devil, wrestling to banish lascivious dreams and temptations of hideous, fascinating coarseness, Michael would eventually wrench himself free of these nightmares.

Their congress would be above all this – or beyond it; something unearthly, undulating, above all aquatic, the congress of two lithe, playful young conger eels. He measured himself carefully all over and rang Lillywhite's.

'I'm sorry, sir, we do stock raincoats but we don't have one in those dimensions.'

'Can you make one?'

'One moment, sir.'

Long pause. Michael rapidly chain-smoked two and a half cigarettes.

'Sorry to keep you waiting, sir. It's not usual, but I understand it could be done. It would be expensive.'

'Money is no object,' said Michael.

61

Rawbones was always moving. He couldn't stay anywhere more than five months, perhaps six. He'd take the same few possessions, increasingly battered, and stick them around. They gave him the feeling that fundamentally he never moved.

He always loved the new place passionately, the more squalid the better. (In the same way he loved new people passionately, and loved them the more if they were in desperate straits or in despair.)

It didn't, therefore, surprise Ivan to find Rawbones living in New York with a new young wife.

They drank a good deal, but Rawbones this time became much drunker than Ivan. The stamina seemed to have gone out of Rawbones's drinking. He reeled about as they walked back to his apartment.

He wanted to piss. He emptied a pail of garbage and (surprising refinement) used that. He required support. Ivan listened to the sound of the piss hitting the pail like the milk on the farm. The delicate crystalline structure of the foaming bubbles on the top of the milk. The warmth of it. The thick veins on the udder of the cow. The sweet smell of it, the foamy, milky smell in the cold early morning. Little Na pouring it into a pan.

He turned his head away.

Rawbones kept lying down in the gutter. He lay on his back refusing to get up. 'Oh, for Chrissake! Get up, will you,' said Ivan, hauling the sodden painter to his feet.

Rawbones lay down for the eighth time. Ivan stood looking at him. He knew he would continue to like Rawbones, more or less no matter what. What was friendship? Rawbones was generous and kind, there were those magnesium-flare moments . . . but it had nothing to do with that. It was more like love.

Perhaps it was love. Something that happened when they finally made the apartment suggested it was, though this only occurred to Ivan afterwards.

'I want ya to sleep with Cathy,' said Rawbones in a slurred voice as they came to the door. Ivan was now actually carrying him.

'Why?'

'No, no, I absolutely insist. I *wan'* you to. I wan' you to fuck lovely Cathy for me, for us – doan thank me. It's a pleasure, a real pleasure. I insist – go on – have her!'

Cathy was a strapping, golden-haired, buck-toothed, freckled, rather coarse-looking American girl about forty-five years younger than Rawbones. She was healthy and vigorous and smelt faintly of fresh horse. (Here lies buried the real birthplace of the famous Uni-Vac glue-extruder top.)

But it was some time later, thinking of Cathy, that he suddenly saw that having them both make love to the same girl was the nearest Rawbones could manage to making love to Ivan himself. And vice versa.

62

The mackintosh or rain cape arrived. It looked like the skin of some giant aquatic bat or aerial whale.

The endless permutations and variations and repetitions of thinking about Elfreda had worn a Grand Canyon in his brain.

To love someone for twenty-nine, or thirty-five or forty years. To be tempted by other women, invited to go with them, even to 'sleep' with them – and yet *still* to love her. Was that not something?

At least she was a secure torment. It was a form of fidelity, even marriage.

Darling Elfreda
I can't forget you. I don't know what to do or which way to turn. You are always in my arms and will be until I die. Until we both die. Do what you must – but don't forget.

63

Rose-Anne staring out of the window at the rain, shoulders hunched, tense with misery.

She had begun to say 'Are you all right?' more and more frequently, her face 'concerned'. He realised this was a reproach, a continual reminder of her great love which he didn't acknowledge by being insufficiently 'all right'.

Yet even then there had been things that brought them together. Her late miscarriage was one. They were united in love of the rejected foetus. Ivan put her in the most expensive room and filled it with flowers.

The second day, when things still hung in the balance, a telegram arrived from Rawbones. A haemorrhage. Would Ivan please come?

'I'll tell him I can't,' said Ivan.

'No, you must go,' insisted Rose-Anne. 'Don't worry about me. I'll be fine, hopefully.' She gave a brave little smile.

'Are you sure? He's got dozens of friends.'

'I know how important he is to you,' she persisted. 'I wouldn't want to come between you. I'll be fine, honestly,' she reiterated.

'But – ' said Ivan.

'Now don't argue, darling, I insist.' Rose-Anne smiled sweetly, tossing her head.

64

About this time Michael developed a persistent little dry cough that wouldn't go away. It sounded odd, coming from his huge, corpulent, damp frame, as if a wizened old dwarf had taken up residence inside him.

He thought it was probably an anxiety symptom and took to spending longer periods in the meditation rooms of the basement, with their now quite numerous rows of silent, opalescent, golden jars, some of which were rather cloudy. His train of thought at the start of these visits was invariably the same. He thought how extraordinary it was that he had not struck on this earlier, at Cambridge, say, or even at Inkpen. So much had been needlessly lost.

He had a similar invariable sequence when he lowered a fresh specimen, using the fine Wordingham Georgian silver sugar tongs, into a demijohn of formaldehyde. He thought how Henrietta had planted the idea, how it had grown in him, seeming more and more relevant, and how in the end it had become the most obvious thing in the world. He next remembered how he had resisted her invitation to the bath and that led him to contemplate thirty-five or forty-five or fifty or however many years it was of continuous love, which led him in turn to think again that however painful it sometimes, even always was, at least it was a secure torment, that this was a form of fidelity and so, in effect, a common-law marriage. Elfreda was his wife.

He followed these identical sequences not once, but hundreds of times. And there were dozens of other sequences, also continually followed. There was a sequence set off when he cleaned his remaining teeth. Another sequence set off when he opened a tin of sardines. A sequence in the bath. A sequence when he set out for Calvino's. Searching among the piled manuscripts of his journal, he would come across an entry written five years before. He would find that he had passed a morning more or less identical to one last week, itself identical to one three months before and indeed to countless other mornings stretching into the remote past. Weeks passed with hardly any alteration in routine and pattern, without a new thought, new reaction, new emotion, or even new physical sensation. It often seemed that time had stopped passing.

Michael had a fantasy that everyone would be compelled to keep an intimate personal journal by law. Some would be several million words long. All journals would be preserved and, at death, handed over to be stored in huge central buildings. There were people who spent their entire lives in these buildings, reading.

He ran quickly through this fantasy every time he sat down to write his journal.

65

Some natures cannot appreciate, only regret.

In the end, Ivan learned that this was the case with Rose-Anne.

The incident that started it – he could still remember it quite clearly many years later – took place in a wagon-lit from Paris to London. Ivan had surfaced to find that he had left his reading lamp on. A faint light from below showed that Rose-Anne had done the same. Ivan leant out and looked down at his sleeping wife.

Her face had been completely transformed. All the tiny muscles about the eyes had relaxed, allowing the eyeballs to swell against the delicate silk-thin tissue of their lids, the eyes themselves to widen. Her pulled-in mouth, too, had opened like a small, pink parachute. Her whole face had softened and moistened and seemed to glow. Although he had seen her asleep many times, he had never seen her like this. He was seeing her as nature had meant her to be.

Suddenly Rose-Anne's lids lifted and they were looking at each other. At once, her pale skin seemed to ripple, to quiver, to shrink – and she was herself again. On an impulse of pity, Ivan reached down his hand to her, but her eyes had already closed.

This extraordinary but minute moment had sparked off the explosion that was to blow them apart.

'What were you thinking when you were looking at me in the train?' Rose-Anne had said suddenly when they were going to bed the following night. Journeys always made her tense. She had drunk rather a lot and still held a large whisky nightcap in her hand.

'I'm not certain,' said Ivan, not wishing to tell her exactly what he'd thought. 'Yes, I remember. I was thinking how beautiful you looked.'

'Nonsense,' said Rose-Anne. 'Don't lie to me.'

'I'm not lying.'

'Do you think I'm a perfect fool? I know perfectly well what you were feeling. You were thinking, *God*, she looks ugly! You've thought that for years.'

'That's not true,' said Ivan, astonished at this outburst.

'Don't interrupt me,' said Rose-Anne, who was trembling violently. She swallowed half her whisky. 'I've bottled all this up so long I've thought I'd go mad. Do you think I haven't seen it all? From the start you've treated me like dirt. The first night we went out, you said, "I suppose I ought to fuck you." Was it so hard? Was it your *duty*? What about me? What do you think I *am* – a sex object? Well, I'm not. I'm a person, a person with thoughts and wishes and feelings. No, don't interrupt. You never let me talk. Later on, quite soon, you said I *couldn't* talk. Yes, you did – you said I could only talk with my cunt or something equally disgusting. Then that party – you've forgotten of course, typically male – at Putney. You didn't talk to me all evening. You thought I was a bore. Well, frankly, I thought *you* were a bore. You've never loved me. Do you love me? Go on, *do* you? Do you love me? You see. A woman needs to be told she's loved. You can't answer. You hate the sight of me. Do you remember when you turned the lights out in Venice? You were into some sex-symbol fantasy, no doubt. You've spent all our marriage, these last five years, trying to humiliate me and make me feel inadequate. That meal we gave when we got back from our honeymoon. OK, I don't expect you to pretend you like something if you don't. But *in front of other people*! At least I'm loyal. Do you remember in Italy that time, at Castellina? How you made me dance alone? I was the laughing stock. Even Italian men don't treat their women like that. Why have you always had jobs that take you away? You've never remembered my birthday – except twice, on the wrong day. Oh, God, I hate you! I could cry. I often cry and you don't notice. In the night. And the final injury, the real injury, was when you made me pregnant and then left me when I had a miscarriage. At my most vulnerable, you left me. A trial separation. I want a trial separation. You've *ruined* me.'

Since Rose-Anne's feelings and emotions had all been destroyed, she had become a dealer in second-hand emotions. For this reason she was a mistress of cliché. And the tremendous cliché of her rage revealed – indeed, actually was – the skeleton of her emotional and married life. It was a structure of grievance.

The second thing Ivan had noticed was his reaction when she had screamed at him to tell her if he loved her. He suddenly realised he hadn't the faintest idea what she meant. From this period there entered his life another of his key phrases: the springs of love are frozen. Though whether it applied to himself or Rose-Anne he was never certain.

All this, of course, took place many years in the past, whatever that means – the head having only the haziest grasp of this linear concept.

66

There was one sentence that always struck Michael from the book from which he'd copied many sentences: '. . . beat life like a dinner bell, yet there is one hour that won't ring – the hour of disentanglement.'

Did this mean someone else had loved as he had loved, suffered as he had suffered? He didn't believe it.

Michael knew that it was possible to think of the same woman every single day, many times a day, for fifty-seven years – or was it a hundred? It was also possible to be miserable every day for 157 years. Did the bell-beater know that?

He began to be haunted by the fear that he might *never* see Elfreda again. His grandmother was now nearly ninety-seven. Although her mind was as active as ever, her body was very feeble, little more than a collection of arthritic knots. She, too, might die soon. With his usual combination of reactions, Michael heaved himself into a visit.

Standing at the window of her bedroom, he was astonished to see that the council houses of Inkpen were now within a hundred yards of the vicarage.

'Why did you let them build so close, Granny?' he said. 'This is absurd. You're more or less in the village now.'

'How could I help it?' croaked Mrs Wordingham. 'You kept on turning out the tenants, you kept on telling me you needed more money for your book. I had to live.'

'I see. Yes. I hadn't taken it in.'

'How is the book? Have you finished writing it yet?'

'It isn't exactly a question of writing,' said Michael absently, still looking with some guilt at the advancing houses. 'That is – yes. Yes, it's nearly finished.'

'What will you write next?'

'Nothing.'

Mrs Wordingham was propped up among five or six large pillows in her large, hot bedroom. The central heating alone must cost about a council house a year. Her legs didn't raise a ripple on the wide sea of their eiderdown. They might have been amputated. She was nearly bald. One eye was milky with a cataract.

After a while, 'That's a nasty cough, Michael,' she said. 'You smoke too much. You must take some linctus. There used to be some in the bathroom.'

There was another pause. His grandmother let her head loll and closed her eyes. Suddenly she opened them. What she said nearly caused Michael to faint.

'Wasn't it odd, that woman writing to me after all these years?'

'What woman?'

'That woman – what was her name? A Pole – the one you ask about.'

Michael sat, almost fell, on to the end of her bed. His mouth went dry and his heart fibrillated. His cough rasped uncontrollably. 'At last,' he whispered. 'Do you mean Elfreda Smitten?'

'That's it,' said his grandmother. 'Wasn't it strange?'

Michael stood up and began to walk agitatedly up and down, groping for his cigarettes. 'Why didn't you tell me this? When did she write? Where's the letter? Was there an address?'

'Don't stump about like that,' said his grandmother. 'You're making the room shake. I did tell you.'

'No, you didn't.'

'I put it in my last letter, the one about the electric blanket.'

'I never read letters,' said Michael impatiently, running his nails down his cheek and pulling on his cigarette.

'What?' said his grandmother.

'I don't like letters,' said Michael. 'I keep them, but never read them. I hope you haven't thrown Elfreda's letter away.'

'What do you mean, "never"?' said his grandmother, beginning to pluck at her sheets. 'Do you mean you have never read *any* letters? The whole of your life?'

'Yes,' said Michael. He went over to a chest of drawers upon which lay a number of papers.

'None?' repeated his grandmother faintly. 'How have you survived?'

'Survived? Perfectly well. I can't find it here. I have a solicitor. I still use Halsey Pinkerton. I have a GP.'

'No, no,' said his grandmother. 'I don't mean that. I mean how – what I mean is – I mean, have you never read any of my letters?'

'No,' said Michael. He turned from the chest of drawers. 'It's not here.'

His grandmother was staring at him. At last she said, 'I'm too old to face unpleasant facts any more. I shan't believe you.'

'For goodness' sake, Granny,' said Michael. 'Can't you see this is an emergency? Where is that letter?'

'I can't see why you want it,' said Mrs Wordingham. 'Especially as you apparently don't read letters. It wasn't in the least interesting. It'll probably be in that basket on the chair by the window.'

With fat, feverish fingers Michael scrabbled through bills, brochures, buttons, bottles of pills, scissors, reels of cotton, spare spectacles, letters from this and that. When he found it he recognised it at once. Love's clairvoyance. It was an address in Battersea.

'I'll have to go now, Granny. I'm sorry.'

'But you've only just got here.'

'I know,' said Michael, clutching the letter, bending to kiss one of the ample spaces of pink, hot scalp. 'I'll come again soon.'

'Soon,' said his grandmother. 'I know your "soon". I'll be a hundred and four. I'll be dead by then.'

Her voice, frail but penetrating, floated after him down the corridor. 'Don't forget the linctus.'

67

Coming home.

How odd the English were! Ivan had forgotten this in his years away. Their reticence, for instance. Professor Osaka Itagaki had explained this to him once in the common room at Chicago University. (The standard of chit-chat had been alarmingly high. Sometimes he had been reminded of Alexis. 'Itty' had been particularly deft.) English reticence was the same as the studied understatement of tenth-century Japan. In a society where everything was known, anything overexplicit came like a thunderclap, was unneeded and exhausting. In Russia and America, with wide divergences and quite different class systems, openness was essential.

But was it home? In England, at first, he'd felt Russian. In Paris, English. In America, European. In the end he didn't feel he belonged to any country, not even Russia. Nevertheless, if someone said 'Russia' or 'Russian', Ivan instantly felt happy and had an absurd sense of communion, of pride, or had, quite often, to feel defensive.

When it was impossible to return, it had been easy to dismiss or forget these rare flashes. Recently, however . . . He had begun to think of little Na again. How old would she be? In her nineties, he supposed. Surely she would be dead? He wished he'd seen her just once more. The smell of hot corn, just cut.

Rawbones rang up.

'Ivan? I feel terrible. I'm on the wagon. Let's meet for a drink. Do you know the Wheatsheaf?'

It had been the voice of an old man. Ivan suddenly wished he'd said no.

68

It wasn't raining but it looked like rain. That is, there was some cloud in the sky. Not that it mattered. He would have worn the mackintosh/rain cape/aquatic bat uniform if she'd been in the Sahara.

Voluminous as it was, he could scarcely buckle the belt across his stomach. Michael took it off. Then he took all his clothes off and rebuckled himself in. What the hell.

He walked over to the mirror. He turned this way and that. Not bad. Not bad at all. Slim, too – the belt had a corseting effect, to a degree. Strange how erotic rubber felt to him.

He'd wait a little longer, till bathtime. He didn't want to risk arrest. But in Edna Street, once inside the door, he'd fling the cape aside. All would be revealed. Everything. His tender bleeding heart.

'Oh, my love, my love,' intoned Michael, humming a refrain. 'I'm coming at last, my love, my love, at last I'm coming . . .'

69

When Ivan reached the Wheatsheaf, Rawbones had already – it was twelve noon – reached a stage where he couldn't have got on a wagon if it had pulled up beside him and let down a lift.

Yet, miraculously, he could still function. 'Look at that, Ivan,' he said, extending a hand the colour and texture of Bombay duck, sprouting a clutch of age-spotted, nicotine-yellow fingers. The fingers were trembling and dancing. It looked as if Rawbones were trying to type a letter after a terrible fright. 'Some days it's not how much you drink that stops the shakes but precisely *what* you drink. You have to find the exact mix. It can take all day.'

There was about two inches left in the bottle of red wine beside him.

'What is the key today?' said Ivan. 'Would you like to change to beer?'

Rawbones swayed, concentrating, staring at the bottle, looking across to the bar. 'I think I'll try a triple Drambuie,' he said. 'That's done the trick in the past.'

Ivan bought a pint of bitter and the Drambuie. Rawbones took the glass and emptied it in one gulp. Then he filled it with the rest of the wine.

'Do you know anywhere to live, Ivan?' he said. 'We really need only a very large bedroom, where I can paint, and somewhere to piss and shit. Kitchen's not necessary. I've discovered you can live without eating. *Virtually*. A sausage now and again.'

'No,' said Ivan. 'I'll see what I can do. Where are you now?'

'Tooting. Hell on earth. And the landlords! The land*ladies* in particular! You'd've thought after all these centuries, landladies would have learnt they can't always be paid on the dot. Damn this fucking cigarette!' After three more attempts he managed to get flame and tip together long enough for combustion. He looked at it waving about in his shaking fingers. 'You know, I'll tell you what I think's required – a sodding great brandy.'

While this was going down, Rawbones said, 'The difficulty about moving is all my paintings. You can't just slip the painter and glide away in the night. It's pantechnicon work. Sylvia – you've met Sylvia? She's my – let me think. How many times have I been married? Have you ever noticed, no matter how many times you marry, you always marry the same woman? You think, Thank God, *this* time I haven't got a neurotic. Then, six months later – bang, crash, sob – you're right back to square one. Same old neurotic, different name. But what was I saying? Money. Yes, dear old Sylvia couldn't earn a penny to save her fucking life. Not a farthing, if farthings still exist. But it's all my sodding paintings. Do you know, I was working it out. I've only sold one painting in the last ten years.'

'That's nonsense,' said Ivan. 'I've bought at least three myself.'

'Friends don't count,' said Rawbones. 'Not that I'm not grateful. You saved my life each time. No, this was an unsolicited, off-the-cuff, off-the-street, straightforward, bona fide buy – except that I very slightly lowered the already ridiculously low price. And I haven't even delivered it. Now there *is* a girl – the one that bought it. You ought to meet her. What's your marital status at the moment, Ivan?'

'No status,' said Ivan. 'Divorced. I'm completely free – more or less.'

'Well, I'll introduce you to Sofka. Just what you need. Do you know, I've discovered the most astounding and marvellous thing. There are girls who actually prefer, who actually *fancy* old men.'

Ivan had felt himself go cold. He could feel gooseflesh at the back of his neck. 'What did you say she was called? Did you say Sofka?'

'Sofka. As a matter of fact, she doesn't know this, but I've had her on ice for several years. That's why I never delivered the painting. But I'm too old for that sort of thing, even if she did fancy me. I'll give her to you. The number's at home. Give me a ring.'

During the next week Ivan fell in love. He wouldn't have believed it possible, given the rather slender grounds. But he'd once read, in one of the American psychoanalytic journals that lay thickly on the table at the Think Tank, about the case of a man who'd fallen in love with a woman's shadow.

He thought of Sofka the entire time. He rang Rawbones repeatedly. He was never in the pub whose number he'd given. How old was she? At one time, anyone under fifty was a girl to Rawbones. Now Ivan guessed that all women were girls. He decided she was twenty-nine. He was old enough to be her father. She wouldn't mind. He became filled with love; at the same time he was as light as air; he floated, suspended from champagne bubbles. They would marry. He would take her to Russia.

Finally, late one evening, Rawbones was in the pub.

'I can't hear you,' he shouted. 'What number? There's rather a racket here.'

'Sofka,' yelled Ivan. 'That girl you told me about.'

'Sofka?' shouted Rawbones. 'Who's Sofka? Oh yes, Sofka. I didn't know you knew her.'

Every time he heard the name Sofka, Ivan felt ill with desire. 'Her telephone number,' he said hoarsely. He found it difficult to breathe. His love was strangling him. 'Give me her telephone number.'

'I can't hear what you're saying,' shouted Rawbones. 'Come to 172 Dradnor Street. It's behind Tooting Bec station. Come tomorrow afternoon. Not too early. Sylvia and I are late risers.'

It was clear from a glance that Rawbones was not there. The long room, into which Ivan had finally managed to explain his way, smelt of stale drink and cigarettes and was stacked with paintings. There were also the Kelim (now half a Kelim), the tea tray from Morocco (all colour gone), the carved wooden head of Christ and the other things Ivan remembered at Cambridge, Malaga, New York and all the other places Rawbones, Bedouin-like, had pitched them. There was a large unmade bed in the middle of the end wall with two full white chamber pots, one on each side of it. The liquid in the pot on the left-hand side – a rich peat colour, a liquid for making whisky with – had its surface dotted with little black boats, the spindly ends of Rawbone's roll-ups. On an easel was the 'work in hand'. It appeared to be, but the light was bad, the so far headless body of a naked man standing against a pale-blue background.

'Who is this Sofka woman?' said Sylvia. She lit a cigarette, and Ivan noticed that she too smoked the Albanian bootlaces. 'I've never heard of her. All that he complains about is that he hasn't sold a painting.'

'He didn't tell me her other name. Just Sofka.'

'He probably didn't know it. If he's bothered to keep her number at all she'll be under "S" anyway.'

Sylvia handed him a battered exercise book, alphabetically organised.

Sofka: 627 1176, 589 5001, 356 3734. There was a huge randy question mark against her name.

'Which painting shall I take?'

'I wish you'd take the lot.'

Ivan selected the smallest he could find – a five-foot by four-foot hillscape. Four unrelated figures (Rawbones's characters never had eyes) cavorted on the green mountain.

'How is he?'

'Well, when he's sober – desperate. He's obsessed with not having sold anything. The other day he said he'd never really properly sold a single painting in his entire life.'

'But it's such rubbish,' said Ivan. 'I told him. I've bought three myself. Much admired. I'd have bought more, only you have to live in a hangar. Why doesn't he count friends buying?'

'God knows. The trouble is it's getting impossible to get through to him. He's hardly ever sober. He didn't come back last night.'

'Remind him about van Gogh.'

'Poor Sam,' said Sylvia, running her hand through her grey hair. She sat down on the bed. She looked sad and beaten and about a hundred. 'He's not van Gogh.'

Desire makes cowards of us all. Ivan waited till the following evening so that he could have two large whiskies before telephoning. The third number was answered.

'Hello.'

'Is that Sofka?' Ivan squeaked, suffocated by love.

'What?' said the lovely voice. 'I couldn't – but yes, that's me.'

Ivan cleared his throat. 'I'm sorry. I breathed in something.' He coughed violently again. 'I am sorry. You don't know me. My name is Ivan. I'm a friend of Sam Raeburn's.

Apparently you bought a painting off him once and he never gave it to you. He wanted me to drop it off.'

'How amazing! I'd given that up long ago. It must have been – Christ, I don't know. Years ago. I was a student. But yes, fine, great.'

Her voice was a low seductive burr, with an attractive gurgle in it. Ivan thought he detected a trace of Russia in its rich timbre.

'Tomorrow evening?'

'OK. Do you know the address? 53a Halton Road. It's off Canonbury Square.'

All day Ivan was suspended from his golden bubbles. They wafted him, intoxicated, along Halton Road, the hillscape a postcard under his arm.

She was beautiful. There was no question about that. Beautiful and clearly Slavonic. She glowed. She shone. Her blue eyes twinkled. Ivan wanted to crunch her in his arms that second.

'Ivan Khuchevsky. I'm sorry. I only know you as Sofka.'

'Innes,' she said. Contralto, almost a bass. 'And I *thought* you said Sofka. It's Sonya, actually.'

'*Sonya?*' said Ivan, staring at her.

In that instant he had the most extraordinary feeling. He suddenly felt very heavy; the huge, ungainly painting, too, put on several stone and wrenched itself free from his armpit. With a single ripple, like Rose-Anne in the train, the woman opposite him became quite plain. Ivan felt his love drain out of him and vanish.

Terrified she might notice, he immediately asked her out to supper.

But the lesson of the experience was perfectly obvious. The Great Love of his life, really the only love, had after all been Sofka. He had been in love with her ever since that brief time in Ruibinsk. At first it seemed ridiculous that a Great Love could be based on an acquaintance that had lasted only a few dozen hours. A moment's reflection made it clear that, of course, it was precisely and only those particular loves that could possibly become Great or that had a chance of lasting intact for thirty years. With a single bound, he joined the ranks of Dante, Petrarch and Kane.

But this realisation was accompanied by one less flattering. It suddenly seemed to Ivan that he had never really possessed or been possessed by a woman. He was a virgin. All his women had just been used as substitutes for Sofka, or as screens to prevent him seeing her. Perhaps the solution was to go and find her.

70

On Monday 4 August, Michael – complying with one of the conditions of his conditional release – attended the consulting rooms of Dr Ambrose Gordon in Devonshire Place.

There was rather a long silence. Michael ran his nail slowly down his cheek.

At last Dr Gordon smiled at him. He was about seventy with a friendly, rather vulgar face, like a retired and successful second-hand car salesman.

'It's a bit tactless of me to refer to this,' he said, waving some official-looking pieces of paper, 'and I won't again. That side of it really doesn't interest me in the least. There is no morality in the therapist's consulting rooms. Nevertheless –' he glanced down, holding a pair of steel-rimmed spectacles to his eyes – 'I understand you never reached this . . . Elfreda?'

Michael coughed. His cough was continuous now. 'No,' he said. 'At the last moment my heart failed me.'

'But, all the same, you . . .' Dr Gordon read again. 'It must have been quite spectacular. *Very* spectacular. You seem to have had, well, the only word is brainstorm. Some sort of brainstorm.'

Michael coughed. 'Yes,' he said in a low voice. 'That describes it. A brainstorm.'

'Well, that's what we have to get to the bottom of, you and me. We'll have to explore why you feel the need to be so large.

But the most important thing we'll have to find out is why you chose this woman Elfreda. If you did indeed choose her. I see there is no record of her attending the proceedings. Indeed, there seems to be some doubt that she exists. Does she exist?'

'Of course,' said Michael, shifting into sudden irritability as if Dr Gordon had pricked him.

'You're sure? She really, physically exists?'

'*Exists*? Are you mad? We're married.'

'Oh, I *see*. Your wife. Your estranged wife.'

'Not estranged. On the contrary. Not quite wife. Common-law wife. Let me explain.'

It will take many visits, thought Dr Gordon.

71

Three weeks after the Sofka incident, Rawbones killed himself. He blew his brains out in such a way that the resulting matter should have added itself in the appropriate place on the latest painting – the space left free for the head. Typically, perhaps – though it was a tricky shot and one by its nature not susceptible to practice – he missed and went all over the room. A note, scrawled when he was extremely drunk, seemed, by the repetition of the word 'sell', to indicate despair over his painting.

Ivan was shattered by his death. Rawbones had been the first person to make proper friends with him when he'd arrived in England. Counting that moment as a second birth, he had known and loved him all his life. He felt some essential bond tying him to the West, even to life itself, had been broken.

Many people had equally strong feelings. Rawbones's powers of attraction had never completely vanished. The memorial service was packed. Ivan sat at the back, crying. In the pub afterwards he heard two people talking about his friend, their friend.

'What did it matter if he didn't sell? The point was not the paintings, but that he was a painter.'

'Anyway, he *did* sell. I bought one at the last show. In fact, it was nearly a sell-out.'

Sylvia fairly quickly got drunk. 'I'm the seventeenth Mrs Raeburn,' Ivan heard her say. Later, he found himself next to her while she supported herself on the arms of the black-bearded critic Symons. 'The electricity bill is £349,' she was saying tearfully.

Symons was extremely influential, even powerful, and very fat in a rather curious way. Ivan had met him once with Rawbones and had noticed how it looked as if he'd swallowed a chest of drawers. He was pressing his big, angled stomach close to Sylvia. 'The man was a genius,' he said. 'A genius. I shall personally see to it that he has a retrospective at the Hayward.'

Ivan turned away, feeling the tears start in his eyes again. He was reminded of an image that always came to him when he read that So-and-so had been rehabilitated in Russia: a commissar bending and yelling at a skull, 'It's all right! You've been rehabilitated!'

Rawbones and Sonya/Sofka between them were responsible for Ivan's accident. Some days later, going obsessively over these events as usual, he drove at speed up a twisting one-way road. Suddenly, rounding a corner, was an enormous lorry bearing down on him. Without thinking or pausing, Ivan wrenched the wheel and drove through the front window of a restaurant – fortunately closed and empty.

When they finally cut him free, one of the things that surprised the firemen was that the steering wheel had been snapped in two. Ivan was holding one half of it clenched in each hand.

He was unconscious for eighteen hours. When he opened his eyes, he was in a dimly lit hospital room surrounded by screens and connected to drips, wires, an oxygen mask and a urine bag.

Eventually there was a nurse.

'What's happened to me?'

'You had an accident. You have a hairline fracture and bad concussion. Nothing dangerous, but Dr Bantry wants to do some more tests.'

'My head aches.'

'I'll see what you can have.'

To Ivan's surprise, instead of some miraculous elixir administered by needle, he was given two humble paracetamol. His headache diminished.

He rapidly improved over the next two weeks. Drips and wires and the urine bag were dismantled. He wasn't allowed to read but they moved him to a new room. He was made to totter up and down the corridor. He was touched to receive flowers and visits. Francis Wyatt came and several other people from the Reuters office. Sylvia called and, a surprise from the past, Davie McBride.

'Och – so they caught up wi' you in the end, laddie?'

'No, Davie. It was my fault apparently. I'll lose my licence and I hope not worse.'

On the day of the tests, he woke early, nervous and restless.

'What will they do to me? I hate pain.'

'There won't be any pain. You should ask Dr Bantry.'

'What are you going to do with me?'

'You received a very severe blow,' said Dr Bantry, the young man, almost a boy, in charge of his case. 'I need another EEG and I want to do a scan. That's all. You'll feel nothing.'

'Could I have a sedative?' asked Ivan. 'I don't know why, I feel very nervous this morning. A tranquilliser, I mean. This sort of thing is very agitating – wires and scans and drips. I thought they'd stopped scans on pregnant women. I know I'm not a woman, but I imagine the brain is just as sensitive as a foetus. Especially the elderly brain after severe battering. I can feel a lot of nervous energy in my head. I might blow your machine in this state. I respond well to Ativan.'

'No,' said the boy surgeon. 'I'm sorry, but we mustn't have anything interfere with the brain pulses. Try and relax, Mr Khuchevsky –'

'Kooch – Kooch,' Ivan interrupted. 'Not Kuch. Double O, as it were.'

'I'm sorry, Mr Koochevsky. I know just how you feel, but I promise you it's absolutely painless.'

'I don't suppose you do know how I feel,' said Ivan, clutching the edges of the operating table or whatever it was. He'd had a sudden feeling he was about to levitate. 'Have you ever had a scan or an EEG? All who sentence should be sentenced.'

'Try and relax,' said the child prodigy. 'Don't hold on like that. Lie back and relax. Let go.'

'If I let go,' said Ivan, 'I'll hit the ceiling.' But he knew he hadn't said anything. Only his throat had moved.

He didn't burst the EEG machine. Quite the reverse. As it was turned on, he felt a marvellous, beneficent surge of power cleansing him. In a few seconds, his cortex was effervescing; light flowed down his veins so that he could feel himself glowing. He floated an undetectable one millionth of a micromillimetre off the operating slab. *Pulse*, went the power, *pulse*, pause, *pulse* pause *pulse* . . . He was interested, experiencing this long, perhaps endless moment of complete serenity and happiness, to notice that he could see clearly through Dr Bantry's transparent skin and skull to the faintly pulsating outline of his brain inside.

It was many years since he had experienced the extraordinary peace that followed.

Later in the day the young doctor came in to see him.

'There's no further physical damage that we can detect,' he said, sitting matily down on the bed. 'But I think I'll keep you in another day or two, none the less. I'm struck by this. Look.' He unrolled a narrow length of elegantly lined paper for Ivan to see. 'Your EEG,' said Dr Bantry.

Ivan looked at the pathetic, crazy attempts of his brain to communicate. How it must have longed for the power of speech.

'These spikes are suggestive,' said Dr Bantry. 'Do you see what I mean? A slow wave of a third of a second, then a spike. We were getting three or four such episodes a second.'

'Really?' said Ivan politely.

Dr Bantry rolled the scroll of Ivan's brain's enigmatic message up briskly.

'Tell me,' he said, 'have you at any time in your life suffered from epilepsy?'

'No,' said Ivan, suddenly nervous. 'Do you mean my brain has been damaged after all? Am I going to have fits?'

'No, no. I very much doubt it. But I'd like to do some further tests – and these could affect how your accident was regarded. There's a drug, Epilin, I'd like you to take for a couple of days and see how that affects the EEG.'

He unrolled the scroll and studied the hieroglyphs again. Ivan waited. Eventually, Dr Bantry said, 'Of course, it would help to know if you had anything like that as a child. *Petit mal* or anything of that nature? Do you know?'

'No,' said Ivan.

'Could you find out?'

'No,' said Ivan. Then he suddenly felt very peaceful again. 'Yes,' he said, 'I suppose I could try.'

72

Yes, it did take many visits.

On 16 August, in time for the 18 August session, Michael dreamt that he was following an owl on a bicycle. Eventually, he found himself sitting on the owl's knee. Dr Gordon asked him if he noticed anything significant to the dream in the consulting room. Michael, feeling he was in a child's game, looked everywhere but could see nothing. Eventually, Dr Gordon pointed to a small owl clock on the cupboard above his own head. During this session he also said, 'We all have to learn to become our own fathers and mothers.'

'I don't remember my father and mother,' said Michael.

'Are you sure?' said Dr Gordon.

On 25 August and 1 September, Dr Gordon began to learn

something about the nature of Elfreda. The 8th and 15 September were passed in almost total silence. At the end of their session on 22 September, Dr Gordon said, almost dreamily, as if reminding himself of something he was in danger of forgetting, 'The aim of analysis is to put the patient in touch with reality. We have some way to go.' He often came out with gnomic sayings of this sort. Although they sometimes irritated Michael, they stuck in his mind. Perhaps that was why they irritated him, or perhaps that was why they stuck. By 29 September he had dreamt he was climbing a series of cliffs and ravines. He ended up trapped at the bottom of a ravine. There was a cave. He went into it and felt safe.

'What is the cave?' asked Dr Gordon.

Michael coughed and reached for his cigarettes. 'My anus?' he hazarded at last. He was learning the language.

'Perhaps,' said Dr Gordon. He also said, 'Just as each cell contains in the DNA the blueprint of your whole body, so every dream contains your entire psychology – your problems and their solution.'

On 6 October and 12 October, details of his house began to leak out. The meditation rooms. 'I'm a collector,' said Michael. 'I collect myself.' He added, after a pause when Dr Gordon failed to react, 'I am also a book,' and laughed a trifle hysterically.

Dr Gordon did not laugh. The gnomic slogan for this week was, 'I cannot cure you. I can only help you to accept.'

On 20 October – nothing; 27 October – nothing. On 3 November Michael flatly refused to believe a suggestion, or rather a suggested interpretation, Dr Gordon offered. Dr Gordon said, 'It is often very difficult to realise that we are acting in accordance with terrible memories we cannot – will not – recall.'

On 10 November Michael said, 'Do you mean I can't love? Can't even form a relationship? I hate that word.'

'Do you think you can, at the moment?'

'Will I ever be able to?'

'Oh, yes. We haven't got very far yet. We will. You will

dream us there. The dream is the golden gate to the unconscious.'

Writing out his cheque at the end of the session, Michael wanted to say, '*Golden* gate is *right*!' But that week, the week of 17 November, he dreamt of an owl again. This time, though, it was the owl's spectacles that were important. Michael suddenly remembered the woman with spectacles who had haunted his childhood room. He found it very difficult and for some reason painful to recount this memory. He sweated and coughed and had to chain-smoke three cigarettes.

Dr Gordon urged him gently on. 'The analyst has to be a disturber of the peace.'

Finally, Michael finished. He lit a fourth cigarette. 'Do you think she was *real*?' he asked.

'I don't know,' said Dr Gordon. 'Who did she remind you of?'

'I think she was real,' said Michael. 'I think I'll go and ask my grandmother. Would it be important if she was real?'

'Anything you can find out or remember about your childhood is important,' said Dr Gordon. There was a silence. Sometimes Michael thought he could hear the ticking of the owl clock, though it was electric and soundless. 'Try and think who this woman might represent,' said Dr Gordon.

'My mother,' said Michael, not thinking.

'And so?' encouraged Dr Gordon.

At the end of the session, Dr Gordon said, 'That cough's been going on far too long. I thought it was a nervous symptom. It may be, but we should check. I know a very good chap at Guy's. I'll give him a ring this afternoon, and I'll give you a note. You ring him tomorrow. Try and do it before you go to your grandmother – if you *do* go, that is.'

Michael had noticed that on the whole Dr Gordon always tried to let him go on an uplift, encouraged, yet sometimes seemed unable to resist inserting something vaguely disquieting, like his cough this time.

It was then discovered that he had forgotten to bring his chequebook. It irritated Michael that Dr Gordon would think this was significant, and irritated him that Dr Gordon also knew this knowledge would irritate him. He tried to smile unirritably but could only manage a curt 'I'll send it'.

73

Ivan found no difficulty in getting a temporary posting to Moscow.

'Well, it's a bit late, but as you know, you were always supposed to go to Russia for us,' said Francis Wyatt. 'And in fact, with what's going on there now, we need more correspondents.'

'I suppose I'll be all right,' said Ivan. 'Technically, I must still be a deserter from the army.'

'That won't matter. I just hope you'll be careful. Tim Chambers – you've probably met him, Timbo – thinks law and order will completely break down this winter. The past is irrelevant. Anyway, surely you're a naturalised British citizen?'

'Yes,' said Ivan.

Naturalised citizen – as though that were possible.

Ivan's life in the West had often – perhaps always – felt unreal. Looking back, it now seemed like a long preparation for something that had never happened. Perhaps what he'd always been preparing for was his return.

Not that he expected his return would do much good. He'd seen too many expatriates to suppose the wrenched-out roots could take again, the severed nerves rejoin. Nor did he any longer believe in his destiny. The lesson of Boris, the magic powers, even the memory of the events that had given rise to it, had all died years ago.

Except, except . . . he did sometimes wonder, Perhaps I was right after all. Secretly, he still believed some cure lay in Russia – even if it was only something about his health when a child for Dr Bantry. Just as secretly, although he knew Sofka would be old and grey now, even dead, he somehow also thought she would be the young and beautiful girl he had, apparently, always loved. Secretly, he believed he was going to find some deep, healing power that would make permanent the peace he had felt for a few moments when he had said he would go back.

Ivan, that is, had at least four complicated and contradictory reactions to his decision to return to Russia. But the last and most important of these was simple and contradicted nothing. It was just an overwhelming hunger to see once more, before he died, the barns and animals, the huge fields of Taschla. To see the fields, since it would be winter, stretching grey-white and frozen to the horizon. To skate once more upon the ice of the Wiga. To sit and warm himself in front of the big, blue-tiled stove. And to hold, to be held by – oh, please God, let her be alive – his little Na.

74

Mrs Wordingham seemed to have had a *coup de jeunesse*.

'Still not reading letters?' she almost snapped from the billows of her pillows. With her one eye she looked like some very ancient, slightly mad pirate.

'I'm going to try,' said Michael. 'I've been very busy.' He sat down on the massive ship of her bed, causing it to list heavily to starboard. He remembered, as he always remembered when he sat on her bed, how her nightly goodnight-story visits used once to tilt his own small craft. Now she was the child.

'What have you been doing, darling?'

His contretemps with the police had not got into the papers. She knew nothing of that terrible humiliation.

'I've started my autobiography.'

'Oh, darling – how thrilling! How absolutely thrilling! What will you put in? Your career in rugger? An account of your published works, of course. I wouldn't mention the servants, if I were you. You were on the committee of London Zoo, weren't you? And then your trips abroad. Naughty boy not to send post-cards. Your love affairs. Oh, Michael – a packed life!'

Michael stared at her, coughing. So, she'd finally flipped. A *coup de démance*. He suddenly felt old and alone. And did it mean he was too late?

'Listen, Granny,' he said. 'When I was very small, still in the tower room, a woman came to visit me in the middle of the night once. A ghost, I thought. But perhaps she was real. Did my mother wear spectacles?'

'Rosemary? Good heavens, no! She had excellent eyesight. In any case, your mother didn't look after you. Your nanny did.'

'My nanny?' said Michael in astonishment. 'I didn't know I had a nanny. Who was she?'

'Nanny Trudie. You loved her. Such a pity she had to leave. You were very small – barely four.'

'Nanny Trudie? It means nothing to me. Did she have spectacles?'

'I believe she did, now you mention it. I can't really remember. She and your mother didn't really hit it off, but that wasn't why she left. The war was virtually fought single-handed by women.'

'Did you ever hear from her?'

'We kept in touch for a bit. She wanted news of you. I think I heard her son was killed, if she had a son. I believe she had an old father in Israel. What was her name? I rather think she had to go out there and look after him. He was a doctor, I seem to remember. She gave up writing.'

'Is she alive? How old is she?'

'She was a bit younger than me. She'd be ninety or so, if she is alive. Ninety-five, perhaps. I haven't the faintest idea. Goldsmith, *that* was her name. I was trying to remember it. Trudie Goldsmith.'

Michael began to cough. He got up, holding one fat hand in front of his little mouth.

'I think I must try and find her. I wonder if she's still in Israel. Did she write from there?'

'No – as I say, we lost touch. I didn't employ her, you see. I suppose as you get older . . .'

Michael walked up and down. 'I shall have to go. Did you keep her last letter? There might be a sister or something. But no, you never keep things.'

'Go?' said his grandmother, plucking at her sheets irritably. 'Where? Why?'

'To London, to the Israeli embassy. To Israel if necessary.'

'But you can't!' cried his grandmother. 'In any case, how will you pay? If you read letters, you would have read the letter from Pinkerton saying I'm going to have to cut your allowance.'

'I'll let out a room,' said Michael. 'I'll let the whole house if need be.'

'Please don't go, Michael! Not just yet. Last time you shot off like a bullet. Stay a day or two at least.'

Michael stayed three days, consumed with impatience. In the evenings he read *Nicholas Nickleby* aloud to his grandmother. He spent most of the day on the telephone.

75

Ivan found at first that he could hardly speak Russian any more. Slowly, it began to come back.

Taschla was some distance from Moscow. He was warned the train would take at least eighteen hours, if it left at all. Better to travel at night. Russia seemed to be running down. He discovered that people looked back to the days of his youth as to a golden age.

There was no taxi. Eventually he persuaded a man with a car to drive him. He would pay in dollars.

At the signpost 'Ruibinsk 307 kilometres', he had to speak.

'You see that signpost? I remember how excited I was seeing that when I ran away from home. Ruibinsk was my goal.'

'You ran away from home?'

'Yes. This road will take us to Taschla. Not more than 40 kilometres now.'

He looked and looked. The bleak, flat land, the empty, pitted road, the solitary trees whose bare branches had been made knuckled and knobbly, bent and twisted and arthritic from the cold winds off the plain, the whole desolate scene was beautiful to him. Home. Home. Home!

'Look at the Wiga. How full it is! The snows will come soon.'

And then – 'There it is! Taschla! Left – go down this track. But it's a road! They've surfaced it. At last!'

This seemed the only change. Except, no – there was another one, and it was immense. The copse beside the river, the mound covering the remains of the old house, the privy, all had been cleared away and two large prefabricated barns – corrugated roofs on a frame of steel – erected on the site. They must have found his books – Alexis's books – rotting in a heap, and the chests.

For the rest, Ivan might have been sixteen again.

The barking of two dogs brought a spare, tall man out of the farmhouse. His chin had the usual six-day stubble. Shave on Sunday. Ivan's name seemed to mean nothing. He was Dmitri Voynichov. So, Ivan had lived here once, had he? His expression said, so what? Slow, suspicious silences. At last – 'Look round if you must. Please yourself.'

Ivan moved slowly towards the stack yard. There were four tractors out now; they had had to rely on the State Tractor Enterprise. One of the old looseboxes was full of fertiliser.

But he had moved back more than forty-five years. There was the gate Boris had beaten him for swinging on. They still kept wood in the small barn. The weight of the pine logs in the panniers. The smell of warm milk, the foamy surface. 'Have you collected the eggs yet, Ivan?' The harness room, leather smells, hot horse, snow on the backs of chickens, the thunder of rain on the big barn roof, safe in the hay with Mikhail. Memories so thick they pressed on him, made him condense and become tiny again, so that he expected at any moment Mikhail would wave from the door of the big barn, beckoning him in.

And yet, standing in the grey November light between the straw stacks, listening to the past, looking at it, Ivan could not quite feel he had come home. Home was buried somewhere still deeper in his childhood, in his babyhood. For the first time he allowed himself to think the name and see the form of the only person, or the only person bar one, he wanted to see in the world – and one who was almost certainly dead.

The driver of the car and Dmitri Voynichov were standing, not talking, smoking. Wasn't there another Voynichov? This must be his grandson. Ivan came up to them. His journey into the past and his return had been instantaneous, outside time.

'There was an old woman. Well, she must be dead, she'd be – oh, well – over ninety. She used to live here. Natalia Ivanovna Mikhailova.'

'Natalia Mikhailova!' cried the man Dmitri, for the first time animated. 'So you did live here then? Well, you said so. Of course you'd know Natalia Mikhailova. Dead? She's not dead. I'll be dead before Natalia Mikhailova. She's getting on, of course. As you say. Ninety-four last name day. Ivan Khuchevsky, did you say? Ivan. Yes, now I think about it, she does talk about you. She certainly used to. Yes, that's right.'

'Where is she?' said Ivan, his heart beating.

'Well, where do you suppose? She hasn't changed much over the years. No, she's much the same.' Ivan remembered the maddening slowness of the peasant, the need during the repetitive days to spin out each rare new event. 'Well, you'll find her by the stove in the kitchen. She sleeps downstairs now. She can't manage stairs. From October you'll never find her far from the stove. Her bones give her trouble in winter now. Come – I'll take you through to her.'

Ivan suddenly ran ahead, unable to restrain himself. All the same, the same smell of cabbage and dog and cold stone floor. Electric light bulbs without shades.

Little Na was asleep beside the big blue stove. She was

tiny, as though time had rolled her up prior to departure. She was nearly bald.

Ivan stood looking down at her. Suddenly her eyes snapped open, one of them a milky white marble from cataract.

'Who's this? Who's that? Who are you? I don't know you.'

'Yes, you do, little Na! It's Ivan.'

'Ivan? Ivan who? Who's Ivan? What a funny way you speak.'

'Your Ivan, little Na. You remember. Boris was my guardian. I flew away. Your Ivan.' He knelt down and took her hands, the dry skin tight over distorted knuckles.

The old woman peered at him. She put out one hand and ran it down his nose. She whispered, 'Why, yes. So it is.' She suddenly cackled. 'Well, you've taken your time and no mistake. If you'd left it much longer I wouldn't have been here.'

'Aren't you pleased to see me?'

She reached out her hand, trembling a little with age, and touched his cheek. 'Of course I'm glad to see you, you silly boy. Give me a kiss.'

He stood and lifted the little black bundle out of her chair and held her against his chest. How odd emotion was! He could feel tears running down his cheeks.

'Don't squeeze me so hard, Ivan. We old women break easily. You'll have me in pieces.'

Once comfortably in her chair, she made him pull up another and sit beside her.

'So you've come back. Well, I knew you would. No one believed me but I said, "He promised. He'll come one day." Mind you – the fuss when you left! You wouldn't believe! Do you know those two boys you used? The ones that flew you away?'

'Yes.'

'Guess what happened to them.'

'I can't.'

'Ten years! Ten years they got, the both of them. I couldn't help being sorry for them. It's a pity they're not here to see it. Everyone dies. I don't know why I don't die. Ninety-three, ninety-four, whatever I am. I didn't want to go on like this. Have you got any children?'

'No,' said Ivan. 'I married, but we didn't have any children. We're divorced.'

'Everyone gets divorced nowadays,' said little Na. 'Well, perhaps you're happier. But I'd have liked to see your children. What do you do?'

'I work for Reuters. That's like a reporter. Like working on a newspaper.'

'A newspaper,' said little Na. 'I haven't read a newspaper for . . . These are strange times we live in. Dmitri tells me we may buy Taschla back. Full circle. You didn't know Daniel, did you? Or Ossip? You'd have liked Ossip. A gentle boy, like you. Boris has gone. Well, of course you know that. What am I saying? He was a hard man on you. Oh, many's the time I wept at what he did to you. I tried to stop him, you know. I did my best.'

'I know you did, little Na.'

'Well, he got his deserts in the end. God saw to that. A terrible end he had, but he deserved it.'

'I had a hand in that, little Na.'

'Did you now? It was always a mystery how he went. I can't say I blame you. You're sure you did? You were always an imaginative little boy. I can remember you standing dreaming. Full of dreams you were, my little Ivan.' She reached out her frail hand and brushed his cheek. 'Perhaps you imagined it.'

'Perhaps. Na, there's something I have to ask you. Did I ever have fits when I was young? Epilepsy?'

'Fits? You mean convulsions? Not while I knew you. No, as I say – you were a dreamer. And then you had too much energy. Always in a hurry. Opposite sides of the same coin.'

Ivan felt his heart beating. He breathed deeply. 'There's something else I always wanted to ask you. Did Boris ever tell you he had a message for me?'

'Not that I remember. What sort of message?'

'Something I was to do. Something my father told him, perhaps.'

'Not anything he told me. I think he expected you'd take over Taschla from him eventually. He was very angry when he found that – well, I don't know what he was. A nice man. That man that ran away and gave us all that trouble.'

'Alexis?'

'Alexis. That's it. What was I saying?'

'Little Na, try and remember. Did Boris ever mention my father and mother wanting anything for me?'

'Well, I don't know. I don't think they'd've told Boris if they had. He wasn't that close to them, as I heard. But they'd gone a long time before I came.'

'Not that long, surely? I can just remember them going. I suppose it was the funeral. I was about four or five, standing in the yard.' Ivan looked at the ancient photograph of his memory, a photograph which gave off, like an almost vanished odour, a just detectable pain.

Little Na looked at him with her single sharp eye. 'That's your imagination again, Ivan. Your father and mother were both killed when you were three months old.'

'Three *months*?' cried Ivan astonished. 'Nonsense! Are you sure?'

'As sure as I'm sitting here,' said little Na. 'Antonina told me. You remember Antonina? Antonina said it was three months after they'd got the wet nurse in. Your mother couldn't feed you and they had to get a nursing mother in at once to feed you. It was a blessing in disguise, it seems, because three months after that they'd gone.'

Ivan had a confused sense of his past flying about in his head. 'A nurse?' he said. 'I never knew I had a nurse, a wet nurse. How long did she stay? I don't remember her.'

'Oh, she was there a good long time. She only left about eight months before I came. So you'd have been about five. It would be her you remember going. She had a little boy of her own.'

'How strange,' said Ivan slowly. He supposed little Na must be right. Yet nothing altered. He strained to see who was disappearing in the old photograph but it remained as it had always done. Himself standing in the mud, staring across the plain. At the same time what she said didn't seem completely unfamiliar.

'Do you think my mother and father would have told her if they had special plans for me?' he said at last.

'Like as not, like as not,' said little Na in her comforting voice. She always wanted to find things to please him, to soothe him. 'They must have been close, in the circumstances.'

There was another silence, while Ivan tried to people the blankness of his early memory.

'Was her son called Mikhail?' he asked suddenly.

'That I don't know,' said Na. 'But what was her name? She was a Jewess, you see. I remember Antonina telling me that. That was why they didn't talk about her too much. She was the only woman they could get in a hurry. But it was a worry, her being a Jewess. Natalia Judah!' cried Na triumphantly. 'That was her name! I knew it was a Jewish name. Natalia Judah. It's true what they say about the old. I can't remember a thing that happened last week, but I can remember the name Natalia Judah.'

'Where did she go? How old was she?'

'Well, I suppose she was about my age. As to where she went, that I can't remember. I don't think I ever knew. That town Ruibinsk comes into my head, but that may be because that's where you went, you rascal.'

'I've got to go to Ruibinsk anyway,' said Ivan.

There was another long silence. At last Ivan said, 'Isn't it strange? The most amazing things can happen to you, terrible things they must have been – and you can remember absolutely nothing at all.'

76

The estate agents sent a brisk, talkative young man who dealt with their 'furnished lets'.

At least, on arrival he was talkative. He was soon

speechless. 'I want as little as possible to go,' said Michael, as they inched between the piles of books and old newspapers. He indicated the toppling heaps of magazines, journal manuscripts, unopened letters, the boxes of bottle tops. 'This is more valuable than you think.' Piles of damp towels lay in the only corner of the bathroom not occupied by collections. The bed hadn't been made for a month. Mrs Inch had given notice one afternoon when, Michael being out, and having been consumed by curiosity for three years, she had finally got into the meditation rooms in the basement.

It was in the first meditation room that the agent at last managed to speak. 'What are these?' he asked.

'Isn't it lovely?' said Michael, aware for the first time in his life of a faint odour, not entirely pleasant. 'So calm, so peaceful. You should see it in the evening sunlight.' He noticed with irritation that the young man was surreptitiously holding a handkerchief over his nose.

They walked between rows of shelves, the demijohns and Kilner jars ranked to the ceiling, and into the next room and the one adjoining, all similarly fitted.

'What's that?' said the agent, his voice muffled.

'My appendix,' said Michael. 'Anything perishable is in formaldehyde. Like all these, for instance.'

'Yes, I was wondering,' muffled the agent. 'What *are* those?'

'I should have thought it was obvious, though it is true they are rather cloudy. You'd see better without that handkerchief.'

When they emerged, the agent drew a deep breath. 'This will have to go,' he said.

'You mean the meditation rooms?' said Michael.

'Yes.'

'All of it? The entire collection?'

'Yes,' said the agent. 'I couldn't even show it like this.'

'I would have thought it was a feature,' said Michael shortly. 'You haven't seen upstairs. In that case, I may keep the basement.'

The agent was trained to flatter and charm. As they forced their way upstairs he tried to think of something to say but he could think of nothing.

'We can't get out on the roof,' said Michael, indicating a retractable metal ladder badly buckled, its first six rungs wrenched out. 'But that's another feature.'

As they retraced their steps, the agent said desperately, 'Plenty of potential cupboard space. What's in here? Another room or airing cupboard space?'

'Don't!' cried Michael. 'For Christ's sake, don't –'

But the agent had already pulled open the door. An avalanche of paper flowed out, for a moment knocking them back against the wall, pouring over and then on either side of them.

'I'm sorry, sir,' said the agent, as they pulled themselves free. 'I didn't realise . . .'

'Letters. They're my grandmother's letters,' said Michael.

The agent began ineffectually to push them back. 'They don't seem to have been opened,' he said.

'Yes,' said Michael. 'Don't bother to do that. It will take hours, days.'

Downstairs, the agent once again drew breath. 'I'm afraid it will all have to go if Smiley and Pinkerton are going to handle it.'

'Do you mean everything? All? Every single thing?'

'Yes,' said the agent.

'You realise this is my life's work?' said Michael. He towered above the young man and stretched beyond him on either side. He looked like a giant squid about to envelop and ingest its prey.

'I'm sorry, sir,' said the agent. 'I don't necessarily mean destroyed. It can be stored. We have a storage facility. But it can't stay here.'

There was a silence. Michael suddenly found he didn't care. He was his book. As for the rest – what did it matter? His life, his hope, his recovery, were in the future. That is to say, in the past.

'Do what you think best,' he said, coughing. 'I leave it entirely to you. You can get me for the next week or two at the Hotel Eden on the other side of the square.'

77

Natalia Judah was, in the end, surprisingly easy to trace. This was because she was Jewish.

The director of the Citizens' Central Registry was a small, jumpy, fawning, bald man, whose features came to a point like a vole's. Ideal for registers, thought Ivan, as he sat waiting for these to be brought into the director's office.

'It was all to have gone on computer by next year, but in the present state of affairs . . .' The director spread his pawlike, pink hands helplessly.

Silence.

'So how do you find Ruibinsk, Mr Khuchevsky? What a pity you could not come in the spring.'

'There was a big building here – the Tcheksna. What happened to it?'

'The Tcheksna building?'

'It was in the main square – Nevsky, was it? I think it was once the seat of the regional government. When I was here, people lived there. Thousands of people.'

'So you've been here before!' cried the director. 'What an honour! I mean, what an honour you should wish to return. But of course, I know the building. I was muddled. It *is* Tcheksna – but only since last year. Before that it was the Brezhnev Building. The army had it. Now – who knows?'

A young woman entered, carrying two large, red-bound registers.

'Now we'll find her,' said the director. 'It's our boast that no one who has lived in Yaroslav can escape our files.'

He dived into the pages as into a burrow, muttering to himself as he scampered up and down the columns. The burrows seemed blocked. The register was discarded and the second opened. 'Suspected Jewish . . . half-Jewish . . . single . . . married . . . divorced . . . resident . . . temporary . . .' muttered the director, scurrying.

'Did she try and emigrate, by any chance?' he said at last, beginning to look harassed. There was a piece of fluff on the point of his nose.

'I don't know,' said Ivan. 'Possibly.'

Once more the director disappeared. Here the tunnel lists were much shorter. Suddenly he surfaced.

'Why didn't you say so at first?' he cried. 'Here we are. Natalia Judah, born 1897. Hm, hm. *Ah* – applied to emigrate 1952.' He looked up and coughed. 'Of course this was many years ago. Such a thing would never happen now. A spell in a labour camp.' He looked down. 'Hm. Hm. Hm. Yes – *here* we are. Granted a visa to Israel on compassionate grounds in 1979. So there you are. Your friend is in Israel. I knew the files wouldn't let me down.'

'Alive? But of course you can't know.'

'Well, a very old woman,' said the director. 'But you will find out. I understand Israeli officials are very efficient at this sort of thing. A call from your bureau in Moscow . . .'

'There is one other thing,' said Ivan, his heart beginning to struggle in his chest. 'I met someone when I was here. She would have been born about 1931 or '32, I think in Ruibinsk. Sofka Alkhanova. They lived then in the Tcheksna building. Do you have any trace of her?'

When the director emerged from the warren of the Ruibinsk registers this time, he looked astonished.

'But I knew her!' he said. 'Well – I *could* have known her. I knew of her. Would you believe it? Her husband worked in this very building. Sergei Petrova. Not this section. In census returns. But I was conscious of his presence. A fine man.'

'And Sofka?' said Ivan eagerly, standing up.

'Alas, I have sad news,' said the director. 'Sofka Petrova died some years ago. Cancer. A tragedy.' He slowly closed the register, as though interring her.

'Dead?' said Ivan. 'You don't mean that. Are you sure? Do you mean divorced?'

'Dead,' said the director. 'Yes, I fear so. I fear so. A very lovely woman, I believe. Was that so?'

Ivan sat down. He was panting. Dead! Was it true?

'Was that true? I understand,' said the director.

'What?'

'I seem to remember they said Sofka Petrova, the late Sofka Petrova, was very beautiful.'

'Yes.' There suddenly came into Ivan's head a fragment, some lines he must have read somewhere: 'it was barred with stakes'. Death. Death was the enemy. He had to hurry.

'. . . I believe I heard something like that – isn't that so, Mr Khuchevsky?'

Ivan stood up. 'What? What are you talking about?'

'That the late Sofka Petrova was a talented poet in her youth. I think I heard something of that kind.'

'I don't know,' said Ivan. 'I have to go now. At once. I may already be too late.'

78

Dr Gordon put the X-rays down on his desk. He hated breaking that sort of news. One reason he had become an analyst was that the neuroses were rarely fatal.

It seemed the unpleasant task would not be his after all. Michael, enclosing his cheque, had written some time before to say he was planning to leave for Israel, for Tel Aviv.

A pity. With the appearance of the dream mother, the introjected screen figure, a fantasy, would have begun to move aside. Slowly, they would have got somewhere.

Now – Dr Gordon picked up the plates and looked at the massive blur on the left. Virtually a lung within a lung. He doubted he would ever see his patient again. Geoffrey, at Guy's, guessed six months at most, quite probably less. There was evidence of secondaries in the lymph. He couldn't get hold of Michael Wordingham.

79

The Beersheva Geriatric Hospital and Hospice was, in fact, about 30 miles south of Beersheva, right on the edge of the Negev Desert.

It was a bit cooler when they got moving, but Ivan cursed himself for taking the bus. He had nearly taken a taxi. The hospital had said that she had turned ninety-eight three days before, and was very frail. She was sensible, but she could die at any moment. She could have died at any moment over the past six months. She could live to be ninety-eight and a half, ninety-nine. Who could say? Women of her sort were remarkable.

For an instant, he had drawn back at the cost of the taxi ride. Israeli inflation made the sum sound so enormous. And the bus had been there, right outside the Tel Aviv Public Telephone Exchange. He wasn't mean, but over the years he had become more economical. How terrible if this door, this last door, should, because he was economical, shut too – 'barred with stakes'.

It was a landscape for death, bleached skeleton-white by the sun. Even goats could have found little in the rock and dust of the bare mountains through which, after five hours, they drove with such maddening slowness.

80

Michael felt that he was melting. He had been assured in London by their embassy that it would be pleasantly cool. He might as well have gone to the equator. He would be reduced to a skeleton. In fact, he had noticed over the past six weeks that he seemed to be losing weight, but this . . .

He pulled himself together. '*How* much?' he said to the taxi driver.

The Israeli took a piece of paper and scribbled something. They seemed mostly to speak English but their accent was incomprehensible, especially when your head was aching and humming and you were melting and dripping great chunks and blobs of yourself into pools on the pavement.

Michael looked at the paper. It seemed to be a million pounds, but the chart the hotel had given him showed it to be about a hundred.

'Very well.' He clambered in, coughing, lighting a cigarette, moving into the middle of the back seat because it irritated and embarrassed him when taxi drivers asked him to do this.

The road south ran through orange groves that would soon be flooding the supermarkets of England. How green and glossy the leaves, how orange the oranges! Like Christmas decorations. The air flowed into the taxi, warm as camel's milk, thought Michael poetically. He'd given up his journal when he'd left Drayton Gardens. The thousands, tens of thousands of pages would by now have been incinerated. Who cared?

The road turned left – Mash'en, Rewaha, Qiryat Gat. They were really all Arabs, of course. Ridiculous to quarrel.

When they'd passed the road off to Qiryat Gat, the land became rapidly more barren. First intimation of the still distant Negev, no doubt. The noise from the driver's radio was Arab too. Michael closed his eyes and felt himself becoming detached. He thought, I shall just look like a large, late-middle-aged man asleep. But before he underwent this infinitesimal transmogrification, the driver shattered him with a frightful blast on his horn and forced an unfortunate bus – itself now honking furiously – practically into a ravine. They veered past. Michael closed his eyes again.

He opened them as the taxi struck gravel. They were circling a small hill – a green hill far away without a city wall. He might have known the golden thread would end here, at his childhood.

81

The arrival, after the six-hour bus journey, was like some cameraman's trick in a commercial. As they swung over the last pass, in the middle of the aridity, the glare, the grey-white monotone of scree, wadi and bare hot rock, he could see, far below and right along the desert's edge, a swath of violent crème de menthe green.

Beersheva Zin was not the largest of the Israeli reclamation areas but it was one of the most successful. It was built above an enormous underground lake, or reservoir, whose water had been laid down 25,000 years before. The Geriatric Hospital and Hospice had been built there because of the dry air and the relative remoteness from hostile borders. A small general department served the farming community.

On one side, the arc of the hospital complex looked out over a desert blooming at this point with rank upon rank, regiments of orange and lemon trees. On the other side it held in its curve a large artificial mound, like a huge, bright-green breast. The grass, he knew, would also seem artificial, like the grass you found on Spanish lawns – tough, springy as plastic, already almost the flesh it was destined to turn into.

The bus swung slowly round this and stopped at the tinted glass doors of the main entrance. In front of them, a dusty, white taxi waited, no doubt the one that half an hour before had tried to kill them. Ivan stepped stiffly down on a glinting ground of crushed rock. It was like walking on diamonds. He could feel his heart beating. At last something momentous was about to happen. This was what he had been preparing for.

The young woman in the reception cubicle checked his name and time of arrival and handed him a small plastic card with his name already printed on it, to be pinned on his lapel.

'The bus leaves at 1800 hours. All visitors must be out of the wards at 17.30. Please hand in your pass and check out before you go.'

'Is this my pass?'

'Yes. You want Ben Gurion Ward. That way up that corridor, and then left at the intersection. The first ward you come to.'

'Thank you.'

Corridors – dream symbol of the Search. Hospital corridors were the modern Styx, the passage from life to death. It was indeed dreamlike, as though he were standing still and the corridor was flowing steadily backwards past him. Nor, at last, was he alone. There was, in the distance, a companion in the dream, an elderly fat man. He for some reason was moving at a creeping pace. His huge hunched back, the way he stumbled, palming his way along with his right hand, suggested that he was not well. Perhaps he was a patient, in which case he was dying. Every patient in the Beersheva Geriatric Hospital and Hospice eventually died, sooner rather than later.

Thinking he might need help, Ivan hurried, and they reached the intersection at almost the same time. But the fat patient had already turned right towards the Golda Meir Ward. Watching him stagger along, Ivan had the hallucinatory sensation that his own shadow – grossly distorted by the pervading air of death – had suddenly detached itself and set off in the opposite direction.

Michael pulled himself along the corridor towards the ward, leaving damp and not very clean palm prints on the gleaming pale-green tiles of the wall.

The sister pointed to the bed at the far end of the ward, now full of evening sun. 'Don't tire her – she had a bad night. Ten minutes.'

He could hear the faint rustle of old lungs. Hands twitched at the folded-back sheets as his grandmother's hands twitched. The smell, faint and familiar, of the meditation rooms. He found he was trying to tiptoe.

The old woman in the bed lay propped by pillows, her

hands now quite still again, lifeless. Her skin had that delicate, almost transparent thinness of immense age – much spotted, something no longer flesh and blood, yet not quite the grey wax of corpse. His old nanny.

He sat down and pulled a chair close, fairly close. Had this been the face in the night? She was not wearing spectacles. He could not recognise her. Time was passing. He reached out with his hand, then drew it back. Suddenly her eyes opened. She was alive. They stared at each other, then her eyes slid away.

'You don't know me but you looked after me. During the war. Do you remember Inkpen?'

He thought she nodded, her lips were moving. He forced himself closer. 'Do you remember my grandmother Mrs Wordingham, her vicarage at Inkpen?'

'I remember.'

'Did you wear spectacles then, can you remember?'

The old woman looked towards him, and then her eyes wandered. He suddenly realised she was blind. 'My son died, you know. Only sixteen. They wouldn't let him come with me and he was killed there. That is why he never comes to see me.'

'I'm so sorry.' He felt a pang of guilt.

Her eyes were shut again. Precious moments were passing. He pulled his chair closer, maddeningly prevented by his bulk from getting as close as he wanted.

'Can you remember – did you come into my room the night before you left?'

Her eyes opened pointlessly, looking to his right. 'You were very sickly as a child. Only I could soothe you. I don't think your mother wanted you. It's often the way.'

There was silence again. The ward was flooded with light, the russet sun of tinted glass. He felt the dream sense of being unable to move his limbs – so near the truth, so far from it.

'Listen, please try and remember. First you left to do war work, then you had to come here and look after your father, the doctor.'

'Doctor?' She looked away, her eyes slowly closing. Don't die.

He waited, then took a deep breath and said in a low, urgent voice, 'This is so important. Please try and remember if you came into the turret room and stood at the end of the bed before you left.'

'What?'

'You see, if it wasn't you, it might have been my mother. My grandmother could be wrong.'

'I can remember so little nowadays. So little.' Her voice was faint and wandering, hardly audible, and she was pulling at the sheets again. 'Very little. Nothing.'

'Did you say nothing? You mean no one came? No one at all?'

'No – very little,' she whispered. 'Nothing any more.'

The ward sister tapped him on the shoulder. 'I think that's enough. We mustn't tire her. You can come back tomorrow.'

He stood up to remove himself from the sister, and with difficulty bent over. He wanted to ask the question yet again. Did you come into my room the night you left? But all at once some tremor from that pain of long ago shook him. 'Why did you go?' he said. 'Why did you leave me?'

'Very little,' muttered the old woman, her eyes now fixed on him. 'Nothing. Very little. Nothing any more.'

As he left the ward, Michael realised he wasn't at all well. It was not just the feeling of intense agitation. He'd suspected for months, of course, that he'd got cancer, and had chosen to leave, or flee, when it was about to be confirmed. But now the pain, which had been growing for weeks, had suddenly become intolerable. It was becoming impossible to breathe. The pain had spread to his armpit. He could feel it flowing down the nerves of his left arm. He was in a hospital. He should report it.

The ward Ivan entered was exactly the same as every other ward in the hospital. The patients, regardless of how poor or how rich, were approaching the lowest common denominator of humanity – or the highest, depending on your beliefs.

'The bed at the end. The sun's just reached it,' said the ward sister. 'Don't stay long, she had a bad night.'

The lowest common denominator. All faces look alike

near death. He sat down and felt himself enveloped, as so often in those old people's homes long ago, by the smell of incontinence and vitamin B.

His nurse. How strange to think that, once again a baby, a child, he should be locked up somewhere in that ancient skull. The old woman didn't seem to be breathing and he wondered if she had died. Then her eyes slowly opened. They stared at one another.

After a pause, he said gently, 'You won't recognise me, but you were my nurse once. Do you remember Taschla?'

She was staring at him, but slightly to his right. She couldn't see. He thought her lips had moved.

'Do you remember Taschla, the farm?' he said a little louder.

'I remember.'

'Would you mind if I asked you something about those days?'

Suddenly she moved restlessly and pulled at the sheets. 'My son died, you know. They took him from me when he was sixteen and put him in a camp. He died there. That's why he never comes and sees me.'

'I didn't know that. I'm very sorry.'

She shut her eyes again. He wanted to say, was he called Mikhail? but there were more important things. 'Can you remember – did I have fits as a baby, as a child?'

Her eyes opened again, staring at the ceiling. 'You were sickly as a child. Only I could soothe you. I don't think your mother wanted you. It's often the way.'

The sun passed through the tinted glass. How hot hospitals were. He tried again.

'Did they have to take me to hospital? Do you remember if the doctor often came?'

'Doctor?' Once more she closed her eyes.

Time was slipping away like her life. He had to ask the most important question of all. How astonishing that his entire life could be framed in a single sentence. 'This is most important: did my father or mother leave a message for me?'

'What?'

'Did they tell you something? Some important message you were to hand on to me? Please, *please* try and remember.'

'I can remember so little nowadays. So little.' He could hardly hear her. 'Very little. Nothing.'

'Did you say "nothing"? They said *nothing*?' He put his ear to her mouth.

'No – very little,' she whispered. 'Nothing any more.'

He became aware that the ward sister was standing beside him. 'You can come back tomorrow. She's tired out now.'

He stood up and looked down at her and all at once he remembered standing in the yard and then remembered remembering. Echo after echo all the way down his life. He bent forward. 'You shouldn't have left me,' he said. 'You shouldn't have left me.'

'Very little,' muttered the old woman, her eyes now fixed on him as if she could see. 'Nothing. Very little. Nothing any more.'

81

Nothing. Ivan stood in the corridor outside the ward with his head down, eyes shut, pinching the skin between his eyes with the thumb and first two fingers of his left hand.

Suddenly, the most terrible cry rang out. Looking up, he saw at the end of the corridor leading to the Golda Meir Ward opposite him his inflated shadow again. It was swaying, groping and seemingly trying to hold on to the wall. As he watched, the huge figure raised its head once more and howled.

The sight, the noise, struck Ivan like an electric shock. He heard behind him an answering and equally terrible cry and then realised, fleetingly, as he raced forward, that the cry had come from him.

Michael was just aware of a rush towards him. His eyes were shut, as if against the rushing. He would have fallen if he hadn't been caught. To Ivan, the encounter, the last thing he was to know, had a curiously familiar feel, as if he'd heaved on some heavy, hot, often worn overcoat.

82

There was a vague awareness of some noise or other in both wards, almost totally muffled by the highly efficient, air-locked, air-conditioning doors. In reception, too, insulated in its rose-tinted cubicle, the sound was infinitesimal.

When, at six o'clock, the pretty, golden-curled young Israeli realised that the two male visitors had failed to check out and hand in their passes, she rang Ben Gurion and Golda Meir; she also asked the bus to wait.

On learning that they had left the wards half an hour before, she at once alerted security. There had never been a terrorist incident at the remote Beersheva Geriatric Hospital and Hospice but, as at all state hospitals, the procedure was extremely strict and thorough.

When a brisk preliminary search turned up nothing, a full alarm was raised and a much more intensive search, continuing well into the night, was instituted, alert now to the possible concealment of explosive devices as well as the presence of the two intruders. The bus was allowed to depart only after it too had been searched. The taxi, also searched, elected to stay. It had not been paid.

Not only were all the wards searched, but the roof areas, the kitchens and basements, the surgeries and the operating theatre, and even the environs of the hospital. But they found nothing, not a sign of a bomb or Semtex or a device of any kind.

As for the two men, they had disappeared without trace; like phantoms or ghosts, they had vanished as completely (and as incompletely) as characters in a book after the final page.

AUTHOR'S NOTE

The figure of the Shaman Detu is based on a character of the same name in an extraordinary book, *Into Africa*, which the author, Keith Nicholson Price, was kind enough to let me read before publication.